FUMBLED hearts

USA TODAY BESTSELLING AUTHOR

MEAGAN BRANDY

Editing: Jenn Wood at All About The Edits

Proofreader: Cat Parisi at Cat's Eye Proofing and Promo

Dedication

To the girl who was told she couldn't,
but proved the world wrong when she did.

Synopsis

After months of refusing, I finally agreed to make the move to Alrick Falls. My family thought it was best - that a new scene would be good for me - and I was sick of having the same conversation.

So here I am, and the plan is simple. Smile through each day and avoid her at all costs.

It's perfect.

Until the cocky quarterback comes into play.

The last thing I want is his crooked grin and dark brown eyes focused on me.

Yet here he is, constantly in my space, pushing me, daring me to care. Telling me what I think and feel, as if he knows.

He doesn't know anything. And I plan to keep it that way.

He's the persistent playboy who refuses to walk away. I'm the impassive new girl with nothing left to give.

Things are about to get complicated.

Chapter One

K ALANI

Come out with me tonight, she said. It'll be fun, she promised.

Yeah...not so much.

I drag myself out of the corner I took cover in, eyeing the American Pie-like movie scene playing out in front of me. Only, in this version, it's ridiculously handsome males and far too sexy females parading around in a hormone-driven buzz, letting loose at the hands of alcohol. I mean, I get it. People can never be who or what they want. They can never be honest and upfront.

Alcohol does one of two things for you in high school: gives you the courage to tell the truth or the freedom to forget it. So, they party, get drunk, hook-up, do and say stupid shit, and in the end, they take a page from Jamie Foxx and "blame it on the alcohol."

Take, for instance, the Pretty Woman, Julia Roberts lookalike - pre-makeover, that is - who was just hoisted up onto the coun-

1

tertop by some tall, dark-haired beast of a guy whose face I can't see. She's biting down on her bottom lip and rubbing her knees together, clearly trying to excite this guy who, no doubt, only sees a faceless vag.

She spreads her legs and pulls him between them. Instantly, he dips his lips to her neck and she wraps her legs around his back. They're three sheets to the wind and he's got something she wants.

Yeah, all this is happening mid-party, and no one seems to give two shits.

Awesome.

In order to get to the other side of the room, I have to weave through the bodies crammed onto the makeshift dance floor. Brushing body parts against drunk, horny high school seniors I don't know doesn't sound like a good time, but it appears to be my only way out. So, I dodge a grope here and an elbow there, and make my way out of the slosh zone, earning only a few dirty looks along the way.

Petty asses.

When I round the corner into what I'm assuming is the living room, I let my eyes roam. All the furniture's been pushed against the tan-colored walls. A few people are passed out, while others are making out on the sheet-covered couches, and there's a beer pong game going on smack dab in the center.

At least there's hardwood floors.

I watch as a big burly guy tosses the little white ball, effectively landing it inside the red cup on the opposite end of the table. Cheers erupt around the room.

The opposing team grumbles as one of the guys picks up the cup, downing its contents in seconds. I stand there, watching them play for a good twenty minutes, only turning to leave when the girls hanging around start stripping down to help "motivate" the players. Their words, not mine.

I'm about two feet from the door when my gaze is pulled to the stairs.

A beautiful girl with white-blonde hair descends, looking like a model on her runway. A large, dark-haired figure over her shoulder catches my attention and my eyes lift. I can't quite make out his face from here, but I can tell he's smirking and his shirt is hanging from his left hand.

My attention turns back to the girl and, imagine that... suddenly, she looks a lot less beauteous, and a lot more bimbo. Her modelesque strut now looks like a runway show for a pro-ho.

And I'm pretty sure that's bleach-blonde, not beach-blonde.

With a shake of my head, I look away.

I've been here for an hour and I'm already labeling these people I know nothing about.

But honestly, am I labeling or just being observant?

I sigh. No matter how I try and spin it, it's shitty all around.

Face it, Kalani, you're being a judgmental bitch.

Once I make it out the front door and into the fresh air, I inhale deeply, trying to clear my senses. Nothing like leaving a party feeling as if you just stepped out of an Abercrombie and Fitch store. Cologne and spray tan overload.

I stand there for a few minutes, looking around, watching as people mill in and out of the house, then pull out my phone and send a quick text to Mia, letting her know I'm out.

As usual, she replies almost instantly.

Meems: boo-hoo, bitch. You lasted 5 seconds.

Me: close. Just add 57 minutes to that and you're right on the dot. Congratulations!

Meems: thank you. Thank you. I'll prepare my speech soon, but in the meantime...be careful on your way home. LUVS!!

I smile at my screen before stuffing it back into my boot and begin the short walk to my house.

It's early November, so there's a nice chill to the air.

I've been in Alrick Falls for three weeks to the day. Tonight was the first time I agreed to go out with Mia and her friends. While it wasn't a horrible night, per se, it wasn't much fun either.

I mean, I like to party and have a good time. Or at least, I used to. But that party felt more like a brothel house. The guys, all too attractive for their own good, with their sexy smirks glued in place, were passing out drinks left and right. No doubt trying to loosen up all the girls - pretty sure most of 'em were already 'loose' - while the girls paraded around in "barely there" clothing, batting their eyelashes as they knocked back every drink thrown their way. Maybe that's how they get what they want, with a little liquid courage.

There was a time I liked kickin' back with a group of friends, laughing, dancing, and singing. But this is a new place, with new people, and I don't feel much like participating in their charades. I'd rather eat junk food and watch movies.

As I'm thinking it, I realize how shitty it sounds.

Maybe that's my problem. I'm being bitchy and judgmental because this isn't my home. Spending my senior year in Alrick was never part of the plan.

I guess I can try not to be such a buzzkill; have some fun while I'm here. That way, Mia doesn't have to explain to her friends why her cousin is such a "snooty biatch." Then, after I graduate, I'm out.

Yep. Headed straight for-

My train of thought stops abruptly as I take in the sight before me.

"What the hell..." I mutter as I peer at the fancy jeep-looking thing stopped in the middle of the dark street.

I wait a beat to see if it starts going again, but it doesn't. It appears to be parked in the middle of the road, still running, lights on and everything.

Instead of doing the logical thing a girl should do when she's alone in the dark with a creeper car close by - like running - I make a stupid horror film decision and walk toward the vehicle because, that's smart.

The closer I get, the better I can see. Not a jeep, but a fancy Hummer. A sexy, sleek, black one, with all-black rims.

Very presidential.

As I approach, I hear Sublime's "Wrong Way" blaring. Looking around, I realize the sound of the music is flowing from the open sunroof.

At five-foot-two, I'm too short to see through the window, so I tap lightly. "Hey, you alright in there?"

No response.

With a frown, I make my way to the back of the beauty before I freeze.

What the hell am I doing?

This is the exact shit your parents warn you about when they give you the "don't talk to strangers" lecture. Only, I'm pretty sure what I'm about to do borders more on "the dumbest idea ever."

"Fuck it." I reach up, grabbing ahold of the spare tire on the back of the vehicle. Gripping it tight, I push up from the bumper, laughing as I hoist myself onto the roof.

If the owner catches me doing this...

I crawl on my hands and knees until I'm at the open sunroof. Leaning over cautiously, I peek inside.

"Oh, shit," I whisper, taking in the sight before me.

And, oh, what a sight. What. A. Sight.

The driver is slouched in the seat, his head dangling away from me, so I can't see his face. His right arm is through a black t-shirt while his left is bare, the material bunched around his neck, like he never managed to get the other arm through. I can see half his washboard stomach, and damn... the boy works out. I let my eyes travel over him, because why not? I've already reached a whole new level of cray.

His hair is thick, short on the sides and longer on the top, the color of dark chocolate. If the letterman jacket on the passenger seat is any indication, he's an athlete. Looks like one, too. All broad shoulders and strong arms.

5

Huh. Seems he was in a real hurry. Didn't even have time to button up those designer jeans.

Ending my appraisal, I inch my hand in the truck, lightly poke the top of his head. "Hey, you alive?"

A gargling sound comes from the dark-haired stranger, and his head falls back. He lets out a breath, causing me to jolt back.

"Ugh..." My nose wrinkles. "Someone was drinking the good stuff."

Now that I can see his whole face, I realize it's the playboy from the stairs. Maybe even the same guy who was playing with the redhead earlier.

He looks like a grown ass man, but since he was at the party, I'm guessing he's around my age. He's handsome though, that's a given.

Bet he knows it, too.

His eyebrows are dark and thick, with eyelashes to match, and his face is clean-shaven, with small, perfectly trimmed sideburns. Following the invisible trail from there, I take note of his strong jawline, sculpted to perfection, then lift my eyes slightly to find a bottom lip that puffs out a bit further than the top, a perfect contrast, really.

A half-hearted sigh escapes me. "Bummer." Perfection brings ego, which translates into one thing: asshole.

"Hey, dumbass. You alright?" I ask, frowning.

"Pfft, I'm fine," he slurs, his chin dropping to his chest.

I roll my eyes. "Sure, you are. I'm coming in."

He lets out a drunken chuckle. "Usually, it's me who's coming when I'm in." He laughs harder, one knee lifting slightly, clearly amused by his own joke.

"Hilarious," I deadpan. Yep. Guy's a tool. "Look, you're drunk. Switch seats and I'll drive you home."

He doesn't move, so I reach in again and give the guy a little shake.

Nothing.

"Lovely." Pursing my lips, I consider my options. He's massive, so moving him won't work. I could call the cops, but that feels like a bitch move, even though it's his own damn fault for being irresponsible.

"I can't believe I'm doing this." I curse myself under my breath, and glance at the houses surrounding me. Not wanting to put my boots on the luxury seats, I use my arms for support and lower myself into the cab until my knees hit the center console. After adjusting the volume on the stereo, I peek at the guy before leaning across the driver's seat. Searching around, I try to find a lever, but my hand barely reaches the side of the seat.

"Shit." I perch on my knees and lean all the way over him.

God, if someone drives by right now... it looks like I'm giving some serious road head.

I stretch, reaching damn near to the floorboard, finally finding a small lever. Unsure of how it works, I quickly push, slide, and pull. One of them works, because the driver seat starts to fall back. I quickly let go so I don't end up giving the guy whiplash. Or get puked on. That would suck.

The guy laughs and grabs me, pulling me back with him, and a ridiculously girly squeal escapes me.

My torso is now lying sideways across his chest, ass still semi in the air.

"If you wanna play..." he slurs, rubbing his nose in my hair. "Mmm...you smell soooo sweet," he continues to mumble before he's snoring again.

His voice is low and rough, and ridiculously sexy.

Don't go there, Kalani. Don't do it.

Man, I bet this guy gets the pick of the puss.

He's got game in his sleep.

I gotta get us out of here.

I wait a minute, making sure he's out cold, then climb the rest of the way across, sliding my legs between his. Squeezing my eyes shut, I move at a snail's pace, lowering myself down so I'm sitting

7

on his lap. I stay completely still for a few seconds, just in case... well, I don't really know. But it seems like the best idea at the moment.

I'm sitting on his thighs, squished against the steering wheel, so I reach down trying to find another lever to move the seat backward, but instead I find a fancy button.

The seat reverses, which causes the back to lift. I gasp when my back meets his steeled chest. The second I shift my body to get into a more comfortable position, two large hands fly to my hips, gripping them like a running back does a football: tight, hard, and close to his body.

My body temperature spikes as I put the vehicle in drive and head down the road. Only then do I realize I have no idea where I'm going.

The heater -or his heat currently poking my ass- is too much, so I roll down the window and head to the only place I know.

I pull into my driveway, which was only a minute drive from where I hopped into the vehicle originally and turn off the truck. As soon as the vibration of the engine stops, I become hyperaware of the stranger beneath me.

The strong rhythm of his heart beats against my back as his exposed skin warms me through my clothes. Deep, hot breaths fan across my neck, making me slightly light-headed, despite my lack of drinking tonight.

It seems I'm not the only one who feels the shift in the air as the guy is now running his nose along my shoulder. I really shouldn't let him do that. He could be a crazy person. Or worse, a Broncos fan, but it feels so good.

My eyes widen when his dick twitches against my ass, and I scramble into the passenger seat. Apparently his 'heat' wasn't all the way nuked if you know what I mean, because that was definitely...more.

I decide I'm going to leave him there, in his seat, to sober up.

Then, come morning, when he feels like Woody Woodpecker is paying him a visit, he can be on his merry way.

I take the keys out of the ignition and toss them on the passenger side floor; close enough for a sober person to find, but not a drunken fool. I allow another look at the guy - he really is adorable - then hop out, careful not to slam the door.

After taking a quick shower, I throw on a thong, my Halestorm concert t-shirt, which has definitely seen better days, and hop in bed. I fall asleep within minutes; my devil cat, Nauni, beside me.

I roll myself onto my stomach, squeezing the pillow over my head to drown out the pounding at my door. When it continues for a good minute, I groan, and throw myself out of bed, ready to ring Mia's neck. I gave her a key to avoid this exact situation. I love my sleep. I need my sleep. This is something she knows.

Scowl in place, I fling the door open. "Where the hell is your ke-" I stop short.

It's not Mia. Nope. It's Mr. Perfection in all his still half-naked glory.

At my door.

And man is he tall. Ginormous compared to me, but not freakishly so. More like six feet of vagina waking, no K-Y needed temptation. Trouble.

My eyes drop to the jeans stretched nicely over what look to be thick, strong thighs. Pants still unbuttoned, I skirt past the no-fly zone, and feast my eyes on his yummy tummy.

Yep. Still rock solid. I continue my appraisal upward until his mouth is in my line of sight, when I snap back to reality.

There's that self-satisfied smirk again, the one he was wearing at the party.

I want to punch it off his perfect face.

My eyes lift to his, and damn it all to hell. They're a deep dark brown, almost black in color, and right now his lids are half-closed as he stares at me.

I watch his eyes as they roam over my body.

I'm fully aware I'm only wearing a very small, very thin t-shirt and thong. The bottom of my freshly waxed prize is surely peeking out, and my ass is exposed. I guarantee my nips are hard as rocks from the breeze sweeping through the door, but I'll be damned if I allow him to think I give two shits what he thinks, not with that "I'm the man" look on his face, smug bastard.

As soon as his dark eyes meet mine again, he speaks. "You must have really worn me out." His voice is deep, and raspy from sleep. "Didn't even make it down the drive before I passed out."

My eyes shoot wide.

At my reaction, he puts his hands up in front of him. "Hey. Don't go gettin' all offended." He smirks. Again. "That's a compliment coming from me."

This guy...

"Okay. Whoa." I lift my hands this time. "Just... whoa." I gape at him. "You've lost your damn mind if you think you-"

"Look," he cuts me off, a miffed sigh leaving him. "I'm not interested in hashing things out. You should know the drill." He drops his gaze to my hard nipples and, without a doubt, this egotistical asshole assumes it's my body's reaction to him. "I don't go in for seconds, so you might wanna put those away." He motions lazily toward my chest. "You know, so you don't embarrass yourself."

I'm pretty sure my jaw hits the floor. Seriously.

What the fuck?

What. The. Fuck.

"Um, hi. First of all, it's cold." I squeeze my boobs. "This has nothing to do with you. Second, let me break it down for you, Mr. Hugh Hefner-in-training." He grins at that. Dumbass. "That," I point to his groin, "was nowhere near this," I say, giving a little

WWE "suck it" smack to my crotch, speaking like I'm addressing a kindergarten class.

His eyebrows pull into a deep frown, and his hands find his hips in a lazy, thoughtful motion. It's almost comical how confused he looks.

I release an annoyed sigh, deciding to get this over with. "You," I push my index finger into his chest, "were passed out drunk in your truck in the middle of the road." I shrug. "Figured I'd do my good deed for the day - though, now I'm thinking I should have left your ass there – but I drove you here since I didn't know where you lived. Thought you would wake up and take off by morning." I motion my hand toward him. "Clearly, I'm a dumbass for that 'cause here you are."

He smashes his lips into a tight line, glances at his truck, then back at me.

"You're saying you brought me to your house... and we didn't have sex?"

"Yep."

"Sooo..." He looks pointedly from my naked legs to his open fly. "We didn't have sex?"

I stare at him blankly.

Those dark eyes of his narrow before he shakes his head unbelieving.

With a quick glance over his shoulder, he looks back at me with a dark brow raised. "Guessin' my phone's not in your house?"

A laugh bubbles out of me before I can stop it because there it is folks, the reason he had to come to the door.

His eyes narrow further.

"K. I get it now." I nod. "This isn't part of the play 'em to lay 'em routine and clearly you have a serious case of selective hearing, that or you're way too cocksure for your own good, so let me try this one more time, maybe a little slower and see how that works?" I mock, not letting him respond before continuing. "You were

Passed. Out. I drove you here so you didn't get yourself arrested. End. Of. Story."

He scowls past me as he scratches the back of his neck. "Huh." Then, his head pulls back, as his eyes widen, a look of horror crossing his face. "Wait," I think he might hurl, "you drove my Hummer?"

What part of... ahhh. So, the big boy is attached to his toy.

"Sure did." He looks seriously disturbed, so I add, "Of course, that was after I climbed up the back in my boots. Then, crawled across the top and dropped in through the sunroof, heels first." That's not a lie. The small heel of my boots did go in first, with extreme caution, but he doesn't need to know that.

"Thank goodness the center console was there for me to step on," with my knees, "or I might have fallen."

And bam. He's full-on fuming now.

Eyes bulging, jaw tight, chest heaving; he's officially going to lose his shit.

I'm not gonna let him.

"Right. So... bye." I slam the door in his face as fast as I can.

I go back to my room and climb into bed, listening as the Hummer's engine roars to life. A few minutes pass before I hear it pull away.

Sleep doesn't come so easy after that.

Chapter Two

K ALANI

Mia and I slide into a worn black booth at Wicker, the small pub downtown.

It's cute, has the typical diner set-up with a counter and bar stool area blocking the kitchen, black booth seats wrapping all along the walls, and black granite-topped tables placed sporadically around the room, ketchup and hot sauce bottles in the center of each one.

If the sports memorabilia covering the walls is any indication, this place is all about supporting their local athletes. According to Mia, this is the hangout spot for all the high schoolers. Looking around, it appears to be true, there isn't an adult in sight. Even the waiters and waitresses seem to be around our age.

"Hey, Mia, how's it going?" A cute, blond-haired guy asks, setting a couple waters down in front of us.

"It's going. I'm here for my 'cure the hangover' meal," she laughs, then touches her temple, wincing.

"Ahh, yes," he chuckles. "So, water and The Grease Monkey for you?"

"God, yes," she says with a moan, slouching further into her seat.

He glances at me. "Holding out on me, huh, Mia?"

"Shit, sorry." She places her hand on my shoulder. "This is my cousin, Lolli. Lolls, Ryan. His family owns Wicker."

"Hey." I smile.

"Nice to meet you... er... Lolli?" His eyebrows rise just a little. And bless his heart, he tries to hold back a grin.

"It's okay, you can laugh. I promise it won't offend me. And to answer your unasked question; no, it's not my real name."

He smiles and gestures to Mia. "Her idea, right?"

"She definitely makes sure it's a constant."

He nods. "So, what'll it be, Lolli? You create your meal; we deliver."

"Well, I don't need to recover from a hangover, so how about you surprise me? Just know, I'm hella hungry."

He rubs his hands together excitedly while looking me over, as if that'll help. "Alright. You're a breakfast kind of girl," he declares.

I can't help but laugh. "Okay. That's a little creepy, but your food witchery mind-reading thing totally works, because I am indeed a breakfast girl." I sigh wistfully. "I'd eat it for every meal if I could."

"I knew it!" He grins triumphantly. "Considering it's well after 3:00 pm, that's the answer I was hoping for." He winks before walking away.

Once he's out of earshot, I decide to spill the beans. "So, I had quite the interesting night last night."

"Yeah, you had a whole jello shot all to yourself." The smartass dazzles me with spirit fingers. "Crazy."

"Har, har, biatch. I was actually talking about after I left the party." I circle the rim of my glass with my finger.

Mia flips her long red hair over one shoulder, resting both elbows on the tabletop. Hands clasped together; she lays her chin on her fingers. "Do tell, oh mysterious one." She wiggles in anticipation.

I take a deep breath. "I jumped in a shiny truck with a total stranger, who was passed out by the way, drove him to my house, left him in the driveway, and went to bed. I woke up to a pounding on my door. Thinking it was you, I opened it, tits and ass on display all day. Guy was smug. Thought he had some fun in my hoo-hoo land, didn't believe me when I told him he didn't, and had a fit when I told him I drove his truck. The end."

I take a drink of my water, and glance up at Mia.

Bad idea. I choke-laugh-spit all over myself.

She stares at me, her mouth wide open, brows drawn in.

It only takes a few seconds for her to work through my word vomit.

"Are you serious?" she shrieks. "He was so high and mighty he couldn't believe you hadn't slept with him?"

"Yep." I laugh at her stunned-stupid expression. "It was as if the idea of being alone with a girl, and not fucking her, was inconceivable."

She shakes her head back and forth. Her brows go from lifted, to pinched, then back to normal in a clear sign of acceptance. "Yeah, with the top football team in the area, we kind of have a lot of big-headed, sexy shitheads," she laughs.

"Yeah." I nod, replaying last night in my mind.

"I can feel your brain thinking. What is it?"

"I don't know." I swirl the straw through my drink. "Now that I think about it, he kind of seemed like…"

She tilts her head, those green eyes searching. "Like what, Lolls?" she says in a soft, attentive tone. I don't think I like it.

"Like…" I roll my eyes and sit up straight. "Okay, so, he

couldn't believe we hadn't slept together, but I think it was a little more than that." I look up at her. "I don't know. It was weird. I don't think he's used to girls doing decent things for him." That evokes a laugh from me. "Well, nonsexual friendly things, and I honestly think he just had no idea how to take it." I look past Mia's shoulder.

She giggles. "Well, based on what you said, I would have to agree." She wiggles her eyebrows. "So...?" I know what she wants.

"What?" I tilt my head back, fanning myself.

"That hot, huh?" she grins.

"Totally."

We're both still laughing when Ryan walks up, food in hand.

"For you, milady," he says as he places a large plate with two slider burgers, a fried burrito, a bowl of homemade mac, and gravy-covered fries in front of her.

"Daaamn, Meems," I stare at her food in awe. "Can you seriously eat all that?"

"You don't know my life," she snaps as she digs in.

"And for you, Lolli... T's French toast with hash browns, and scrambled eggs. I even took a chance and brought you strawberry syrup."

"Ooh-ho-ho." Mia wiggles her eyebrows at Ryan. "You did good, boy."

He grins and looks to me for confirmation, but all he gets is a thumbs up and a not so appropriate moan, because the goods are already causing an orgasm in my mouth. He walks away with a smile, so I guess he's satisfied with my response.

We sit in silence and inhale our meals. It's a quick and satis-fying adventure, before paying the bill and heading to Mia's house.

She pulls into her driveway and kills the engine to her Red Jeep Wrangler.

"You coming in?" she asks.

"No, I'm gonna get my crap ready for hell tomorrow, and crash out early."

"It won't be so bad, Lolli, I promise. You've met some of my girls already. You just gotta give it a chance." She gives me a sad smile.

"I know." I sigh, before shifting my body to face her. "I actually wanted to apologize to you."

Her head jerks back, and she frowns. "For what?"

"For being such a drag the last few weeks. You've been stuck spending most of your time watching movies with me when you should be hanging out or something."

"Hey, Grease is a classic," she jokes, nudging me in the shoulder.

"Really though, thanks for that, but I'm seriously done moping around."

She raises a skeptical eyebrow at me.

"I'm not kidding! Might as well let loose and have some fun while I'm here. Once school's out, I'm leaving and-"

"Okay, stop," she cuts me off, laughing. "You can't get me all high on a 'let's party', then knock me down with thoughts of you leaving."

"Ugh, you're right." I let my head drop back against the headrest. "I'm bad at this stuff."

She tilts her head to the side, and replies, "Try to get to know people."

"Right." As in, yeah right.

"Seriously though, Meems," I say, as we step out of the Jeep, "I'm just your cousin who moved in next door to you for senior year, okay? They don't need a backstory."

"I hear you, Lolls, but remember, this town is all about football, so..."

"Yeah, I know."

We part ways as she calls out, "Be ready at seven sharp, chickadee!"

I throw a peace sign over my head as I walk to my door.

The second I walk in; my bitch of a cat is at my feet.

17

"Yes, I know. Pet you, feed you, clean out your box. I'm on it." She follows me into the kitchen and watches as I pour food into her bowl.

After taking care of all her crap, I grab a water from the fridge and head to my bedroom.

When it was first decided that Alrick Falls was where I would complete my senior year, I didn't realize that meant living directly next door to my Aunt Kara and Uncle Ben. I guess I was hoping to be at least a couple miles away. Close enough if I felt like stopping by, but not close enough to have to see them – and by *them* I mean her - on a daily basis. I think she knew that which is why she was quick to jump on this place the minute it was available, thinking it would be good for me to be "close to the family." I can't really fault her for it, her heart's in the right place. Regardless, right next door is a bit much and she knows it.

I do like the house, though. It's a basic one-level home with a two-car garage and a hella big backyard. There are three bedrooms: a master and two average-sized rooms, and a hall bath.

The first thing I did when I crossed into Alrick Falls in my rental car was pull over at the hardware store to purchase paint.

The kitchen is now a deep burgundy with mocha-colored countertops and cabinets, while the living room, along with the rest of the house - other than my room - is a charcoal gray with white trimmings. The red suede couches and black furniture help bring it to life, but my room is by far my favorite.

The walls are a deep, teal blue color, matching the pillows that lay on top of my black comforter perfectly. A California king-sized bed is pushed up against the wall with a small black nightstand next to it. My long black dresser along the far wall has a TV perched on top, and that's it. Mia says it's weird not to have a mirror in my room. Apparently, the large closet doors that are actually two huge mirror doors don't count - gotta love her quirks.

She's really the only positive I could come up with for this entire situation. Being only a year apart in age, she and I have always been pretty close, and this time together will be good for us. It makes the whole "waiting a year to go back to school thing" worth it. Now I can sit idle while she soars through our final year of high school.

Yippee.

I've been lying on my bed staring at nothing for at least three hours, watching as my room grows dark, the light disappearing with the sun.

With a sigh, I roll over and reach into my nightstand drawer, feeling around for the Polaroid camera my parents gave me last year. For the first time, I consider walking the few blocks to the meadows, but decide against it just as quickly.

I call for Nauni, the devil cat. She jumps up, curls herself beside me, and we fall asleep.

Chapter Three

K ALANI

As soon as the last curl drops from my fingers, I hear the front door slam. Knowing it's Mia, I continue studying my reflection in the mirror.

My dark, almost black, hair is shiny, and reaches the middle of my back, even with the big barrel curls I gave it today. I went light on the makeup, using a nude color shadow, and adding a thin line of black liner to make my blue eyes pop, a little blush, mascara, and voila. I look like I care, but not like a hooker.

I decided to wear my stretchy, dark blue skinny jeans with a white, crew cut tank top, my black leather jacket that reaches just below my oversized breasts - thank you, genetics - paired with my favorite black knee-high boots.

I'm fluffing my hair out as Mia comes around the corner.

"I don't know why you don't take the master. This room is..." She trails off. "Hells bells. You. Look. Smokin'." She slowly shakes her head back and forth, admiring my outfit. "That jacket, with those boots...just, damn." Crossing her arms, she releases a sigh. "The boys of Alrick High are gonna looove you."

I laugh. "So, I have your seal of approval?"

"Nope." She spins on her heels and walks out of the bathroom.

I follow her into my room where she picks out a pair of silver hoops. "Once you put these on, you'll have my approval."

I loop them through my ears, not because she told me to, but because they're hella cute.

She hooks her arm through mine and pulls me toward the door. "Okay, chickadee, let's roll. We have a grand entrance to make."

"I thought the cool kids were supposed to be fashionably late?"

She squeezes my arm and bounces with fake amusement. "Funny, Lolli, you should be a comedian."

"Nah, I couldn't handle the night shift."

"Right, the cat lady needs her sleep."

"Damn straight. However, I think you have to have more than one cat to be considered a cat lady. Or at least like the one you do have."

"Whatever."

We hop in her jeep and are pulling into the school parking lot far too soon. It literally only took three minutes to get here.

My eyes roam, taking in the dozens of teenagers milling around all different types of vehicles, chatting with friends as they arrive.

I glance down when Mia's hand clamps on to my knee. "You'll be fine, Lolli."

Ah, right. Of course, she takes my hesitation as nervousness or fear or something, 'cause that's what a "normal" girl my age would be thinking if she were in a new town and a new school.

Probably shouldn't tell her the only thought going through my head right now is what a waste of time my being here really is. Not to mention completely unnecessary.

Yeah...that might make her sad or whatever.

I look over at her. "I'm good, Meems, promise."

"I know." She gives me a sad smile, before shaking her head. "Gah! Okay, this is going to be fun, remember? You said yourself you're ready for some fun. This is the first step. Now..." She reaches into her purse and hands me a light pink color lipstick. "Put this bad boy on, it'll last all day," she says, as she pulls out a hot pink one for herself, and carefully applies it to her lips.

She's wearing a pair of white skinny jeans, a pink flowy top with a crop jean jacket, and a pair of her famous wedges. Yes, her toes will freeze but she doesn't care.

Her deep, dark red - like, Jean Grey red - hair is pulled back into a high ponytail with man-made curls bouncing all around. The dark color compliments her fair skin well, and with her large green eyes covered in a light golden shimmer, she's simply stunning.

She notices me studying her and winks. "Ready?"

"Let's do this."

As we make our way across the parking lot, at least a dozen people greet Mia in some sort of way. I see the curious glances directed at me, but so far, no one has approached.

"Okay." She hooks her finger over her shoulder. "This is where I leave you. If I'm late to first, my teacher will ring my ass, and I still gotta stop at my locker. Text me a pic of your schedule when you get it?"

"Yep."

"You'll be fine, Lollipop." She nudges me forward. "Now, go."

I purse my lips and stare into the office. Now I'm not nervous, but even I gotta admit this shit's fucked up.

I never should have agreed to this.

I approach the counter, and a cute older woman with frizzy brown hair and round glasses greets me with a smile.

"I've been at this high school for forty-something years. I know every face that passes these halls, and, sweet pea, I don't recognize yours. I'll bet you're my newest addition to Alrick High?" she kindly assumes.

"That, I am." I grin. "I was told I needed to pick up my schedule."

"And right you are, young lady." She beams at me and reaches to her right, picking up a manila folder. She opens it and hands me two sheets of paper. "This here top one is a school map, just in case you get lost, and the second paper is your schedule. I noticed, in your transcripts, you've already completed your requirements for Physical Education, yet it appears you've chosen PE as your elective?" she inquires, tipping her head down to peer at me over the rim of her thick glasses.

I laugh lightly. "Shocker, I know, but I actually enjoy PE. Thanks for looking out for me, though."

She sighs, before smiling. "We're going to get along just fine, you and me. Now hurry yourself up, the bell already rang. My name is Mrs. Evans. You come to me if you need anything, okay?"

I nod my agreement, and walk out, looking to my schedule. First up, Chemistry, Room 148.

After one wrong turn, I'm standing outside of the room.

Taking a deep breath, I turn the handle and walk into the classroom. Thankfully, the students are still milling around, so I approach the teacher's desk.

A middle-aged woman with curly blonde hair turns to me, looking a little annoyed. "Well, hello. You must be my new student. I'm Ms. Nolan. May I see your schedule?" She's already reaching for it as she asks.

With a fake smile, I hand it over and force my gaze to stay on hers, since the class went from a loud chatter to crickets in thirty seconds. Probably at the word "new."

To high school guys, new is code for fresh meat. For high school girls, it translates into one word: competition. I, for one, don't want to be either.

"Let's get you introduced." She steps up next to me and places her hand on my shoulder. "Okay everyone, it appears I already have your attention, so let's get this meet and greet out of the way so we can begin."

She glances back down at my schedule quickly, "Class, this is-"

She's cut off by a squeal I'm all too familiar with. "Shut up! You're in this class?!"

Ms. Nolan responds before I can. "Nice of you to join us, Ms. Edwards. Now please, have a seat." I swear she rolls her eyes.

Mia ignores her and throws her arm over my shoulder. "Everyone, this is my cousin-"

"Sit. Down. Emiliana." the teacher tells her sternly.

"Yeah, yeah. I'm going," she mumbles as she walks away, and I follow her with my eyes. The second she plants her ass in her seat, I see the large figure sitting a few rows behind her.

Drunk Guy. No fucking way.

His arrogant smirk is already on his lips as his gaze sweeps over my body.

This dick seriously thinks he had a piece?

"Okay, so why don't you take a minute to introduce yourself," I hear from my left, but I'm too busy scowling at the asshole in the back of the class.

I watch as he leans over and whispers something into another super-hot guy's ear, whose head jerks to look at me, as a sly grin crosses his lips. He then fist-bumps drunk guy.

I think I hear the teacher grunt in frustration, but my attention is pulled to Mia when she giggles. She wiggles her eyebrows at me, before nudging her head toward the teacher.

I turn to Ms. Nolan. "What?"

She sighs heavily. "Class, this is our new student. Please make her feel welcome."

"What if she's already been welcomed properly?" Drunk Guy's smug voice calls out from the back of the room.

Mia's eyes widen, and she jumps up to keep me from getting

suspended on my first day. "Watch your shit, Nate!" she snaps. "She is not the one."

"Nathaniel! That will be enough, and Emiliana, watch your mouth in my classroom."

Damn. Nathaniel. That's a good name.

Mia ignores her and hurries through the introduction. "Everyone, this is Lolli. Lolli, this is everyone. There. We're done."

Ms. Nelson looks down at my schedule she still holds in her wrinkled hands. "Your schedule doesn't say Lolli; therefore, that's not the name you will go by in my class."

Man, she is a bitch.

"Why don't you introduce yourself?" She smiles but doesn't even try to make it look genuine.

I turn back to the class; all the students are staring at me. I catch Mia's eye and she winks.

Just for kicks, I make eye contact with the guy I now know as Nathaniel, or Nate. "I'm Kalani Embers." His dickhead smirk never leaves his face, but his eyes tell me he's curious.

My gaze turns playful, and I purposely look from him to an attractive guy with kind, familiar eyes sitting a seat up and to the left of his. There's something soft and welcoming about him. "But most people call me Lolli." The guy smiles at me, and out of the corner of my eye, I notice Nate sits taller.

"Right, Kalani, why don't you grab a seat," Ms. Nolan grits out.

"I don't know about you Ms. N., but I wanna know one thing," Nate's super-hot friend begins as he gives me his best smirk, his voice shooting for sexy. "How'd you get the nickname, 'Lolli'?"

"Enough, Austin," Ms. Nolan demands, at the same time Nate smacks the back of his head.

"Kalani, please have a seat so we can get started."

With a quick glance around the room, I find three open chairs. One toward the front - a smart person would grab that one - one to the right of Austin, and the last, right in front of Nate and conveniently next to the guy with friendly eyes.

I lock my stare with Nate's as I make my way toward him and his buddy, choosing the seat right in front of him.

"Hi," I whisper to the cute guy next to me as Ms. Nolan begins her lecture.

"Hey. I'm Parker." He extends his hand to me, an easy smile on his lips.

"Hi, Parker." I hear an irritated sigh come from behind me but refuse to turn around.

His smile grows larger, and he starts to say something, but Ms. Nolan demands all our attention.

"Okay, everyone. The semester is closing in on us, and since a new student has joined us, today is the perfect day for a review." For the next forty-five minutes, we get lost in the world of protons and neutrons. Before I know it, the bell rings, and students jump out of their seats, hurrying to the door.

"So, where you headed next?" Parker asks.

"Umm..." I pull out my schedule and groan. "Ugh, shoot me." I look up at him, pouting. "Statistics."

He laughs lightly. "I take it you're not a fan?"

"Hell no, I'm not a fan. Numbers hate me."

"What room? I'll walk you," he offers, just as Mia bounces up to me.

"Hey," she acknowledges Parker before turning to me. "Ms. Nolan's a real sweetheart, right?" Her voice drips with sarcasm.

"I think she just needs to get laid or something." Mia nods in agreement, while Parker chokes on his gum at my response.

"I suggest," Ms. Nolan's voice booms over us, "you all get your belongings and get a move on."

Mia snatches my schedule out of my hands and looks it over as we walk out of the classroom. "Looks like you're on your own the rest of the day as far as classes go."

Parker's head peeks over Mia's. "I got her in Phys Ed." He turns to me then, his brows shooting up. "Why you taking PE?"

Mia rolls her eyes and slams my schedule into his chest. "Because she's a freak like that. Even purposely takes the stairs and shit." She actually shudders at the thought. "I'll see you at lunch. Meet me by the doors and we'll walk in together." Not waiting for a response, she struts down the hall.

Parker walks me to my next class, then heads off to his own.

So far, each period has dragged, becoming more and more boring than the last, and government is proving to be even worse. Sure, I'm in a 'read my dirty thoughts' staring contest with the good-looking guy across the room, but even Mister Hazel Eyes isn't enough to drown out the nonsense coming from the cutesy girl next to me.

Every. Time. This guy smirks or shifts in his seat – his attempt to spark my fire, I'm guessing - she giggles and sighs, then proceeds to tell me his life story, as if I care. I should probably be grateful that she's being friendly instead of catty, but damn.

How long is this class?

Unable to listen to any more of her babbling and unwilling to suffer through the whispered conversation of the classmates surrounding me, I excuse myself and head for the restrooms.

I swear to God, if I hear one more person talk about the great and glorious Nathaniel Monroe and his performance, be it by mouth or other appendages, I may rage out like an athlete weaning off 'roids. Oh, look! Speak of the douche and he shall appear...

I smirk and lean against the locker, watching him and a pretty brunette adjust themselves as they shuffle out of the girls' bathroom.

As soon as they look up, they spot me, both freezing. It only takes a second for them to realize they aren't necessarily busted, and I watch as their panicked expressions transform.

Nate, still a bit tense, meets my gaze and holds it, one brow raised a fraction of an inch, almost daring me to care. The girl holds her head up high, looking all too proud of herself for their little bathroom hoorah.

When she looks to Nate, finding him looking at me, she frowns, then reaches up to pet –yeah, pet – his chest with her hand.

She opens her mouth to speak, but without looking her way, he jerks his head just a teeeeny bit and her hand halts, then drops. Realizing she's being dismissed, she takes it in stride, a saucy grin forming on her lips. "See you later."

He doesn't acknowledge her and she acts like she doesn't care, sashaying down the hall.

Good for her.

I watch her for a moment, grinning, then turn back to Nate, who has yet to move an inch. "Fun times?"

He takes a single step toward me and keeps his voice low. "You're the one out here listening. Tell me," he tilts his head slightly, taking another step, a vapid smirk on his lips, "did she sound like she was having fun?"

I bite the inside of my cheek to keep from laughing at his failed attempt at seduction.

I mean, come on. He just walked out of a nasty ass bathroom with some chick, and I'm supposed to... what? Bat my lashes, giggle, full on girly sigh?

Seriously?

My face must depict my thoughts, as usual, because his smirk falters slightly. I'd even go as far as to say he looks a bit ashamed, embarrassed maybe, but he catches himself and quickly reverts to the 'cool kid' persona. His posture is strong and tall, his shoulders wide, and his feet planted a fair space apart. He's the picture of confidence and carelessness, but those eyes tell me he's not sure. About what, I don't know.

"Sorry to break it to you, but I was a bit too late to the show to catch the credits."

"I'm sure your memory can help you out."

"And I'm sure yours will bite you in the ass when the drunken fog you're clearly in wears off, and you remember what garage you parked your car in this weekend, if you catch my drift." I kick off the locker and step past him, before spinning around. Sticking my hands in my back pockets, I lock my eyes on his, and push through the door with my elbows. "Girls only." I grin, as the door swings shut, erasing him from my view.

Once lunch rolls around, Mia meets me outside the cafeteria doors as planned. She throws her hands up in a praising motion. "You survived."

"Hardly." I check my back pocket to make sure I remembered my cash. "My teachers are assholes, the females are bitches, and the guys all look like they stepped out of Sports Illustrated magazine. Like, a 'Sexiest Men of the Year' edition." I shake my head, not at all understanding. "This shit ain't normal."

She giggles and links her arm through mine, dragging me into the lunchroom's common area.

"I almost came on the spot when this sexy blond-haired gem of a guy squeezed by me in Government. Rubbed me in all the right places if you know what I mean." She busts out laughing, and I hear a familiar choke behind me. I turn to find Parker standing there, staring at me with raised eyebrows.

"Hi."

"Hey," he says, clearly not sure if he should laugh or run.

"Let's get this out of the way, okay?" His eyebrows pull together slightly, as he waits for me to continue. "I'm hella loud and tend to blurt out whatever I'm thinking, overly sexual or not, and I can be completely inappropriate. Basically, I'm like a guy."

"With a tight body," Mia adds, shaking her head in agreement.

I continue, "So, what do you think about that?"

He smiles wide and throws his arms around Mia and me. "I think you're my new best friend, Lolli."

"I can handle that," I reply with a smile.

He laughs and pulls us further through the doors.

The cafeteria is large. To my right is a smaller corner, with about twelve circular tables scattered around and long tables lining the walls. Those are filled with students working away on their laptops, while the circular tables seem to occupy several different study groups.

The left side is a wide-open space filled with dozens of long tables and chairs. These tables are filled with students eating, chatting, and all the other shenanigans you'd expect to see during a high school lunch hour.

The concessions run along the entire back wall. "Damn." There are at least a dozen different options.

Mia rolls her eyes next to me. "Right? It's way too much, but the town loves its athletes. Gotta keep 'em fed good."

"Yes, they do. We wouldn't be two-time champs without good meals," Parker teases.

"I should have known you played," I tell him, looking at him closer. "Your shoulders are massive, and I'm bettin' your thighs are rock solid."

Parker's cute. Okay, he's crazy fine. The top of his dirty blond hair is wavy and sticking up in no particular direction, while the sides are shaved a little shorter. His eyes are a light, icy blue and go well with his summer tan that's just starting to fade. The gray Henley he's wearing fits him like a glove, drawing attention to the aforementioned shoulders, and conforms slightly to the tops of his ribs, giving away a torrid physique. He's kind of got a Paul Walker thing going on.

"Earth to Lolli." Mia snaps her fingers in my face, effectively pulling me out of my daze.

"What? He knows he's fine. How could he not?" Parker laughs, a huge smile on his lips. I look him over again. "I was right about the thighs, wasn't I?"

"I'm starting to think you're the one who needs to get laid," Mia mutters as she walks off to her line of choice.

I look at Parker expectantly, making him chuckle. "Man," he

says, shaking his head, "you're something else." He leans in and whispers in my ear playfully, "They're gigantic."

When I wiggle my eyebrows in response, he laughs loudly. "Go eat," he says, shaking his head as he walks off.

Once we get our food, Mia leads us to her usual spot in the cafeteria. She and her friends take up the three tables in the farthest back corner, next to the doors that lead outside to the picnic area.

"Whuddup?" she says, as she sets her tray down.

"Hey, Mia. Hey, Lolli," her friends Ashley and Alyssa greet us. These girls have been Mia's best friends all through junior high and high school, so I've met them several times over the years.

Bet they star in a lot of these guys' fantasies with their exotic looks. Tan skin, long, sleek dark hair, with eyes to match, but polar opposites in personalities. While Ashley is quiet and reserved, Alyssa is loud and crude. I like Alyssa more.

"Why are you looking at them like that?" A grating voice questions me from my left.

I look over to find the leggy blonde from Saturday night sitting on Austin's lap.

"Because they're hot and worth a second look," I answer. Duh.

Austin laughs his ass off, Ashley blushes, and Alyssa blows me a kiss.

"Are you a lesbian or something?" she asks, scrunching up her make-up caked face in disgust. Of course she asks, as if it's a disease. Rigid bitch.

"Nope." I don't elaborate. Fuck her.

"You sure about that?" she snaps, clearly trying to get a rise out of me.

I'm two seconds from ripping into her but stop short when a hard chest presses against my back. Not sure how, but I know exactly who it belongs to.

"Oh, trust me," his deep voice drips with confidence. He waits until I glance over my shoulder and make eye contact with him to continue, "She's no lesbian."

I want to smack that smirk right off his handsome face.

The bimbo, who's no longer sitting on Austin's lap - shocker - purses her lips and crosses her arms over her chest. "And you know this how, Nate?"

Hmm...there's a bite in her voice. She's jealous.

"Come on, Liv," Austin teases, reaching out to flip her hair. "You know Nate's always the first to get acquainted with the women in this town."

Liv is fuming, Nate's still smirking, dick, and Mia is simply waiting for it, a knowing grin on her lips.

But how to play this? If I don't argue it, I look like a ho. If I do, the bitch gets satisfaction.

Good thing I don't give a shit what other people think about me.

I turn around, extremely slow, bringing Nate and I chest to chest, giving him my best 'pretty please with a naked me on top' face.

It works.

I get exactly what I'm waiting for.

"You're wasting your time, Gorgeous," he says, shaking his head. His words say one thing, but those eyes scream another. "I already told you, I don't double dip." I hear Liv scoff behind me.

Perfect. She just told me exactly what I needed to know.

This guy thinks he slept with me that night when really, he slept with her, just as I assumed. But Little Miss Perfect Legs just confirmed it wasn't her first time around, and dude doesn't remember the second. This is gonna be so much fun.

I have to fight extremely hard not to laugh.

I smile coyly, placing my hands on the edges of Nate's letterman jacket. Running my fingers over the buttons, I play the part, biting my lip as I look up at him through my lashes. With a tight grip on the collar, I lift myself onto the tips of my toes, bringing my mouth a few inches shy of his. I turn my head, tilting it up just a bit so I can speak into his ear.

"Think about it, Handsome," I tell him, loud enough for everyone to hear, purposely choosing those words so everyone thinks I'm begging him for more.

Ignoring the gasps, giggles, and whispers around me, I lean in even further, so now we're flush against each other.

"Think reeeal hard, asshole." My voice is a sultry whisper for only him to hear. "Because, I can promise you this... if I fucked you," I swear I hear him groan, "you can bet your ass you'd remember it." I let my lips brush his cheek as I lower my feet to the ground.

Nate's eyes are wild and lust filled as he stares at me, searching for a sign of a lie.

He won't find one, so I decide to throw him a bone by quickly flicking my gaze toward Liv, then wait for confirmation of something I've already figured out.

It's only a few seconds before his eyes shoot wide in realization. Bingo.

I pat his chest patronizingly. "So much for no double dippin', huh?"

His chin drops to his chest with a curse.

I start to turn around, but he catches me by the wrist before I can, pulling me back in. Out of the corner of my eye, I see Liv stomp off.

"You realize what this means, don't you?" he whispers in my ear, his voice oozing sex. "Now you can come home with me after school."

I smile wide, and when he grins in triumph, I can't help but bust out laughing.

His smile goes limp as he studies me, eyes narrowed, curious and confused. I do my best to compose myself quickly, but it's easier said than done.

"Damn," I say through a laugh as I dab at my eyes. "You're making me mess up my makeup." I point a finger at him playfully. "That's a serious offense for a girl wearing black eyeliner."

His brows are still pulled together, but I see the grin he's trying to hide.

We stare at each other for a second before it gets awkward.

"Aaany waaay... good luck with the clinger," I say as I motion toward the direction Liv stormed off in.

I start to walk away, but he stops me. Again.

This time, he grabs ahold of my elbow. I look from my elbow to his face, raising an eyebrow.

Nate scratches the back of his neck, his face pinched in confusion. "So, that's it?"

Now my brows pull in. "What do you mean?"

"I mean, you're not going to throw shit at me, or scream and yell in my face or something?"

"Um, no?" Why would I do that?

"Okay," he says, his tone skeptical. "And, just so we're clear, you're not coming home with me?" The poor guy looks so thrown off.

"I mean, sure," I shrug. "I'll go home with you." He starts to perk up, but it's short-lived. "If you want to hang out, watch bad TV, and eat hella junk food, then I'm totally game." I smirk. "But something tells me that's not what you had in mind."

"No. Definitely not."

"I'm guessing you don't get told no very often?" I raise an eyebrow in question.

"Never." His hands find his trim hips.

I laugh, walking backward so he can't reach out and grab me. "Later, Nathaniel."

"Everyone calls me Nate."

I smile. "Everyone calls me Lolli."

This time his grin does slip, and he nods slowly. "Later, Kalani."

I laugh. "Touché."

At the table, I sit down next to Mia, who is openly gaping at me.

"What?"

"Don't 'what' me, what the hell was that?" she says, a gossipy fire in her voice. "I know that little show just now wasn't about the fun from first period, so spill!"

"Remember the guy I was telling you about at Wicker yesterday?"

Her eyes widen. "No!"

"Yes." I open my Dr. Pepper and take a drink.

She squeals and grabs onto my arm. "Oh, my God! That's Nate Monroe."

"And that's supposed to mean something to me because...?"

She rolls her eyes. "He's Alrick Falls, baby. Seriously, his ass can do no wrong around here. He's our star quarterback; been on Varsity since freshman year. He's actually halfway decent, just a slut."

"Cool," I respond flatly because I super don't care.

"He's got major scholarship offers rolling in. I'm surprised you, of all people, haven't heard of him, or came across his name. He and I are just friends, known him since elementary school, but pretty much all the other girls around here fall at his feet."

"Figures." I take a bite of my croissant sandwich. Mmm... so good.

"Did he just ask you to go home with him?"

"Yep."

"And you turned him down?" Her smile couldn't possibly get any bigger.

"Uh-huh." I look around. Where did my chips go?

"Ow!" I whine through a mouthful of bread when she pinches me. "What the hell was that for?" I narrow my eyes at her.

"For giving me one-word answers," she snaps. "That shit gets on my nerves." I laugh at her and she scowls in return. "You do realize you're probably the first girl to tell him no, right? And I mean, first ever. As in... EVER!!" She's looking at me with wide eyes.

"So what?" I shrug. "He's a big boy. He'll be alright." I don't think for a second my rejection has any effect on him. "Besides, there are dozens of girls around here who, I'm sure, are willing."

"Wow," she says, a teasing edge to her voice.

"What?"

"Are you a lesbian?" The last word doesn't leave her mouth completely before I'm throwing pieces of bread at her and she's laughing hysterically at herself.

Once we catch our breath, we turn back to finish our food. During conversation, I glance behind me to find Nate staring at me from his seat.

Raising an eyebrow, I hold his gaze, and shake my head back and forth.

Not a chance, buddy.

He holds steady for a few more seconds, but as soon as his lips twitch, he turns his attention to the dark-haired girl so desperate to gain it. She's perched at the end of his table, leaning toward him, her arm slightly touching his.

Curious about his 'vagina voodoo', I prop my arm on the back of my seat and watch the Nathaniel Monroe Rope-A-Ho Show. Picture this:

First, he gazes at her. She, of course, responds with fake shyness. He knows it's an act, but she doesn't know he knows it, and dips her chin down just a bit, peeking at him through her lashes. I watch one side of his mouth turn up as he runs the pad of his finger down her left arm. This draws her in a little more.

Nate leans into her now, whispering something – no doubt, something dirty, sexy - in her ear, causing her to giggle. He pulls back a little, enough to look her in the eyes, giving her no choice but to notice when he drops his gaze to her lips.

As soon as she licks them in response, he pulls back more and goes in for the kill, giving her his game-winning smile. Let's hear the applause because there it is, ladies and gentlemen... the infamous blush. And just like that, she's ready to strip down and do the dirty-dirty.

It would almost be impressive if it weren't so damn typical. With a smile and a shake of my head, I turn around and rejoin the debate of matte versus gloss.

Chapter Four

K ALANI

I walk to my next class, ready to rock this shit out and get the day moving. That is, until I enter English and see Liv perched on a desk near the front of the class, legs crossed, palms face down on the desk.

The second she notices me, her face shifts from flirty to 'fuck you' quicker than the D-line at the recognition of a trick play.

Then, the funniest shit I've ever seen happens.

She stands, juts her jean skirt-clad hip out, and crosses her arms over her chest, as two other blondes flank her, mocking her position. It's quite comical, to be honest.

They're cute, not nearly as attractive as Liv is, but that's usually how it goes. The Countess never wants her followers to stand out over her.

When I grin, she stands taller, her eyes narrowing.

She gets all up in my personal space. "You're new here."

I'm not sure if she wanted a response or not, but when I don't give her one, she opens her mouth again. "Mia may be your cousin, but don't think that brings you to my level." Her eyes narrow even further, her body shifting to a more aggressive stature. "Stay away from him."

I laugh. Loudly. This girl's hilarious.

As I catch my bearings, I look up at her and I freeze, mid-fun.

She's not...surely, she's not serious?

"Wait." I put my hand out in front of me, my head drawing back a notch. "Are you for real right now?"

"Do I look like I'm joking to you?" she sneers.

Oh, hell to the no...

I take a step forward, forcing her to step back. "What's the matter, Liv?" I goad her, knowing damn well who the him is she's referring to. "Afraid you won't get round three?" Her eyes widen just the slightest, but I was waiting, so I caught it.

Yeah, Bitch. I know you've only had him twice.

"You little-" She's cut off as the teacher enters. She looks back at me briefly, before taking her seat at the front.

Once everyone is seated, I go through the whole new student ordeal for the fifth time today and walk to the back of the class, where there are several open desks, and take a seat.

Just as the teacher is about to start, she stops, a frown forming on her round face. Crossing her arms, she leans back against the white board, and waits.

Nothing happens for a good three minutes. She just continues to stand there, and I'm starting to wonder if she's all there. Right when I'm about to pull her crazy card, the classroom door opens and the room shifts.

The pheromone levels rise as a handful of Alrick High's finest walk – no, stalk - through the door.

The guys in the class look away, as the females maneuver themselves into position, pushing their tits out and twirling their hair.

Idiots.

The first through the door is the manwhore himself.

Nate commands attention when he walks. All tall and broad, and far too alluring for his own good. It's hard to explain, but you can't really take your eyes off him. His robust shoulders in that tight gray t-shirt and dark jeans don't exactly hurt, either. If he wasn't such a self-proclaimed sleaze, I may or may not let him play a part in my dirty fantasies.

Once he's completely through the door, I zone in on the treat right behind him. It's the guy from my government class I was telling Mia about earlier. He has that silky blond hair you want to pull on, with green eyes, and a perma-smirk on his lips. His hair is spiked slightly, but free of products. He's about five-eleven; solid, but not massive. I'm guessing his contribution to the team is speed.

The cornerback, maybe?

He's delicious.

"Kalani?"

My attention snaps to the front of the classroom and giggles erupt around me.

"Honey," the teacher gestures with her head. "Would you mind moving a seat back so the boys can sit?"

I look to my left then, and see Austin, Nate, and two monstrous guys – definitely linemen - smirking at me.

Wait, where's...

I look to my right.

There he is. Sexy government guy is sitting directly next to me.

When I smile, he winks.

"Is there assigned seating in this class, Ms. Arella?" I ask, not taking my eyes off government boy.

"Well," she pauses. "Technically, no, there's not, bu-"

"Then I'm good," I say, before turning back to her.

"Oh." She seems like she's not sure what to say. "Oh, well, yes, of course."

She then faces the guys, as do I. Nate is the only one still standing. He's scowling at me, so I give him my biggest, brightest, sweetest smile. Teeth and everything.

He keeps his scowl in place but can't hide the small smile creases at the corners of his eyes. I think I hear him take the open seat directly behind me, but I don't look to confirm.

"Ms. Arella!" Liv shrieks from the front of the room. "You can't just let her take his seat like that!"

"Olivia, please," she says on a sigh. "Let's get class started, shall we?"

Liv or 'Olivia' whips around in her seat and tries to burn me with her gaze. I, being the sweet girl I am, blow her a kiss, making sure the smooch sound is nice and audible. She narrows her eyes a little more before swiveling back around, huffing and puffing. I do my best to cover the laugh that makes its way up my throat.

As expected, the class is boring and uneventful, and forty something minutes later, we're dismissed.

Right as I stuff my notebook into my bag, the guy from my government class kneels next to my desk.

I clasp my hands under my chin and lean on my elbows. "Hi there."

He smiles. "I'm Jarrod."

"What can I do for you, Angel Face?"

Lick you? Bite you? Both?

"Come by Wicker tonight," he says, looking at me like he wants to eat me.

If he plays his cards right, I just might let him.

Just as I'm about to say 'abso-fucking-lutely', Nate pipes in.

"Sorry man, she's busy."

My head snaps toward him. "No. No, I'm not." I stand, crossing my arms over my chest, glaring at this delusional dumbass.

"Yes. You are," he says in a stony voice, his eyes hard and focused on me, as if I'm supposed to care.

41

Jarrod chuckles from beside me. "I'll talk to you later, Lolli," he tells me as he walks out of the classroom.

I turn back to scowl at Nate just in time to watch Liv slither her way next to him.

His jaw ticks in annoyance, but his eyes are still trained on me, so I give him a 'karma's a bitch' smirk.

"What, Olivia?" he snaps, reluctantly turning toward her.

I take the opportunity to make a clean getaway and head to my final class of the day, PE.

Mr. Prescott greets me with a frown, thrusting a lock and locker number into my hands, and waves me off to get changed, telling me to meet him on the field.

I make it a point to rush my ass and am exiting the locker room in less than three minutes.

As I step around the corner of the gymnasium to get to the track field, I see nothing but a shit-ton of muscles. The big, buff, sweaty, sexy kind. And for some godforsaken reason, my eyes find Nate.

His shirt, much like everyone else's, is sleeveless and ripped from the armpit to the waist, and his black track pants lie perfectly against his trim hips.

They fit him real good.

All the guys seem to be following his lead as they begin to stretch. He's definitely the Alpha of this group. That thought reminds me of the stunt he pulled in English. Not that I wanted to jump on and ride the Jarrod train the first chance I got, but from what the curly-haired girl in government - okay, apparently, I did listen to a bit of her rambling - said, he actually dates, unlike the other players on the team. Ha! Players.

Speaking of Jarrod...

"Hi, Lolli," he purrs with a sly smile as I approach.

Yeah... I'd ride it.

When I don't respond, just gawk at him, he turns his grin to the group behind him then back to me. "You do realize seventh period PE is for the football team, right?"

"It was either this or first with the freshman class." I peek around him. "Yeah, clearly made the right decision." I wiggle my eyebrows at him.

With a chuckle, he moseys on over to the Magic Mike crew-in-training.

There really should be some kind of limit; only so much steaminess allowed in one place. Like a max capacity of muscle mass.

I sigh. "I'm gonna go to jail."

"Jail, huh?"

I look over to find Parker walking up next to me. "Oh, yeah," I tell him, watching as the guys start stretching their legs, tilting my head to follow their actions. "Definitely."

He throws his arm over my shoulder, dragging me toward Mr. Prescott, who is now beckoning me with his finger.

"I'll bail you out," he says playfully, nudging me. "So, you're ripe then, huh?"

"More like rancid."

"Rancid?"

"Yeah, you know, stale, overripe, fucking shriveled." The last word leaves me on a pout and Parker bends over laughing. I roll my eyes and shrug his arm off my shoulder before making my way over to the teacher.

"Ms. Embers." He gives a little jerk of his chin. "Have any trouble in the locker room?"

"No sir, I undressed and redressed myself just fine."

He blinks.

"Ms. Embers, I can handle your wit, but try to remember you're in a class full of," he pauses to find the right words, "overly-stimulated young men." He pulls his brows in. "You might want to refrain from any words that relate to... well, basically anything female-related."

"Uh..."

"I think that might be a problem, Coach," Parker says, a teasing edge to his voice. Placing his hands on his hips, he continues, "Lolli here is worse than half these boys."

Mr. Prescott sighs, pulling his Oakley's from his salt and pepper hair. "Just keep to the track or the weight room and you'll be fine."

"I can do that," I tell him eagerly.

He looks from me and Parker, to the group of guys behind us, and back to me. Putting his sunglasses on, he turns to leave, mumbling, "This should be interesting."

I would have to agree.

As soon as he's out of earshot, I turn and narrow my eyes on the shithead next to me.

"Aww... don't be mad at me, Lolli Bear. You're my new favorite person," he says, as he makes a show of slowly approaching me, as if I'll pounce, then envelops me in a hug.

"Yeah, well," I begin with zero enthusiasm, "you're not so bad yourself."

I laugh when he playfully gasps in mock appreciation and hug him back briefly.

"So, how old are you?"

"Eighteen. Nineteen in April."

Parker's eyebrows disappear into his hairline. "Shit, I better start saving," he says seriously.

"Saving?"

"Yup." He motions to all the hotness surrounding me. "Look around, Lolli. A body like yours surrounded by all these assholes. You're definitely going to jail." He barely gets the last word out before he's bellowed over in laughter at his own dig.

Before I can stop him, he's calling out, "Hey, dickheads!"

"Is this necessary?" I yell-whisper through my teeth.

He laughs harder.

Dick.

"Raise your beater meter if you're officially primetime, boys. We've got a full-grown, wild-woman on our hands." He chuckles and I can't help but laugh, too.

I watch, amazed these guys understood Parker's bullshit, as a hand goes up here and there, taking note of whose hands are raised, because, well, it's good to know, right?

Jarrod's hand is one of the first to rise. He shoots me a wink when I catch his eye. A few other guys I've seen throughout the day raise their hands as well.

"Does this mean I'm outta the race for your heart, Lolli?"

I turn to Austin, who has both hands down.

I tilt my head playfully. "Still need mommy to sign your progress reports?"

"Eighteen in May." He spreads both arms out. "I'm the baby."

Next, Nate catches my eye. I look down at his hands, then back at his face, raising an eyebrow.

He smirks and takes off down the track. And the fun is over, because as expected, his boys follow.

I squeal when Parker smacks my ass and takes off. Spinning around, he starts with a backward jog. "It's okay, Lolli Bear." He smiles wide. "That party you cut out on this weekend..." I nod my head, my eyes narrowing slightly. "That was my birthday party." Laughing, he turns and takes off full sprint to catch up to the group.

I laugh and drop down to finish the last of my stretches.

I take a minute to watch the team, observing how well disciplined they are, even in something as simple as group laps.

Four lines, single file, even speeds. All hanging back, running in place when someone falls behind; a pat on the shoulder or a gentle push in the back where encouragements needed.

It's a beautiful thing to watch, the camaraderie.

A true smile hints at my lips for the briefest of moments before it's gone.

I breathe in and out before taking off, entering the land of free winds and piercing silence. A place free of judgment and expectation and...emotion. Stone cold numbness. It's all right foot, left foot, back straight, eyes forward. Distance. Point A to point B.

Pure nothingness.

Perfection.

Chapter Five

K ALANI

Walking out of the girl's locker room, I head straight toward Mia's Jeep.

She's sitting on the hood talking to a couple of people, but as soon as she spots me, she waves them on, and smirks.

That's never good.

"Hey, hoochie," she says slyly.

I cross my arms, narrow my eyes, and wait.

She huffs. "Fine, I heard you and Nate have a," she wiggles her eyebrows up and down, "date this afternoon. That didn't take long." She looks mighty pleased with herself.

"Wow, word really travels fast around here," I tell her, my annoyance obvious. "And fuck no, we don't. That guy from my government class, Jarrod Hollins -"

"Ooh," she cuts me off. "He's a good one."

I ignore her and continue. "Asked me out and Nate ruined it."

"Well," she leans back, propping herself onto her elbows. "Word is, Nate's taking you home after practice today."

"Yeah, that's not happening."

"Hope you're ready to tell him that." She tips her chin, motioning behind me.

With a huff, I turn to see him closing in. I go ahead and let my eyes rake over him.

His track pants have been traded for a pair of black football pants.

I was right about the thighs; nice and strong.

"Give me your bag, I'll throw it in the Hummer, and then you can come watch me practice." He says it like he's talking to an old friend and this is routine.

I gape at him for a few seconds. "Huh?"

He reaches out and tugs on my shoulder strap. "I'll put this up for you," he says again, placing his hands on his hips casually.

"You're delusional if you think this is happening," I snap.

"Don't be difficult, Kalani," he huffs.

He fucking huffs, like I am being unreasonable.

I drop my bag on the ground and push a finger into his chest. "Listen hotshot, I get it. You're used to being the shot caller around here, but I," I motion to myself, "am not from around here."

"You not a woman of your word, Ms. Embers?" he asks, a cute, I'd say innocent, if I didn't know any better, smile on his lips.

I stomp my foot, like a damn child. "I never said I'd go with you."

"Flip on it." He raises a dark brow.

"I...what?" I hear Mia giggle from behind me, clearly enjoying this shit.

"Come on, it's mostly fair." He nods to Mia, and the bitch tosses him a quarter.

Because she just happened to have one in her hand?

"This is dumb. Fine. Whatever." I roll my eyes, propping my hip against the side of the Jeep.

He lets out a deep chuckle. "Alright, heads I win, tails you lose."

I purse my lips, nodding.

He throws the quarter up and it lands on tails. Mia starts laughing and hops off her hood.

"Guess I'll see you later, Lolls," she grins, jumping into her Jeep and turning it on. She shakes her head, her brows high into her hairline. "I can't believe you fell for that," she giggles, dropping her shades into place. "Byyee." The bitch speeds off, officially leaving my ass high and dry.

"What just happened?" I ask, utterly confused.

Nate smirks, a deep, dangerous, naughty smirk, and completely ignores me. Bending down, he grabs my bag, throws it over his shoulder, and heads back toward the field. "No time to put this away. Coach will lay me out if I'm late."

He keeps walking while I stand frozen in place, trying to figure out what the fuck just went down.

He's about halfway across the parking lot when my mouth falls open in shock, then quickly transforms into a huge smile. "You tricked me, you little shit!" I shout, laughing all the while.

He doesn't turn around but throws his head back on a laugh.

I catch up to him and shove him lightly in the shoulder. "That was damn good, Nathaniel Monroe. Damn good," I tell him, a smile still on my lips.

He shrugs. "My dad used to pull that shit on me. For the longest time, I thought it was luck, or a trick coin or something, because he always won. Took me a whole summer of yard work before I finally figured it out." He chuckles.

He walks up a few stairs and sets my bag down on the first bench seat in the bleachers. "All right, I gotta get out there." He looks over his shoulder at the boys warming up on the field, then back to me. "You," he points a stern finger, "stay put. You wanted bad TV and junk food? That's what you're getting."

My nose wrinkles. "I did say that didn't I?"

He smiles, all cocky like. "You did."

"Uh-huh," I tease, "and you're sure this is about what I wanted, and not about you, how did Austin put it..." I tilt my head and place a finger to the corner of my mouth. "That's right," I snap my fingers. "About how you have to be the first to get 'acquainted' with the women in this town."

"Well, I couldn't let Jarrod beat me to it, now could I?" he smirks.

I cross my arms, feeling irritated all over again, remembering how he stepped in where he wasn't wanted. "That was fucked up."

"I'm much better, trust me."

"I doubt it," I shoot back.

He steps forward, his dark eyes blazing with intensity.

"Monroe!" We both turn toward the field to see Mr. Prescott's clipboard-clad hand raised as he uses his other to point at his watch.

I turn back to him, only to find he's already halfway down the stairs.

I debate grabbing my bag and walking home. That, or calling Mia's bitch ass and making her come back to get me. But I do neither. No, I play the good little servant girl, listening to the words of a man-boy on a power trip and sit my ass down.

Shrugging to myself, I decide I'm going to enjoy this for my own selfish reasons. Hot athletes in tight pants, grinding, pushing, and engaging in the most intricate dance of all.

Football is an art, really. A hand-selected bunch, each for very different reasons, pieced together to form the biggest and best, most in sync, combination of fight and fury. There's nothing gentle about the way these boys work.

The boys line up. The QB, Nate, calls out, letting them know what he needs of them. They get into position; a typical pass formation of five down linemen and four receivers, but at the last second, the defensive line shifts right.

"Interesting," I mutter to myself, leaning forward slightly.

The ball snaps and Nate drops back, plants his back foot, and steps forward into the pocket ready to fire the ball, but my eyes zone in on the line. I watch as the O-tackle and guard are forced to step left into their gaps to cover their blocks. This leaves a gap in the center, a perfect opening for the middle linebacker to swoop in and make the sack, easy as pie. Only he doesn't. A wide smile takes over my lips.

It's a test run.

A perfect setup.

I don't see the throw, but when the offense cheers, I know the pass was successful. I laugh, knowing what's coming.

The boys set up, now at the sixty-one. One, two, hut, but this time the D-line shifts left.

"Here it comes," I whisper, my leg bouncing in anticipation.

And sure enough, the offense doesn't see what's happening until the right outside linebacker swoops in and takes down their QB.

"Sack." I smirk at my perception.

Nate hops up, brushes it off, and lines his boys up again.

He's running a hurry up offense, so I'm almost positive he didn't evaluate that last play, which means it's bound to happen again.

As if on cue, same play, same result. He lets out a loud curse as he huffs back into position for the third time, now set back to the fifty. I sneak a peek at Mr. Prescott and he's got his hand covering his mouth, a deep frown creasing his forehead, but he's not making any corrections.

What the hell?

My anger rises as I prepare for the same conclusion.

I'm on my feet as soon as the ball's snapped. I hear the roars of the boys, the defense fired up, and the O-line cursing and barking about preserving their quarterback, but I'm on a mission.

I stomp right up to Mr. Prescott and jut my hip out. "What the hell, Mr. P.!"

He does a double take before resting his scowling face on me. "Ms. Embers, what the hell are you doing on my field?"

I ignore him. "Why do you keep letting him run that? He's getting nailed every time!" I shout. He eyes me, but as soon as Nate calls out, his gaze zips back to the field.

If he's not going to acknowledge me, I'm giving his ass my play by play.

"Balls on the forty-four, because he's losing yards. QB's running a no huddle hurry up offense, i.e., no time to adjust coverage. It's an obvious pass play formation." Mr. P. cuts me an irritated look out of corner of my eye. "Ball's down and ready but look at your defense." I point. "The defensive line shifts left. Watch your offensive tackle," I rush to say, just as it plays out in front of us. The O-tackle blocks the outside gap, leaving the inside gap open for the middle linebacker to swoop in and make the sack. Again.

"See!" I yell, turning back to Mr. Prescott, who is gaping at me.

"The offensive line needs to be able to spot these things at first go-round. I mean," I scoff, "how much more obvious could it be, really? They set the shit up perfect, first play." My hands are flailing all around. "A standard play across the board, with zero adjustment, and the D-line shifts?" I tilt my head. "Seriously? It was perfectly executed on the offensive side, boys rush in, receiver's deep, and free of coverage. All was good, except the obvious brilliance from your D was overlooked.

"And it worked!" I take a deep breath and look up at Mr. P., who's looking at me like I sprung two heads.

"What?"

"How the hell did you read that?"

My gaze snaps to the field to see Parker walking toward me, a huge, proud papa bear smile on his face. I take note of the embroidered C near his right shoulder. "Defensive captain?" I quirk a brow, a grin taking over my face.

"You know it, baby." he laughs. "Playing safety allows me to see everything. Helps me spot the gaps."

"Okay, Hero." I nod, then jerk my chin toward the field. "That your play?"

"It was. First time trying it out." He unsnaps his chin strap, pulls his helmet off, and wipes the sweat from his forehead with his wrist.

He squints one eye. "Was it really that easy to read?"

A cackle bubbles out of me. "Obviously not. It worked... like, five times," I tell him.

He nods, his grin growing. "Good."

"That test run," I point to the field. "That was good. Perfect, really. They didn't see it coming. Test one way, execute another. Keep 'em guessing." I nod, thoroughly impressed.

Parker leans in, his warm breath close to my ear. "That's 'cause I'm smooth as silk, Lolli Bear. Smooth as silk," he whispers, making both of us laugh.

"I have no idea what's happening right now," Mr. Prescott says, his irritation evident.

We both look over at him.

He points at Parker. "Not sure why your helmet is off your head or why you're over here." He turns the finger on me. "And you... hell, I don't know what to say to you." He scratches at his chin, eyes narrowed. "Embers, huh?" he inquires.

"Uh, yeah," I answer hesitantly, but still looking him in the eye.

His lip twitches and he looks away, nodding.

My gaze returns to the field to find the entire team's eyes on me. Curious if he's shooting daggers at me, I sneak a quick peek at Nate, finding him simply watching me, intrigued.

I cup my mouth with my hands. "Well, you all heard the get

down." I turn to the O-tackle. "Okay, number..." oh hey, it's Austin, "Number Nine, screw the adjustment. Stay on your guy, no matter what. It's all an illusion. A mind fuck if you will. Obviously, we're hoping the opposing team won't see it, but you guys need to be prepared in case someone comes at you with a similar play. Let's see it in action." I shove Parker in the shoulder. "Get out there, Hero." I shoot him a wink.

He laughs and plants a sweaty kiss on my cheek, before jogging back on the field.

"You heard the boss lady. Line it up, boys," Parker calls out and everyone gets into position, the offense now knowing what's coming.

"Wait!" I wail.

"God damn it, Embers," Mr. P. barks, hitting his leg with his clipboard in frustration.

"You!" I yell, pointing at the middle linebacker who keeps getting the sack. "Chillax, alright? Your QB needs to be able to play the game on Friday. He can't do that if you keep laying him out. Save that shit for the opposing team, eh?" He laughs loudly, then makes a show of angling his back toward me so I can view the last name on the back of his practice jersey. Hollins.

Jarrod.

Oh, shit.

"Alright, boys, stop fuckin' around. Get this done. Ms. Embers." He shoots me a look, like he's trying really hard to be mad, but can't figure out why he's not. "Sit."

With a slight pout, I start to walk back to my seat in the bleachers.

"Ms. Embers," he calls and I turn to him.

With his head, he motions toward the players' bench. So, with a smile, I plant my ass right at the fifty-yard line.

After a while of watching the boys on the field, my eyes haze over and suddenly I'm in a different time, a different place altogether; yet, it's all familiar.

The smell of the dew-covered grass, the loud cracking sounds that take over the air - a testament to the hard work and effort given from the players. The gusty winds and crisp frosty air rustles the last of the rust-colored leaves from their branches.

Closing my eyes, I take a deep breath in, welcoming the razor-sharp November air.

Man, I've missed this.

A small smile graces my lips for a half a second before my eyes fly open.

Panicked, I jump up and head straight for my bag. The second I pick it up and prepare to bail, I'm hoisted up and spun around by a very happy, very sweaty, Parker Baylor.

He drops me and bends to whisper in my ear, "Where you going, Lolli Bear?"

He pulls back to look down at me. "You were 'bout to bolt."

Evasion isn't lying, right?

"Perhaps I was." I force a grin. "Perhaps I wasn't."

"Uh-huh," he laughs. "Your ass was on a mission; Operation Escape Monroe's Hooks." He laughs harder when I smack him on the back of the head. "We usually head to Wicker after practice a couple days a week. We're going there after showers. You in?" he asks, squeezing me tighter.

I'm about to respond when a throat clears behind us.

I turn, still in Parker's arms, to see Nate standing there, helmet in hand, sweat dripping down his temple, and looking pissed. I purposely lean into Parker's chest, my back to his front.

He looks away. "I'm gonna change and we'll head out."

"Can we go to Wicker instead?" I ask, just to be polite because I'm going, whether he likes it or not. I think he knows it because he reluctantly agrees, before stomping off.

Parker waits a good forty-five seconds before he chuckles into my hair. "You're a mean, mean woman."

With a sigh, I pull myself out of his grasp, and turn to pat his chest. "I am indeed. Now, go change. I don't want to get there way before you."

"Afraid to be alone with the infamous," he uses a dreamy schoolgirl voice, "Nate Monroe?"

"Afraid, no." I deadpan. "Annoyed? Most definitely."

He smiles. "Uh-huh, okay, Lolli Bear."

"Whatever, you better hurry your ass up. This is your fault."

His eyebrows shoot up. "My fault? How the hell is this my fault?"

I roll my eyes. "Okay, fine, it wasn't your fault, but you could have warned me or something."

His eyes flicker over my shoulder as he leans in to kiss my temple. "See you in a bit."

As he passes, I turn to find Nate already at the bottom of the stairs, waiting for me.

His hair fresh and wet – fastest shower known to man, I'm guessing.

"Ready?" he asks, his tone irked.

I sit down and cross my legs, folding my hands in a patient motion over my knees, and look at him with a cheesy smile on my face.

"What the hell are you doing, Kalani?"

When I don't move an exasperated sigh leaves him, and he runs both hands down his face. "Let's go."

Still, I don't move, just keep smiling.

He narrows his eyes, but it only takes about ten seconds for him to crack a smile and shake his head.

"See. That wasn't so hard." I jump up and throw my bag over my shoulder, walking down to meet him. I stop two stairs from the bottom, bringing us eye level, and narrow my gaze on him. "No brooding allowed."

He steps forward, bringing us a breath away. "Rule for a rule?" He quirks an eyebrow.

Something in the pit of my stomach flits, making me nauseous or, well, I don't really know. It's strange, which pisses me off. So, naturally, I purse my lips, mask my face, and push past him.

I'm not falling for that...

He chuckles and snatches my bag off my shoulder, leading me to his fancy pants ride.

To ease the tension, I head toward the driver side; you know, for old times' sake. His eyes narrow, but he can't hide the amusement laced in them as he steers me toward the passenger door.

"Not today?" I ask over my shoulder.

Leaning in, he whispers, "Not ever. Now, hop in."

The rest of the night goes by in a frenzy. That'll happen when you put thirty rowdy guys with fresh adrenaline pumping through their veins in one place. Throw in the new girl who had to show her shit at practice and it's a damn circus.

Everyone fired off question after question: Where did I learn it? How long have I been a fan? Where did I come from? Was I single and taking marriage applications? That one was good.

I smiled, played polite, and answered most questions with a question, but all in all, it was fun. And when I told Nate I was getting a ride back to my house from Parker, he frowned and walked out, the dark-haired girl he was playing with at lunch under his arm.

Good times.

Hopping out of the shower, I brush my hair and teeth and drop onto my bed. I call for Nauni and she jumps up, snuggling into my side.

"Today was a good day, Nauni," I whisper, running my hand down her back and across her tail.

Reaching over to my nightstand, I pull out my camera and set it down beside me.

I could just snap a picture. Of the wall. The window. Nauni. It'd be easy. Insta-photo, Polaroid and all, but the thought makes me want to puke and I like my bed too much for that.

My phone beeps next to me.

Picking it up, I find a text from Mia.

Meems: you alive or did the dreaded thing called high school win out?

Me: better call the coroner.

Meems: hmm... wonder if the autopsy will show death by feral females - aka jealous bitches - or hard up hot heads – aka the ENTIRE football team...

I bust up laughing, which scares the shit out of Nauni.

Me: definitely the latter.

Meems: yeah, figured. Heard you let your football flag fly today?

Me: not a big deal, Meems.

Meems: oh, but it is. However, since I love you, I'll play along... good job you.

I can't help but smile.

Meems: my mom asked about you today. Guess she figured you would be over for dinner. Talk about your day and what not.

Me: and what not.

Meems: yeah.

I gnaw at my lip, unsure of what to say; an extreme rarity for me.

Meems: see you in the morning, Lollipop.

Thankful she gave me the out I needed, I sigh, toss my phone on my nightstand, and put the camera back in the drawer.

Today was a little crazy.

I forgot how chaotic a single day in high school could be. I made a friend in Parker; one I can tell will go the distance. I see something in him that I see in myself. He's spunky and free spirited, but there's more going on behind his blue eyes, something he pushes away, like me. I think he sees it too, and for that, we'll balance one another well.

Then there's Jarrod, a good-looking guy I might be able to kill time with. That is, if he's not a total dud and doesn't backpedal after Nate's little "she's busy" stunt. Shithead.

Right. Nate, the broody, sexy superstar looking to add another hit to his helmet. I wouldn't be opposed to it if he wasn't such a privileged ass about it. Assuming, instead of putting in the legwork. I've dealt with over privileged assholes all my life, kids of high-profile people who think their name or status means they get what they want at the snap of a finger.

Yeah, me and those kids never got along.

Then there's the bitchy blonde who clearly thinks Nate belongs to her. And shit, maybe he does. Who knows?

So, yeah. One day in and I have a friend I never wanted, but now plan to keep, a guy to play with, a guy to fend off, and girl to watch out for.

Throwing myself onto my back, I stare at the ceiling.

Fuck high school.

Chapter Six

K ALANI

Two weeks in and mostly everything remained the same. Liv was still a raging bitch, PE was still my favorite class, Nate never failed to frown in my direction, and Mr. Prescott was still both irritated and curious about me.

Every day, I continued, on my own accord, to show up to practice. It was the second day when I discovered cheer also practiced at the same time, on the same field. It didn't take me long to figure out Liv was team captain. To say she didn't particularly like that I was watching the boys' practice was an understatement.

Mia knew my first week was a lot to take in, so when the weekend came, she didn't hassle me too much about going out. I told her I needed some R and R and she was okay with it. Well, she accepted it. Begrudgingly, of course.

Last Friday had been the team's bye week, so I'm excited to go to the game tonight.

Apparently, so is the whole damn town, I think, searching the bleachers for a place to sit, Mia in tow.

She squeals, pointing to the second bleacher from the bottom that's half-bare in the center. "There!"

I shake my head, leaning close so she can hear me over all the noise. "There's a blanket down. Those seats are taken."

"Oh, I know they are," she says, pulling me toward the section, a deep smirk in place.

"Mia, we can't take someone's seats."

"You're right, but these," she steps over the first bleacher, not caring that she's bumping into people all around her, "are our seats. Well, your seats, but I get to bask in your glory."

I squeeze by the front row, careful not to nail anyone with my bag, and sit down next to her. "And who, dare I ask, saved these seats for me?"

"It appears Mr. Hollins is ready to make his play, Ms. Embers." She wiggles her eyebrows. "Rumor has it, he's coming for you tonight."

A smile finds my lips. "'Bout damn time. I thought Nate scared him off with his He-Man act. Luckily, he's chilled out."

"Yeah, something's up with him. I went to Wicker last night with Ashley and Alyssa, and Ryan said he hasn't been in since Monday, which is totally out of character for him."

Eyes on the field, I shrug. "Maybe he wasn't hungry?"

She barks out a laugh. "Hungry? Shit, Lolli. It's not about being hungry." She thinks it over for a second. "Well, I guess it is." She laughs again.

I turn to look at her, frowning.

"Lolli," she gapes at me. "Wicker is where all the girls go, knowing damn well the guys will be there. It's basically a one stop shop for the team. Fill up on carbs, then burn 'em off." She grins.

"Shag 'em and bag 'em."

"Pick 'em and stick 'em."

We both laugh.

61

The lady in front of us turns around, shooting daggers at Mia.

"Oh, hey, how you doing Ms. Asia?" Mia asks, overly animated and clearly amused.

The woman scoffs and turns around.

Mia laughs and leans into to whisper in my ear. "'Member the story I told you about the guy I got caught dry humping on the bus freshman year?"

I nod.

"That's his mom." She laughs. "Did I tell you she was the one driving said school bus?"

Now we're both laughing.

She turns in her seat and I look back out at the field.

"Anyway," she shrugs, digging her lipstick out of her purse. "Something's off with Nate."

"Maybe he has a girlfriend or is hooking up with some chick and doesn't need to go to Wicker."

She scoffs. "Um, no. That's the least likely scenario."

The conversation is cut off as we stand for the National Anthem.

The game starts out on a high note, with a Knight running the kickoff back for a touchdown. All the boys are on point, Nate included.

Watching him, his precision, his fluidness... It's so obvious his heart is in his hands, in the form of rubber and laces. The moment it leaves his hand, you know it's going only where intended. He has full control.

Passion in its deepest venue.

In the end, the boys take the win thirty-four to thirteen.

As we pack up to leave, I hear my name being called from below. I turn, finding Jarrod at the bottom of the railing. He rips his helmet off, his blond hair slick with sweat.

"You found your seat," he shouts.

"That I did. Good lookin' out."

He grins. "Let me take you to the party tonight."

Right, the party. As much as I want to hang with him, I don't want to go to a party. I'm about to turn him down when I remember I told Mia I would try the whole normal high school senior thing.

I walk up to the metal bar and lean over, into his space. "You gonna feed me first?"

His green eyes light up. "I can do that."

"Then, I can definitely go with you."

He laughs, stepping back. "Let me get fresh for you." He holds up both hands, his helmet still in one. "Ten minutes. Stay there," he says with a wink, and I can't help but think of the last person who told me to stay put.

My eyes seek him out. He's standing next to Mr. P. and a gray-haired man, a pleased smile taking over his handsome face. In my peripheral, I see Liv. When I turn to meet her stare, she flicks her gaze to Nate, then back at me, her eyes narrowing so low I'm surprised she can see.

When I toss her a flippant smile, she flips me off.

It's the perfect hate-hate relationship.

Jarrod and I end up at a small taco shop.

Our conversation is light and easy. He tells me he plans to play ball in college, but eventually he wants to go into business with his father. Apparently, he owns a computer programming company that helps create and edit commercial ads. Interesting enough, I guess.

He asks me what I plan to do after high school, so I tell him I plan to channel my inner pixie, fly to Neverland, bunk with Wendy, and become best friends with Tiger Lily.

All in all, it was fun. So, when he asks me to go out with him again, I agree.

By the time we pull up, it's around ten-thirty, and the party's in full swing.

He turns off his truck – a white Dodge Ram, locked and loaded, chrome everything - and opens his door. He looks to me before stepping out. "You ready for your first official Alrick High party?" I just smile, not telling him I was at one a few weeks ago.

As we walk up the steps, he places his hand on my lower back. It's a sweet, yet unnecessary, gesture.

"So, whose place is this?"

"Parker's dad's house," he responds as we walk through the door.

Relief washes over me. Parker's place I can do.

Jarrod senses it and removes his hand, his eyes cutting away then back to me.

I can't help but laugh. "Just ask, Hollins. Don't be scurred," I tease.

He laughs, nodding his head, urging me through the entryway and into the kitchen. "All right." He hesitates for a beat. "So, you and Parker..."

So, he's not bold enough to ask. Shame.

"Are just friends. I plan on keeping him around," I hold his gaze. "Indefinitely."

He lifts his hands in surrender, a grin on his lips. "Message received," he laughs, reaching out to brush my arm with his finger-tips. "Want a drink?"

"Sure." I nod. "If you can find me something with a cap or twist top that has yet to be popped or twisted, I'll have a drink."

"Smart girl."

I turn to mingle but stop when I feel his hand on my arm again.

"I'm not about to leave you here for some other guy to try and swoop in."

"Paranoid much?" I laugh.

"Definitely," he says with a smirk.

64

The night continues with ease. We mix and meander through the house, chatting about nothing with different people. Jarrod is very attentive. I know he wants me to have a good time, to feel included, and he's doing a good job. But I just need to breathe, get some fresh air. My facial expression must show it because Parker finds his way to me, a knowing grin on his lips.

"Jarrod, my man." He slaps him on the shoulder. "I'm stealing Lolli for a while."

Jarrod looks at me for confirmation. I should probably feel bad, but I have been hanging out with him for the last few hours.

With a smile, I rise to my toes to speak in his ear so I don't have to yell over the music. "I'm gonna hang with Parker. If I don't see you before one of us heads out, thanks for tonight." I drop a quick kiss to his cheek before lowering to my feet.

His smile seems a little forced but he nods, dropping his head to kiss my cheek as well.

Parker tries to hide his grin but fails miserably. Throwing his arm across my shoulder, he pulls me through the house.

"You looked like you needed an escape," he laughs.

I smile and wrap my arm around his lower back. Leaning my head into his side, I sigh. "Ahh, Parker...my Knight in tight Calvin's."

He busts out laughing. "You like these, huh?" He reaches down and snaps the top of his briefs that are slightly sticking out of his faded jeans.

"It's quite sexy, yes, but...question?" I pull back to look at him.

He quirks a brow.

"Not that I don't mind the view, but why aren't you wearing a shirt?"

He backs away from me, eyes bright with mischief and glazed from alcohol. He shifts his hips, swinging his arms around, and sings, "All the girlies love me..."

I bend over laughing, hard, crossing my legs to keep myself from pissin' my pants. "Oh, my God, stop!" I laugh, pushing through the back door, out into the night. "If you start doing the Dougie right now, we are officially no longer friends."

He gives me puppy dog eyes, puffing his lower lip out and when I narrow my eyes at him, he pushes it out more.

With a grin, I drop down to the grass and look up at the open sky. "Fine. That was adorable. Now quit before I bite your lip off."

He laughs and goes to take a seat next to me, but someone calls his name from the back door. Turning back to me, he frowns. "Shit, I better go see what's up." He shifts on his feet lightly. "My, uh, my dads' would kill me if something happened to their precious James Dean shrine." He laughs nervously.

"They have good taste. James Dean was a badass. I'd have to kick your ass just the same."

His smile is one of pure appreciation. The fact that I didn't blanch at his revelation not lost on him.

He reaches for me, so I place my hand in his, allowing him to pull me up and we walk back into the house. "These boys better watch out, Lolli Bear." He kisses my temple. "I might decide to keep you to myself," he teases.

"Parker, you and I would be phenomenal," I gush and follow up with a dejected sigh. "Too bad your sexy doesn't do it for me."

He laughs, releasing me. "You good?"

"Yeah, I'm actually gonna cut out. If you see Mia around, tell her I'll catch up with her later."

"Want me to find someone to take you? Or I could walk you," he offers.

I scrunch my face. "Nah, I'm good."

"Alright, but if you don't text me in twenty minutes, I'm sending out my Calvin Cavalry," he laughs.

"I may not text you just to see that."

He pushes me lightly. "Get out of here."

I make my way out the door and into the cool, quiet night. I'm rounding the driveway, turning onto the sidewalk when his rough voice calls out and wraps around me, warming me in places I don't want it to.

I turn my head over my left shoulder to find Nate sitting with his back against a tree.

"Hey."

"You leavin' already?" he asks, his tone friendly, which makes me uneasy.

"I am. You run out of one night stands to keep you warm on this chilly night, Handsome?" I joke, but he doesn't smile; he just gazes at me.

With the slight frown on his face, he looks a little disappointed, which makes no sense, so I face forward and continue walking.

"Kalani," he calls out.

I mask my confusion and turn back to him.

"I'm sorry I acted like a dick that night," he says into his lap before lifting his dark brown gaze to me.

His eyes are so open and earnest and...sexy.

Yeah, no. Not happening.

I give him a one-sided smile. "Sorry for trying to put a hole in your seat."

His head snaps up, his eyes wide. He looks so adorably horrified; I can't help but laugh.

"I'm kidding, chillax."

He breathes a heavy sigh-chuckle of relief.

"So, um..." I hook my thumb over my shoulder, "I'll see you later." I begin walking again.

"Kalani?"

Damn it.

I turn back around. "Yeah?"

"Thanks for bailing me out that night." The corner of his lips lift slightly as he tosses a piece of picked grass from his hand. "You didn't have to do that."

"Wow," I tease, unsure how else to act. "An apology and a

67

thank you, all in one night? I didn't think you had it in you, Monroe."

"I didn't," he says, not missing a beat, not elaborating, but not looking away either.

I nod my head, refusing to allow myself to try and decipher his meaning.

Hopping up, he dusts off his jeans and I permit myself a good look.

His hair is perfectly messy, and his black jeans fit him just right. Paired with a dark gray long-sleeve shirt, and black Palladium boots, he's every girls wet dream.

He's looking at me, but I can't read his expression.

And then I make a bad move, out of pure curiosity.

Or pure stupidity. I'll decide which one later.

"You still owe me bad TV and junk food," I say flatly, and kind of in a rush.

His eyebrows shoot up for a millisecond before a ridiculously seductive smirk takes its place on his lush lips. "I do."

"Well," I shrug, "I don't have cable, but I own a plethora of horribly hilarious movies, every season of Law and Order, and a shit ton of junk food."

"Sounds like a good time." He's eyeing me, no doubt an internal debate going on in that perfect head of his.

I look at him over once more.

Yeah, this is happening.

I turn and start walking.

"Wait, seriously?" he says, his voice that of an excited little boy headed to his first pro game.

I don't turn around. I can't see that look on his face because I may jump him.

"Go home. Change. See you in twenty."

"Kalani?" I hear his smile.

"Yes?" I call out, still walking away.

"Don't wear that Halestorm shirt."

I freeze mid-step. The world must be turning on its fucking axis because I swear to God, if I were looking in a mirror, I would see a hint of pink on my cheeks. A fucking blush.

I don't blush. Ever.

I start walking, faster this time.

I swear I hear him chuckle and I want to strangle myself for liking the sound of it.

"What the fuck did I just do?" I ask myself as I make my way to my house.

Chapter Seven

K ALANI

Something is wrong with me. Seriously fucking wrong.

I let out a frustrated sigh as I hastily throw on some black leggings and an off-the-shoulder royal blue tee.

I blow through the house and into the kitchen, pulling out all the junk food I can find, then make my way into the living room and toss it all down on the coffee table. As soon as I reach for the remote, I hear the rumble of his engine.

A minute or two ticks by, and still no knock.

Perplexed, I walk to the door and swing it open. I'm greeted with the smell of leather, grass, and sweetness, accompanied by an apprehensive Nate. Relief fills his features as soon as he looks at me.

I laugh, tilting my head. "Second thoughts?"

He shrugs. "I wasn't sure if I should knock or not and I don't have your number. I didn't wanna get you in trouble or whatever."

I grin, pulling the door open wide. "It's fine, just us. Come in."
He walks in and loiters in the entryway.

He's changed into a pair of red and black basketball shorts and a long-sleeved black thermal shirt that fits him perfectly, nice and tight over his pecs and arms.

I step up next to him. "The movies are on the back wall, go ahead and pick one." He nods and I follow him into the living room. The second he passes the threshold of the carpet, the bitch strikes.

Nauni jumps out of fucking nowhere and attacks his ankle.

"Shit!" he jumps, eyes round as saucers. His body shifts awkwardly to avoid stepping on her, which makes him bump into me, knocking me over the side of the couch.

Laughing so hard I can't breathe, I tuck and roll off the side of the couch - a sight to see, I'm sure. Tears rolling down my cheeks because of it. When I look up at him, he's shaking his head, hands on his hips.

"You could have warned me," he chuckles.

I nod through my smile. "Yeah, I could have. But that was much more fun."

"Now you have to pick what we watch," he says, plopping down onto the couch.

"Fine." I hop up and pop the movie in, scooping up my cat on the way back to the couch.

"What's the little shit's name?" he asks, nodding toward her.

"This is Nauni, the she-devil."

Please don't ask.

His lips twitch.

He's totally going to ask.

"Nauni, huh?"

"Yep." I turn my attention to the screen, preparing the movie on the PS3.

"As in..."

I close my eyes. "Yes. As in Kalani's Punani."

He tries real hard to hold it in, I'll give him that, but it's a lost cause. He laughs so hard; he hunches over and grabs his ribs. "I was legit attacked by your pussy."

I cross my arms and legs, sitting Indian style on the couch. "You let me know when you're ready for me to push play." I squish my lips to one side to try and cover my smile.

He reaches out and grabs a peanut butter M&M. Popping it in his mouth, he throws his hands up in surrender, but can't help himself and has to get one more in. "Can I at least pet her?" He teases, and I roll my eyes, reaching for the remote.

Just as we settle and I press play on The Sandlot, my phone rings on the table.

"Hero" by Enrique Iglesias streams through the air, and I laugh loudly.

"That sneaky bastard. Hand me that, please." I motion toward my phone, a wide smile on my face.

With a small scowl on his face, Nate picks it up and hands it to me.

"Why hello, Hero," I answer the call, seeing Nate's scowl deepen out of the corner of my eye.

"Lolli Bear!" Parker shouts.

"Love the new ringtone, by the way."

"Oh shit." He laughs. "I forgot about that. I hit the nail on the head on that one, didn't I?" he asks, sounding mighty proud of himself.

I roll my eyes, amused. "What can I do for you?"

"You didn't call me. You promised me you would," he says, louder than necessary. Alcohol is clearly his best friend tonight.

"Indeed, I did, but I forgot." I give him my pouty voice. "Forgive me?"

"Always, beautiful."

I laugh a little. "Okay, Sir Calvin, I'll call you tomorrow."

"Why you trying to get me off the phone?" he asks suspiciously.

"Because, Nosy Rosie. Handsome and I are trying to watch a mov-" My eyes shoot wide and I slap my hand over my mouth as soon as I say it.

"Whoa, wait. WHAT?" Parker yells with a laugh.

"Shit." Hanging up immediately, I throw my phone on the table like a hot potato.

I peek over at Nate and he looks pissed, just as I assumed, he would.

With a shake of my head, I drop my face into my hands as he stands from the couch. "Nate," I speak through my fingers, "I am sorr-"

"Don't worry about it, Kalani. I get it," he says, his voice holding a little bite. "Can't have people thinking you're hanging out with the school playboy, right?"

My jaw drops, and I stare at him. "Is that what this is about?"

"Is that a serious question?" he challenges, his face a mixture of anger and hurt.

He thinks I'm hiding the fact that he's here. And that... bothers him?

"Look." Now I'm getting pissed. "I told him you were here because, duh, you are, and he was buggin'. I freaked because I thought, after I opened my loud fucking mouth, that you'd be pissed I told him you were here. Preserve your reputation or what-the-fuck-ever." I wave my hand in the air, bringing it down on a slap against my thigh.

He shakes his head, unbelieving. "But you didn't tell him I was here, Kalani, that's the point. You freaked out because you knew he'd ask you who was here." He narrows his eyes. "But nice try."

I give him my 'you wanna fuckin' bet' face and answer my phone that has yet to stop ringing, choosing to place it on speaker this time.

"Hello again, Hero," I say with a nasty grin, my eyes pinned to Nate's.

"Nate's there?" he instantly fires off in excited confusion.

My smirk deepens when Nate drops his eyes to my phone, his brows pulled in. "He is," I tell him as I sit back on the couch, extending my legs to the coffee table in front of me.

"Liar!" Parker accuses.

"I don't lie. Ever." I tell him, tuning into the movie, grabbing some caramel corn while I'm at it.

Not a care in the world.

Parker laughs. "I know, that's why you're my favorite."

"Ditto."

"Let me talk to him."

"Speaker."

He barks out a laugh. "Nate!"

Nate places his fists on the edge of the couch and drops his chin to his chest. "Yeah?" he answers reluctantly.

"Oh shit, this is good." I picture Parker rubbing his hands together. "Lolli Bear?"

"Yes?" I answer, purposely adding a hint a sexy.

His smile is evident in his voice. "Can I tell Jarrod?" Nate's eyes pop up to mine, obviously wondering why he'd ask me that. "Please tell me I can go tell him you came to the party with him and went home with Nate?" I watch as Nate's jaw ticks, realization setting in, though I'm not sure why he cares.

"I'm a big girl, Hero. I could care less what you tell him," I answer him honestly. "You may want to ask your QB here, though." I shrug, for bitch factor since he's watching me. "Bad blood and all that but make it quick. Scotty's about to shit his pants when he finds out that ball was signed by the Great Bambino."

Before Parker can respond, Nate butts in, his fiery eyes locked on mine. "Tell him thanks for keepin' her company," he pauses, eyes torching me, "but I'll take it from here."

I lift a single eyebrow at him and take in the smirk he gives me in return...

This is bad.

Parker's laugh booms through the phone, bringing my attention back to my screen.

"Lolli Bear?"

"Yeees?"

"Call me to post your bail," he howls.

His laugh is the last thing we hear before the line goes dead.

"Well... that was fun."

I look up and into Nate's eyes, and pat the spot next to me. He drops down, placing his elbows on his knees, eyes locked on the TV screen in front of us.

"Listen," I begin, "I know we don't know each other from Tom, Dick, and Harry, but one thing you should know about me, Nate, is I dance to the beat of my own drum." I shrug, even though he's not looking at me. "Always have. I won't lie or hide or sugarcoat things, and I sure as shit don't care what other people think. If you're here, it's because I want you to be. Plain and simple."

He nods, blowing out a deep breath. "Right. You just, uh, threw me off for a minute, that's all." He chuckles, a low, husky sound. "Not something I'm used to."

"Yeah, well..." I trail off because what do you say to that?

He looks at me and grins, then we sit and watch the movie in comfortable silence.

When the credits start rolling, I look over to see Nate has passed out. With his arms crossed at his chest, feet propped up on the coffee table, he looks thoroughly relaxed. Too relaxed and at home, in fact, so I kick him.

"What the..." He jolts, glancing around briefly before his eyes settle on me, and he grins. "I passed out."

I nod. "You did. Now go home. Movie night is over."

Nate stares at me for a second, then shakes his head, laughing lightly. He stands, stretching his long, tanned, toned body, and glances from the TV to me. "Sorry, I guess I was beat."

"You had a long day," I tell him, following him to the door. I open it and lean against the frame, looking up at him. "Good game tonight, by the way."

His eyes light up and his smile is all too conceited. "Thanks."

I laugh, crossing my arms across my chest as the breeze makes its way in the door. "Get outta here before that hot air you're full of makes me sweat."

He takes one step out, then hesitates before turning to face me. "I can't tell you the last time I just chilled out and watched a movie on a Friday night."

"I bet." I straighten and begin pushing the door closed.

His dark eyes look right into mine. "Night, Kalani."

I nod and shut the door, leaving him standing there. I hear him chuckle as I walk back toward the couch.

Bastard.

My phone chimes from the table the second my butt hits the sofa. I laugh out loud when I see the message that pops up.

Unknown number: thanks for the wild night.

Right as I'm about to hit send, asking him how he got my number, a second text comes through.

Unknown number: Parker sent me your number the second he hung up on you. Said you'd never give it to me. Save it.

I program it and text him back.

Me: I think he was right.

. . .

I may have.
Probably.

Handsome: glad he has my back then.

Me: don't get it twisted, Monroe. If it came down to you and me...
he'd pick me.

Handsome: funny. I think I would, too.

I stare at his text.

Handsome: choose you, I mean.

I still don't text back.

Handsome: night, Kalani.

I toss my phone on the floor and make my way to my room, Nauni
hot on my heels. I throw myself in my bed, and the two of us fall
asleep together as we have every night for the last year and half.

The next morning, I wake to the sound of my front door
slamming and twenty seconds later, my bed dips. I throw my

covers off my face to find Parker's baby blues shining back at me, a smile on his lips.

"Mornin' sleepyhead. Certain someone keep you up all night?" He wiggles his eyebrows and I hit him in the face with my pillow. His laughter booms and I want to punch him.

I'm about to ask him how he got in, when the culprit herself walks in, carrying a box of my Waffle Crisp, wearing the same thing she had on last night.

I raise an eyebrow at her. She shrugs, popping some dry cereal in her mouth.

Parker laughs. "Someone fell for Austin's charm last night."

"And the night before," Mia adds with a laugh.

"Congratulations, assholes. Now go away. I'm sleeping," I tell them, rolling over and tucking myself under the blanket.

Parker wraps his arms around me and scoots in. "Lolli Bear, we're hungry."

My voice is muffled by my blankets. "Then go eat."

"You're the only one who knows how to cook," Mia whines. "Come on, pleeease?"

When I don't budge, she goes in for the kill.

"Parker needs his energy; he played his little heart out last night."

God damn her, pulling the athlete strings.

I throw my blanket off my head and cross my arms.

She grins from ear to ear, knowing damn well she won.

I turn to find Parker giving me his puppy dog eyes and groan.

"Fine." I shove him, but he doesn't budge. "Get out of my bed, you big brute."

He chuckles, squeezing me harder, then releases me and stands.

"I'm going to rinse off really quick," Mia says, as she walks out the room and into the bathroom in the hall.

"Come on, Lolli Bear." He reaches down and scoops me up, bridal-style. "Feed me."

Parker carries me to the kitchen, sets me on my feet and hops up on the bar stool while I start pulling the stuff out to make French toast.

Once everything is set up and ready to go, I turn on the Keurig and make a quick cup of coffee.

"You want one?" I ask him, not bothering to turn around.

"Nope. I'm still a growing boy," he jokes.

I settle in on the stool next to him, waiting for Mia to get out of the shower before starting breakfast.

"So." Here it comes. "You and Nate, huh?"

I narrow my eyes at him.

"What?" he asks innocently.

"You gave him my number."

"I did."

"Why?"

"'Cause, it would have taken you a minute to swallow your pride and give it to him yourself."

I smile into my mug, knowing he's right.

He's still looking at me expectantly.

I roll my eyes. "We watched a movie. He left. The end."

His eyebrows shoot up. "Really?"

I stare at him blankly, making him laugh.

"Shit. Good job, Lolli Bear. You're officially the only girl at Alrick High with the willpower to hold out on my boy."

"What about you, Hero?" I change the subject. "Any girls fall at your feet last night?"

He shakes his head. "Nah, the downfall to being the party thrower. Gotta keep shit in check."

"Okay," Mia walks into the kitchen, looking fresh and clean, hair up in a wet, messy bun, donning a pair of my sweats and a t-shirt. She pops a pod in, making herself a cup of coffee, and leans her elbows on the counter. "Now, you feed me."

"And me," Parker pipes up.

"Us. Feed us," Mia corrects herself.

We eat and chat about the night before, the game, and my first few weeks at school. Mia grills me about my night with Nate. Parker covers his ears when she tells me about Austin and his 'preferences'. I really didn't need to hear it, but girls will be girls.

The morning transitions into the afternoon and, before we know, it's nightfall. It was, quite honestly, one of the most relaxing days I've had in a long time.

Mia looks up from her phone with a huff. "Alright, guys," she says. "I'm going home. My mom says I'm required to show my face for a few minutes today." She stands and walks to the front door. "Night," she calls over her shoulder before leaving.

Once she's gone, I tell Parker to pop a movie in and give me a minute. I take a quick shower, throwing on a pink tank, a matching pair of sleep shorts, and fuzzy slipper socks.

I reclaim my spot on the couch, laying across it, and Parker squeezes himself behind me.

"No movie?" I close my eyes.

"I was too comfortable to move," he laughs.

I smile and kiss the arm that's under my head.

We lay there in the quiet, just relaxing, but I can feel him thinking.

After a while, Parker clears his throat softly.

I hate this part.

This is why I prefer solidarity.

As if on cue, he whispers into my hair, "What's your story, Lolli Bear?"

A friend who's curious, he's simply asking, and my throat closes.

I don't do deep shit.

I laugh. I joke. I make inappropriate comments.

I don't share.

Parker's great, and in the short time I've known him, he's somehow become my best friend. And while I'll always be honest and loyal...I don't share.

I open my mouth to tell him so and, praise the Dr. Pepper gods, I'm saved by the bell.

I look back at Parker with creased brows.

"Mia?" he guesses.

I shrug, "Come in!" I yell, having no energy to attempt moving.

When the door opens, Parker lifts his head to see who has walked in, then looks back at me with a huge smile. He kisses my temple and hops off the couch. "I was just leaving," he says, a hint of laughter in his voice.

My eyebrows pull in, and I sit up to look toward the door.

Nate.

Chapter Eight

K ALANI

Nate's standing in my doorway, looking every shade of sexy, a little uncomfortable, and a lot pissed off.

"Sorry, man." Jaw set tight; he turns to leave. "I'll go."

But Parker makes it to him in a heartbeat.

"Oh, no." He grabs Nate's shoulders and turns him toward me. "You stay. I'm out." Parker turns to me and winks. "Call me tomorrow," he tells me, laughing at my scowl as he walks out the door.

Nate looks from the closed door to me.

"Hey," I offer.

His scowl deepens a bit. "Hey," he says, sounding as puzzled as he looks.

"Are you gonna come in or just stand in the doorway?"

His scowl doesn't quite go away, but he walks toward the

living room, looking around before crossing the threshold of the tile to the carpet.

I grin. "It's safe. I locked Nauni in the back room for the afternoon. She kept jumping up and swatting at Mia's bun."

His face relaxes just a hair. "Mia's here?"

"Was," I tell him, confused by his reaction.

His scowl deepens again and I can't help but laugh.

"So, what's up? Jonesing for another wild night?" I tease, wiggling my eyebrows at him.

"Did I interrupt something?" he asks, still standing at the head of the couch.

"No." I reply, holding eye contact.

He raises a dark brow, his eyes hard. "You sure about that?"

"Be a man about your shit, Nate," I tell him, leaning back against the cushion. "If you wanna know something," I lift my hands, "ask."

"Fine. You and Parker fucking around?" he accuses, sounding all too sure of himself.

Zero hesitation. Nice.

"If by fucking around, you mean fucking all around, as in, on this couch," I look down and run my fingernails across the red suede. "On the floor," I peek up at him through my lashes, "and on my bed," his brows are practically touching his eyeballs now, they're so furrowed, "then, no." I smirk. "We're not 'fucking' around. But if you mean, are we friends, homies, compadres, then, yes. Yes, we are."

His eyes roam my face, trying to decide if he believes me or not. He either does or realized it doesn't matter, because he sits down, runs a hand down his face, then turns to look at me.

"What?"

He doesn't say anything, but after a few seconds, he shakes his head and looks away.

"You eat yet?" I ask, simply to change the subject.

"I have a pizza in my truck, actually," he admits, looking around the room. "Thought maybe you wanted to watch something." He glances at me briefly.

"Why you nervous?" I razz him.

His eyebrows shoot up. "I'm not nervous," he quips, rubbing the back of his neck.

"No?" I challenge, biting my lip to hold in my grin.

"I don't get nervous, Kalani," he snaps, sounding just as exasperated as he looks.

"Alright." I try hiding the laughter in my voice. "You're not nervous." I shrug one shoulder. "But you did bring me pizza, right?"

He finally smiles, a nice easy one. "I did."

"Well, get your ass up and go get it. I'll grab us something to drink."

He doesn't say another word but stands and walks out the door to get said pizza.

I'm just making my way back to the living room with paper plates, Ranch dressing, and two cans of soda when the door opens and closes.

I look over my shoulder when I don't hear his footsteps, and find his eyes zoned in on my legs. Or maybe my ass.

It takes him a minute to meet my gaze, but when he does, a look of possessiveness passes through them briefly. Weird.

He sets down the pizza box and opens it. I pass him his plate and drink and we both grab a few slices. As soon as I start to take my first bite, he breaks the silence we've settled into.

"I'm sorry." He shakes his head and sets his plate down. "You're telling me you invited Parker over here wearing that," he motions with his eyes only, "and you're just friends?"

As much as I want to punch him for basically calling me a slut, and definitely calling me a liar, both of which I'm not, I don't. I'm going to assume he thinks he's asking a completely rational question. It's not his fault no one's ever thrown him a curve ball, football player and all. So, deciding to fuck with him, I mask my pissy bitch and go for nonchalant.

"No, actually." I shrug. "When he carried me out of my bed this morning so I could make breakfast, I was still wearing what I had on last night when you were here." I look back at my food to keep myself from laughing at his manic expression. "I didn't change until after I took a shower about an hour ago, hence the wet hair." My face is blank as I look at him.

Oh, shit.

His jaw is set so tight, I'm afraid he may break a tooth. His eyes are hard around the edges, and unblinking. As strange as it seems, I'm pretty sure he's honestly crazed right now.

"Parker?" His tone is scary.

And exciting.

It's scary that it's exciting.

"Yep." I make sure to pop the 'p' and hold eye contact.

"He was in your bed?" I swear he sounds like the Hulk right now, about to flip his shit.

"Uh-huh," I breathe, continuing to spur him on.

"Don't fuck with me, Kalani."

I must be asking for it, whatever it is.

"I'm not," I say innocently, and he growls.

Actually growls.

I finally let my smile break free. "I woke up this morning to him jumping on my bed, demanding breakfast, while a hungover Mia took a shower. Then, we all kicked back and watched movies all day." I'm full-fledged laughing by the end of my explanation, or confession, whatever it was, but neither of which he deserved.

He searches my face. Once he's satisfied, he releases a long breath, his eyes narrowing in on me. "That wasn't funny."

With the sudden need to lighten the mood, and not marvel in my own thoughts about why he would care, I channel my inner Heath Ledger - the Joker version. "Why so serious?"

His smile is instant and he chuckles. Leaning forward, he

places his elbows on his knees, a go-to move of his, I've noticed, and turns to look at me. "You're something else, you know that?"

"So I've been told," I say with a smile and he nods. "Can I eat now?"

He nods again. "Yeah, brat. Let's eat."

"Question?"

He shrugs.

"This masterpiece in front of us…" A smirk forms on his lips; he knows what I'm getting at.

"I overheard you tell Austin he owed you a pepperoni and jalapeno pizza for helping him in class. Figured it was a safe choice."

I smile. "It was a fan-fucking-tastic choice."

Nate grins, and we settle in eating.

"So, what'd you make for breakfast?" he asks a few minutes later.

"French toast and bacon."

"I like French toast and bacon."

I turn, giving him an amused smile. "Is that right?"

"It is," he responds, taking a large bite of his pizza.

I laugh and take the bait. "Well, then it's settled, Handsome. I guess I'll have to make French toast and bacon for you some time."

"How about tomorrow?" he asks, looking me right in the eye.

"You sure you won't be sick of me by then?"

He shakes his head. Slowly. Purposefully.

"All right," I swallow. "Tomorrow it is, but don't expect me to wake up before nine." I wince. "Make that nine-thirty, that's hella early as it is. Understood?"

His eyebrows lift. "You're serious?"

When I look at him like I'm not following, he explains. "You're actually agreeing to make me breakfast?"

"Uh… yeah?" I draw out.

He reaches for his napkin and wipes his hands. "I'm holding you to that."

"You do that." I laugh, not at all understanding his reaction.

After setting my plate down, I lean back on the couch. "Okay, I am officially stuffed."

He kicks off his shoes and turns to me. "Can I ask you something?" he asks, suddenly serious.

No. "Sure."

"How'd Parker know you were talking about me?"

I blink at him. "Huh?"

"Last night. You didn't mention me by name, but somehow Parker knew you were talking about me." His lip twitches. "How'd he know that?"

"How long's that been on your mind?" I ask, amused.

"All night last night, and all morning and afternoon today. The drive over...and the entire time we've been sitting here."

I narrow my eyes at him. "Why, Nathaniel Monroe, are you trying to stroke your ego?"

He shrugs, unashamed, his eyes full of delight.

"Alright." I turn so I'm facing him, sitting with my legs crossed on the couch. I lean in, locking my blues to his browns, and speak slowly. "He knew damn well who I was talking about because I told him I think you're absolutely, ridiculously, totally and completely, unfairly," I roll my eyes, "attractive. Ergo... Handsome." I wink. "Though, I imagine hearing these things is nothing new to you."

Somewhere during my little speech his gaze did a one-eighty.

No more signs of a playful Nate. No. He's officially checked out.

He's staring at me, eyes hooded. Not moving, not blinking, just... staring.

And I can't move.

Can't retreat back to my corner.

Can barely fucking breathe.

"What else?" he rasps. His voice... that damn voice is drop dead sex.

87

Fire spreads through my veins, heating me from the inside out.

"What else what?" I ask, low and breathy. And turned the fuck on.

"What else have you imagined, Kalani?" he dares.

"Your hands," I admit, admiring them, not bothering to try and hide the sheer desire in my voice. "They're your instrument; your hardware, if you will." My tongue darts out, wetting my thirsty lips. "Large. Strong." I steal a glance at him, finding he's fixated on my mouth, his eyes the darkest shade of brown I've ever seen.

My attention turns back at his hands, and I examine them deeper.

His knuckles are wide and thick with a rugged and manly exterior; yet, somehow still graceful. Maybe it's because I know what they're capable of – on the field anyway.

But off the field...

A chill runs down my spine at the thought.

"I bet they're rough," I whisper to myself, imagining the feeling on my soft skin. "Calloused. A product of..." Shit. "Devotion," I say on a swallow. When his fingers flex, my eyes fly back to his. This time he's looking right at me.

This is bad.

Eyes ablaze, he holds me captive, unable to look away if I wanted to.

I don't want to.

Slowly, ever so slowly, he reaches across the single cushion separating us and gently wraps his long fingers around my sock-covered ankle.

Pulling it toward him, he places my foot flat against the soft suede, wedging it between his thigh and the back of the couch, my leg now bent between us.

When he lets go, he looks to his hand. Placing the tips of his fingers on the outside of my calf, he feathers them painfully slow up to my knee, then down my thigh, stopping at the curve of my hip.

My breathing turns electric, coming in spurts, heady and heavy.

Moving in, he lifts my right leg and sets it down on top of his left. He scoots even closer, erasing the distance between us.

Nate brings his mouth within inches of my ear. "Are they?" he whispers, resting his forehead on my exposed shoulder. "Rough, I mean?"

I shiver. The feel of his hot breath against my skin, mixed with the tips of his hair grazing my neck...

Fuck. Me.

"I can't tell," I manage to pant out, dropping myself back against the arm pillow behind me, forcing him to follow.

He takes my move for what it is, an invitation to continue, to show me.

The pads of his fingers find the waistband of my sleep shorts. He scratches at the elastic with his nails, before sliding his hand up and flattening his palm against the incline of my hip. And when he runs his hot palm up and across my ribs, I'm officially catapulted past ignition and straight into combustion.

I was right. I was oh so very right. His hands are erotically tough in the best possible way.

His forehead still rests on my shoulder, so when his hand slides back to my waist, I feel his once deep breaths turn ragged.

And I can't take anymore. I have to taste him. Like, right now.

Turning my head, I use the tip of my tongue to lick the helix of his ear. The instant my tongue touches his skin, a gravelly, and not so ladylike, sound leaves me. He tastes like citrus and sweat and sex.

"Nate," I whisper, sounding as desperate as I feel.

He groans, gripping my hip tighter, but makes no other move.

I say it again.

His response is a nip to my shoulder.

My back arches off the pillow as I gasp, causing my body to shift lower.

This gets his attention.

He moves so he's hovering over me, eyes wild, breathing erratic. Needy.

I tilt my chin up as he lowers his head, and our eyes lock onto each other's. His mouth opens, as does mine, but he doesn't kiss me. No. This Lothario grazes my bottom lip with his teeth, teasing me - a perfected sport, I'm sure - before disappearing into the crook of my neck, kissing, licking, biting.

This is so, so good.

He kisses across my collarbone, up my throat, across my jaw, then finally – fucking, finally - his fevered lips descend on mine, and -

"Well, this is interesting."

He curses under his breath, right as I whisper, "So close."

Mia is dead.

So. Fucking. Dead.

How did I not hear the door?

Nate stands, adjusting his shirt, among other things.

"Mia." He addresses her with a nod.

"Nate," she mocks.

And I cover my head with a pillow, trying to come up with one good reason I shouldn't throw her ass out and get my key back.

"I brought chocolate chip cookies," she sings, but that is so not enough right now.

I sit up, huffing, my face the picture of rage, I'm sure, fully intending on unleashing it on her, but the little bitch throws the gauntlet.

"The unbaked kind." She smirks.

Cookie dough, my one true guilty pleasure in life.

Damn her.

I'm assuming my face reverted quickly if her obnoxious laugh is any indicator.

She looks at Nate. "When it comes to Lolli, everyone's second best next to chocolate chip cookie dough."

Nate smiles, nodding his head, as if that doesn't surprise him one bit.

It's unnerving.

"Aren't you supposed to be at Shawna's party?" Mia asks him, still standing in the same spot.

I'm waiting for him to make an excuse, dodge the question, and shuffle out at the speed of lightning, but Mr. Monroe is full of surprises.

He walks over to Mia, motions for the bag in her hands - which she gives to him, eyeing him with a bewildered expression - then plops down on the couch, right next to me.

"Nope," he tells her, not bothering to turn around and look at her. "I'm right where I want to be."

I look back at Mia, who's still frozen in the same spot, and shrug, a clear 'I have no fucking idea' look on my face.

"Uh, alright then. I..." She hooks her thumb over her shoulder. "I'm gonna go."

"Bye, Mia," he sings.

She doesn't respond but locks the door on her way out.

I turn to Nate just as he looks at me and we both double over laughing.

I reach over and snag the bag from his hands, eyeing him suspiciously.

"What?" he quirks a dark brow at me, a playful smile on his lips as he settles into the cushions.

"Gotta say it," I tilt my head slightly. "I was expecting you to make some excuse about a forgotten assignment or something else as equally lame as to why you're here."

He narrows his eyes and gazes at me for a few seconds before turning his attention to the suddenly fascinating pizza box on the coffee table. "Why is that exactly?" he asks the pizza box.

My brows lift. "Well..." Then I think about it and come up

with nothing. I watched him parade around at that first party with two different chicks and I see the way he is with girls at school. "Honestly, I have no idea. Guess I jumped the gun on that one. I mean, you clearly have no shame in your game." I shrug.

He leans forward, resting his forearms on his knees, and cuts me an irritated glance over his shoulder. "I don't play games, Kalani." When I scoff at him, he turns his massive body toward me. "I don't." His voice is adamant. "I always make it clear. They know what it is and what it's not. That's how most of 'em prefer it." He lifts a shoulder. "Bragging rights." He looks away and I get the feeling he's a little embarrassed or maybe ashamed. Not that he'd ever admit that.

"Sooo..." It's clear I don't believe him. "You're saying they don't want to be carried around on your arm?"

"There are always some who want more, but we've got to be careful. We're all viewed as meal tickets at this point."

"Seriously?" My brows pinch. "Like, Varsity Blues shit?"

His lips smash into a tight line, and he cocks a brow so perfect I could draw that shit on.

"You know." I roll my wrist. "Star player and cheerleader in 'love', he gets hurt, gets dumped, then she goes balls out, trying to get his buddy with a whipped cream bikini?"

He throws his head back, laughing, and I watch as his Adam's apple bounces up and down. "Yeah, Kalani. Just like that."

"That sucks. Guess I get it, though."

He glances back at me, a small smile now tipping his lips. "I may not play games, but if I want something," his gaze flicks to my mouth, "I make sure I get it." His eyes are meaningful, his smirk deadly. "I just never found anything I wanted to keep before."

Before.

Before.

Shit.

I shove the bag of cookie dough into his chest. "Here, have some."

He leans back and laughs, pulling out a nice big chunk of heaven.

Then, we watch Angels in the Outfield in comfortable silence while eating raw cookie dough.

Chapter Nine

K ALANI

Beep.

Tired of staring at the blank white walls, I lay my head down on the stupid scratchy blanket.

What? Have these things been washed, like, a gazillion times?

No wonder people hate hospitals. It's nothing but bad food, uncomfortable bedding, and never-ending white walls. Everywhere you look, it's bleak.

Empty.

Lifting Papa's hand, I place mine under his, and lace our fingers together. Instantly, I can breathe. I'm safe. Closing my eyes tight, I gently squeeze. "I'm here," I whisper.

Beep.

His once strong hand lies motionless in mine. "Remember the first College Bowl game you took me to?" I ask softly, knowing he can't respond. "I got to go down and meet the players before the game." I smile at the memory.

"I was so scared, Papa," I whisper, the first tear spilling from my eyes.

"I didn't want to go," I remember, biting the inside of my cheek to try and stay strong. "You bent down in front of me and asked me what I was afraid of, and I told you I didn't want to be alone, and you," I take in a shuddered breath, "you grabbed my hand, and told me that you had me. That no matter what, you'd always have me. Then you squeezed my hand, like you always did, and told me to be brave." Tears now fall from my eyes at an unstoppable rate.

"That nurse said I have to say goodbye to you. Doesn't she know we don't do goodbyes?" My attempted laugh comes out as a broken whimper and I quickly slam my free hand against my mouth to hide the sound, then force myself to look at his face.

He looks like my Papa, but he doesn't. His big blue eyes are closed, not shining and bright. His ever-present laugh lines, nowhere to be found. I just want to hear his voice, see him smile. Just one more time.

Beep.

I squeeze his hand.

I'm here.

"I'm...scared, Papa. I don't know how to be brave." I nod my head frantically. "But I will be." I reach up and run my fingers over his silver eyebrows. "For you, I will be. Always." I let my hand slide down his face.

"You can go to sleep..." More tears stream down my face, but I have to be brave. "Go to sleep, and I'll wake up for you."

"Ms. Embers?" a soft, hesitant voice calls from the doorway, and I drop my head back down.

Beep.

"Please, go." I hear the desperate plea in my voice. When I hear a soft cry, I look up at the nurse standing in the doorway.

Tears fall from her eyes as she shakes her head back and forth, opening her mouth, then closing it.

She says nothing.

Beep.

"Please...can you give me this time?" I say, my voice getting louder, tighter. "I just need more time."

"Ms. Embers, I'm afraid there's been an accident..." She trails off, her eyes focusing on the floor.

My body tenses, and I immediately place my other hand on top of Papa's, caging it. Shielding him.

I'm here.

Beep. Beep. Beep.

I jolt up in my bed, gasping for air.

It takes a few seconds for my eyes to focus on the room around me.

Teal walls. Not white.

I drop back onto my pillow but freeze when I still hear the beeping.

My breathing ceases, then I realize my alarm is going off.

Scrambling onto my knees, I rip it from the wall and toss it on the floor.

I hurry off my bed, throw on a sweatshirt and sweats, and storm out of my room.

Once in the entryway, I lace up my sneakers and bolt out the door.

Not bothering to stretch, I take off, full stride. The moment my feet hit the pavement; I can breathe again.

I focus on the leaves' movements.

I focus on the roll of my foot.

I focus on the chilled air as it stuns my lungs.

I focus on everything around, yet nothing at all.

Perfection.

In a rush, I burst into the house, slam the door, kick off my shoes, and strip out of my sweatshirt. By the time I make it to the bathroom, I'm naked.

I step into the shower and turn it on, hissing as the cold water hits my skin, but I don't move.

It only takes a few seconds to heat and I turn, soaking my hair the rest of the way.

With a deep inhale, I lean against the shower wall, eyes closed.

Stop, Kalani.

I curse myself for acting like a little bitch and hurry to finish my shower.

After throwing on a pair of black joggers and a light pink, V-neck t-shirt, I brush my teeth and hair, turn on a random playlist, then head into the kitchen.

Right as I pull the eggs out of the fridge, the doorbell rings.

I glance at the clock on the stove and smirk.

Nine-twenty-nine.

"Good morning, Nathaniel," I say as I open the door, sweeping my hand out as his permission to enter.

He gives me a bright grin. "Hey."

I can hear the excitement in his voice, which is ridiculous.

"Hey yourself." I walk past him and he follows.

Once I get my coffee going, I glance up at him. "Why are you smiling at me like that?"

He shrugs from his spot on the barstool but does nothing to hide his smile.

It's a nice smile. The left side rests just a hair higher than the right, but not in a cocky way. Well, not at the moment, anyway.

He has perfect movie star teeth, too.

I roll my eyes.

Of course he does.

"Here." I hand him a freshly-brewed cup. "I only have Peppermint Mocha creamer. If you don't like that, well, too damn bad, I guess." I shrug my shoulders, making him chuckle.

After switching the burner on to heat the pan, I get the mix ready.

"Interesting morning?" he muses.

My brows pull in and I turn to him, wondering what the hell he's referring to.

He motions to my clothes sporadically thrown around the entrance.

I turn back to the stove. "I went for a run and was in a hurry to get in the shower after."

He laughs.

It's fake as shit, but I don't care to know why.

I place the first few slices in the hot pan, then pick up my coffee cup. Leaning my hip against the counter, I shift to face Nate.

His brows pinch together as he stares at me. "You alright?"

I straighten my spine and turn back to the task at hand. "'Course. Why wouldn't I be?"

It sounds strange, but I can feel the weight of his stare on me. "You seem, I don't know, upset." He lets out a deep breath.

I steady my breathing before glancing back to him, giving him a sideways smile. "I'm good, Monroe." Last names are much less personal.

His deep brown eyes narrow, searching my face, before he nods.

I watch as he rolls his broad shoulders, taking a drink of his coffee.

"You sore?" I ask.

"A little bit, but nothing out of the norm."

"How do you treat it?" Reaching up to get the plates out of the cupboard, I glance at him when he doesn't answer.

His eyes are eating up my midriff that's now exposed. When my feet are once again flat on the tile, his eyes raise to mine and an unapologetic smirk plays on his lips.

I roll my eyes, making him chuckle.

God, that sound...

Get a grip, Kalani.

I place the syrup, powdered sugar, butter, and bacon on the bar.

"I don't usually do much. Ice packs, for sure. If it's hurting continuously, I'll throw a heat pack on it. It'll be fine come Monday."

I put the French toast on a platter and walk over, sitting down next to Nate. "So, you just deal with it all weekend? That's hella dumb."

He laughs. "I guess, but not much you can do. It's the name of the game."

"Uh-huh. Here." I push the pile toward him. "Grab what you want."

I place a slice of French toast on my plate, spread on the butter, shake on a yummy amount of powdered sugar, and top it off with a layer of syrup. I bring my first bite to my lips when I realize he hasn't moved.

I look up at him and he's staring at me with a strange expression on his face. "What?"

"Nothing." He grins.

I drop my fork to my plate and turn toward him. "Spill it."

"You're just full of surprises, that's all."

"You said you liked French toast and bacon. I said I'd make you some. You said yes. What the hell is surprising about that?" I'm agitated because he's...I don't even know what he is, but I don't think I like it. "You were well-aware I was making breakfast. So, stop being weird and eat." I turn back to my food and take a huge bite, my eyes rolling back at the deliciousness.

Nate makes his plate and begins eating next to me.

"What I meant was, you're a breath of fresh air," he mutters between bites.

I look over at him and flutter my eyelashes. "That's because I'm shiny and new," I say with a mouth full, making us both laugh.

"Nah, you're just...different, that's all."

What a line.

I grab another slice and add all my goods.

"You'll be high on sugar by the time you're done," he teases.

I smile. "My grandpa always said I'd be bouncing off the walls in no time." He laughs and I freeze.

I jump off the stool and turn toward the hallway. "Be right back."

I hold my breath until I step into my room. Shutting the door behind me, I lean against it.

What the fuck?

Why did I just say that?

I never, and I mean ne-ver, talk about...stuff.

I'm like a Starbucks menu. What you see is what you get, however, the true connoisseur, or those closest to you, know about the secret menu; things others don't know about. But that shit's never advertised, and it sure as shit isn't volunteered information.

So, yeah...what the fuck?

Closing my eyes, I place my palms against my temples and give my head a little shake. When I open them, I see it.

The cord to the alarm.

You!

Of course. The dream, or flashback, has me all jacked up in the head right now.

That's all it is.

Okay. Okay. Rolling my shoulders, I release a deep breath.

That being the reason for my word vomit I can handle.

I walk into the kitchen, my head held high, and take my seat next to Nate.

"So, did you have fun at the game on Friday?" Nate asks, his attention on his plate.

I look up at him, and he glances at me briefly and winks.

Why he's giving me the out, I don't know, but I take it.

"It was fun. You guys played great. A few quirks here and there that need fine-tuning, but I'm sure Coach P. will handle it."

His face is a mixture of shock and amusement.

I can't help but smirk. "You thought I was going to sit here and gush over how well you played, and how good you looked doing it?"

"I figured, yeah," he replies honestly, leaning back in his stool.

"And that, bucko, was your first mistake."

He eyes me. "I'm beginning to understand that assumptions are not the way to go when it comes to you."

"Correct you are." I set my fork down and turn toward him. "If there is one thing you need to know about me, it's that I'm honest, Nate." His brows are pulled in, like he's completely focused on what I'm saying, his eyes holding mine.

"If you ever need to know something, ask me." I shrug my shoulders.

"Why?"

"Why, what?"

"Why are you always honest?" His eyes roam my face.

"I don't see the point of being any other way. Dishonesty is a pointless trait. All it does is cause problems and distrust." I hold his dark gaze.

I really should just shut up, but I'm already right there. "I may not care what others think about me, but I refuse to give anyone a reason to doubt me. Honesty is the only way to avoid that. Plus, if you're honest, people know what to expect. No one gets caught off guard."

He breaks eye contact, clearing his throat in the process. "Good to know."

I hop off the stool and start cleaning up.

"Do you have plans today?" Nate asks, his voice straining for indifference, but when I glance at him, I find him moving imaginary food around on his plate.

With a grin, I set my plate in the dishwasher. "I have zero plans, Handsome."

He brings his dishes to the counter, and sets them down by the sink, before leaning his back against it. "Feel like coming to a barbecue with me today? A bunch of guys from the team will be there."

I mock his stance on the opposite side of the kitchen. "A barbecue?"

He nods, holding my eyes hostage.

Licking my lips, I agree.

"Yeah?"

"Sure." I shrug. "Why not. I'll call Parker to pick me up."

His brows crease for a moment, but he recovers. "Yeah, alright. I better head out."

I nod and walk him to the door.

"So, I'll see you there, then?"

"Guess you will."

Before I realize what he's doing, and before I can stop him, his rough hand grazes my cheek as he tucks a piece of stray hair behind my ear.

"Thanks for breakfast, Kalani." His tone is low, soft.

For some reason, I have to tell myself to breathe.

"One more thing..."

"What?"

"The barbecue, it's kinda for my sister and her fiancé."

"Go home." I frown.

A grin takes over his face as he walks backward out the door. "See you in a bit."

Closing the door, I pause in the entryway.

Yeah. This might be a bad idea.

Chapter Ten

K ALANI

It's just after 1:30 pm when Parker turns down a dirt road that leads to a large, beautiful home. Once the house is in full view, my mouth drops open.

"Shut the fuck up. Is that..." I squint, leaning forward in the cab of his truck.

Parker cackles next to me. "Nate's mom has got the hots for Tom Hanks. His Pops delivered." He smiles, pulling his blue Chevy to a stop.

I hop out before he has the thing off and gawk at the sight before me.

The white, two-story home sits in the center of a perfectly mowed and edged spread of the greenest grass. The screen-covered front door sits dead center, surrounded by long windows bordered in forest green shutters.

Six long, white pillars run from top to bottom, acting as

supports for the covered patios on both levels, with a knee-high railing that runs along the base. The bottom level stretches slightly longer and curls to the right where there's a small extension of roof top and a short set of stairs.

"Oh, my God." My eyes slide right. "Holy shit!" My brows climb. The swing.

The swing!

Parker throws his head back, laughing, wraps his arm around my shoulder and starts dragging me around the side of the house.

I pivot my heels into the grass. "No! Wait... I-" I give Parker my best 'pretty please' expression.

"Uh-uh," he backs away. "Nope. You're not sucking me into that shit." He gestures toward my pouty face.

"Pleeease?" I beg. Grabbing ahold of his shirt, I pull him closer.

"Hey."

We both whip around when we hear Nate's voice.

"Thank God," Parker exhales, using Nate's distraction to rocket away from me. "You deal with..." he glances at me, horrified, "that."

I can hardly stand still at this point.

Nate looks back at me with his brows pulled in. "What's going on?" He cuts a quick glance in the direction Parker headed.

"Your house..." I start and he begins to grin. "This is the Forrest Gump house."

He laughs and walks toward me. "No, it's a replica of the Forrest Gump house."

I nod, my eyes bulging. "Put me out of my misery, Handsome," I beg. "I gotta swing on the swing." I clasp my fingers together in a prayer-like position.

He puts a hand out for me, his eyes shining.

With a squeal, I pass him, smacking his arm out of the way, only to stop at the stairs and take a deep breath before climbing them.

When I reach the swing, finding it swaying slightly in the light fall breeze, I glance back at Nate. He's leaning a shoulder against the first magnificent pillar, watching me. I smile wide, then turn back to the swing.

Running the tips of my fingers along the light wood from one side to the other, I wrap my palm gently around the metal support it hangs from and, once again, glance back at Nate.

He gives the subtlest of nods, so I lower myself onto the seat, slowly leaning back. Closing my eyes, I take a deep breath, only to release it shortly after with a laugh.

"What?"

I smile. "You smell like your home," I tell him, leaning back, my eyes closing once again.

"I don't even know what that means," he laughs.

"You don't need to. Come. Sit." I pat the spot next to me.

When the bench-style seat shifts with his weight, I settle in more, but don't open my eyes.

It's quiet for a few minutes, other than random voices floating around from the other side of the house.

"I really want to climb that overlay and sneak in your bedroom window, just so I can say I'm a badass like Jenny was. Granted she was, what, eight?"

Nate laughs, bumping his shoulder into mine. "I wouldn't be opposed to that."

I chuckle, dropping my head back again. "I bet you wouldn't."

"And what do we have here?" A silky, smooth voice beacons our attention.

He drops his chin to his chest on a curse.

I look over to see a beautiful girl with short, brown hair, dressed to the nines in a long-sleeved, royal blue maxi dress, a silver scarf around her neck, glaring my way.

"Hey, Ken," he grumbles, narrowing his eye at the girl. But the look on his face is more, I don't know, curious in a gleefully annoyed kind of way.

"Hi," she says to him, but keeps her dark eyes on me.

And here we go...

"So," she purses her lips, "you the girl Nate invited today?" she interrogates, crossing her arms over her chest.

Not bothering to move, I answer, "One of many, I'm sure."

Nate tenses beside me.

She shifts her mouth to the right, her eyes squinting further. "Why didn't you come here with him?"

My brows lift. "Uhhh, because I didn't want to."

She lets out a humorless laugh. "You didn't want him to pick you up?" she accuses. "Please."

Mmm... yeah, I'm done.

"Check it out." I sit up and lock my eyes on hers. "I'm not some harlot looking to be seen on his arm. Personally," I cut a glance at Nate, "I'd rather he be throwing a ball with it, than have it hangin' around me like some sorta prize," I snap.

Bitch.

Her eyes narrow even more, but I notice her foot begin to bounce and her mouth's pinched tight.

I don't have time for this.

With a sigh, I drop back against the seat. "Look, if you've got some itch you need scratched, don't waste your time on me," I tell her, as I tilt my head to look her over.

Without a trace of skin showing, she's still what a girl who cared would call a triple threat: tall, tan, and curves for days. Her face is naturally pretty, smooth with high cheekbones and a classy amount of make-up. Her perfectly placed hair and straight posture screams high maintenance, not that that would stop a guy like Nate, but still.

She's every bit as perfect as a porcelain doll.

"Yeah," I nod, impressed. "You probably won't even have to beg."

Her mouth drops open in shock, while Nate doubles over in laughter.

I look at him like he's gone mad, then turn back to the girl.

"Oh, my God!" Her brown eyes sparkle and gleam.

Maybe she's bipolar?

She bounces on the balls of her feet, her eyes flying between Nate and me.

My gaze flicks to Nate, who simply winks and leans back on the swing.

"I'm Kenra Monroe." She thrusts her thin hand in my face but is quick to pull it back and smooth down her sleeve.

Monroe.

Oooh.

"Overprotective sister?" I raise a brow at her.

With a pop of her shoulder, she says, "More like, sniffing out the skanks." Nodding, she continues, "I'm impressed."

Before I can respond, she turns to Nate, her brows disappearing into her hairline, eyes wide. "Don't let mom get ahold of her."

They have some weird brother-sister mind-reading moment, resulting in Nate smirking at her, and her jaw dropping, again.

"What?" I ask, looking between the two.

"Nothing," she answers too quickly, releasing a breath as she stands taller. "Come on." She grabs my arm, pulling me to my feet. "I'm dying to see how all this plays out."

Allowing her to drag me away, I turn back to Nate and glare.

He stands, grins at me, but makes no move to reel his sister in.

Awesome.

NATE

As we make our way around the corner, I watch as she takes everything in.

Her eyes follow the grass line out to the trees that box in the property.

She can't see it from here, but there's a small stream that runs along the Grove, wrapping around the hillside.

Her eyelids are low, telling me she appreciates the simplicity of the land. I kinda thought she might.

When my sister turns, she catches me staring, a crease forming on her forehead as she looks from Kalani to me.

I shake my head, earning a sad smile in return.

Mr. Prescott spots her first. Breaking away from his conversation with my uncle, he turns to her with a smile. "Ms. Embers, great to see you."

She waves. "Hey, Mr. P."

The smile she gives him is her standard go-to. There's little to no effort there, an exercised smile I've noticed she gives when she feels like being polite.

Gorgeous, but void.

Not like the one I saw a few minutes ago.

Back on the porch, when she smiled over her shoulder at me, my stomach bottomed out, putting me off balance. I had to lean against the damn post to keep from making a fool of myself.

Her long, dark hair was flowing over her shoulders, blowing lightly in the wind, making me want to wrap it around my fist and pull her to me, kiss those lips she's got polished a pretty pink today. Her eyes were creased at the edges, leaving her dark lashes fanning over her cheekbones. The contrast of dark against light, made her eyes shine an impossible shade of blue. I'm not a clumsy guy, but this girl's got me trippin' over myself in every which way and she doesn't even know it.

That smile she gave me; I've never seen it before.

It was real.

Lethal.

I want to see it again.

"Save her!" I'm ripped from my thoughts when my sister hisses in my ear.

I chuckle, not taking my eyes off a very animated version of Kalani. "She can handle her own. Trust me." I smile, watching her hands fly all over the place as she gives the four-time State-winning coach a lecture in proper coverage I'm sure he'll never forget.

Kenra punches my shoulder. "I'm not talking about them. Shit, both Uncle Jim and Mr. P. are ten seconds from adding her to their wills, what with that freakish football jumbo she's spittin' at em'."

Then I see him moving in. I take a half a step forward, only to have my sister stop me with a palm to the chest.

I frown at her.

She shakes her head back and forth. "Too late now, brother."

Jarrod steps up to Kalani, wraps his arm around her shoulder, and steers her toward our friends who've gathered in the furthest back corner.

When Kenra starts laughing, I turn my narrowed eyes on her.

"What?" I snap.

"This is gonna be fun."

"What is?"

"Watching your role reversal."

When my brows pull in, she rolls her eyes and looks back to Kalani.

"You like her and she hasn't the slightest clue," she observes. "And I'm betting, even if she did, she wouldn't give a damn." She turns, smiling wide at me. "I think it's safe to say, you've been friend-zoned."

"You don't know shit," I grumble.

She smiles even wider. "Say what you want, little brother, but I have a feeling you'll be the one doing the chasing this time around."

I groan and follow behind the smiling bastard who wants his arm ripped off, a humming Kenra behind me.

The second we walk up, I hear Liv's nasally voice mumble something hateful from my right, but don't bother looking.

She's always looking to start shit.

"Why does mom still insist on inviting Liv to all these things? No one can stand her, not even you."

"Just because we're not friends doesn't mean Dad and Mr. Richmond aren't. She doesn't want him to feel unwelcome just because his daughter's a bitch."

"Right."

"Whuddup, Lolli?" Austin grins.

Kalani glances around the group. "Well," she breaks from Jarrod's hold and starts walking toward Parker, who has his hand held out for her, "I'd go with your typical 'hard dicks and helicopters', but since Liv is here," she tosses a gelled-up smile, "I'd say the chances of getting an STD is pretty up there."

The group erupts in laughter, causing some of the other party goers to glance our way briefly.

"Nice to see you, too, Lolli," Liv bites out, flipping her fake blonde hair over her shoulder.

"Aww," Kalani places her right hand over her heart. "Fuck you very much, Liv." She smiles and drops onto Parker's lap.

She's there for a whole five seconds, before I pull her ass right back up and down onto mine.

She frowns at me and I frown right back.

I don't say a word, just look over at Kenra, who's grinning like a fool. A grin that falls flat the second Parker speaks.

"Hey, Ken," he says quietly.

My brows pull in as I study her. Her shoulders grow tense and she starts rubbing at her palms, something she does when she's nervous. Finally, she glances his way, but only with her eyes.

"Congratulations on the engagement," Parker leans forward to tell her and she drops her gaze to her lap, a quiet "thanks" leaving her.

Before I have time to dwell on that weird ass interaction, Liv pulls a Liv and starts runnin' her mouth.

"Real classy of you, Lolli. Bouncing from one lap to the next in seconds," Liv grins smugly.

"Better than two beds, or do you disagree?" Kalani holds eye contact until Liv looks away.

"Looks like you may have met your match, Olivia," my sister chides, dropping down to sit on the grass.

Liv's look of pure disgust is pointed right at my sister – her former best friend. I'm still trying to figure out exactly what happened there. I have my suspicions, but Ken refuses to talk about it. "You couldn't keep up with me, Kenra," she accuses. "What makes you think she can?"

Kalani tries flying off my lap, but I hold her hips in place.

If she thinks she's punishing me by pushing that tight ass down on me as hard as she can, she's dead wrong.

I might ask her to do it again.

"Listen up, you over-privileged bunny," Kalani starts. "I don't give a shit who you are, where you came from, or what trash can you end up in, but don't think for a second you can sit there and insult the person this party is for. So, take your free drink, fake nails, and bad attitude, and move along."

She settles into my lap, but when she notices Liv's eyes cut to mine, my firecracker decides she's not done yet.

"Oh, and if you're here for Nate, he's under me right now, so you might wanna give him a ring later."

"Burn, bitch," Kenra adds, laughing alongside the rest of the group.

Liv stands and turns her glacier gaze on Kalani. "I always get the last laugh." Her face turns predatory. "Right when you think you've got it all figured out; I'll make sure it all blows up in your face."

"I'll give you the last word, Liv," Kalani grins. "I'm thinking you need it."

Liv stomps back to her car, peeling out on her way down the dirt road.

A couple hours later, I walk away from the volleyball game we've got going to grab a water out of the ice chest.

"How'd you keep her away from mom this whole time?"

I grin, bringing my water to my lips. "Simple. Invited half the team." We both laugh. "She's been stuck refilling dishes most of the day. By the way, where's the groom-to-be?"

"Flight delay," Kenra shrugs a shoulder, looking down at her ring, then pulls her sleeves over her hands. She looks up at me. "I like her, Nate," she continues. "She's...real."

Not taking my eyes off Kalani, I nod my head.

"Be careful, Nate." I look at my sister then, finding a wrinkle in her brow.

She reaches up, grabbing ahold of my shoulder. "She seems content the way she is," she tells me, holding my gaze. "Don't push, but don't back out."

My brows pull in as I stare at my sister. She seems... off. Different somehow.

She definitely isn't acting how I imagine a glowing bride-to-be would.

I'm about to ask her when I see a flash of black out of the corner of my eye. Turning, I find Kalani not so casually sneaking around the front of the house. I couldn't help the smile that takes over my lips if I tried.

I drop a quick kiss to Kenra's cheek, then make my way to our front porch swing, knowing what I'll find when I get there.

KALANI

. . .

With my toes, I give myself a healthy push, then settle into the swing.

I close my eyes and lay my head against the woodgrain seat, crossing my fingers that the sway continues since my feet don't reach the ground.

The sun is beginning to set, causing the glow to shine under the awning, offering a small sense of warmth on this chilly November evening.

I feel him walk up, but don't open my eyes, figuring he'll speak when he's ready.

"Can I join you?" he asks a few minutes later, his voice sounding thicker than normal. Sexier.

"Yes," I whisper into the air, not wanting to disrupt the peaceful element surrounding me.

Once he's settled, he scoots his body next to mine so our arms and thighs are brushing each other. His body is warm, blanketing me with the simplest of contact.

"Is it alright if I swing us?"

My smile is wide, but I still don't open my eyes. "Please."

We sit, swaying together ever so slowly, as the sun dances lower on the other side of my eyelids.

Thoroughly relaxed, I release an appreciative sigh. Turning, I find Nate's glossy eyes open and on me.

"Have you always lived in this home?" I murmur.

He nods and I shift my torso toward him, bringing my knees up to rest my chin against them.

"My parents have been together since high school. Prom king and queen, and all that." He rolls his eyes. "She told him what she envisioned in a home and family, and he didn't stop until he got everything he thought she deserved."

"They're good people?"

He smiles. "Yeah. They're like the poster couple for what a marriage should be. My mom always says they probably love each other more now than they did then."

"So, you're not your typical 'bad boy from a broken home' then, huh?" I tease.

He chuckles and rubs the back of his neck. "Nah. Not a 'bad boy' at all, just like to have fun." He sighs. "Too much sometimes, I'll admit, but I know that's eventually what I want - what they have. When I have my girl, I'll be good to her." He holds my gaze, his voice earnest.

Not sure why, but I believe him.

"Did you sit here a lot, on this swing, with your parents?"

Unblinking, he nods.

"I would have, too." My words are spoken in a tone I don't recognize.

I think about looking away, but his lazy gaze holds mine. There's a message his eyes are trying to convey that I can't quite catch, but it prompts me to reveal. "I live by myself."

I have no idea why I just said that, but my heart's not racing and my eyes aren't fogging because of it. I'm not getting lost in my own head and preparing for paralysis. No. My pulse spikes and my pupils dilate because this playboy in front of me is looking at me like he never wants to look away.

Nate's fingers come up and skim across my cheek, leaving a trail of fire behind them. Gently, he tucks my hair behind my ear, sliding his hand down until the piece slips from his fingertips.

My skin begins to tingle.

"Kalani..." he trails off, his body leaning toward mine.

His eyes are fervent and open, and I gotta go...

I hop up so fast I have to squeeze my eyes tight for a few seconds to regain stability.

I don't look back at him, and he doesn't follow.

Like a true godsend, Parker walks around the corner right then.

"Ready?" he calls out, cutting Nate a curious glance.

"Yep," I answer, walking past him.

Right when my hand reaches the handle of Parker's truck, Nate calls out, "I'll catch you later, Kalani."

My body denies me of the breath I need once I process his double meaning.

Hopping into the truck, I slam the door, earning a glare from Parker and a laugh from Nate.

Let's pray the quarterback can't catch as well as he can throw.

Chapter Eleven

K ALANI

Tomorrow night is the last playoff game, the one that will determine if the boys go to the Championship, so we all decided to have dinner together at my house.

We've been talking football, going over their game plan, for the last twenty minutes and apparently, our sports talk isn't entertaining enough for Mia because she takes the first opening she can and changes the subject to what to do after.

"Shawna's having another party," Mia informs us, her eyes flitting between Nate and me.

Out of the corner of my eye, I notice Nate go still. "Yeah, and she's gonna keep having parties until the main attraction is open for rides," Austin says, earning a laugh from me.

"Seriously, Nate, put the girl out of her misery already," Parker adds, grinning.

Nate frowns at his plate. "I'm not interested."

"Why not?" I ask. "She can't be that bad. She's got a nice ass and she's pretty. Kinda got a Rachel Bilson look going on. Girl next doorish, but she's got a bit of crazy." I tear off a piece a bread and pop it in my mouth.

While the others laugh, Nate turns his frown on me. "Like I said," his eyes tighten around the edges, "I'm not interested."

Mia scoffs from her side of the table. "Not anymore," she mutters into her cup, looking away when Nate's eyes flash to her.

And suddenly it all makes sense.

"Oh, my God!" I laugh. "She's looking for seconds, huh?" I ask, bumping his shoulder playfully.

The table shakes and everyone freezes when he jumps to his feet. Looking down at me with hard eyes, his jaw tightens. "I am not. Having. This conversation with you."

My head pulls back as my brows climb. "Uh..." I cut quick glances at the others. "Okay?"

His nostrils flare before he drops his chin to his chest on a curse.

Not a second later, Austin pops up. "Dinner was awesome, Lolli, but we better head out." Walking around the table, he slaps a hand on Parker's shoulder. "Big game tomorrow and all."

I nod, half-focused on what he said, half-wondering what the hell Nate's problem is.

"You need some help cleaning up?" Nate asks, looking everywhere but at me.

I can't help but laugh at his weirdness. "Thanks, but I got it."

Parker leans in and places a chaste kiss to my temple. "Thanks, Lolli Bear."

"You're welcome, Hero." I give him a one-armed hug.

Austin gives me a quick hug, before wrapping an arm around Mia's shoulder. "Bye, Lolli." He salutes me on his way out, Parker hot on his heels, leaving Nate standing in front of me.

His chest inflates as his strangled gaze finally returns to mine.

I tighten my lips to keep from grinning. "You alright?"

A deep sigh leaves him, and he nods, heading for the door. Pulling it open, he murmurs, "Goodnight, Kalani," and walks out, without looking back.

And I'm left standing here wondering why I expected more.

NATE

The second the door clicks shut, I dig my fingernails into my palm to keep from opening it again, pulling her in my arms, and biting down on that buxom bottom lip of hers until she begs me to stay.

Once I'm seated in the Hummer, I let out a frustrated sigh. "Fuck." Running my hands down my face, I drop my head against the headrest.

"Interesting evening," Austin teases, from the seat beside me.

Not at all shocked to see him sitting there, I put the truck in reverse and pull out of the driveway. "Where's Parker?"

"Told him to take my truck home." I glance at him, and he grins. "Figured it best if I rode with you instead."

He'd be right. I was one hut away from choking Baylor's ass out for putting his lips on her. Again.

"So, what's up, man?" Austin shoves my shoulder. "Let's hear it."

"I fucked Shawna."

Austin howls in laughter. "Shit, I didn't think it happened yet. Thought for sure she'd get you tomorrow, though." He grins. "Guess that's done with now, huh?"

I frown at the road ahead of me.

"Wait. You're thinking about going at it again?" He hits the dash on a howl. "Damn-"

"What?!" I cut him a glance. "No! I didn't plan to the first time. I..." A groan leaves me.

"What?"

I look at my best friend. If I can be real with anyone, it's him.

"I threw up after," I tell him, as we pull up to Parker's house.

A grin starts to grow on his face, but when my expression doesn't change, his lip lowers back down. "Alright," he urges me on.

"When I left Kalani's house last weekend, Shawna called." I shrug. "Figured, why not. Nothing else to do."

Austin nods.

"It was fine at first, but then she kept rubbing on me and her catcalls were fake as shit, and I... Fuck, I don't know, man."

"Sure you do. Out with it."

My hand comes down and smacks the steering wheel. I turn back to him and narrow my eyes. "Don't give me shit."

Austin lifts both hands, letting me know there's no judgment.

"It felt...fucked up, wrong. I was disgusted with myself after." My stomach starts to turn at the thought. Shawna was desperate and...easy.

"That's new, huh?" He tries to keep his tone neutral, but I've known him long enough to know when he's tripped the fuck out.

I nod.

"Was it Shawna ... or ...?"

That's the million-dollar question.

"I don't know, man." I rub the back of my neck. "I have a feeling it has absolutely nothing to do with Shawna and everything to do with-"

"Your dark haired, blue-eyed wonder?" he too eagerly supplies.

I nod my head, looking out the front window. "Yeah. God," I huff on a laugh. "I sound like a chick."

Then it dawns on me what he said.

My.

I look over to find him grinning like the fool he is. "My wonder?"

"Dude. You pissed on her the second you seen her at school." He laughs. "She's yours, man," he says, before shrugging. "She just hasn't figured it out yet."

"Hmph, yeah, no shit." I roll my shoulder so it doesn't lock up on me, then I ask him something that's been bugging the shit out me. "You think Parker plans on making a move?" I ask, glancing at Parker's house. "They seem real close."

Too close.

"Man, get out of here with that shit. Parker's your friend, and yeah, maybe he and Kalani started some friendship before we all started hanging out and all, but he sees it. Shit, everyone sees it but you two." He laughs. "You guys got some serious something brewing between you. I mean, look, you've barely had your hands on her, and you already can't stick your dick in anyone else without getting sick."

When I glare at him, he laughs even harder, reaching over to shove me. "I'm fucking with you, dude. Chill. But, seriously, you don't need to worry about those two."

When he sees I'm unconvinced, he nods.

"Trust me, Baylor knows it's a loss." His voice is adamant. "A helluva loss," he finishes, looking out his window.

I put the truck in gear. "I'll see you tomorrow."

He nods and hops out.

Right before he shuts the door, he pops his head back in. "Go home, Nate." He holds eye contact until he knows I'm catching his drift. Once I nod, he heads for Parker's door.

As soon as I get home, I strip down and lie back in my bed. Pulling out my phone, I text Kalani.

Me: you were right.

. . .

She responds a minute later.

Kalani: I usually am.

I smile at her response. Only Kalani wouldn't care to ask what about. I like that. I take a deep breath and type out my next text.

Me: I slept with Shawna.

Kalani: ha! I knew it! Ten points for me...

I frown at my screen.

She texted back instantly. What the fuck's up with that?

She didn't even need a few seconds of contemplation? Of rereading my message and processing her thoughts, or feelings of whatever the fuck girls normally do in this situation?

She was completely unfazed by my admission, like she expected it. That, or she just doesn't care.

I'm not sure how I feel about that.

Unsure of what else to say, I end the conversation.

Me: Night, Kalani.

Kalani: Night, QB.

. . .

Tossing my phone on the bed beside me, I turn and groan into my pillow.

She doesn't care I hooked up with Shawna. I'd be lying if I said that didn't bother me.

That thought alone is the confirmation I've been waiting for, everything I need to know. Things become instantly clearer to me in this moment.

I smirk into the darkness. "Game on."

Chapter Twelve

K ALANI

"Come on, Lolli," Mia whines as we exit the field gates. "Come to the party with us." She links her arms with Alyssa and Ashley, who are wearing matching grins, both nodding at Mia's invite.

"Not tonight, Meems." I smile and catch her keys when she tosses them to me. "Next weekend." I wink.

"Yeah, yeah." She rolls her eyes and they walk off to hitch a ride on the party train.

"Bye, Lolli," the twins say in unison and I wave in return.

Once I get home, I strip down to my chonies, throw on an old Nickelback t-shirt and head into the kitchen to make something to eat.

I scan the fridge.

Tacos it is.

I throw chopped chicken in a pan, heat the oil for the tortillas, and grab the fixings from the fridge. I set them on the bar, frowning when the doorbell rings. After a quick toss to the chicken, I run to answer it.

When I swing it open, I come face to face with Nate.

"Uh, hey."

His eyes narrow and he nudges me inside, closing the door behind him.

"Wha-"

"You can't answer the door in a t-shirt," he chastises me. "I could have been a murderer or something."

I roll my eyes and walk back into the kitchen. "Know of many murderers in Alrick, Handsome?" I shoot him a grin over my shoulder. "What are you doing here anyway?"

"That's not the point." He ignores my question. "Look out the window or, better yet, put pants on before you answer your door. For anyone."

He's still frowning.

"Fine. If it bothers you, I'll put pants on." I turn to face him, jutting my hip out. "Here," I hold the spatula out. "Come stir and I'll go get dressed."

He smirks, edging toward me. "I said, before you open the door." He steps in front of me, so I have to tilt my head back to look in his dark brown eyes.

"I'm already inside," he whispers, and my dirty mind takes flight. "No need for pants now." He winks, taking the spatula out of my hand.

It just got real warm in here.

Suddenly in need of air, I lean over the sink and push open the window. When I drop back down to my feet, I look at Nate, who's frozen in place, spatula midair, eyes zoned in on my lower half.

With a smirk, I walk right up to him and snatch the spatula back.

He shakes off his dazed expression and hops up on the counter to my right.

The oil is now good to go, so I start crisping the tortillas.

"Tacos?"

"Yes. You hungry?" I smile up at him.

"Starving," he admits.

"You come over here expecting me to feed you?" I raise a brow.

He holds my gaze for a few seconds, then says, "Just wanted to see you."

I laugh at that. "Man, it's no wonder girls just hand it over." I pull a cutting board out of the cabinet behind us, rushing back to make sure the tortillas don't burn. "You're a smooth talker."

He huffs and hops down. "That wasn't a line."

"Make yourself useful and cut the veggies."

He chuckles and walks to the other side of the kitchen to start.

"You know how?" I ask him, not bothering to turn around.

"I can cut lettuce, Kalani."

I bite back a grin. "Just checking."

Once everything is cooked and ready to go, we decide to eat in the living room. Setting everything up on the coffee table, I pop in a movie and we settle in on the floor.

"Rookie of the Year?" He quirks a brow, amused.

I nod and take a bite of my taco. "Love me some Rowengartner."

He laughs and wipes his mouth with a napkin. "You know, for the football girl you seem to be, you sure have a thing for baseball movies." He reaches for another taco shell.

My face pinches for the shortest of seconds, and I wait for my body to tense, but it doesn't happen. I look up at Nate and see he's focused on eating, his eyes flicking back and forth from the TV to his food. He's not expecting an explanation, or anything for that matter.

I'm not sure what propels me to say it, but it happens anyway. "Football was a huge part of my life growing up." Cutting a quick glance at Nate, I find him now hanging on every word.

Clearing my throat, I continue, "My grandpa was a coach. After a loss or a shit day of practice, he said he needed to clear his mind so he could go into the next day with a clean slate and build off that." I pick at my napkin. "So, when he needed to find a new strategy or make adjustments that weren't obvious to him, we'd watch baseball movies. Rid the house of football altogether." I shrug and take a drink of my water, then finally look over at Nate.

He gives me a soft smile, his eyes earnest. "That's a good idea. I never would have thought of that."

"Yeah." I hop up onto the couch and he follows. "It worked for him."

Grabbing my hand, he traces my fingers with his and I let him. "Did you live with him? Your grandpa?"

"He, uh," I take a deep breath, "stayed with me a lot, but his job had him on the road, so it was never completely permanent. At least, not for long."

"You don't talk about your family much, do you?" His voice is cautious.

I look up, finding he's staring at our hands in fascination.

"Never," I whisper, a crease forming in my brow at his perceptiveness.

Now he looks at me. "Why did you tell me?"

I swallow and look away, but he doesn't allow that. He places his hand on my chin and turns my face back to his. He stares at me, giving a small tip of his chin.

"I have no idea," I breathe.

His gaze flicks from my eyes to my mouth and back. "Kalani..."

I scurry off the couch.

"Are you full?" My voice is tight and obviously shaking, but I don't care. It's self-preservation at this point. Something about Nate throws me off my game and my defense slips. And I'm a defense girl.

"Kalani." His voice sounds pained and that has me ready to flash.

A major factor as to why I don't talk about things is because I can't stand pity. I don't need it and I don't want it.

However, when I flip around to give him a mouthful, my eyes widen.

His eyes are lasered in on my thighs, his chest heaving, causing my breathing to speed up.

His gaze slowly rakes up my body, his perfect teeth sinking into his lower lip as those hungry eyes meet mine.

Oh lordy, no...

I am far too exposed for this Nate to come out and play.

With a strangled breath, I tell him, "You should go."

His eyes narrow in challenge; a hint of a smirk he doesn't dare let slip on his lips.

He sees it, damn it. He knows the last thing on my mind is him leaving, what with my body trembling, nipples poking out to say 'hey', and boobs bouncing around because I'm breathing so fast.

Yeah, fucker. You get me going.

He takes a step closer.

I take a step back.

"You want me to go?" he whispers. I think. That, or my blood is pumping at a dangerous rate because I swear his voice is silky, sexy smooth. The kind of voice that makes you stop in your tracks and rethink everything.

"I'll go," he rasps.

Oh, thank God...

"If," he adds quickly when he sees my relief.

Now the bastard smirks.

"Quid pro quo, how nice of you," I deadpan, causing him to laugh.

"Make me breakfast Sunday and I'll go."

"Deal," I don't hesitate, just stomp to the door. Anything to get him out of here.

He chuckles and smacks my ass on his way out. "Night, Gorgeous."

Even though I roll my eyes, there's a small smile on my lips. "Night, Handsome."

Chapter Thirteen

K ALANI

"So," Nate finishes off his last piece of bacon. "You ignored my call yesterday."

"No, I didn't." I set my dish in the sink. "I turned my phone off so I could sleep."

He nods. "So, you didn't do anything fun? Didn't go out with Mia?"

"Did you see me at the party?" I raise an eyebrow.

He shrugs and looks away from me. "I didn't go to the party. Stayed in," he tells me, rolling his shoulder around.

I sigh and walk out of the kitchen. "Go sit on the couch and take off your shirt. I'll be right back."

He chokes on his coffee and turns to me. "What?"

I roll my eyes as I pass him, heading down the hall. "Nike."

"Again, what?"

"Just do it!" I laugh.

My kit in hand, I walk back into the living room, finding Nate right where I told him to be.

Hovering over his form, I purse my lips.

"What?" he asks.

"Okay, so maybe the no shirt thing was a bad idea."

When I lick my lips, he quirks an eyebrow.

"And why is that?" he teases, brown eyes gleaming.

"Duh! Because all of that," I throw my hand out, "is distracting."

He laughs and it's really not fair how every muscle tightens and becomes more defined as he does.

I frown. "Sit on the floor, your back against the foot of the couch."

With a grin, he does as he was told.

Once he's situated, I climb in behind him and place my legs on either side, careful to keep them from pressing against his tanned skin.

Oil in hand, I squirt some into the bowl and stir in the crushed lavender leaves. I snap the heat pads and set them aside.

"Okay." I knock his arms off his knees and he chuckles. "Sit still and keep your arms at your sides."

He shifts so he can place his arms on the floor under each of my legs.

After I apply a generous amount of the concoction to his shoulder, I set the bowl down and begin rubbing it in.

I don't miss Nate's sharp intake of breath the moment my hand comes down on him.

I rub it all around, covering him in it from his right shoulder blade to the nape of his neck and halfway down his upper arm. Then, I begin to gently massage him, my fingers strumming across the top of his strong shoulder, each one applying a different amount of pressure.

His chin drops to his chest.

After a few minutes, I replace my hands with the heating pad, and start working his bicep the same way.

"What is it?" he asks, his voice low and raspy.

"Lavender and oil."

"What's it do?"

I smile. "It's a natural anti-inflammatory. Has some element that relates to the symptomatic nervous system." Releasing his bicep, I study the structure of his back. "It, uh, helps bring muscles back to their proper form, has a calming element in it that increases blood flow, yada, yada."

I can't stop myself from running a finger down his strong spine. As soon as my finger leaves his skin, his fingers run up my calves, and he begins working my muscles with his firm hands.

I flatten my palm against his lower back, apply a little pressure, then slowly run them up. Reaching his shoulders, I glide them over his collarbone, careful not to knock off the heating pad on the right and push against his pecs with the pads of my fingers.

He looks at me over his shoulder for a moment before closing his eyes and facing forward again.

Pulling my hands back, I begin kneading the trigger points at the base of his skull.

"Mmm..." he moans and my core heats.

My body moves on its own accord, leaning in to kiss his spine as my fingers ghost down his arms and across the side of his ribs.

A smile twitches my lips when his body shudders at the feeling.

"You know," I whisper near his ear, "I totally get why you acted like such a cocky shit when I first met you."

His taut body shakes, his husky laughter flowing through him. "Oh yeah?"

I lean back so I can get the full view. "Oh, yeah. I mean, I can only see your back right now...but the thoughts that are running through my mind..." I laugh because it's ridiculous, but true.

After a few seconds, he responds, his voice low, deeper than usual. "Good to know."

I go back to massaging his shoulders.

"So-" I'm cut off when my phone beeps on the table.

"Check that for me, please," I ask him.

His head whips around. "Huh?"

I widen my eyes and lift my oil-clad hands. "Can you check that for me? I can't exactly grab it." I wiggle my fingers at him.

He furrows his brows, nodding. "Just so we're clear, though, you want me to check it, right? As in, read it? Not just hand it to you?"

I gape at him.

"Hey," he defends. "Most people don't like, or want, other people even touching their phones." His eyes widen to make his point. "And by most people, I mean everyone."

I stare at him blankly.

"What?" He cracks a smile, an adorable innocent one.

"Check the damn thing and turn around." I shove his head playfully, making him laugh. "You're messing up my mojo."

I hear the smile in his voice. "Wow, not even a password, huh?"

"Nope."

He shakes his head. "It's programmed under Speed." He looks at me expectantly over his shoulder.

"Oh, shit." My shoulders slump and I glance at the ceiling. "I forgot." I lift my chin, trying to see the screen over Nate's massive shoulders.

"What'd he say?" I ask him, even though he's still looking at me. "What?"

"You said he. Who is it?" he probes.

My brows lift. "Oh, we're doing this?" I move my hand between the two of us.

He stares at me.

"Okay." I reach over and remove the heat pad from his right shoulder and turn his head so he's once again facing forward. "Think about it. Who's the quickest to get into the backfield?" I smirk, even though he can't see me.

131

Not a second later, his body tenses. "Hollins," he grounds out in whisper, though, I'm pretty sure he's talking to himself.

"Ding, Ding."

He cuts me an irritated look and I watch his jaw shift to the right as he turns around.

"So, what'd he say?" I try blowing a piece of hair out of my face.

"He wants to know ... if you're still meeting for lunch today." His voice is stiff.

With the cloth I brought out, I wipe off Nate's shoulder. "Tell him, yeah. I'll meet him at Wicker at one."

Nate releases my legs and turns his body so quickly I have no time to react. He's now on his knees, facing me as I sit on the couch.

"Hi," I taunt, biting my lip to keep from laughing at how bent out of shape he seems.

His eyes narrow to slits. Placing his palms on the cushions he cages me in, and crouches into my space, his face set in stone. "I'm not telling Jarrod you'll meet him."

"Alright." Shrugging, I hold out my hand, palm up. "Hand me my phone, would ya?"

He shakes his head back and forth. Slowly.

"No?" I raise an eyebrow.

A dangerous smirk forms on his lips and before I can process it, his arm is wrapped around my back and I'm flush against his bare chest.

Leaning in, he slides his lips over mine, his dark, igneous eyes burning into me. Teasing me.

I don't like to be teased.

Right as he goes to pull back, I wrap my legs around his back and smash my lips into his. And when I bite down on his bottom lip for punishment, he growls and forces my mouth open for him.

His tongue brushes mine with perfect precision.

I scoot in closer, pressing my pelvis against his waist, and his hands find my hair. He pulls gently, earning a moan from me.

When my phone beeps again, he pulls back and glances at it, then back at me.

I wait, panting, while he works through his thoughts.

I know he's figured it out when he lets out an irked breath. "You're going to lunch with Jarrod."

It's not a question.

"I am," I breathe out, still trying to recover from that kiss, all the while wanting to go at it again.

His brows pull together and his lips flatten.

He stands and puts a hand out for me. When I place my hand in his, he pulls me up, looking down at me with unreadable eyes. He reaches behind him, picks up my phone, and places it in my palm.

I smile at him and open the new message.

Speed: don't bail. I know you had fun last time.

Nate scoffs. "He's a jackass."

I just laugh and text Jarrod back, letting him know I'm not bailing and I'll be there by one.

My phone beeps instantly.

Speed: there she is. One's good.

Not bothering to reply, I toss my phone on the couch behind me.

Nate's still standing in front of me, so I pat his chest. "I gotta get ready." I circle my hand around my face.

"You're not wearing any makeup." He inspects, in wonderment.

I laugh. "That I'm not."

I watch his face soften as he studies my features, taking in every inch.

I don't think I like it.

Before I can move, his lips lift into a half-smile that roots me in place.

With his eyes following his hand, he reaches up and brushes my still wet hair behind my ear. Though they're not looking into mine, I don't miss the fascination shining within them.

Something stirs in my chest, tightening, making it hard for me to breathe. It's a foreign feeling I can't explain, and completely unwelcome.

Quickly, I slip past him, and walk to the bar to clean up. I don't have to look to know he's following me. I can feel him.

Oh, don't be dumb.

"You need some help?" he asks.

I don't look at him. "No, I'm good. It'll only take a minute."

He's quiet for a moment before his response. "Alright."

"Your shoulder shouldn't give you any more trouble." I laugh. "Well, until after tomorrow's practice, that is." I look over at him to find him moving toward me, his shirt in his hand, allowing me another look.

Goddamn, he's pristine.

His eyes shift back and forth between mine. I'm not sure what he sees, but his eyes take on a mischievous glint.

"What are you up to?" I narrow my eyes in question.

He smirks, leans down to kiss me on my cheek, and whispers, "Thank you for breakfast, Kalani."

Lips pursed, I cross my arms, and tilt my head to the side.

He chuckles and walks toward the door.

"Bye, Handsome," I call out from the kitchen.

"Bye's not gonna work for me, Kalani," he says in a smooth and unwavering voice.

My entire body turns to stone.

"See you soon." This is the last thing I hear before the door closes and my body collapses to the floor.

All I can see are white walls.

Chapter Fourteen

K ALANI

I hear her. She's calling my name.

"Kalani."

Her voice...it's soft, just like I remember.

"Kalani."

Only she sounds clearer now, not muffled by bad reception.

It's nice.

"Kalani!"

Why is she shouting?

Slowly, I open my eyes to see the fuzzy image of my mother kneeling in front of me.

With a shaky hand, I reach out and touch her cheek. "Mom?" I whisper.

"Oh, honey..." she breathes, her voice breaking.

Her face is still blurry, but I can make out her slim figure.

Her hair, long and dark, lays straight against her shoulders.

Squinting, I see a flash of crystal blue eyes before losing focus again.

Shaking my head, I blink rapidly.

When she's still there, still kneeling in front of me, panic takes over and I fly to my feet, frantically looking around.

Burgundy walls. Not white.

The moment my eyes land on her, they harden.

"Kalani..." Her head tilts as she puts her hands out in front of her, slowly moving to stand. "Honey, I-"

"Stop talking!" I shout, my palms flying to my temple, eyes closed tight. Taking a calming breath, I drop my hands, straighten my spine, and lock eyes with her. "How did you get in here?" I snarl.

If Mia-

"I knocked," she rushes out nervously. "When you didn't answer, I got worried and tried the knob." She looks down at the tile. "It was unlocked."

There's a desperate look in her eyes.

"I know I shouldn't have just walked in, and I was going to turn around and leave, but the light was on." She looks at the ceiling. "Then I saw you lying there..." She motions with shaky hands to the spot on the floor.

When I give a sharp nod, she smiles weakly, and I have to look away.

"Kalani, talk to me," she whispers and I want to scream. "Please."

"I can't," I murmur to the ground. "I can't talk to you. I can't even look at you. I'm sorry, but all you are is a constant reminder."

"But-"

"I can't!" I shout. "Please, just... go." Desperate for something to hold onto, I turn and grab ahold of the countertop, squeezing until my knuckles turn white.

I don't let go until I hear the front door close.

Run. I need to run.

I rush to the door but stop short. "Shit." I don't have time before I have to meet Jarrod.

Music is my only option.

I storm into my room, blast Linkin Park's "Numb" as loud as my speakers will let me and get ready for my 'date' with Jarrod.

As I enter the bathroom, I flinch at my own reflection.

Long dark hair.

Bright blue eyes.

I look just like her.

"Ugh!" I grunt out. This is so stupid. This is why I didn't want to come here. I don't need this shit.

I was fine.

I've been fine.

I am fine.

Plugging in my curling iron, I let it heat, while I start on my makeup.

In the beginning when everything went to shit, everyone thought I'd be depressed, suicidal.

I let out a humorless laugh.

When that didn't happen, they thought I was hiding behind my pain. Living in denial. They thought I'd come unhinged at any moment. That my emotions would eventually win out and destroy me.

They were wrong.

So wrong.

What the counselors and psychologists and psychiatrists failed to realize is my emotions could never pull me under.

It's simply not possible.

My emotions could never take over, never swallow me whole.

No.

What they failed to realize is you can't be depressed or suicidal or in pain, and you sure a shit can't break, if your emotions themselves are... lifeless.

Empty.

Sure, I laugh and smile and enjoy myself. And yes, I'm fully capable of getting excited, or becoming aroused. But I don't feel it. Not on the inside anyway. Not where it counts.

I don't get sensations deep within myself that cause distress or discomfort, or anything else for that matter.

Common conceptions don't apply to me; they don't affect me.

I don't get jealous. I don't feel humiliation or compassion or love. Hell, I don't even feel alive most of the time. It's all skin deep. Fun and free-spirited. It is what it is and nothing more. And I love it. It's perfect.

A beautiful simplicity of nothingness.

The ultimate escape.

Chapter Fifteen

K ALANI

As soon as I step foot in Wicker, Ryan catches my eye and motions for me to hold still. He delivers a tray of drinks to one of his tables and jogs over to me.

"Hey, Lolli." He smiles, resting his hands on the black apron at his waist. "I knew you couldn't stay away," he teases.

"It's all about the food, Wicker."

He laughs. "Jarrod said you're meetin' him. Back corner booth. I'll grab you a drink."

I lift my hand in thanks as I make my way over.

I'm almost to the table when Jarrod's head lifts and he spots me.

"Hey," he beams, a nice smile gracing his lips as he hops out of the booth, leaning in to give me a quick hug.

He steps back and holds a hand out, motioning for me to sit as he takes the seat across from me.

"Sorry I'm a little late."

"Don't worry about it." He waves me off. "I'm glad you came."

His smile is infectious and I can't help but smile back.

"Did you order yet?" I glance up at him as I pick up the menu.

"Nah," he shrugs. "I wanted to make sure you showed up first."

I laugh. "Good idea."

Ryan pops over to the table, setting a soda down in front of me. "Dr. P. for you, Lolli."

My eyebrows lift and Jarrod laughs.

He reaches over, clasping a hand on Ryan's shoulder. "Man remembers everything."

"I hear everything, too." He cuts me a glance.

"Oh, I bet you do," I tease. "This place is probably worse than a beauty salon, what with half the junior and senior class here every night."

Ryan laughs. "Don't be mistaken, I get freshman and sophomore dirt, too."

I laugh and lift my legs in my seat to sit Indian-style. "Alright." I set my menu down and look at Jarrod.

"You decided already?" he asks, amused.

I smile and slowly shake my head. "Nope."

They both stare at me, wide-eyed and grinning, making me laugh.

"I'm in an indecisive mood today, boys." I tilt my head and wiggle my eyebrows playfully at Jarrod.

His green eyes hold mine. "What do you have in mind, Ms. Embers?"

I raise an eyebrow. "How about a spin on 'I'll show you mine if you show me yours'?"

Jarrod chokes on his water and Ryan laughs his ass off. He hits Jarrod with his elbow. "I told you she's a spitfire."

Jarrod nods, never taking his pretty greens off me. "I'm game if

141

you are." He licks his lips and I have absolutely no doubt his double meaning stands true.

He looks like he wants to skip the whole eating part and go straight for the nitty gritty.

With my forearms on the table, I lean toward Ryan. "Mr. Wicker, if you would, please bring me Mr. Hollins' favorite dish, and him mine."

Ryan's brows pull in and Jarrod sits back on a chuckle. "You sure about that?"

I look at Jarrod and he sweeps his hand, giving me the go ahead. "Yep." I bounce in my seat.

"Okay." Ryan shakes his head, walking off.

I look back at Jarrod and rub my hands together. "This is fun."

He laughs, bringing his hand up to scratch the scruff on his chin and I let my eyes appraise him.

His blond hair peeks out from underneath his Michigan ball cap. The dark blue makes his green eyes shine brighter. He's wearing a white, long-sleeved thermal that fits him a little too tight, so his muscles are visible. They're not large but defined.

I reach across the table and rub the hair on his jaw. "I never noticed this. It looks good on you." He grabs my hand as I go to pull it back.

He kisses my knuckles, giving me a crooked grin. "I'm beginning to think everything looks good on you." Right when I'm about to roll my eyes, he leans over and pulls a leaf out of my hair, making us both laugh.

"I was about to call you on your cliché, so points for you." He grins at my playful banter.

"Well, then I guess I won't waste time telling you how good you look."

I nod and place my straw to my lips. "And I won't sit and pretend like everything you say is hilarious, if in fact, it's not." I wink and take a drink.

He scratches his chin, eyeing me. "You're something else, you know that?"

"Yeah." Releasing a breath, I play with my straw. "That's what I keep hearing." I glance out the window.

He squints his eyes, clearly about to ask me what I mean, but Ryan walks up with our plates.

At the same time, Jarrod and I say, "What the fuck is that?" We look at each other and bust up laughing.

"Hey, you asked, I delivered. Enjoy guys," Ryan says, before rushing off.

I'm still laughing when I reach out and grab onto Jarrod's arm. "Okay." I look to my dish in horror. "Explain this to me, like right now."

He's still grinning. "That's the Poor Man's Plate."

Eyes wide, I nod. "Uh-huh, and are you a poor man or was this a drunken experiment that ended up working out?"

He tries to hold it in but fails. "Okay, yeah, it was a drunken experiment, but it's delicious." He picks up his fork and cuts off the end of the gravy-covered hot dog. "Try it," he says, as he brings it to my lips.

I narrow my eyes at him but open up after a few seconds.

As soon as the bite touches my tongue, I can tell it's all the wrong flavors for me but chew it and try to keep my nose from scrunching.

Once I swallow, I turn to his hopeful eyes. "That shit's nasty."

He drops back against the seat, laughing.

"Okay," I pick up my fork and stab into the peanut butter, cream cheese, and syrup-covered French toast on his plate. "Your turn. Open up." I lean clear across the table and twirl the fork around in circles.

He opens his mouth and takes the bite like a champ. I laugh loudly when his face scrunches.

With a shake of his head, he reaches for his water, taking a long pull. "Damn, Lolli, how do you eat that?" He licks his lips and shudders. "Ugh."

"Me?" I laugh. Tucking my knees up behind me, I point to my plate. "That shit's ridiculous."

We eye each other's plates.

"You know this was a win-win situation, right?" I ask him.

He looks disturbed. "Yeah? How is that exactly?"

"All we have to do now is trade and we'll each have our favorite dish." I pick up his plate and set it in front of me, moving mine in front of him. "See. Perfecto."

I take a quick bite. "Mmm.... so much better."

Jarrod nods, taking a bite of his disgusting ass food. "I'm glad you suggested switching. I don't know if I would've manned up and admitted I didn't like it if you hadn't."

"Really?" I ask him, unbelievingly. Because honestly, that's super unattractive.

If a guy can't even be honest about food...

He nods and take a drink of water. "I can almost guarantee I'd be sitting here right now, forcing myself to eat that crap you call food."

I smile, leaning over the table. "Well good thing I'm the one with the balls then, huh?" I tease in a quiet voice.

He takes my cue, not knowing I'm trying to test this out and meets me halfway, placing a peck of a kiss on my lips.

He pulls back, eyes playful, and whispers, "You taste nasty."

I bubble up with laughter, but it quickly dies in my throat, lodging there like a ball of powder sugar would.

My body turns rigid, causing my brows to pull in and my eyes to tighten. I must look as off as I feel, because Jarrod asks if I'm alright, but I don't respond.

On its own accord, my head turns to look over my shoulder, and there he is. Standing just inside the doorway, staring right at me. His crooked ass grin in place.

Nate.

What the fuck?

I narrow my eyes and he smirks in return, but then he takes in mine and Jarrod's proximity and his gaze hardens, those dark eyes slicing from my date to me.

Planning to ignore him, I turn back to Jarrod, but he's not focused on me. Nope. He's looking behind me, his jaw growing tenser by the second.

I know he's coming over here. There's no way he wouldn't.

I keep my eyes locked on Jarrod's, watching as he goes on the defense. He leans back, slouching into his corner in a cool, calm, and collected kind of way; though, I'm thinking he's anything but. He casually lifts his arm, laying it across the back of the booth, his other holding onto his water glass.

He tilts his head to the side and jerks his chin, acknowledging our uninvited guests as they walk up.

"Wassup, Hollins?" Austin booms, as he throws himself into the seat next to Jarrod. He wiggles his brows at me when I look at him. "Lolli, how you doin'?"

"Peachy Keen, jellybean." I give him a sideways smirk.

"Not sick of French toast yet, huh, Kalani?" Nate smirks, and I see Jarrod's head shift toward me out my peripheral.

Please, boy. You think you're going to make me squirm? Negative, Ghost Rider.

I keep my eyes locked on his as I take another bite, scraping the fork with my teeth to be annoying. "That's not a thing."

Nate laughs and sits down.

Right next to me.

"What can we do for you guys?" Jarrod boldly asks and I raise an eyebrow at the boys.

Austin laughs. "We interrupting something?" He doesn't let anyone answer before he speaks again. "Some of the guys are meeting here in a few. Want to join us?"

"Sorry man, but" he looks at me and I give him a forced smile, "me and Lolli are hanging for a while."

"Yeah," I say, taking another bite. "Stop trying to steal my date, Nine."

Nate scoffs and I reach down to pinch his thigh.

He doesn't even flinch.

"Fine, fine. You can have him for a while," Austin teases. "Oh hey, Hollins-" Austin starts asking him something but I have no idea what.

All I can focus on is the large hand that's making its way up my thigh.

I turn to look at Nate and the smirk that I know is on his lips. I fully intended to narrow my eyes, but the instant our gazes lock, his cocky smile falters. Those dark eyes search my face and his brows pull in, causing his forehead to wrinkle.

Why does he look worried?

"Nate?"

Both our heads snap toward the other two people occupying this table, one being my seemingly annoyed date.

"What's up?" he asks Jarrod in a bored tone.

"I said I'll hit you up later." Jarrod holds eye contact with Nate, whose smirk only grows.

He squeezes my thigh before sliding out of the booth. "You do that," he tells him, then turns and winks at me before making his way to the other side of the diner, Austin chuckling behind him.

After a few awkward moments of silence, Jarrod and I get back into a good flow of conversation – football.

We talk while I pretend I can't sense Nate's eyes on me.

Jerk.

Once we've finished our meals, Jarrod reaches across the table and grabs my hand, giving me his most charming smile.

I try real hard to make it set me off in some type of way, but it doesn't. It's attractive, that's for sure, but it's a practiced and overused smile that I don't care to see.

Damn.

When he leans over the table, I decide to meet him halfway.

Maybe his kiss will redeem himself for the smile. But when his lips touch mine, I can't help but notice how pinched tight they are or how they're the wrong size. They're not...commanding.

So much for wishful thinking.

He pulls away and stands with a smile. "Be right back. I'm gonna hit the bathroom."

My phone beeps so I pick it up and shake it in the air. "And I'm gonna check that." He grins and walks off.

I pull up my messages and laugh out loud.

Handsome: you're killing me smalls...

Reaching around, I grab the back of my seat, my gaze finding his. His mouth is in a tight line, but there are crinkles around his eyes so I can't quite gauge him.

My phone vibrates in my hands and he lifts his in the air.

I turn around and look down at my screen.

Handsome: don't kiss him again.

Um...what?

Who does he think he is?

And why do I feel like I just took a double shot of espresso?

First things first...

Me: one, don't act like you watched a lick of that movie. You fell asleep remember?

. . .

Handsome: I accept your offer for a redo.

I roll my eyes at my screen. Before I can respond, another message comes through.

Handsome: let's hear number two...

I know for a fact he's smirking right now.
    Dick.

Me: I'll kiss whoever I want.

Handsome: good. Nothing for me to worry about.

Okay, Mister Confident.
    With a sly smile, I type out my response.

Me: what did we decide about making assumptions when it came to me, Monroe?

With a winking smiley face emoji, I hit send.
    His response doesn't surprise me. Not even a little bit.

Handsome: don't kiss him again.

. . .

Smirking, I turn my head and wiggle my eyebrows at him.

His chair slides back as he stands. Leaning his hip against the edge of the table, he crosses his arms over his chest. I'm not even going to comment on how that move makes the sleeves of his t-shirt stretch tighter around those concrete biceps of his. The ones my hands were rubbing on this morning.

He's challenging me, but as my eyes rake over him, I can't even be mad.

Apparently, I'm not the only one who appreciates the view because two girls I recognize from school slide right up to him. One leans into his side, running her hand down his arm, while the other mimics his stance directly in front of him.

He glances down at them briefly, then back at me. I raise my eyebrows and mouth "nice" with a huge smile on my face and his eyes narrow more.

Laughing, I turn around right as Jarrod steps up to the table.

He wipes his hands on his khakis.

I hate khaki.

"Ready?"

I pop out of my seat, finishing off what's left of my disgustingly watered-down soda, then turn back to him with a smile. "Yep. Thanks for the invite."

"You're welcome." He smiles, throwing some cash down on the table. "What do you have planned for the rest of the day?"

Quickly glancing at my phone, I see it's only 2:15 pm. "I don't know. Probably drag Parker to the store with me." I scrunch my nose. "I'm running low on junk food."

He chuckles and steps toward me.

I can tell by the way he's looking at me with his eyes half-closed that he's gonna kiss me. I smile, knowing Nate's watching, but Jarrod assumes it's for him and grins.

He reaches out, places his hand on my forearm, then leans down.

I tilt my head back the slightest bit.

Just as his lips touch mine, an arm wraps around my middle and pulls me back. Hard.

Jarrod's eyes shoot wide open, then narrow, all in the same second. His eyes drop to the arm around my waist then dart to the brazen man-boy it belongs to. "What the fuck, Nate?" His eyes slice to mine.

I simply shrug one shoulder non-committedly.

Don't ask me.

Jarrod's brows pull in and his head jerks back.

Nate's grip on me tightens.

And me? I'm too curious to see how this pans out to say or do a damn thing.

"Back off, Monroe," Jarrod seethes. "Go back to your groupies." He throws an arm out, motioning to the direction Nate came from. "Lolli, came here with me."

I feel Nate stand taller behind me. "Yeah, well. I never should have let that happen."

Let that happen?

Let that happen?

My eyes widen as my mouth drops open.

Oh, fuck to the no...

I go to turn, but as if prepared for my reaction, Nate's free hand finds my hip, effectively rooting me in place.

Bastard.

Jarrod lets out a humorless laugh. "You've got to be kidding me." He places one hand on his hip, while the other motions toward me. "You got a thing for her or something?"

Nate ignores his question and turns us both. His hand still locked around me, he shuffles us toward the door in awkward movements.

I hear Austin's obnoxious laugh and throw my middle finger over my head at him right before the door slams behind us.

Chapter Sixteen

K ALANI

As we exit the diner, Nate lets go of my waist and quickly grabs onto my wrist, pulling me toward his truck. He makes sure we're out of sight from the restaurant windows before he cages me in, his chest firmly against mine, my back against his Hummer.

Eyes closed, he rests his forehead against the window just over my left shoulder, his arms set stiff at his sides.

I think about shoving him off, calling him out for his macho-man act back there, but when I feel his chest heaving against mine, I don't.

His breathing is erratic.

Angry.

Excited?

Brows pulled in, I lift my right hand and place it over his heart. Sure enough, it's beating wildly. Uncontrollably.

I can feel the heat of his body under my palm.

Unsure why, but not necessarily caring, my hands find his shoulders. Gently, I drag them up and down his forearms.

Tension rolls off him instantly, as if my touch is soothing in some way.

On their own accord, my hands glide up and over his firm deltoids, down his solid chest, then back up until my fingertips graze the edge of his dark brown hair.

When his strong hands find my hips, gripping them like a lifeline, a small moan escapes me and my forehead drops to his chest.

My hands slide further up, loving the sharp feeling of his fresh crew cut as it flits across my fingertips.

With a slight bend, he fits his left foot between mine, his thick thigh now pushing into my center. Turning his head, he skims his nose painfully slow over my cheekbone, his hot breath cascading over my jawline, both leaving a burning trail in their wake. His lips brush up my chin, stopping once his top lip is settled between my upper and lower one, but still a breath's space away.

"Want to tell me what happened in there, Handsome?"

At this point, we're both breathing heavily. The pressure of his heaving chest against my now sensitive one is an intoxicating feeling.

His eyes open lazily, but he doesn't answer. Not that I thought he would.

He takes one look at my dilated pupils and flushed cheeks, then smashes his lips into mine, instantly growling into my mouth as he does.

My hands wrap tight around his head, pulling him in as he presses his thigh harder against my core, rocking his hips into me.

Overwhelmed by the sensation, I pull back on a gasp, my head falling back against the truck.

Like a true quarterback, he takes advantage of the opening. His head drops into my neck where he sucks, then blows cool air, only to make the spot hot all over again with his perfect mouth. Perfect tongue. Perfect lips.

Goosebumps roll down my spine.

Shamelessly grinding into him, I feel his dick, hard and thick against my hip.

His hands snake behind me, giving my ass a nice, firm squeeze.

When another small moan leaves my lips, he pulls away with a growl, putting a good three feet between us.

We stand there staring at each other, our chests rising and falling at rapid speeds. His hands on his hips, mine on my throat, our eyes locked.

He tips his chin toward the truck, so I turn and climb inside.

"Buckle up, brat," he tells me through a smile, before shutting the door and jogging around.

Once we're stopped in front of my house, I turn to find Nate grinning at me.

"What?"

With a chuckle, he shakes his head and looks out his front windshield. "I don't know what I expected to happen today when I showed up at Wicker, but that definitely wasn't it."

"Since your playbook is open, let's hear the version that went through your head beforehand."

He grins deeper. "Figured I'd go in there, make him ball up a bit. Thought maybe I'd corner you by the bathroom or something; kiss you so you'd be thinking of me during your date."

I giggle. Giggle.

Now I want to punch myself.

Clearing my throat, I speak, "Wow. While that's original and all," I grin at him, "I kind of like the real version better."

He chuckles.

My mouth drops open in thought. "Did you see Jarrod's face?" I ask, smiling. "That alone was worth the bitchin' I'm sure I'll hear from him later."

Nate's body goes rigid, and he turns to look out his side window. "You thinking about going out with him again?"

"Well, that depends," I tell him, earning an irritated look. "You plan on showing up and dragging me off again?"

"Yes." His answer is instant. Firm.

My eyebrows jump.

"So, maybe you should just give up the whole dating thing altogether." He grins at his suggestion.

"So, I should be more like you then?"

His brows pull in slightly.

"I should just skip the pleasantries and go straight for the pleasuring?" I give a 'meh' look and nod my head. "I guess I could get on board with that. I mean, it's not like I'm a virgin, so it's really not that big of a deal, right?"

He's out of the car and pulling me out my door before I have a chance to enjoy the raged look on his face. Tossing me over his massive shoulder, he rushes to my front door, while I laugh my ass off and enjoy the view of his tight butt flexing with each step he takes. He reaches back, grabs my keys out of my hand, opens the door, and quickly marches inside.

Still laughing, I smack his butt. "Set me down, shithead!"

He doesn't reply but turns right, heading down the hallway. "Anyone besides Mia have a key?" he asks.

An airy, almost nauseating, but not, feeling filters through my stomach and my brows pull in.

"Kalani?" He stops in his tracks.

"Uh, no. No one."

"Where?"

I already know what he's referring to. "First door on the right."

Once in my room, he sets me down on my bed and hovers over me. His eyes are dark, determined, and zeroed in on me.

Not taking his gaze off mine, he trails one finger from my collarbone, down my arm and across my now exposed stomach.

My lips part as I wait for his next move.

His long, thick, black lashes are half-mast as he leans over me, dark eyes burning within them. His hair is just long enough on top for me to run my fingers through.

Apparently, my hands agree, because before I can stop, they're gliding through his hair. I watch, mesmerized, as the dark strands flow through my fair fingers. It's enticing.

When a soft sound leaves Nate, my gaze flicks back to his.

His eyes are closed, his brows creased, making small lines appear on his forehead.

Slowly retreating from his silky hair, two of my fingers trace the lines above his eyebrows. His eyes open as my fingertips skim down his temple, his cheek, across his jaw.

My lips twitch. "You really are incredibly handsome," I whisper.

My brows shoot high, my gaze on him as soon as the words leave my mouth. I've said them before, but not like this.

His face is a perfect mask, giving nothing away. "Kalani?"

I swallow. "Yeah?"

"Tell me what you just said in the truck was no more than you being you and trying to get under my skin?"

"What?" A sly smile forms on my lips. "I'm not a virgin."

"You know damn well that's not what I was referring to." His eyes are narrowed on me now, but he can't hide the playful gleam floating in them.

I grin and maneuver my legs to the outside, so he's now on his knees between them. "Did it work?"

"Oh, it worked." His grin is simply sinful.

"Yeah?" I squirm against my pillow.

"Yeah." He licks his lips. "Looking at you gets under my skin." He drops down an inch. "Thinking about you fucks with my head." Another inch. "Hearing that raspy, sexy ass voice of yours gets me riled up," he rumbles quietly, his body now brushing mine. "And touching you? Touching you sets me on fire," he whispers.

"Yeah," I breathe, bringing my legs up to wrap around him. "Fire."

"Seeing another guy touch you..." He shakes his head, brows pulling in further. "I can't handle that." He brushes a teasing kiss across my lips, making me whimper like a desperate ho when he retreats. "So, how about we make sure that doesn't happen anymore?"

"Yeah, okay." I'm a hussy at this point.

He shakes his head and drops his mouth to my ear. "You're not hearing me, Kalani." His voice vibrates down my spine.

"Mmm..." I moan, closing my eyes. "Don't let you see me with another guy. Got it."

He lowers his body against mine.

I gasp when his thickness presses into me, right where I want it. "Handsome," I whisper.

His lips push down on my throat. "Tell me, Kalani." His hot breath brings goosebumps to my skin's surface. "Tell me. No other guys. Just me."

"You're bossy," I breathe and wrap my legs tighter around him.

"That's because you like me bossy." He gives me more of his weight, and his husky voice caresses my ear. "Tell me."

"Yeah, okay. Just you," I tell him, my chin lifting.

He pulls back instantly, his eyes flitting back and forth between mine. "You said it yourself, you don't lie."

"Nate?"

"Yeah?"

I wrap my arms around his neck, pulling him toward me. "Move," I demand as I lift my head, sealing our mouths together.

He doesn't disappoint.

With a deep growl, he takes control of my mouth, owning it like nothing I've ever experienced before.

Every stroke of his tongue, mine mirrors. Every roll of his hips, mine follow. Every move he makes, my body anticipates.

It's the strangest, most thrilling sensation I've ever felt.

His hands find my hips, where he uses them as a steeling force, creating more pressure.

My hands glide up his sides, pushing his shirt up. He breaks our kiss long enough for me to pull it over his head.

I moan into his mouth as my hands make their way down his masterful pecs and abs. Once I get to his V, that glorious V, I trace each side with my pointer fingers. Not stopping when I reach the band of his jeans, I dip my fingers in, sliding to the center, where I unbutton them, then run my knuckles over the hardness in his boxer briefs.

He rips away from my mouth, panting wildly into my neck. One of his hands slides under my shirt, cupping me over my bra. I grasp him over his briefs, and when I squeeze, he thrusts his hips forward, pressing my hand harder around him.

Fast like a NASCAR pit crew, he lifts to his knees, pulling me with him. Yanking my shirt off, he slams his mouth into mine again. Next, he unclasps my bra, slides the straps down my arms, then lowers me back onto the pillow, my boobs bouncing as I hit the bed.

"God damn." He drops and flicks my nipple with his tongue, earning a whimper from me. "So fucking perfect." He squeezes my left breast while sucking my right nipple into his tepid mouth.

"Ohmygawd." I squirm under him, my hands finding their way back to his dick. I pull his briefs to his thighs and grip him hard.

He's thick and silky and wanting.

As Nate switches to my other boob, I begin to pump him.

I start slowly, working my hand up and over his tip, then back down.

When he bites down on my nipple, my back arches, offering him more, and his hips begin to thrust, driving himself faster as he works with me to bring himself relief.

When a sound that can only be described as a moan-growl leaves his mouth, I bring my free hand up. Yanking on his hair, I direct his hungry mouth back to mine.

"Fuck, Kalani," he moans into my mouth, his fingers pinching and twisting my nipples.

"I can't fuck you," I pant, between kisses.

He laughs into my mouth.

"You can't fuck me either."

"Stop talking."

I nod as he assaults my neck with his tongue.

His hand slides from my left breast and down my stomach, where he flicks open the button to my jeans.

Gently, he bites down on my shoulder as his middle finger glides down the center of my thin panties, then back up, stopping right where my body's calling for him.

He adds a second finger, then slowly circles my clit. Like a firework, my body lights up. Starting at my core and fanning out through my stomach and thighs, not stopping until my toes curl, heat takes over, and I know I'm close.

Not wanting to finish alone - and not caring to know why it matters - I pump him harder, faster, feeling the thick veins bulge under my fingers.

He lifts his head and watches me as he makes his next move.

He maneuvers his fingers to where my clit is pinched right between the two, and when he begins squeezing and rolling it between his fingers, my hips lift off the mattress.

"Wha...shit," I croak, turning my head into the pillow.

Gripping my chin, he turns my head back to look at him. Dropping his forehead to mine he pinches my clit harder, pumping his hips faster while I grip him like a vice.

I watch his eyes darken, feel his forehead tighten against mine. Right as my core clenches, fire takes over my body, releasing the ultimate orgasm, and I squeeze him impossibly tighter.

Tilting my chin, I grab ahold of his bottom lip and bite down, right as his body shudders on top of mine, coating my stomach with his warm, wet, finale.

His face when he comes is the sexiest thing I have ever seen. Hard and taut and ravenous.

Applying pressure to my clit, he holds still, letting me ride the pleasure train to a complete stop.

"You look good like this." His voice is deep and gravely.

"Like what?" I pant.

His sexy smirk finds his lips. "Flushed and under me."

I roll my eyes and hit him in the chest, causing him to laugh and roll off.

Hopping up, I make my way to the bathroom to wipe off my stomach. Grabbing the shirt that's hanging over the towel rack, I throw it on.

When I turn back, I expect to find a fully clothed Nate ready to make his getaway, but instead I find him lying in the same place I left him, arms crossed behind his head, eyes closed, dick out.

"What are you doing?"

He smiles but doesn't open his eyes. "Relaxing?"

"Get your ass out of my bed and go home." I pick up the water bottle on my nightstand and take a drink. "I got stuff to do before tomorrow."

His grin slips some as he slowly rises from the bed. After buttoning his pants, he pulls his shirt over his head and walks toward me, an unreadable expression on his face.

I grin up at him as he wraps his arms around my lower back. "Is this how it goes?" I ask. "A nice 'thanks for the fun, sugar'. Maybe a kiss on the head, then you bow out?" I laugh. "'Cause if it is, it's totally not necessary."

Something passes in his eyes, but it's gone quickly. Dropping his arms, he scratches the back of his neck and steps back. "Walk me?"

I laugh. "I can do that."

Once we reach the door, he looks to me, those eyes searching. For what, I'm not sure, but I don't think he finds it because his shoulders drop an inch.

"See you tomorrow," I tell him. I start to open the door but he halts my movements.

"Wait. Can I ask you something?"

No. "Sure."

"Did Jarrod do or say something to you today to make you uncomfortable or upset, or anything?"

My head jerks back. "No. Why?"

"No?" he challenges, raising an eyebrow.

"I said no, Nate. And if he did, I would have handled it myself." I yank the door open. "I told you before, I handle my own shit."

"Alright." He frowns.

"Why did you ask me that?" I ask, biting on the inside of my cheek.

Reaching out, he tucks my hair behind my ear, smiling weakly when I swat his hand away. "No reason."

"Liar."

His eyes tip up, but his chin drops to his chest, and his chuckle is forced. "See you tomorrow."

Shutting the door behind him, I lean against it and wonder what he meant.

Chapter Seventeen

K ALANI

I set my bags down and walk outside to help Parker with the rest of my groceries.

My brows lift when I see he has every one of them in his hands and a twelve pack of soda under his right arm.

"You need some help there, Hero?" I tease.

He grins, the receipt hanging out his mouth. "Nope. I could add you to the load and still carry more."

I usher him forward with the swipe of a hand.

After setting everything on the countertop, he heads into the living room, and plops onto the couch while I start putting stuff away.

"So," he calls out. "A little birdy told me a certain quarterback made an interception today."

"Weird." I toss the chips and popcorn into the cabinet. "I

wasn't aware quarterbacks played defense." I glance at him with a raised eyebrow.

"Exactly!" He shouts in excitement, hopping onto his knees to face me, his forearms resting on the back of the couch.

I toss the gum into the drawer nearest the fridge, closing it with my hip, and lean against it.

"Exactly, what?" I laugh, shaking my head at him.

"Quarterbacks don't play defense. That's rule number one in football for dummies." He grins and I roll my eyes. "But my boy never played by the rules."

I kick off the counter and grab another bag to unload. "I don't doubt that."

"But he did."

"You weren't even there, so shut it." I stand on my tiptoes to hide the Waffle Crisp behind all the paper products.

Ha! Try and find them there, Mia.

"Hear me out, alright?" I go to nod but he narrows his eyes. "And not with those blinders of yours."

I open the fridge to put away the milk with one hand, while reaching around and flipping him off with the other, making him chuckle.

"So, I heard Jarrod tried to kiss you, and Nate swooped in."

"Yeah," I roll my eyes. "He was a real Captain Save-a-Ho."

Parker bellows over in laughter.

"What's your point, anyway?" My tone is bored.

He shrugs, a grin still on his lips. "Maybe he likes you."

"Yeah. Maybe."

When he sits back on his heels and puffs out his chest, it takes everything in me to hold back my laughter.

"Or maybe he's never had to work for ass before and really, really wants to be the first in line to," I wiggle my eyebrows, "break me in."

"You win!" He yells, dropping himself back. "That's definitely the reason!"

Even though he can't see me, I smile in triumph, but my head takes a second to catch on to the gleefulness of being right.

"So, what's the plan, Stan?" I call out.

He groans. "I'm out of here, actually. My mom is headed to my dad's to pick up some old photos or something for my senior page in the yearbook. I get to go play referee."

"I don't envy you," I laugh, pulling out what I need to make a sandwich. "But real quick, I've been meaning to ask..."

He grins. "What?"

"Did you hook up with Nate's sister?"

His eyes shoot wide and he chokes. "What?"

My mouth drops open. "Shut the fuck up! You did!"

"No!" he's quick to rush out, "I did not."

"Okay..."

He groans. "She... showed up at my house one night, crying over some bull shit she shouldn't have been dealing with in the first place. She was drunk, so I let her crash." He looks away. "In my bed."

"And..."

"And apparently, I decided to sleep in my bed too 'cause I woke up with my arm around her, my morning wood appreciating her ass."

When I bust up laughing, he rolls his eyes, and makes his way to the door.

"Bye, Lolli Bear. I'll call you later."

Once the door shuts behind him, I walk over and lock it, a triumphant grin on my face. I read Kenra's bashfulness when she saw Parker. She was remembering his dick against her ass. There's definitely more to that story than Parker chose to share, but who am I to push when I don't participate in show and tell myself? Not that he would have budged. Parker is as loyal as they come and that wasn't his story to tell. It's one of the many reasons why he's the shit and will forever be my best friend.

With a smile, I walk back into the kitchen.

163

Right as I do, Nauni comes out of hiding.

"I'm on it." After finishing my sandwich, I pour her food in her bowl and make my way to my room.

Once my clothes are off, panties included, I jump under the covers and tuck the blankets under my chin. My mind begins to settle and I take a deep refreshing breath. Instantly, my senses are invaded and my eyes fly open.

Nate.

He's all over my blankets. His grassy fresh sweetness, mixed with leather and man and...

Shit.

Burying my face in my pillow, I sigh.

This is not good. Not. Good.

As I walk into Alrick High, my eyes bulge.

The walls look like a kindergarten class threw up on them. Hand-painted posters cover the walls, surrounded by shiny gold, red, and black crepe papers. They look like mashed-up balls but are supposed to resemble flowers. I think. Matching streamers hang from the ceiling at all the entry and exit points. A large poster hangs crookedly in the middle of the hallways with big bold painted-on letters reading "Knights Kingdom."

An arm wraps around my shoulder. "Cliché, isn't it?" Parker laughs in my ear.

"Very." I smile up at him. "Morning, Hero."

"Mornin'," he grins.

"I like it." Mia shrugs, falling back in place next to us. "We are the Knights." Fluttering her eyelashes, she gives us a bow. "And this is our kingdom."

Parker releases me, bends and hoists Mia in the air. "That's right, Mia." He turns so he's facing me. "Where's your school spirit, Lolli?" Grinning, he reaches up and gives her ass a good smack.

"Damn it, Parker! Put me down!" she laughs.

"Hey now…"

We turn to see Austin walking up with a smile on his face.

Parker laughs, setting Mia on her feet only long enough for Austin to swoop her up and spin her around. She throws her head back and plays the part, making all of us laugh along with her.

"What do you say, wanna be the princess to my prince, Ms. Edwards?" He smiles up at her.

She quirks a brow. "Why not the queen to your king?" she teases, sliding her hands around his neck.

He plants a quick kiss to her lips. "Because we already know who the king is." He laughs, turning his head to look over his shoulder, and our eyes follow suit.

And there he is, the unofficial king of Alrick High himself.

Nate's striding down the hall, looking all kinds of tempting. How he makes a plain black tee and jeans look like a walking, talking, life-size ad for Guess, I'll never know.

My eyes collide with his.

People call out to him, pat his arm, do everything but flash him to get his attention as he meanders down the line, but his dark eyes never leave mine.

I know what those eyes look like when pleased.

A throat clears behind me.

I turn to find Liv leaning against a locker, a nasty smirk in place.

With a roll of my eyes, I turn to my locker she just so happens to be leaning next to. "Why, might I ask, have you decided to grace me with your presence?"

She stops admiring her manicure and narrows her eyes at me. "I told you once, I'll tell you again." Her eyes flick over my shoulder quickly.

He's getting closer.

"Stay away from Nate. He's better than you'll ever be. You may pretend to be a part of the football world, but he's going somewhere in it." She stands up taller. "He doesn't need some wannabe getting in his head."

I close my locker and lean one shoulder against it. "You're right, Liv." I nod my head with a smile on my face. "He is going somewhere." I eye her for a few seconds. "You plannin' on going with him?" I raise an eyebrow.

"I've been accepted on early admission to every college I've applied to." She crosses her arms, smirking like she's won something.

He's almost here.

I laugh. "Let me guess. They all happen to have Division 1 teams?" Her smirk falters a little and my mouth drops open in humor. "Oh, my God, they do!" I gape at her. "You plan on picking based on who he commits to."

"Listen, slu-" She cuts off and plasters a huge, silky smooth smile on her lips. One that falls right off as his chest comes flush against my back.

One of his large hands wraps around my waist, and he brings his mouth to my ear. "Good morning, Kalani."

"Handsome," I answer, biting the inside of my cheek to keep from laughing, my eyes trained on Liv's.

He lifts his head, jerking his chin in the wannabe Barbie's direction. "Liv."

She forces the corners of her lips up and pushes her chest out. "Hey, Nate," she practically moans, and I couldn't hold in my eyeroll if I tried. "Can I talk to you?" She cuts me a quick smirk. "In private?" I swear to God, she just slithered.

"Actually-" He's cut off when the bell rings.

"That would be the bell." Stepping back from me, he grabs on to my elbow and pulls me away from the lockers.

Throwing his arm protectively around my shoulder, he calls out, "Bye, Liv," never bothering to turn around.

As soon as we turn the corner, I bend over laughing, shrugging Nate's arm off in the process. "That was pretty smooth there, Handsome." I look into his eyes, finding them narrowed in on me. "What?"

He opens his mouth to say something but decides better of it. Shaking his head, he walks ahead of me into class.

By the time lunch rolls around, I'm beyond starved. Food in hand, I go to take a seat next to Mia, only to have Jarrod drop down before me and pull me onto his lap.

My brows shoot up and I grin at him. "Hi."

I set my Funyuns and drink on the table, strategically keeping my Twix in hand. Never know when a thief with a sweet tooth might come along.

He smirks at me. "Hi, Lolli."

Ugh...

His clammy hand runs down my left arm. "I think we need a repeat of our date from Sunday." He leans in as I lean back. "We didn't quite make it to the good part, now did we?" he whispers. His voice is striving for seductive, but his eyes have a hardened glare behind them.

"You mean the food wasn't the good part?" I joke, and shift to stand, but he misses the hint and adjusts me on his lap.

He pushes my hair over my shoulder. "I was referring to-"

Somewhere behind me, I hear an "Oh shit," before I feel him.

I turn to find Nate making his way through the tables. Unfortunately, turning involves a shift of my waist and I feel a little excitement from Jarrod – no pun intended, but in this case, sadly, it works.

Nate sees my eyes widen and drops his narrowed gaze to where Jarrod's body and mine are touching. His jaw ticks and there is no doubt he knows exactly what just happened.

He masks his rage on a blink and casts me a warning with his eyes, telling me to 'run girl, run,' unless I'm ready for what's coming.

Curiosity did kill the cat after all...

He's almost to me now, his eyes burning into mine, but the closer he gets, the clearer they become – for me.

You'd never see it – or believe it, for that matter - with the way his body's moving. With his arms hanging loose at his sides, his easy strides, a shadow of a grin tipping those lips, and his chin held high, he oozes confidence. Or smugness, depending on how you look at it.

His face is a cold mask for all those around him to see, but for whatever reason, I see the vulnerability hidden deep in his dark orbs. He's not hiding it from me. He wants me to know what he wants; what he's hoping for... secretly begging me for.

I give it to him.

Never breaking our eye contact, I push Jarrod's hands off me and stand right as Nate's feet land in front of mine, bringing us chest to chest.

His eyes shine instantly and I don't even care it's his cocky smirk that comes out to play. "You forget what you promised me last night, Gorgeous?" he whispers for only me to hear, his eyes narrowing.

My tongue slides out to wet my suddenly dry lips, I shake my head. Because, no, I didn't forget. I also didn't think for a second he was serious.

"Good." He winks.

Next thing I know, his soft lips are on mine.

His kiss is more demanding and territorial than anything, but right now, I don't mind.

Not giving a damn about the gasps and giggles and screeching chairs, I throw my hands around his neck and kiss him back. Not even caring when my candy falls to the floor.

Chapter Eighteen

K ALANI

By the time Wednesday rolls around, I'm beyond done with the social buzz around school. Yes, Nate and I hang out.

Whoopty-fucking-doo.

It's not like it's a big deal. Nate 'hangs out' with a lot of girls. Plain and simple. If I were a guy as attractive and talented as he is, and had girls throwing themselves at me left and right, I'd probably do the same thing. Tupac said it right, "I ain't mad at cha."

Seriously, though, do they not realize the only reason he's still hanging around me is because we haven't had sex? Everyone knows his golden rule is to hit and quit it. He's the king of the smash and dash.

To say I don't understand what the fuss is all about is the understatement of the year. Which is exactly why I skipped football practice today.

I need a fucking break.

From everything.

I ran five miles and did mad crunches in PE, but my mind is still racing, so I throw on my running shoes and head out the door.

A few hours and dozens of achy muscles later, I'm lying on my bed, watching my fan go around and around when a text comes through. Picking up my phone, I see it's from Nate.

Handsome: you missed practice.

I roll my eyes.

Me: you're perceptive.

Handsome: what are you doing?

Me: nothing.

I sit in beautiful silence for a few minutes before his next text comes through.

Handsome: can I come do nothing with you?

Me: no.

My reply is instant. All that's left to do now is wait for his persistent ass...

And three, two, one... my phone rings. Shocker.

As soon as I answer, I hear his laughter boom through the speaker and something inside of me eases. A breath full of tension I didn't realize I was carrying releases.

"Why not?" he asks, laughter fueling his voice.

"Because, we're supposed to have fun, and I just want to sit here. You don't need to be here for that." You shouldn't be here for that.

When he doesn't respond, I pull the phone away from my ear, making sure I didn't lose him.

"Nate?"

I hear some shuffling and then he answers. "Yeah, I'm here. Sorry, I was stepping out of the locker room real quick."

Glancing at the time on my newly purchased, music-operated, alarm clock, I see it's ten past six. Practice just got released.

"It's fine." I begin counting as the fan circles above me.

Nate clears his throat. "What if I want to do nothing with you?"

"I don't really care. I said no."

Twenty-five, twenty-six...

"Kalani..." His voice is gruff, determined.

I already know how this is going to go. I say no, he shows up anyway.

Squeezing my eyes shut, I answer, "I'll unlock the door. Let yourself in." I hang up quickly so I don't have to hear his crap about leaving the door unlocked, blah, blah, blah...

I do as I said I would, then climb back into bed and assume the position.

Fifty-three, fifty-four, fifty-five...

NATE

I hustle back into the locker room with more of a punch in my step, grab my shit and hit the showers. Not wanting to be a smelly bastard, I try to take my time washing, but knowing Kalani's door is unlocked has me on overdrive, so I'm out of the shower in record time.

"Pussy on the brain, Monroe?" Jarrod jabs from his locker three spaces down from mine.

"Shit," Joey, one of my offensive linemen begins, "one pussy's more like it. Boy's whipped." He laughs and playfully swats me with his towel.

Of course, I was expecting it and make quick work of snatching it from his hands.

"You not denying it, then?" Jarrod asks, his eyes pinched at the side.

I know he's still got a hard-on for Kalani, that much is obvious in how jumpy his eyes are every time she's around.

I should knock him out.

"Nothing to deny, Hollins. I know where I want to be and yeah," I pull my shirt over my head, grabbing my wallet and keys, "that happens to be where she is."

"Safe to say you won't be heading to Wicker tonight?" Austin asks, jumping into the tail end of our conversation with a smirk.

Walking backward toward the door, I give them a sideways grin. "I'm done at Wicker, boys." I salute them and walk out, ignoring their jabs and catcalls.

On my way to Kalani's, I run by the grocery store to get some reinforcements.

I've noticed she has these moments where she...I don't know. It's almost like she allows herself to be free, but when she stops and thinks about it, realizing she's enjoying herself or...enjoying me, she pulls back.

I've seen it happen on the field before. She'll smile and get a small light behind her beautiful blue eyes, but as soon as it takes over her features, lighting her up the way she was meant to shine, she turns to stone.

I decided a long time ago that I want her, but I want my Kalani tonight. The Kalani I know only I get to see.

The one that smiles through her eyes and drops her head back on a laugh, making that long dark hair seem impossibly longer. The laugh where she raises her soft little hand over her heart while the other playfully rests on my shoulder.

Yeah, I want to see her tonight.

Once in park, I kill the engine and jog to the door.

The second I turn the handle; a woman yells out from behind me.

I turn around, and my eyebrows jump into my hairline.

Holy shit, Kalani looks just like her mom.

"What do you think you're doing?"

Damn, Kalani's gonna age real nice.

"Hello?" The dark-haired woman waves as she walks closer. "Why are you just walking into this house?"

I'm cooking up a lie in my head when I remember Kalani said she lives alone, so I go for bold and pray to the football gods it's the right move.

"She's waiting for me." I hook my finger over my shoulder. "She left it open so she didn't have to get up." I unintentionally crack a grin when I say this.

That girl loves her some sleep.

It's clear she's not necessarily happy with my response considering the way her brows pull in and she glances off. We both stand there for a moment before she nods to herself and turns, heading back to the car parked on the curb.

After a deep exhale, I walk in and find Kalani lying on her bed in an oversized pair of sweats and t-shirt.

I set the bag from the store down next to the bed and drop beside her.

She doesn't say a word, so neither do I.

After a good ten or fifteen minutes, she breaks the silence.

"I had to restart."

I turn my head toward her in question. Without looking at me, she gives a small jerk of her chin.

"The fan. I was almost at seventeen-hundred." She shrugs, then turns to me.

As soon as her glacier blue eyes are on me, I smile. "Hi."

Kalani gazes at me for a moment, her eyes vacant, but I keep my smile in place and I'm rewarded when her blue eyes grow brighter and a small smile plays on her lips. And, of course, a playful eyeroll.

"Hi, Handsome."

I smile wider and feel like a jackass, so I turn to the fan.

"Handsome?" Her voice, so quiet, lost, and unsure, slices right through me.

"Yeah, Gorgeous?" I palm the center of my chest.

"I'm going to tell you a story, but I need you to distract me after."

173

"I can do that," I mutter quietly.

I place my hand on the mattress, so my left pinky is brushing hers.

"She's not my mom." My brows pull in and I turn back to her, but she's staring at the fan now.

"My window's open, so I overheard." Her voice is different right now. Almost hollow. I don't like it, but I know her well enough to know if I ask the wrong question, she'll make a joke and shut down on me.

"That was my Aunt Kara, Mia's mom. My parents are dead."

Shit. I never thought about why Kalani lived alone. I guess I just figured her parents were assholes and not around or something.

"My Aunt Kara?" she begins. "She was my mom's sister. Her twin."

I swallow.

"Identical."

Fuuuck. I'm trying real hard not to react, but... fuck! My hand is twitching to reach out and touch her, but I don't. Instead, I dig my fingers into the comforter beneath me, and hold my breath, waiting – hoping - to hear the story that broke my girl's heart.

"My parents, they were cool. Photographers. We traveled all the time. It was fun at first, but after a while, I was tired of missing all the normal kid stuff. Friends' birthdays, school functions, and crap. Stupid stuff that I could care less about now, but back then... it mattered.

"I kept complaining, so my grandpa, my Papa - he was my dad's dad - said he'd stay with me for the few months a year that he could, and on some of his off weekends. He had been wanting to for years anyway but didn't want to step on my dad's toes."

I wonder if she even feels the story she's telling me? Her idle tone tells me she doesn't.

"So, the day I turned fourteen, I begged my parents to sign papers to emancipate me, so I could always stay home, even when

174

Papa wasn't around. I was a good kid, as far as I never got in any actual trouble, so they agreed." She shrugs into the pillow, her eyes still following the fan around.

"I had to get a work permit, and a little job to get the state papers signed off on by the courts, but it worked."

"After that, my parents hardly ever came home. I didn't mind. I got to do whatever I wanted and hang out with my gramps more often than ever before." She adjusts her pillow and crosses one leg over the other.

I stay frozen in place, waiting for the hit.

"They came home three times a year. Super Bowl, Fourth of July, and my birthday…" She takes a deep breath, then turns her head toward mine.

I don't move.

She searches my eyes, for what, I'm not sure, but once she's satisfied, she continues, her eyes still trained on mine. "My grandpa showed up to surprise me the day before my seventeenth birthday. My parents were due in that day, but their flight was delayed, so they wouldn't be getting in until the next morning. He didn't want me to wake up on my birthday by myself." She turns back to the fan.

"When I woke up on my birthday, I found him hunched over in the kitchen. He was making me French toast."

I remind myself to breathe.

"Once we got to the hospital, he went through hours of testing before they finally told me he had congestive heart failure, CHF. Apparently, he'd had it for the past few years and he'd had a heart attack. They kept draining the fluids from his lungs, but it wasn't working. They couldn't keep him stable; said I only had a couple hours with him."

Her head jerks toward me and she glares.

"Why don't you ever say goodbye to me?"

My brows jump at her sudden and unexpected question.

"I pay attention. I hear you say it all the time, to other people, but you never say it to me." Her tone is accusatory, as if she's upset by it, but I can see the importance of the question in her eyes. I don't even think she realizes how badly she wants my answer, maybe even needs it, but I can feel it.

Cautiously, I lift my right hand and tuck her silky black hair behind her ear. Flattening my palm, I let it rest there against her soft skin.

I prop myself up on my elbow and slowly lean down to press a kiss against her lips. She doesn't pull away, but she doesn't give in either.

I whisper against her lips, my eyes locked onto hers, "Because, for some reason, the thought of saying goodbye to you does something to me. I don't like it. It makes me feel like I'm losing something."

Her lids lower the smallest of fractions and, for a split second, she allows herself to lean into my touch, then quickly looks back to the fan, forcing my hand to drop.

"My grandpa didn't allow goodbyes; said that's not something he and I would ever have, a goodbye." She releases a sharp breath. "Anyway, he was about to die. Just after midnight, the nurse came in to add the cherry on top."

I can't handle it anymore, I reach out and pull her to me, tucking her little body into my arms.

Now I can breathe.

KALANI

"Anyway, he was about to die. Just after midnight, the nurse came in to add the cherry on top."

Nate's strong hands grab ahold of me and he pulls my body against his. I can feel his heartbeat against my palm. It's kind of...soothing.

When his hand comes up and begins running through my hair,

I get lost in my words and the memory I haven't allowed to surface in over a year.

"You can go to sleep..." More tears stream down my face, but I have to be brave. "Go to sleep. I'll wake up for you."

"Ms. Embers?" A soft, hesitant voice calls from the doorway, and I drop my head back down.

Beep.

"Please, go." I hear the desperate plea in my voice.

When I hear a soft cry, I look up at the nurse standing in the doorway.

Tears fall from her eyes as she shakes her head back and forth, opening her mouth, then closing it. She says nothing.

Beep.

"Please, just...can you give me this time?" I say, my voice getting louder, tighter. "I just need more time."

"Ms. Embers, I'm afraid there's been an accident..." she trails off, her eyes focusing on the floor.

My body tenses and I immediately place my other hand on top of Papa's, caging it. Shielding him.

She continues, her voice pained, "It's your parents..." When her eyes finally meet mine, I know. It's clear as day, right there on her pretty, round face.

"They're dead, aren't they?" I think I say aloud, but I can't be sure, because the moment the last word leaves my mouth, the beeping stops and the searing sound of a flatline drones on.

I look down and my grandpa... My Papa. My best friend.

Gone.

My body starts to convulse, my mind flipping like flashcards, as dozens of thoughts and images fly through my brain. I can hear my pulse in my ears and nothing else. The nice woman's lips are moving, as are the officers now standing behind her, but I don't hear them.

Then, suddenly, my body seizes, air flows through me, and I feel...nothing.

Standing, I offer a nod to the men and women in the room, thank them, then walk out. Never once setting foot in that hospital again.

Nate's grip tightens around me and I allow myself to settle into his arms.

"How did they die?" he asks in a tight voice.

"Car accident. Nothing spectacular. Just bad timing, I guess."

I can't help but scoff at that. Bad timing alright. My parents and grandpa all died on my seventeenth birthday. All because they wanted to be there to celebrate with me.

"So, your aunt..."

I nod into his chest. "Is a perfect picture of my mother." I release a deep breath. "She tried to pull the guardian card, since she was the only adult left who I was related to, but my lawyer shut her down quick. Turned out, she had no idea my parents had emancipated me. She did everything she could to have it overturned, but it didn't work. It was all in good faith on her part, but it was the last thing I wanted."

"So, you lost your grandpa and parents in the same day, then stayed there alone?" His voice is thick with emotion. "Why, Kalani?" His arms tighten around me protectively.

The answer is simple.

"Twins, Handsome." I don't say anything else because that alone is enough.

He whispers after a few minutes, "So, you're eighteen..."

I nod. "I had good enough grades when everything went down, so I didn't have to finish out the last two months of my junior year. They dropped, obviously; went from solid A's to hardly passing C-minuses, but I didn't care. I wasn't about to go back, regardless." I shift, laying my chin on my hand so I can look at Nate's face.

"When my senior year started, I signed myself out and took the year off. I had a lot of business things I had to handle, since everything that belonged to my parents and grandpa was signed over to me. After that was done, I just hung around."

Nate starts running his hand through my hair again and I smile.

"Anyway, Mia and my aunt ganged up on me and begged me to come here and finish out school when, really, I should have just gotten my GED, but whatever. I knew they were worried and I had nothing else to do for a while anyway. So here I am," I say, rolling my eyes.

We lay there in silence for a few minutes, staring at each other, before Nate kisses my hair and shifts out from under me. "I have something for you."

I look up at him as he makes his way to a bag I didn't see him bring in.

"What is it?" I ask, curious.

"Nope," he smiles, and I could kiss him.

He's trying so hard to act nonchalant after everything I told him and, once again, I find myself wondering why that makes my body seem... lighter.

I make my way around my bed and step into his chest.

Instantly, his arms come around me, barricading me in their safety. I tilt my chin up and we seal our lips together.

Mine, thanking him. His, telling me - showing me - that my words were heard and felt and appreciated.

When a small crack forms in the center of my chest, right where my rapidly beating heart lives, I pull out of his embrace.

Nate says nothing, but grabs the bag, asks me to get my shoes and a sweater, and meet him in his truck.

I change into a pair of black yoga pants and an oversized hoodie, choosing my Uggs over my Chucks.

I hesitate at the front door.

My brows pull in as the fingertips skim slowly over my lips.

A smile pulls at my mouth, but my phone beeps from my boot before it takes over.

Handsome: it's okay to want something. No pain, no gain.

I'm wondering if he's right.

"What are we doing here?" I ask when we turn down Nate's long driveway.

He glances at me quickly, a nervous smile on his face, before focusing back on the dirt road. "We're hanging out."

I roll my eyes, of course, but I can't stop myself from smiling.

I like it out here.

"Alright." Nate parks his truck and unbuckles his seatbelt. "Give me a minute."

My brows jump and I try to object, but he's gone too quick.

Not a minute later, a soft light flicks on, illuminating the swing, and my anxious feet take me right to it.

When I reach the top stair, Nate walks out the front door with a goofy grin in place, two blankets in hand.

I follow him the last few steps to the beautiful escape.

He folds one blanket, laying it across the seat part of the swing, then motions for me to sit. He reaches for my feet, removes my boots, then joins me, covering us both with the other blanket. We settle in next to each other, his feet planted on the floor to sway us, mine tucked underneath me.

He sets the mysterious, white grocery store bag in my lap.

I smile at the bag.

"I have cousins who are twins, Mason and Arianna."

My lip twitches and I peek up at him. "Yeah?"

"Yep. Same age as us. Mase plays football, too."

"Hmm... what's Mason look like?" I smirk and he glares, earning a laugh.

"You know," I sigh. "It sounds stupid, but the worst part wasn't even losing them all, like you'd think it would be."

"No?"

"Nope." Releasing a deep breath, I continue, "The worst part was that my Grandpa didn't tell me he was sick." I tilt my head and look over at Nate. "How could he not tell me? He was my best friend and he didn't tell me he was dying."

Nate's hand moves to rest on my thigh. "I can't say for sure," he gives me a small smile, "but if I had to guess, I'd say he didn't want you to worry."

I nod, my lips in a flat line. "Yeah, I figured that, too."

Nate lifts his hand and rustles the plastic bag, drawing my attention back to my lap.

I untie the knot and peek inside.

Once I see it, my head falls back against the wood, my laughter echoing around us. I don't lift my head but turn it to look at Nate.

He's staring at me with parted lips, his eyes bright and unblinking.

When I see his hand move out of the corner of my eye, my lips twitch in anticipation.

As expected, maybe even wanted, it skims across my cheek until he reaches my hair, where he tucks it gently behind my ear. His hand rests there, in his spot.

And all I want to do is lean into him, get as close as possible, and maybe stay there... for a while anyway.

The thought alone is enough to make my throat grow thick.

"What are you thinking right now?" he whispers.

"You first," I croak out instantly.

His whispered response is as quick as mine. "I'm thinking about how beautiful you are." His eyes roam my face and I bite the inside of my cheek. "About how soft your skin is." He runs his fingers down the side of my neck, my body shivering under his touch. "How, as strange as it may seem, I want to see you smile this way every day, for me... at me."

It's my turn to search his face and, as I do, it's the first time I don't see the overzealous playboy, but a guy searching for something more in a girl who has nothing to give.

And for the first time in what seems like forever, I feel a ping of sadness, right in the center of my chest. Because right now, I wish I could give him whatever it is he's looking for.

He sees it, but in true Nate fashion, he doesn't push. He gives me the pass I need. "Okay, you have to share," he says, snatching the bag from my fingers.

I laugh and wait as he opens the prepackaged cubes of Nestle's chocolate chip cookie dough. Setting the package on his lap, he winks and passes me a few pieces.

All I can do is stare at him.

When he turns to me, tilting his head in question, I simply smile and face forward again.

An hour or so later, we're pulling in my driveway.

"Thanks, Nate," I turn to him. "For tonight, all of it. I haven't talked about any of that since it happened. Not to anyone." I shrug.

His face gives nothing away, but he jerks his chin in response, silently thanking me for trusting him.

The moment my feet pass the threshold of my house, I feed Nauni and am overcome with nostalgia.

Unwilling to wallow, I throw on my running shoes and head out the door.

Chapter Nineteen

K ALANI

"Lolli Bear!"

I turn to find Parker running toward me, an unshakable smile on his face.

My eyes bulge when I realize he isn't slowing down, and within seconds, I'm squealing and being thrown over his shoulder, spinning around.

"What the hell, Parker?" I laugh, then grunt as my stomach smashes into his shoulder.

"We're three-time State Champions, Lolli! You're coming to the party tonight if I have to carry you there myself."

I think about telling him I already fought with Mia about it and lost, but why burst his happy bubble?

"Okay, Hero. I'll go to the party."

"Ye-"

"If you put me down."

I'm on feet in two seconds flat.

"Perfect." He smiles and throws his right arm over my shoulder. Kissing my temple, he asks, "You gonna drink with me tonight, Lolli Bear?"

"Actually," I take a second to think about the crazy week I've had, "a few drinks sound pretty damn good right now." I smile, wrapping my arm around his waist.

We're laughing as we reach the group of people waiting around for everyone to head to the party.

My eyes instantly find Nate's.

His eyes instantly find my fingers wrapped around Parker's side, then Parker's arm around my shoulder.

I wait for him to meet my gaze again, but instead his shoulders tense, and he turns for Austin's running truck.

Parker's oblivious but gives me a small nod as I slip away from him and the conversation he just started with Blaine, the tight end.

A few girls pile into Austin's cab seats and Nate's reaching for the front handle right as I approach.

"Good game, Handsome."

His biceps flex and he slowly turns, a deep pinch in his brow as he looks down at me.

"Hi, Lolli!" The girls giggle in excitement in the back seat.

I laugh, waving. "Hey, guys!"

One leans over the front seat, and I see it's the dark-haired girl from my government class, Casey. "You going to-"

"She's coming," Austin's quick to interrupt her on a laugh.

She smiles and throws herself back against the seat.

"You're going to the party tonight?" Nate asks, his tone accusatory.

"I am." I hold his eyes and ignore the scoff he gives me at my answer. Boys will be boys, after all. "You gonna drive me or not?" I raise an eyebrow at him.

It takes a second, but finally, his smirk appears and he pushes off Austin's truck. "See you there, my man," he calls out, not bothering to look back when Austin protests.

Nate steps into my space, so I'm forced to look up at his perfect face.

Me being this close to him makes me want to kiss him, so I raise onto my toes. Right as my arms wrap around his neck, his slide across my back, pulling me closer.

"You really want to go to the party tonight?" His eyes search mine, a weary expression on his face.

I nod. "I could use a few drinks. Been a long week, Handsome."

He blows out a breath, looking around in thought. "Yeah, it has."

"That was your last official high school game."

He nods, glancing at the stadium lights as they shut off in the distance. "We have the annual spring game the school puts on for fun, but yeah. Season's over. It's crazy."

I grin and pat his chest. "You'll be playing under bigger, better lights in no time." I wink at him when his brown eyes make their way back to me.

The corner of his mouth starts to crook up, but it falls flat, quickly transforming into a frown when Parker plants himself next to us.

"Ready, Lolli?" He smiles, bouncing from one foot to the other, clearly eager to get his grown man on.

Laughing, I shift in Nate's arms, feeling his body tense immediately. I can only assume it's because he thought I was moving away from him, considering he relaxes a second later when I turn to lean my back against his chest. "I'm going with Nate."

"NO!" I hear from my left and right, and suddenly, Mia's standing there with us.

My head jerks back and Nate's arms tighten around me.

"Uh..." I look back and forth between the two.

185

"Nate is riding with Austin and the floozies in the back. You," she points to me, "are riding with me and Parker."

Something's fishy, and it ain't the floozies.

I narrow my eyes at Mia and stand taller. "Why?"

She cuts a quick glance at Nate, her eyes flying back to me as she shrugs. "I have a quick pit stop to make and I need you to go with me." She smiles a big, cheesy smile I can't help but laugh at.

"Fine," I roll my eyes. "Get that ugly ass look off your face and wait for me by...wait. Whose car?"

Mia bounces away, lacing her arm through Parker's. "My Jeep. Be there in five."

When I step out of Nate's arms, he grumbles, "What was that all about?"

With a quick glance in the direction the two headed off in, I shrug, turning back to Nate. "You never know with Pebbles and Bamm-Bamm."

He nods, a crease forming between his thick brows as he watches them hop into Mia's Jeep.

"Alright, guess I'll see you in a bit." I pull out of his embrace.

He looks back at me, his eyes tight. He doesn't say anything, just nods, leaning down to kiss my forehead, before walking back to Austin's truck.

As soon as I jump into Mia's Jeep, I start, "Okay, assholes. Spill it."

Parker, who's in the driver seat, howls in laughter as he takes off, while Mia squeals from her spot in the passenger seat. "Tonight is going to be so much fun!"

And that's all I get until we're walking into my house a few minutes later.

"Okay, Lolli." Mia shoves me into my bathroom. "Quickest shower of your life, go. Shave whatever needs shaving, hair in a hairnet; we don't have time to dry it." She picks up one of my curls and nods in approval. "Thank God you did your hair before the game." Then she's running down the hall. "Be right back!" she yells before I hear the front door close.

I don't bother arguing, because, what the fuck's the point?

On a curse, I slam the bathroom door closed. "I know this is somehow your fault, Hero!"

His laughter booms from the other side of the door. "It'll be worth it, trust me."

"Yeah, yeah," I mutter and do as I'm told.

Thankfully, I'm a fresh and clean, and an always bare kind of girl, so my 'to be shaved' areas are on point.

Approximately two minutes later, I wrap the towel around me and rip the shower cap off my head, letting my curls hang loose, and head into my bedroom for some answers, but in the short distance from A to B, I hear some commotion.

As I make my way around the corner, I see Parker smirking, lying on my bed with his arms crossed behind his head, and Nate standing in front of him, a scowl on his face.

"Uh." Both their gazes turn to me. "Hi?"

Nate's scowl deepens, while Parker doubles over in laughter.

Then I hear more yelling coming down the hallway.

"What the hell, Austin?" Mia shrieks. "I told you we'd meet you guys there!"

He laughs. "I know, but the guy is relentless. He saw your Jeep in the driveway, saw you, and you alone - as in, not Parker and Lolli - run over to your house, and practically jumped out the truck. What's a man to do?"

"Argggh!" She grunts, her voice getting closer. "You are so not getting any tonight."

She comes around the corner, Austin hot on her heels, and Nate jolts out of his frozen state.

"Shut your damn eyes!" He points at Austin, who stands in front of me, smiling. "You!" He whips around, pointing at Parker. "Get. The fuck. Off her bed and go wait in the living room!"

Parker laughs and hustles out of the room as they all make their way down the hall.

"Give me five minutes!" Nate yells out, then gently shoves me into my room, his chest heaving.

"What the fuck is going on right now?" I ask, my eyes shifting around the now empty room.

Nate drops his chin to his chest, and when he looks back up, it's a slow, scorching perusal that starts at my toes and spreads until the hairs on the back of my neck are standing up.

He has my back against the door and his mouth on mine before I can protest, not that I would.

A needy moan leaves my lips as my legs are lifted to wrap around him. Using the door and his body to support me, his hands trail down my throat, my chest, until they reach the edge of my towel just above my thighs. Right when his hands start to push the towel up further, there's a loud bang on the door.

"Oh, hell no!" Mia yells. "Nate, get your ass out of there and get to the damn party!"

Neither of us move.

After a good thirty seconds of silence, she lets out a humorless laugh. "Okay, fine." I can hear the smirk in her voice. "Get your ass out of there and get to your party, playboy!"

My gaze flies to Nate's and a sexy ass smile takes over his face. "Cat's out of the bag." He winks.

Still a little breathless, I ask, "Today's your birthday?"

He presses his hard-on into me on a roll, and I bite my lip to keep from moaning with my cousin on the other side of the door.

"Eighteen, Kalani." He kisses me, hard, one more time before dropping me to my feet and sauntering out the door.

Bastard.

"You do realize, had you told me about Nate's birthday, not only could I have gotten him a gift or something, but I would've gone home to get ready willingly, right?" I tell Mia as we jump out of her Jeep.

"Okay, first off, you are the gift, honey." She motions toward my body from head to toes. "Wrapped up in pretty shiny wrapping and everything." She shimmies while I roll my eyes. "Second, I call bullshit."

Rounding her hood, I look at her with raised brows.

"Please, had you known, you and Nate would be between the sheets already, party forgotten." She stops and thinks for a second. "To give him credit though, he didn't even want to tell you. Wasn't going to have a party or anything. It was kind of a surprise, well, until he burst into your room, and found Parker lying on your bed 30 minutes ago." She stops to check her lipstick in a random car's window. "Never thought I'd say this, but I think he actually likes you."

When I scoff, she places her hands on my arms, halting my steps. "I'm serious, Lolli." Her eyes grow concerned. "At first, I thought I had to watch out for you, but seeing as how you're all stone cold and shit, I'm starting to think it's him I need to watch out for." She drops her hand with a shrug. "Just be careful. With him. With yourself."

I nod, not at all agreeing with her. "'Kay, well, I'm glad Parker ended up leaving with the boys earlier since we're having this little heart to stone."

"Can I ask you something, Lolli?"

I search her face, nodding.

"Why is it that you and Parker are such good friends? I mean, how did that happen? He's always been a busybody, but he never really took to anyone like he did you."

I stand silently, looking past her shoulder.

I hate sharing, but she must need this. I was wondering if mine and Parker's friendship, the fact that I spend a lot of time with him and not her, affected her. I guess it does.

"Parker...he's...like me, but in an opposite form, if that makes sense. He throws parties, loves big groups, and seeks out big crowds, where I like to be by myself and hate visitors." When her brows pull in, I continue. "He avoids that intimate setting because he refuses to get to the point of showing who he is, Mia, like me. Sometimes, what's going on inside isn't meant for everyone to see. Someone will come along that he'll talk to, but right now, this is what makes sense to him."

"How do you know that?"

"I can't explain it, Meems. It is what it is. We...get each other without having to say it. It works for us."

"Right." She frowns at her feet.

I glance at the house behind me. "Can we get some drinks now?"

She holds eye contact for a few seconds, then smiles. "Yes, Lollipop," she says, shaking her head exuberantly. "Let's get some drinks."

I smooth the edge of my skirt before we walk toward the door.

Apparently, Mia had stashed an outfit at her house for me that was intended for tonight. So here I am, donned in a black tube top and a badass, blood-red – Alrick High Knights red - pencil skirt that comes up just past my belly button and halfway down my thigh. The skirt is a stretchy material, so it forms to my curves perfectly. Paired with sparkly black four-inch heels, and red bow studded earrings, it has to be said... my outfit's banging. My long dark hair is left loose in big barrel curls, with smoky eyes, and red lips to match, and I'm ready to party.

"You sure I'm not going to fall out of this top?" I ask Mia, making sure I'm all tucked in.

"Honey, the D's are safe, trust me. You paid good money for that top." She laughs. "Hence the whole 'no bra needed' thing."

I laugh. "Whatever you say. Let's go inside. It's cold as shit out here and I'm in a skirt like it's summer."

Once we've made it into the house, I don't bother looking around for Nate or anyone else right away. I know they're around, so Mia and I make our way into Parker's dad's kitchen, which acts as the bar tonight.

"What'll it be, ladies?" A kid I recognize from the JV team asks, a proud smile on his lips.

Must be an honor to serve drinks at the QB's birthday party. I can't help but roll my eyes.

I look at Mia, with raised eyebrows.

"Oh yeah. Bartender, DJ, catered food service. He gets all the perks." She laughs. "Vodka cran for me." She blows the boy a kiss.

"And for you, Lolli?" He smiles at me.

"Tequila. Two shots and a lime, if you got it."

"Gotcha."

Within a minute, we have our drinks in hand and exit the kitchen to join the crowd.

"Okay, girl." Mia raises her glass. "To a fun night of the triple D's."

"And those would be...?"

"Drinks, dancing, and dick." She winks. "In that order."

We both double over in laughter.

"I thought you told Austin he wasn't getting any?"

"It's a dead threat and he knows it. Why punish myself?" she says, and we laugh harder.

"Alright, I'm ready." I toss my first shot back, setting the glass down quickly to suck the lime dry.

Right as I bring number two to my lips, my hand freezes, and I look to my right.

Nate's leaning against the wall, staring right at me. As soon as our eyes meet, he pushes off the wall and glides toward me.

He changed, too.

Gone are the faded jeans and white tee. He's wearing a black button-up with the sleeves rolled up to his elbows. The shirt lays untucked over a pair of dark jeans that stretch nicely across his thick thighs and those Palladium boots I love. His face is freshly shaven and begging to be rubbed on, while his hair is stuck in a perfect sideswipe – that natural 'just rolled out of bed', or 'just pulled on', look.

I'd like to pull on it.

I lick my lips.

God. Damn. He's sexy. I may even beg...

"I know I would..."

My head snaps to Mia.

She laughs and walks backward. "Yes, bitch." She widens her eyes mockingly. "You said that out loud. We're dancing, so don't ditch me," she adds as she skips off toward a group of girls.

I return my gaze to Nate and watch as his eyes roam my body. He bites his lower lip and all I can think is how bad I wish it were me. Gettin' bit or doing the biting, I'm not picky.

"You better stop looking at me like that," he rasps, stepping in front of me.

"Like what?" I ask, my eyes still trained on his luscious lips.

His response is to grab my lime from between my knuckles and place the peel side in his mouth. He lifts my hand and I take the cue.

Purely for show, I tilt my head back slowly, and pour the golden liquid down my throat. My head barely makes it back to its righted position before Nate's hands are on the sides of my face, bringing my lips to his.

I merely have a chance to lick the lime, before he releases it and locks his mouth to mine in a deep, needy kiss.

His fingertips run down my neck and body until those rough hands of his find my hips.

I pull back and smile up at him. "Happy Birthday, Handsome."

"Best one yet," he winks, stepping back slightly.

"Why didn't you say anything?" I ask, genuinely curious.

He shrugs. "Because I didn't want you to feel like you had to come out if you didn't want to, and I wasn't gonna if you weren't."

He reaches up and tucks my hair behind my ear.

"But... it's your birthday."

"And I wanted to spend it with you."

When my brows pull in, he smiles and grabs my hand. "Come on, Gorgeous. We need another drink."

I nod and allow him to pull me through the house.

Nate does have special privileges, because our shots are already ready to go and handed to us right as we step up to the makeshift bar.

"You on tequila tonight, too?" I smirk.

"I'm on what you're on."

"Alright," I laugh. Raising my glass, we cheers before knocking back another shot. "I'm on three. What's your number, Handsome?"

"Like he knows," an annoyingly familiar, grating voice says from behind me.

With a roll of my eyes, I turn, giving Liv a fake as fuck smile. "Bet he knows the exact number after you." Her eyes narrow. "Or maybe not." I pop my hip out, like an Olivia clone. "I'm betting it's taken a lot to erase that train wreck of a memory."

Her head swivels, nearly shaking with rage, while her arms cross over her lackluster chest.

"Oh, wait," I mock. "I forgot. Nate doesn't even remember the second time." Her eyes fly to Nate for confirmation, and he coughs to cover his laugh. "Guess you are pretty easy to forget after all."

She flips her long blonde hair over her shoulder before shoving past me.

"You know," I study Liv's stiff posture as she trudges off. "Maybe you should give it to her. She clearly needs some kind of release. Bitch is wound tight."

When he doesn't respond, I look up, finding his eyes narrowed in on me. "What?"

He opens his mouth to say something but is cut off when Austin throws his arm around his neck. "Let's go, my man. Shots!" he yells, dragging a laughing Nate off with him, but not before he glances back, his hand outstretched for me to take.

Shots are being passed in all directions as LMFAO's "Shots" booms through the speakers. I decline, until a smiling Nate holds one out to me.

The music dies down and suddenly Austin's voice takes over.

"Alright y'all. It's December 11th, we just won the State Championship, and it's my right-hand man's birthday!" Everyone cheers. "Who knows when his ass'll disappear with the fine ass lady on his arm tonight...Hi, Lolli," he winks, earning a few laughs and Nate's arms snake around me, pulling my back into his chest. "So, let's wish him a happy mutha fuckin' birthdaaay!"

Everyone yells and we all take our shots.

A little while later, our close-knit group settles in the den where there are less partygoers.

Nate drops down onto the edge of the couch. He tries pulling me down with him, but I evade on a laugh. Spinning to stand behind him, I lean down to whisper in his ear, "It's true, you know, what they say..."

He raises an eyebrow and I smile wide. "Tequila makes her clothes fall off..." I throw my head back, laughing as he chokes on his own spit. Raising my final shot of the evening, I knock it back, sans the lime.

His eyes follow my movements as I wipe my mouth with the back of my hand.

The music has died down some, everyone around growing drunker by the minute, so I decide it's about that time.

"Alright, it's been real, but I'm out like trout," I announce to whoever's listening, turning to leave.

Nate's strong arms wrap around me in seconds. "You're leaving me?" he whispers.

"I am," I giggle.

He sways us slightly. Dropping his head, he nestles into the crook of my neck, his arms tightening around me. "Don't go..." His voice is so quiet I almost miss it.

But I don't. And now, for some reason, my breath gets caught in my lungs, and there's a tightness in my chest.

Tequila. It's the tequila.

Yeah, I got to go...

I take a half of a step.

"Kalani..." His voice is light and almost... vulnerable.

Shit.

With my eyes squeezed shut, I whisper, "Come with me, Handsome."

He freezes, which makes me grin, confirming it was the right move. He wasn't expecting an invitation, but I know he sure as shit wanted one.

Nate stands to his full height and gently turns me so he can look me in the eyes.

There is no indecision in mine and I'm not drunk. Relaxed and horny, sure, but not drunk.

He smiles, grabs my hand, and together, we sneak out of his party.

Chapter Twenty

K ALANI

The first thing I do when I walk into the house is kick off my shoes, press play on my iPod, and make my way into the kitchen for a bottle of water. "You want one?"

"Yeah, please." He takes off his boots and joins me.

"Are you hungry?" I ask him, after I down half my bottle.

A devilish grin comes across his face, and suddenly he starts walking right for me.

With those dark eyes locked on mine, he outlines my top with his fingertips, then runs them down my side, gripping my hips. Lifting me as if I weigh nothing, he gently sets me on the countertop.

His right hand comes up to trace over my lips.

"Red's never looked as sexy as it does spread across your lips." He leans forward and gently bites down on my bottom lip, pulling away until it releases. "Or over your thighs..." His gaze drops to my red skirt, and he pushes it up some so he can fit better between my legs.

I say nothing. I'm dying to see what the hype's all about.

He leans in close, bringing his soft lips to my neck, and kisses his way up my throat until he reaches my ear. "I want you, Kalani," he whispers, biting down gently.

Pulling back, he looks into my eyes.

I leave them open for him to read my desire; I want him just as badly.

When his one-sided smile appears, I wrap my legs around his waist, and my arms around his neck.

"Show me what you got, Handsome."

He scoops me up by my ass and carries me to my room.

I'm attacking his mouth before we make it to the bed.

He fumbles and we drop onto the comforter laughing, which quickly morphs into moans and groans as we undress each other.

In nothing but a black thong, I scoot back on the bed.

Nate's eyes are dark and dangerous and sexy.

He drops his boxers and his dick salutes me.

My mouth waters thinking about what's coming next.

"Condom?" I pant, my eyes still trained on his manhood.

"Got it." He tosses the foil package near my head.

I lay back as he crawls on top of me, kissing my stomach and ribs all the way up. I wrap my legs around his back as he does, sliding along his skin the closer he comes. The feeling sends tingles up my thighs.

His right-hand skates up my ribs, cupping my breast, while his mouth comes down to show some love to the other. When my back lifts, he growls into my skin, switching it up on each nibble.

My fingertips zig-zag through his abs. When I reach his pelvis, I flatten my right palm and slide my hand down, gripping him, hard.

His mouth flies to mine and he pushes his body into me, forcing my hand out.

I reach up in search of the package. Not wanting to break our kiss, I blindly tear the wrapper open above our heads.

Pulling the condom out, I push on his stomach so he lifts, place the condom over the head of his dick and start rolling...

"Honey, I'm home!"

"You've got to be fucking kidding me."

"Bitch."

We say in unison.

"Get rid of her," he huffs.

I nod and he rolls off me.

I throw on his shirt, quickly buttoning it enough to cover the important stuff and walk out my bedroom door, freezing as a thought occurs.

Biting my nail, I turn back to Nate. "But what if she has cookie dough again?"

He pins me with a stern look, and I watch, salivating, as his hand starts to stroke himself. My eyes fly back to his and he tilts his head.

"Right," I croak. I'm gone quicker than a running back on a blitz.

As I come around the corner, I find Mia standing in the entry way.

"Hey, you didn't tell...oh!" She smirks when she looks down at what I'm wearing.

"Yeah, bitch." I widen my eyes. "Oh." I lay my hand out, palm up. "Key."

"But-"

"I'll give it back to you tomorrow, after I buy a 'do not disturb' sign or something, but tonight," I point to the door, "go."

She laughs and slaps the key in my hand.

I walk to the door and swing it open, shocked when I hear a bunch of different laughs coming from outside.

I look out to see a truck full of her friends.

She kisses my cheek. "I was planning on going home with

Austin anyway. His parents are out of town." She runs out the door, heels in hand, screaming, "Pay up, bitches! Told you they were together!"

I can't help but laugh and wave as they drive off.

As I head back to my room, I'm not sure what I'll find or if the mood is dead, but when I walk in, finding Nate lying on my bed in the same exact position he was in when I walked out, his hand still holding onto the base of himself, I'm hot and ready all over again.

With a smirk on my face, I wave the key in the air.

He smiles back, his eyes roaming my body, covered in his dress shirt.

When they lift, connecting with mine again, his arm extends, reaching for me.

The key falls to the ground, and in no time, I'm under him. He's sleeved and at my entrance but holds still.

My legs lay open against the comforter, his strong thighs pressed against mine. I run my nails up his arms, grinning when he shudders.

His right hand comes up, and he runs the tip of his pointer finger down my throat until he reaches the buttons of his shirt I'm still wearing. He doesn't remove it, but slowly undoes each one until it lies open at my sides.

My body is trembling, my heart's racing, and I'm hot everywhere, so when Somo's "Ride" begins to flow through the speakers in the background, I take matters into my own hands, and wrap my legs around his waist. I lock them tight, forcing his pelvis down, his thickness inside of me.

His moan swallows mine as our lips and teeth clash together.

When he's pushed to the hilt, my back arches off the bed, and his warm mouth comes down onto my erect nipples, sucking and biting.

He fucks me to the rhythm of the song, and when my thighs clench around him, his forehead creases and drops to mine.

It doesn't take long for his body to go stiff as mine quivers against him. He moves his forehead to my shoulder, kissing my collarbone lightly as he pushes in impossibly deeper, rolling off and onto his back when my limp legs drop from around him.

Once I can hear more than my erratic heartbeat, I turn to him with a grin, but when I find him staring at me, a stoic expression on his face, my breathing halts altogether.

His right-hand lifts between us. Grabbing one of my curls off the pillow, he runs it through his fingers, watching as it falls from his hand. Brows drawn in; he lifts his eyes to look at me.

And now my heart's beating faster for a completely different reason.

His eyes are weightless, as if he just figured it all out.

Problem is, I have no idea what it is.

When he lifts onto his right elbow to peer down at me, I have to look away. His eyes are too bright and honest, too strong and sure.

Too much.

Before he can speak, because I know he's about to, I stand.

Without looking at him, I tell him, "You can let yourself out. I'm going to take a shower and go to bed."

He doesn't speak while I grab my pajamas from the drawer, or even when I take my towel from the hanger by my door, but I feel his eyes on me.

As I exit my room, I chance a glance at him.

Pinched at the edges, his eyes search mine discreetly, and when his head hangs on a nod, I turn and hurry into the bathroom.

After taking long enough to ensure he's gone, I rush into my room, ignoring the fact that it's well after one in the morning, my hair's soaked, and it's cold as shit outside, and throw on my tennies and rush out the door.

It takes longer for my mind to clear this time, more miles to pass before all I can think about is the ache in my calves and the burn in my lungs.

My mind shuts down, but I don't stop.

I keep running.

I wake up in my bed hours later, not knowing how or when I got there, but that's not what has me on the verge of a panic attack.

What bothers me is the first thing that comes to mind when I open my eyes is how much life might suck here in Alrick now that Nate won't be around anymore.

And, for the life of me, I can't figure out why I care.

NATE

I wake up the next morning with a newfound understanding of the fucked-up reality of last night.

I fucked Kalani.

She kicked my ass out after.

That upset me.

Took a night of shitty sleep to realize that I'm a dumbass and she's stubborn as hell.

That's probably what drew me to her in the first place. Her no bullshit, fire and ice soul, with a bangin' body to match.

She's the perfect mixture of sugar and spice.

I know she's telling herself we're friends, that we're just fucking around. Literally, as of last night.

I grin, thinking about the way her body felt under me, around me.

Mmm... Yeah, she thinks it's over. She thinks last night was a one-time thing.

It wasn't.

I saw it in her eyes. She tried damn hard to feign indifference, to look at me with empty eyes, but she needs to realize I can see right through her. Right into her clear blues. And somewhere in that caged-up, closed-off heart of hers, she knows.

There's more going on here than either of us has admitted.

She wants me. She wasn't looking for bragging rights, or to say she had sex with Nate Monroe, football protégé. Nah. She just wanted me. The hot-headed, hot-blooded guy, with a soft spot for the little blue-eyed, black-haired piece of perfection.

I can't wait to have her again.

And again.

That should freak me out, wanting a girl even more after than I did before. Shit, me wanting a girl again period should have me running, but it doesn't.

It feels damn good. Refreshing.

For the first time, I know what I want, and it's her. Plain and simple. I figured it out a while ago, but last night confirmed it.

It'll be a challenge, breaking through to her, but I perform best under pressure. It's my job as a quarterback: read, revise, analyze, and execute.

I can't help but laugh.

Austin was right, she's mine. She just doesn't know it yet.

Whistling, I throw on my A's hat, grab my keys, and head out the door.

She's about to find out.

Chapter Twenty-One

K ALANI

As I make my way around the corner, I freeze mid-stride when I spot Nate carrying groceries into Mia's house.

She's always putting the boys to work.

Once they've stepped through the door, I sprint past, glancing back quickly to make sure they didn't see me. The moment I face forward, I slam into something - or someone, rather - and I'm knocked backward.

"Whoa." Mia catches me from behind, laughing. "Clumsy, Lolli."

"Oh, my gosh. Kalani!" Her voice stuns me. "Honey, are you alright?"

My eyes fly forward, landing right on my Aunt Kara.

She freezes, as do I.

My body starts to shake, the voices around me are no longer

clear. There's a fog over my eyes, a lump in my throat, and I can't feel my legs.

"Kalani!"

"Move!"

I'm spinning so fast; my lungs can't grasp any air.

"Oh, my God!"

Why won't she stop talking?

"Ma'am, I'm sorry, but you need to move! Now!"

Right when I start to fall into oblivion, two warm hands make their way to my face, keeping me here a moment longer.

The textured hands push past my cheeks, coming to rest right beneath my ears, in his spot. Nate's spot.

"It's okay, Kalani," he whispers. "I'm here."

He's here.

NATE

"Nate, what are you-" Mia starts, before I cut her off.

"Shhh!" Cutting my eyes from Mia to her mom, I give her a warning with my eyes. She needs to stay the fuck back.

I quickly turn to Kalani, who is standing lifelessly in front of me, her face a blank slate and ghostly white.

"Hey." I drop my forehead to hers, keeping my hands rested against the nape of her neck on both sides, my thumbs brushing over her jawline. "Breathe."

Her vacant eyes squeeze shut as she takes in a strangled breath.

"Nate..." She breathes my name like a prayer and my heart starts hammering against my chest.

My right-hand slides further into her hair, and I shift my body closer to hers. "It's me."

Her beautiful blue eyes open, focusing on me, and my breath catches in my throat.

When the corner of her lips twitches slightly, a grateful chuckle escapes me.

"Hi, Handsome," she whispers dismally.

I smile and kiss her forehead gently. "Hi, Gorgeous."

"Why are you here?"

"I came to see you. To get you," I answer honestly.

She scowls at me, some fire coming back into her desolate eyes.

I nod when she challenges me with her gaze.

"But-"

"Yeah, I know," I interrupt, knowing what she was about to say. "Don't care."

She eyes me for a moment before lightly shaking her head, attempting to hide a grin. When her gaze shifts left, her body tenses, but only slightly.

With my palms, I apply more pressure to her face, effectively gaining her attention again.

I'm hoping we have some kind of telepathic connection, or some weird shit, because I really need her to understand what I'm trying to convey.

We must because she gives me a stiff nod.

Her hands come up and case over mine, gripping them tight.

As we lower them together, we both take a step back, straighten our spines, and inhale deeply.

Then, having no fucking idea how this shit's about to go down, I let go of her left hand and step next to her.

She looks at Mia first, who has tears in her eyes and her hand on her chest. Kalani gives her nothing but a shrug, and that seems to be enough for her, because she smiles then, nodding. Guess they have telepathic shit, too.

Her eyes shift to Mrs. Edwards, her aunt, who looks back and forth between the three of us, completely unsure of what to do.

Kalani's face tightens slightly, so I discreetly squeeze her hand, smiling on the inside when her shoulders instantly drop in a fully visible sign of relief.

Her gaze falls to our intertwined fingers before she focuses back on her aunt.

"Hi, Aunt Kara." Her voice is steady. Strong.

Fuck, I want to fist bump right now. Or kiss her, I'm so fuckin' proud.

Nose red, jaw trembling, Mrs. Edwards whispers, "Hi, Kalani," hope shining through her voice.

Kalani turns to me. "I'm going to shower, then we can leave."

She says it like a statement, but she's asking me to take her somewhere, take her mind off things.

I was going to, whether she liked it or not.

Lifting my free hand, I tuck the loose strands of hair behind her ear, and nod.

She turns, offering a tight smile, then walks into her house.

"How the fu-" Mrs. Edwards silences her daughter with a raised palm, her gaze trained on me.

Her eyes are soft, knowing. "She told you." Her tone is a mixture of relief and wonder. There's a hint of mom tone in there, too. The kind you can't decipher, that means something, but you have no fucking clue what.

"She did." I can't help but puff my chest out a bit.

Mia catches my attention when her eyes shoot wide open. "She what?!"

Mrs. Edward steps up to me, gently placing her hands on my shoulders. "She talked to you?"

My throat grows tight at her tender, sincere voice, so I nod.

"Oh, my God." Her hand flies to her mouth when a whimper escapes, but she quickly recovers and rights herself.

"Remember something for me..."

I don't think she's looking for an answer, so I remain silent.

"If she's let you in..." She catches the pinch in my brows instantly, the uncertainty. "Don't doubt it. If she told you, she

206

already did. She has let you in." Her voice is confident, leaving no room for argument.

"Kalani is a free-spirited girl. She picks and chooses who to trust. Once you're in, you stay there. Always. No matter what." She drops her hand and steps back. "Remember that."

I can't help but heed her words as a warning, but nod in acceptance, and make my way into Kalani's house.

The second my ass hits her mattress, she storms into her room, that body wrapped in a towel.

A little one.

"Why the hell did you show up today, Nate?" she snaps, making her way to her dresser.

She's all wet, dripping, and half-naked, and now my jeans are getting uncomfortably tighter.

"And why the hell don't you ever call first?"

Her hair looks longer, impossibly darker when it's wet like that. There's a piece sticking to her neck, in my spot.

My fingers are twitching to brush it to the side, lean in, and suck off the water left behind.

"Hello!" she shrieks.

My eyes fly to hers the second she turns around, and she smirks instantly.

I know it's all over my face.

I want her in a bad way.

She grabs her hair in one hand, lays it across her right shoulder, and slowly runs her fingers through it.

Now my hands aren't the only thing twitching.

She keeps her eyes on mine as she walks my way. Damn, if it don't look like she's putting on a show...

I lick my lips as she leans in.

She's inches from me when she reaches out, snatching a t-shirt from behind me, and returns to her dresser, laughing her sexy little ass off.

"God, Nate. You're such a guy." She pulls her shirt over her head and drops the towel.

It's not quite long enough - the ultimate tease - and I'm on my feet, taking a step closer to her.

"Careful, Handsome."

I freeze.

She slips her feet into a tiny ass scrap of fabric - a thong.

A little pink one.

"You just might put a hole in that poor bottom lip of yours." The tiny piece of cloth makes it up and over her soft thighs and hips.

My eyes fly to hers and she winks. "Off limits now, remember?" She smirks, looking like she's on board for what she just said.

I'm about to call her bluff.

Moving deliberately slow, I let my gaze roam over her until her chest rises and falls quicker, more erratic. Then, I lock my eyes on hers, stepping directly in front of her.

"You okay with that, Gorgeous?" I whisper, skimming my fingers down her arms, eyebrow raised.

"It is what it is, Nate." She licks her lips, her voice dripping with desire.

The left side of my mouth lifts. "But you want me." I wrap her wet hair around my fist.

"Me and every other girl in a twenty-mile radius." She looks to my mouth.

"Fifty, but who's counting."

She rolls her eyes and goes to step away, but her back hits the dresser.

"Guess what, Kalani?" I bring my hand holding her hair around to her back, pulling gently so she looks up at me. "I want you, too," I whisper over her lips.

Her pupils dilate, her little tongue poking out to wet those plump ass lips of hers. "Yeah?"

I nod. "Yeah."

Her hands slide under my shirt, and she smirks up at me. "What are you gonna do about it, Handsome?"

I grin into her neck, squeeze her ass and bring her body flush against mine, letting her feel how hard she makes me. How much I want her.

"What am I gonna do?" I whisper, running my nose up her neck to her ear. "I'm gonna feed you. Then fuck you." When her breath hitches, I turn and walk out of her room. "Ten minutes, Kalani."

I bite my knuckles on my way out to keep from either running back in there or laughing at the sexually frustrated grunts she's throwing around right now.

Walking into Wicker with Kalani beside me feels different today.

By the looks we're getting from the others around, it's different to them, too. I've never brought a girl in here. I've left with a fair share, but never showed up with one. And the fact that it's the same one I left the party with the night before? Well, that's bound to stir up some shit.

She leans in to ask, "Is it just me or is the entire party here right now?"

"Tradition." Taking advantage of her closeness, I slide my arm across her back, and grip her hip.

"Tradition," she says flatly.

I shrug, pull her a little closer, and kiss her hair. "The night after a player's party, everyone comes to Wicker for breakfast. Or lunch, depending on how hard they went the night before."

"The players, as in the team, or..." she teases, a perfect brow raised.

"Funny," I quirk, kissing her hair again.

I don't miss the side glance she gives me after, but I also don't acknowledge it either. She felt it, everyone saw it, mission accomplished.

"You cool to grab a seat, man?" Ryan asks, juggling dishes in each hand.

"Yeah, bro. We're good."

He nods in appreciation. "Hi, Lolli!" he calls out as he rushes off.

She smiles and waves.

After a quick look around, I see a table of my teammates and head in their direction. Choosing a vacant booth that's still in the mix - and not at all because Jarrod has a damn good view of us - I usher her in first, then take the seat next to her.

She picks up her menu and looks it over while I take a few minutes to look her over.

She's wearing a pair of tight, light blue jeans with some pink Chuck Taylors, and a long-sleeved black top that dips down a bit in the middle. She threw her hair up in a cute, messy ball on top of her head and her face is perfect; not a trace of makeup and she still looks amazing. Beautiful.

She turns, catching me looking at her, and sets her menu down.

Unashamed I've been caught, I smile, and grab her hand. Lacing our fingers together, I lay our hands in my lap, and relax into the booth.

She gives me a one-sided grin, and I swear to God, her cheeks turn a single shade brighter. Using my free hand, I run my knuckles over the soft pink that's taken over. When her breath locks in her throat, my heart beats faster.

She feels it. She must.

Her lips are parted and she has a dazed look in her eyes, but it's gone when a cup is set onto the table.

"Sorry, guys," Ryan apologizes, setting two waters in front of us. "It's a madhouse in here."

"I'll take a coffee today, Ryan," Kalani tells him, covering her yawn with her sleeve.

He grins at her, his hands planted in fists on the sides of his black apron. "Long night, Lolli?"

I clear my throat to keep from laughing, while Kalani narrows her eyes at him playfully.

"You were in the damn truck last night, weren't you?"

He laughs, taking a step back. "I was, but even if I wasn't, it's all I've heard about this morning."

"Oh, I don't doubt it. Go get my coffee." She rolls her eyes and pulls her hand from mine.

He smiles and turns to me. "Coffee?"

I nod, then snatch her hand back in mine, earning a half-hearted eyeroll from her. She lets me run my fingers over hers a few times before pulling them back again, opening her straw as an excuse for something to do.

She smiles her thanks to the girl who sets our coffee and a bowl of creamers in front of us. We give her our order, then sit back, relax, and enjoy our warm drinks.

When she leans her body into mine, I wrap my arm around her shoulder and pull her closer.

"Thanks for earlier," she says into her cup.

Turning my head, I run my nose over the lobe of her ear. "Thanks for last night," I whisper.

She flicks her wrist to smack my shoulder, but I catch her hand and bring it to my lips. She shifts so her body's facing mine and watches me run her knuckles along my lips before kissing them gently.

As I lower her hand, her head tilts and she stares at me.

"Okay." Ryan shows up with our dishes and she quickly cuts her gaze out the window. "Two pancake platters." He's gone as quickly as he arrived.

I push her plate in front of her, laughing when she lets out a whimsical sigh just looking at it.

"I'm so hungry right now." Stabbing a piece of scrambled eggs, she dips it into her syrup, then takes a slow, savoring bite.

"Mmm..." Her eyes close and her head falls against the seat. "Soo goood," she moans.

My body comes to life watching her. Eyes closed, head still tilted, she licks her lips, moaning again when her tongue slides innocently over her now sugar-coated mouth, and all I can see is her under me - doing the exact damn thing.

"Keep moaning like that," I whisper, "and I may just take you out to my truck right quick."

Her wide eyes cut to me.

I wink and take a bite off my own plate.

"Promise?" she purrs, laughing her sexy little ass off when I choke on my bacon.

"You're such a brat," I shake my head, leaning over to kiss her hair again, loving that she tries to hide a smile in her coffee mug.

Once Kalani's done, she sits back and gazes at me.

"What?" I smile, letting my hand rub across her jeans.

"Tell me something, Handsome?"

I nod, not missing how her crystal blue eyes have turned a shade darker.

Never breaking eye contact, she reaches up and pulls my hat off my head. "You done?"

"Not by a long shot."

"Good answer," she smiles, lifting my hat to block our faces as she gently places her sweet, soft lips against mine in a kiss that leaves me desperate for more.

She pulls back, laughing, placing my hat back on my head.

"So, what are we doing today?" she asks as we stand.

"I want to show you something on my parents' property." I reach over and grab her hand, tossing some cash on the table.

"Okay."

The entire drive to my house, I keep her soft little hand in mine.

Glancing at the dark-haired beauty in my passenger seat with her eyes closed, a small smile playing on her swollen lips, I know... something happened last night or today. Shit, maybe even a month ago, when she first invited me over for a movie. I guess it doesn't really matter when it happened. All I know is, this girl next to me... I want to keep her here.

Now to convince her that's where she wants to be.

Chapter Twenty-Two

K ALANI

With a smile on my face, I run up the side of the hill, only to slip in the mud when Nate wraps his arm around my waist.

"Shit!" He tucks quickly, so he's the one that hits the ground, and I land on top of him.

Laughing hysterically, I drop my head to his stomach. "You okay?"

He narrows his eyes at me and I laugh even harder, rolling onto my back next to him.

"That was your fault." He nudges me with his elbow, his voice light.

"Oh." I roll onto my stomach, propping myself up on my elbow. "I made it rain?"

"You jinxed us." He laughs, reaching up to brush dirt off my face.

I roll my eyes. "Uh-huh."

He pulls my hair tie out, and my wet hair falls down my back. "Did you have fun today?" he asks, playing with a few strands.

"I did." I can't help but smile down at him.

Nate brought me to his house to show me the stream that runs along the back side of his property. The water stretches out about five feet and runs as far as you can see in both directions. Thick, tall trees stretch from beginning to end on the side that meets his family's land. Some are raised higher as the hillsides lift into small mounds of fresh, feathery green grass.

First, we tried to fish in the pond, but after a good two hours, didn't catch jack shit, so we decided to take a hike instead, and it started pouring on us. So, here we lay, underneath a giant tree, attempting to stay out of the downpour.

"I always liked the rain," I tell him, looking out over the hillside.

The wind's blowing slightly, just enough for the limbs of the trees - some leafless, others full - to bounce around.

"Yeah?"

"Yeah. It's a random escape, the rain."

"How so?" His fingers reach out and he pushes my wet hair over my shoulder, leaving his warm hand to rest there.

"It comes and goes as it pleases, taking with it the remains of the day or the hours before, washing away all traces of attendance, all the memories. Nothing is as powerful as the rain."

"Kinda like you?" he asks, a few moments later.

My eyes slide back to his. He must see my confusion because he gives me a small smile before explaining.

"I can see it, Kalani," he says quietly, running his fingertips down my arm. "You battling with yourself. Sometimes you allow yourself to smile, a real one that makes your eyes shine, only to wash it away seconds later, leaving behind a blank space." He gazes at me. "Like the rain."

I'm not sure how to react, so I just stare at him.

My instincts tell me to get up and run, let the rain wash away the memory of today, like we just talked about. But something's keeping me rooted on this hillside, and I have a sneaky suspicion it's this mystery of a man-boy lying next to me.

When I finally react to his words with a laugh, he releases a breath I didn't realize he was holding and reaches up to brush my hair behind my ear tenderly, sending an involuntary shiver down my spine.

Nate's eyes pinch slightly, a small grimace on his lips. "You're cold." He misreads my body's reaction for the first time. "Want me to call my dad, have him come back here on the ATV, and get us out of this mess?"

I smile at him, reaching down to smooth out the worry lines that have taken over his forehead. Shifting so I'm sitting on my knees, I shake my head and his brows knit further.

My hands grab the hem of my rain-soaked shirt, and I pull it over my head, dropping it down next to me.

Nate sits up instantly, and gently runs his hands up my ribs, across my back, until he has the clasps of my bra in his hand.

His eyes find mine, his hand frozen in place.

"What are you waiting for, Handsome?"

He maneuvers us so his back is against the tree, then he grips me under my thighs, positioning me so I'm straddling him. His right hand comes up to case in my neck, while his left splays across my back, pulling me into him.

Our mouths seal together in a heated kiss, making me desperate to be closer to him. I let my knees spread as far into the grass as my jeans will allow, bringing my center against his stomach.

Right as my hands find the hem of his wet shirt, a throat clears from the other side of the tree.

Nate's head drops back, and he squeezes his eyes shut.

"Hey, Dad."

Oh, fucking lovely.

How did I not hear him coming? I swear, it's like as soon as

Nate's around, all jaw-dropping and irresistible, all Nate-like, something in my head blocks out everything else.

I'm not sure that's normal.

"Thought you and your...friend might need some help getting out of here." He says the word 'friend' as if there should be a question mark after it.

Nate's eyes widen when I wink at him, and he watches in horror as I round the tree. In my bra and jeans.

At least it's a cute bra, though. Matches my Chucks.

With my head held high, I reach out to shake Nate's dad's hand. "Mr. Monroe."

A smile twitches his lips as he holds a hand out to me. "Ms. Embers."

When my head pulls back, he laughs.

"Oh, yes. I've heard all about you."

My scowl flies to Nate, who quickly shakes his head.

His dad's chuckle draws my attention back to him. "I've been married a very long time, so I know what that look means." He grins and holy shit! He looks like an old, hot version of his son. "Rest assured, pretty one," Oh, he's smooth like him, too, "he hasn't shared anything you'd be upset about. He's at least that smart." He winks.

"Okay, Dad." Nate grumbles, stepping around to stand directly in front of me.

This only makes his dad's smile grow into a full-blown grin that makes his dark eyes shine as they shift from me to Nate and back again.

They stand there staring at each other for a good minute. Nate, with his eyes narrowed, Mr. Monroe, with a grin.

"Uh..." The scowl and grin turn on me. "This whole silent brain to brawn thing is super cool and all," both their brows jump, "but I'd much rather not be standing here in my bra."

Then I think about what I just said. "Well, not with Mr. Monroe here anyway."

Nate's head drops to his chest while his dad does his best to cover his laugh with a fake cough.

His dad walks over to the neon green ATV, and Nate grabs at the hem of his shirt.

My eyes watch the show.

His shirt is wet. Soaked, really, so I'm not surprised to see the remnants of water left behind when he peels it from his skin, giving me a nice and slow look at his no-need-to-flex-I'm-that-damn-good abs. As he pulls it over his head, a tiny drop of water makes its way down the center of his chest.

I hadn't realized I moved until his hand closes over my wrist.

My eyes fly to his, finding them dark and dilated, with a hint of laughter.

His dad does nothing to hold in his laugh this time.

Nate releases my hand and pulls his freezing shirt over my head. Instantly, it works like a cold shower would.

He sees the defiance in my eyes and narrows his. "Leave that on," he scowls, bending down to grab mine off the ground.

"I'll leave it on." I step out from under the semi-safety of the tree and am instantly drenched with more rain. "Not because you told me to, so don't get excited, but because I'm riding in the middle and it'd be weird if I didn't."

"I can't wait to get her to the house," his dad grins, his arms crossed over his chest.

Nate grumbles something under his breath then walks to the ATV.

When his dad fires up the toy, Nate's hand splays across my stomach and his thighs press more firmly into my backside.

"No funny business, Monroe," I snap.

"Never," they say in unison, both letting out deep, rich laughs before we're on the move.

Men.

It only takes a minute or two, then we're pulling in front of the off-side garage, where his dad kills the engine.

Nate steps off, offering a hand to me as he does, grumbling when I smack it away and hop off myself.

"Ready?" His dad rubs his hands together in what appears to be excitement.

"Might as well get it over with," Nate mumbles, ushering me forward.

As I make my way up the front steps, I watch my fingers run across the worn, white wood, allowing them to travel up the post a few inches. Once I hit the top step, my eyes lock onto the swing.

The blanket Nate had laid across the bottom is still there, spread out across the seat. I can't help but wonder if we were the last two to sit there; if the blanket's imperfect placement with lumps and creases are from our bodies; from us simply sitting, living.

Despite the sodden clothes I'm wearing, warmth radiates through me in a way I'm not familiar with.

"Hey." Nate's coarse hand skims across my cheek soothingly.

Reluctantly, my eyes pull from the swing to his.

He tucks my wet hair behind my ear, earning a grin from me.

I answer the question his eyes are asking. "I'm good, Handsome."

He nods but makes no move to release me.

"Nate..." his dad says quietly, almost hesitant, like he's interrupting something he shouldn't.

Nate tilts his head toward the doorway where his dad stands. "Ready?"

I nod, unable to take my eyes off Nate.

He drops his hand from my face and we walk through the front door.

"Honey," his dad calls out.

"Oh!" a sweet voice responds. "Did you get to see her? Was she as pretty as he said?"

I turn to Nate with an eyebrow raised.

He smirks.

"Well?" she yells out when no one answers. "Did you?"

Then a beautiful woman in her late forties comes around the corner, wearing a hot pink apron that reads 'Property of Ian Monroe' proudly.

Her hair is dark, like Nate's, and lays at her shoulders, but her eyes are lighter than his, more caramel.

"Oh shit!" she says, then her hand flies to her mouth. "Sorry."

I laugh and walk further into the house, waving a hand at her. "Hi."

"Wow." She looks me over from head to toe. "I can't even imagine what you look like normally-"

"Here we go..." I hear Nate say from behind me, while his dad steps up next to his wife, laughing.

Suddenly her shoulders slump, and her husband laughs even harder, placing a kiss to her hair as if reading her mind. "I want to be young and perfect and in love."

My eyes grow wide, and my body freezes.

"Ma! No." Nate grabs my hand and forces me to move toward the stairs. "Talk to your wife, Pops," he yells as his foot hits the first stair. "We'll be down in a bit."

"Wait, what!" I start to protest. I may not care about others' opinions of me, but I'm not a disrespectful bitch.

"Go on," his mom calls out and my eyes fly to her.

She winks at me.

Winks. At. Me.

Halfway up the stairs, his mother's voice rings out again. "We're going to have a cup of coffee out back!" she tells us, adding in a rush, "Outweigh before you play!"

Once inside Nate's room, he shuts the door behind us.

"What the hell did she just say?" I whisper-yell.

He laughs and walks past me, stopping at his dresser. "Exactly what you think." He pulls out a few t-shirts and sweats. "Weigh out the consequences versus the actions." He turns with a grin, "Aka, no grandbabies allowed."

My brows jump. "So, she just gave us the clear to get down and dirty?"

"Pretty much, yeah," he chuckles, walking toward what appears to be a bathroom in his room. When he disappears through the door, I allow myself to look around.

Surprisingly, his room is clean and neat.

His walls are tan, thank God, with posters of random football players scattered sporadically across them, and a few small shelves, holding trophy after trophy from all his years of football.

There is a large bed, not quite as big as mine, pushed against the left wall, his brown, wooden dresser and closet across from it. The window on the wall opposite the bed has a small gamer chair placed next to it. That's when I notice the cinema-worthy TV hanging from the wall, game consoles beneath it on a nifty hanging stand.

"Damn."

Nate's arm wraps around me from behind. "Big, isn't it?"

"That's what she said."

He laughs, reaching for my hand. "Come on."

He leads me into the bathroom, letting go of my hand to adjust the settings in the shower, so I start stripping down.

"That should be good." He glances over his shoulder quickly, doing a double take when he realizes I'm half-naked, shirt on the floor, jeans halfway down my hips.

"Fuck," he curses, frozen in place, his body still facing toward the shower, eyes on me.

I lower my jeans the rest of the way, pulling the wet material from my body in a not at all sexy manner, but if his labored breath is any indication, he's enjoying it.

I duck under his arm into the steamy shower, his eyes following me. Stepping under the warm water, still wearing my pink thong, I wink at him and slide the door closed.

I wait at least fifteen seconds - long enough for him to fight the internal battle and convince himself to walk away - then toss my underwear over the top of the shower and wait.

Three, two...

The shower door bursts open and Nate charges in, finding me leaning against the wall behind the spray of the water, waiting for him.

He stops in front of the water, his gaze raking over every exposed inch of me, before settling on my face.

"I can make this quick." His eyes ask for permission.

So confident. Sexy.

A smile from me is all it takes for him to lift me by my thighs and press me against the shower wall. Our mouths connect and I'm sinking down onto his bare dick in seconds.

And he wasn't wrong, 'cause with little to no effort, he has me on edge – boy's got moves.

"Shhh," Nate coos, his hand reaching for my chin, bringing my mouth back to his. He kisses me deeply to cover the moan that escapes when he grinds against me, as if he knew it was coming before I did, and I bite into his lip to keep from crying out.

"There you go," he whispers, never taking his eyes off me as I shudder in his arms. He rolls his hips once more before quickly setting me on my feet. Placing my limp hand over his dick, he helps me work him as he comes all over my stomach.

His forehead drops to the wall over my right shoulder, while mine falls to his chest.

After a few minutes, neither of us say anything as we both reach for the soap and clean ourselves off. When I go to rinse my hair of conditioner, Nate's arms wrap around my body from behind.

"Water is getting cold," he breathes into my neck, warming me all over again.

"You tryin' to warn me of some possible shrinkage?" I tease.

"There'd still be plenty, even if there was shrinkage. Which there isn't."

My laughter dies on my lips when his rough hands come up, cupping as much of my breasts as he can fit in his palms.

"Step out of the shower, Kalani. Now," he whispers into my ear. "Or else we'll be in here for a while." He nips at my earlobe. "I have no intentions of being quick next time around."

My head falls back against his shoulder. "I think I'll stay right here then, thanks."

His laughter shakes both our bodies.

Quickly, he releases me, gently shoving my wet body out of the shower, and closes the door.

I laugh when I hear him adjust the setting again, presumably turning what's left of the hot all the way down.

After brushing out my hair, I go to put on the clothes Nate left out for me, but my whole-body fits in one leg of his sweats. "Ugh, Nate. This stuff doesn't fit!" I call out from his room.

"Look around, grab whatever!"

With his okay, I skim through the shirts in his closet, pausing when I come to his jersey. I pull it out, turning it to see his last name stitched in big, bold, red letters, the number twenty-one large and proud beneath it. Smiling, I place it back on the rack.

I end up finding a white wife beater and use it as a stand in for a bra. I throw a navy blue, long-sleeved thermal that hangs just above my knees over it. The black tube socks I pull on are so large there's only a good three inches of skin showing between them and the shirt, so I decide a rolled-up pair of Nate's briefs is enough for under.

Nate comes out of the bathroom, his hair dripping and towel wrapped tightly around his waist, stopping at the foot of the bed I'm currently sprawled across.

"That," he motions with his head to my body. "Yeah. You keep that." His tongue runs across his bottom lip and I can't help but laugh.

One knee starts to lift onto the mattress.

"Oh, no!" My eyes go wide and I fly off the bed. "The safety of the loud shower was one thing, but no way in hell right here, right now, with nothing for your parents to hear but that bed post knocking."

He stares at me for a few seconds before the lust fades and he nods in agreement. "Right." He dashes into the bathroom, shutting the door behind him with more urgency than necessary.

Once he steps back into the room, fully dressed, he makes his way to the door, turning to look at me with a goofy grin in place. "Lead the way, Ms. Embers." He winks.

This should be interesting.

Chapter Twenty-Three

K ALANI

When I was little, I watched my parents interact with each other, as I'm sure most kids did. I remember them holding hands sometimes, and quick kisses on the lips and cheek. I remember my dad's arm around my mom and her head on his shoulder when we would snuggle on the couch to watch a movie. They loved each other. I know they did. But standing here, watching Mr. and Mrs. Monroe, I'm wondering if I even know what that means.

As soon as my foot hit the last stair, Nate snapped his fingers and said he'd be down in a second, before deserting me and running back up the stairs. I shrugged it off and followed the smell of freshly brewed coffee, only pausing when I heard a soft whisper, followed by warm laughter.

So now, here I sit, perched on the edge of a floral print couch, watching two people I know virtually nothing about, float across the cherry hardwood floors in the gentlest sway I've ever seen.

Their noses are kissing, eyes shining into each other's souls as their lips move in a beautifully private conversation. They're oblivious to my spying eyes - as they should be in an ambrosial moment like this.

His arms are wrapped tight around her, her palms resting on his chest as if she can't fathom the thought of not touching him.

My chest tightens. The sight is too tender, too raw and real.

The love between these two strangers is pouring off them in sovereign waves, and I'm about to drown.

When her smile widens as he leans in, I turn away, not wanting to steal any pieces from her. That's when I see Nate standing behind me, a soft, adoring smile on his face. But his eyes aren't on his parents; they're on me.

I turn back toward the kitchen, not understanding why, but needing nonetheless to try to experience such a passionate, unyielding love - if only ever by sight.

But when I turn, finding Mr. Monroe running his fingertips down his wife's temple, watching as he gently sweeps her dark hair behind her ear, all the blood in my body runs cold and I fly off the couch.

Nate sees it, the moment I'm about to bolt.

He's quick.

I don't get a step away before his hands are cupping my cheeks and he's kissing me, soft and slow. Slow and soft.

The muscles in my body start to warm, slowly releasing tension with each stroke of his tongue against mine, and suddenly I'm melting against him.

"Kids?"

We break apart when his mother calls out.

With a wink, Nate reaches for my hand, which I high five and walk past.

As soon as we come into view, a beautiful smile takes over his mother's face. She wipes her hands against her apron and steps in front of me.

"Hi, Lolli. It's nice to meet you," she beams.

And I smile back, a completely genuine smile I didn't know I had, not missing she called me Lolli, and not Kalani, as her son does.

"Nice to meet you, Mrs. Monroe."

"Oh, no..." She laughs and walks around the kitchen island. "Call me Sara." She pulls out several coffee mugs. "And this guy..." she hip-checks her husband as he sets some creamer down beside her, "is Ian. We'll expect nothing else."

"Alright," I laugh and hop up onto the bar stool across from where they stand. As soon as my butt hits the stool, the name clicks and I gape at Mr. Monroe.

"Ian Monroe?" I raise an eyebrow and Nate chuckles beside me.

"Uh-huh." His dad narrows his eyes in a playful challenge, one I'm betting he thinks I'll fall flat on. He's so wrong.

"Wow." My eyes widen. "Two-time College Bowl MVP." I nod my head, impressed by the memory. "You still hold the record for the most sacks in a college championship game."

With a shake of my head, I laugh, continuing, "That last sack, when you made Henry Michaels fumble the ball and Tommy Brown picked it up, running it back for a game-winning defensive touchdown...that's movie shit right there."

"You a stats girl?" Ian tilts his head, gauging me.

"I'm a defense girl." I shrug. "And I remember the good stuff. Store it in my brain for times like these," I tell him, tapping my head with my pointer finger.

His dad grins from ear to ear, his chest puffing out slightly.

"Oh, holy hell..." Sara mutters. "She's perfect."

My eyes fly to her and her stunned face slowly transforms into a big, bright smile that radiates through her eyes.

Nate leans over and kisses my temple, a proud grin on his face.

I don't miss the quick glance both his parents throw his way as he does it.

"We heard you were a fan of the game, but that..." Sara laughs, handing me a mug.

"Fan doesn't quite cover it." I grin. "But yes, I love football."

"Why is that?" Mr. Monroe – Ian - quips, a smile tugging at his lips.

"Fans fade for hundreds of different reasons." I take a slow sip of my coffee, savoring the rich creaminess, all the while biding time.

"Me and football, we go way back. I was literally on the field in the womb." I laugh lightly, looking out the large window that overlooks the hillside. "Football's more a way of life than anything else, in my eyes anyway. I love the hot summer days and cool winter nights. The ambience of the crowd is enough to excite you sometimes, and the smell. But the dedication behind each player," I smile, "that's my favorite part. It's a controllable magic, driven by pure determination that most people take for granted." I shrug, facing forward again.

All three sets of eyes are on me, all wearing completely different expressions, each one overwhelming in their own way.

I clear my throat. "Well, all that and a bunch of muscles in tight wrapping," I joke, bumping Nate's shoulder.

Nate groans, Ian grins, and Sara throws her head back with a laugh.

Crisis averted.

"I bet that will be a treat come college, grown men in tight pants," Sara winks at me. "For you and me both."

"Not funny, woman," Ian scowls at his wife. Walking up behind her, he wraps his arms around her possessively and pulls her against him. She laughs, dropping her head back, allowing him to kiss her forehead, and Nate's arm chooses that moment to snake around me. I force myself to keep my breathing steady.

Sara smiles at me, her eyes dropping to Nate's hand around my body, catching his fingertips brushing up and down my ribs, then back to mine with a newfound softness in them. "Would you stay for dinner?"

Before I can decline, because I was planning on it, both Nate and Ian answer for me. "She'll stay," Nate says, as Ian blurts out, "'Course she will."

My mouth drops open, and I look to Sara, who's laughing lightly. "How the hell do you survive with two Alphas in one pack?"

She steps away from her husband, placing an oven mitt over her right hand. "I had Kenra to help me balance 'em out." She pulls a heavenly smelling dish from the oven. "Now I'm outnumbered and losing my mind." She laughs, smacking Ian's hand when he tries to pick an olive off the top of the cheesy concoction.

"Just so we're clear," Ian raises an eyebrow. "I am the Alpha."

"Got it." I hide my smile while Nate rolls his eyes.

A few minutes later, we're sitting around a picnic-style kitchen table, eating Nate's mom's 'Chicken Enchilada Pie'.

"So," Sara begins, and my mind starts screaming, telling me it's time to bow out, but I force a welcoming smile instead, "you have a very beautiful name."

"Thank you." I cut a glance at Nate, unsure of what to do here. I don't want to be rude, but I'm not so sure I can get through a 'let's get to know you' conversation, as simple as it may be.

His eyes lock on mine, and he brushes his thigh against me, somehow easing my mind in the process. When a deep breath leaves me, he drops his head, grinning into his plate as he goes in for a bite.

Shithead.

"Um," I clear my throat, turning back to Sara. "My parents spent a lot of their time in Hawaii. I guess, on their first trip back after finding out I was on the way, the first person to greet them off the plane was a beautiful woman with dark hair and light eyes named Kalani. They said it was a sign. The fact that I was born with dark hair and light eyes was somehow confirmation it was meant to be." I laugh lightly, stabbing a piece of chicken with my fork. "Of course, it had nothing to do with the fact that I look just like my mom. My parents were total hippies," I tell them, rolling my eyes, earning laughs all around.

"Do you not share that?" Sara tilts her head, her soft eyes shining in my direction. "Not believe in fate?" Her question is genuine, so I answer.

"Not really, no. That would mean that all the bad happens so, in the end, one good thing can. I don't see how so many negatives could ever be worth one positive."

"Sometimes the answers aren't so simple," Ian offers softly. "Sometimes we go through things we shouldn't so, in the end, we come out stronger."

"But are we?" I hold his gaze. "Stronger? Or are we so broken that at the first sign of 'good', we latch on in hopes to forget the bad? To erase it as if that makes it any better? That's not being strong, that's confirming you're weak."

"It's called healing, Lolli, not forgetting. Not erasing. There's always an up after a down," he says quietly, and Nate squeezes my thigh under the table. "It just takes some of us a little longer to find it, that's all."

Aaand bonding time is over.

I laugh it off. This is just a conversation, right?

So why do I want to scream?

With a polite smile, I stand, and nod at both Ian and Sara. "Thank you for dinner and everything today, but I should go." I turn to Nate. "I'll call Parker and wait outside for him."

Nate's eyes narrow and I can see he's about to argue, so I narrow mine in return, sending him a silent message.

You really want to do this right here, right now?

He knows exactly what I just thought, and he doesn't give a shit.

His sexy, troublemaking, panty-wetting smirk takes over his

handsome face, and he stands to tower over me, forcing my head to lift.

"I'm taking you. Give me five minutes. I'll meet you out front," he tells me, before spinning and leaving me standing there.

Stubborn, sexy bastard.

Ian's roar of laughter has my head swinging in his direction. I glance at Sara and find her trying to hold back her snickers.

"My internal monologue doesn't seem to work when it comes to him."

Sara grins, placing her hand over Ian's. "I have the same problem."

Right.

I go to lift my plate from the table.

"Please," Sara's hand comes out, her smile only growing, "leave it."

I wave at Ian, who's still wiping tears from his eyes and head for the door.

Once I step onto the porch, my feet carry me to the swing. Running my fingertips over the blanket, I smile, dropping myself down slowly. The moment my eyes close, I hear footsteps, and they open again to find Ian standing before me.

"Care for a swing?" he asks, raising an eyebrow.

I don't much feel like sharing this place with Nate's dad, but it's his house, and his and his wife's swing, after all. "Sure." I incline my head and pat the seat next to me.

He gives a few pushes before speaking. "About two years ago, I was on a business trip in California." Shit. "I ran into an old friend from college while I was there," he says softly and my body grows tense. "He played for the Tomahawks, my friend."

"He must have been a good football player," I respond, not looking at him.

I see him nod in my peripheral. "He sure was. His coach told him he was a Ferrari with nitrous - inconceivable and priceless."

I bust up laughing, a breaking feeling hitting my chest at the same time, because those words are to a T. "Arthur Miller, running back. First round draft pick."

Ian nods. "Arthur Miller. He was on his way to his coach, or former coach turned owner's, funeral the day I saw him."

I nod, my eyes searching for imperfections in the wood grains on the porch ceiling.

"He doesn't realize, does he?"

"I'm no liar, Mr. Monroe." I purposely go with his last name. "If he ever asked, I'd tell him, but it's completely unnecessary and insignificant. I don't like people knowing about my life because it's my business. I've shared things with him I haven't shared with anyone – not that that's your business - but some things aren't factors in who I am, and that's one of them." I shrug. "So, I now own half of a professional football team. So, my grandfather has two Super Bowl rings and was inducted into the Hall of Fame. Who cares that my parents owned and operated the number one sports photography company in the country? While those things are awesome, they're mine."

He's quiet for a minute or two, before he turns to me.

I meet his stare head on.

"You're right, Lolli." His eyes soften as he nods, but it's quickly replaced with a huge grin. "I like you," he says, making all the tension roll off me and a laugh escape.

"Five minutes, Dad, and you're already hitting on my girl?" Nate walks up with a bag of what I'm assuming are my wet clothes in his hand.

Ian relaxes against the wood, laying his arm across the back of the swing. "Your girl, huh?" He bumps my shoulder and I roll my eyes.

"He keeps saying that," I grumble, making both the heaven-sent, handsome, freaks of nature laugh.

"You are my girl." Nate grins.

"No, I'm not. I'm my own girl." I jump up, frowning. "Take my ass home."

Ian, who is laughing his ass off, yells out, "Night, Lolli. Come back soon."

I don't bother turning around, but wave over my head and walk down to the last step, freezing there when I realize I have no shoes on and there's a huge puddle at the bottom.

Nate notices and jogs over to me with an electric smile, thrusting his arms out.

"You really want me to jump into your arms with your dad watching?"

He nods, his grin growing, and I can't help but laugh.

I place my hands on his shoulders and he gently lifts me off the ground, my legs wrapping around him for support. I bury my face in his neck so his dad doesn't see the jolt of lust that has instantly taken over me. My body better get a grip and quick, because this shit's ridiculous.

When I'm set gently into the seat, a soft kiss placed to my forehead, I have the strangest, most unwelcome, foolish thought. A girl could get used to this.

A few hours later, after tons of snacks and nonsense, Nate starts to rub at his eyes.

"Alright." He throws down his cards and drops onto his back against the carpet. "You win. I quit." He throws an arm over his face.

I uncross my legs and sit back onto my knees. "How convenient of you to concede when I'm seconds away from 'Uno'."

"Any other girl would let me win." Angling his head toward me, he offers me a bemused smile.

I laugh, popping a Skittle in my mouth. "That's because they have an ulterior motive."

He grabs my hand and pulls me on top of him.

Laughing harder, I peer down at him as he absentmindedly runs his fingers through the tips of my hair.

"And you don't?" he stares at me.

"All I want," I lick my lips and watch his eyes dilate, "is to win." I smile and start to pull back, but he's quicker, and rolls us until my back is against the carpet and he's hovering over me.

He plays with my hair some more, while looking into my eyes. "What are you doing tomorrow?"

"None of your business." I grin, placing my hands on each side of his ribs.

"You're still meeting us at Wicker for lunch, right?"

Right, lunch. Parker and Mia mentioned it.

I nod.

He smiles, his hand sliding across my cheek to tuck my hair behind my ear as he tends to do, only this time, he holds steady. The gentle caress of his fingers behind my ear has me leaning into his embrace.

His eyes raid mine as he flattens his palm against my cheek.

There's something in them. Something flowing through him, radiating off him, that he's trying to show me or wants me to catch, that I can't quite reach. His deep brown eyes hold a promise that I can't figure out, and I don't dare ask.

And when he lowers his head to kiss me, gentle and slow, a crack between my breasts has me gasping, followed by a tightness in my ribs I don't quite understand.

He pulls back, kissing my forehead gently, before jumping to his feet. I take his extended hand and allow him to pull me off the floor.

"I'll pick you up at noon."

I nod.

He walks out the front door. "Goodnight, Kalani."

As soon as I hear him pull out of the drive, I throw on some sweats and my running shoes, and walk outside, not bothering to grab a sweater, my phone, or lock the house. Sure, it's past midnight, but what do I care?

My brain is on overdrive and I need to shut shit down.

I run until the only thing on my mind is the pain in my calves and feet.

Until my limbs are physically incapable of carrying me any further.

Until I'm numb.

Chapter Twenty-Four

K ALANI

"You're seriously dragging ass today, Lolli. And you could have at least brushed your damn hair." Mia links arms with me and drags me alongside her.

"I did brush my hair, and my teeth, for that matter. This," I point to the tangled ball on top of my head, yawning, "is a strategically placed knot. It's called a messy bun for a reason."

"And the sunglasses that cover half your face," she deadpans. "What are those, a fashion statement?" I can hear her eyeroll.

"Nailed it, you did."

She huffs.

"What's up, girls?" The boys all greet us as we reach the table.

I give a half-ass wave while Mia smiles.

"Sorry we're late." Mia literally pushes me into a chair.

"Bitch," I mumble, dropping my head onto my folded arms on the table.

"Rough night, Lolli?" Austin laughs.

I lift my finger and flip him off.

"Uh, yeah." Mia snaps. "I went to her house to sleep off my buzz last night and this bitch," Mia explains, "didn't walk through the door until, what?"

Assuming she's looking at me, I lift a shoulder in a shrug. "Three-thirty-ish, give or take."

My head is in my arms, so I can't be sure, but while the other boys laugh, one chair scratches the floor and heavy footsteps carry someone away. My guess is it's Nate.

I texted him when I hit snooze for the first time today, telling him I'd meet everyone here. My plan was to ditch, but of course, Mia figured as much and dragged my ass out anyway.

"Uh-oh," Austin teases. "I'm gonna take a guess here, Lolli, and say you weren't with Nate last night?"

I throw myself back in the chair and lean lazily, knowing what's coming. We've all fought about it a few times in the last couple weeks. "I went running."

"What?!" Parker yells.

"Lolli!" Mia screams.

And I'm done.

Now it's my chair scraping across the floor.

"Check it out," I begin, my black long-sleeve hanging over my pointed hand. "I'm a big fucking girl." I glare at each of them, then remember my glasses are covering my eyes. Rolling my eyes at myself, I continue, "I don't want to hear shit from you guys. In case you haven't already guessed, I don't give a shit. I do what I want when I want. Period."

Mia's eyes soften and Parker gets up to walk around the table but I put my hand out, stopping him. "I get it. It's hard on my body, it's not safe to run alone at night, blah, blah, blah. But maybe you guys should stop and think that maybe it would be worse if I didn't."

"You always go running after you've spent time with Nate." Mia's voice turns accusatory.

"And?" I ask, not bothering to deny it, but pissed she'd blast my dirty laundry in front of everyone. "Sometimes I gotta shut it down."

"Why?" A strong, yet vulnerable voice says from behind me, and my body tenses slightly.

I turn to Nate and shrug. "Because..."

Fuck.

I shrug again.

He shakes his head back and forth, not allowing my answer.

"Fine, you want to know why?" My head pulls back slightly, while my eyebrows jump out from under my shades. "It's because this," I motion between the two of us, "is supposed to be careless, and easy, and fun...and sometimes it's... not." I look away, even though he can't see my eyes.

I know he gets my underlying message.

Sometimes it's more.

"And that's a bad thing?" he questions, his voice calm and even.

"Yes!" Exasperated, I lift my hand, bringing it down against my leg. "You're supposed to be the fun guy, just looking to pass the time, but that's not who you're being at all." I stomp my foot like a child. "You're my paramour."

"Problem with that, Lolli," Austin pipes in. "He ain't married."

I prop my hands on my hips and cut him a pissy glance over my shoulder. "Yeah, well. He isn't mine, either."

Nate steps into my space, forcing my eyes back to his. "Maybe I want to be."

"Want to be what?"

"Yours." He tips his chin.

I gasp and stumble back a step, but he catches me. I hear an "oh shit," a "no fucking way," and a laugh from the three stooges behind me, but my gaze is locked on Nate's chest and refusing to look up at him.

Clearly, he senses it because he bends at the knees and sweeps me into his arms, before carrying me outside.

Neither of us say anything as he puts me in his truck, orders pizza, and drives to pick it up. We don't speak when he gets out to pay, nor on the way to my house. Not when I open the door and we shuffle in, nor when we sit and eat. Not even when I stand and grab his hand, leading him into my room.

I take off my glasses and sandals while Nate empties his pockets and kicks off his shoes. I pull the covers back as he turns on the music, then we climb into my bed.

He tucks me into the crook of his arm and I lay my head on his chest and we watch Bad News Bears.

When the movie's over, Nate kisses my head, and goes home.

I kind of hate he knows what to do and when to do it.

Then again, I kind of don't.

Chapter Twenty-Five

K ALANI

The school is buzzing. Everyone, even those who've probably never even seen a football, teachers included, have Championship fever, and are decked out in their school spirit gear.

Three years in a row, Nate has helped carry this team to the state Championships and came out on top - that's golden.

I'm stuffing my English book into my locker when it's suddenly slammed shut, almost hitting my hand in the process. Whipping around, I come face to face with a smirking Olivia.

"You better back up a couple inches or I'm gonna help you."

She lets out a sadistic laugh, but complies, turning to lean her shoulder against the locker to the left of mine.

"You finally gave it up, huh?" She raises an eyebrow.

"Why are you asking a question you clearly know the answer to?"

"Confirmation." Her head jerks, eyes narrowing.

"Sure, Liv. You want to know?" I cut her a quick glance, reopening my locker. "Yeah, we fucked." Several times now.

She surprises me with her response. "It's about fucking time."

When I laugh, she stands to her full height.

"I didn't realize you were waiting for it."

"Of course, I was." She crosses her arms like a prissy bitch. "You're off the radar now."

Ahh...okay. I get it now.

"Right." I close my locker and lean against it, holding my Chem book against my chest. "The one hit wonder rule. I almost forgot." I smirk at her.

The way she keeps adjusting her arms and glancing away, it's clear she's not sure how to read me.

"You still plan on entertaining him?" she spits out.

I grin. "Now, how could I do that if my lucky number's already come up?"

She grins this time. "Didn't you know, Lolli?" She says my name with a venomous tone. "He only fucks once." She flops her blonde hair behind her. "I've pleased him several times in other ways. Most of them while sitting in that pretty little truck of his." She looks so smug.

"Awe," I coo and her head jerks back. "A hummer in the Hummer, Olivia?" I laugh, nodding my head in fake approval. "Very original."

"Listen, bitch-" she starts, but I cut her off.

"No." I lower my book. "You listen, bitch. I don't normally waste my time on chicks like you," I scrunch my nose. "You know, the ones desperate and self-absorbed, looking to latch onto something bigger and better, out of fear of being left behind or forgotten after your reign here in high school is over." I nod. "But I'm sick of your shit." I step into her space.

Again, she surprises me and holds her ground.

"I'll do whatever, whoever, whenever, where-the-fuck-ever I want, and no threat or warning, or anything else, from you or anyone, is going to stop me." I give her a little shove for good measure. "So back the fuck off!"

The cunt laughs.

Right then, my body tightens and relaxes at the same time.

My eyes dart over Liv's shoulder, finding his immediately. Nate is walking down the hall - headed straight for me.

Her back is to him, so she doesn't know he's coming - doesn't sense him the way I can. I try to keep my eyes on her so I don't give it away, but they refuse to listen, and keep shifting to him as she rambles on about some kind of nonsense I couldn't give two shits about.

I swear, he must define the term 'beauty sleep' because every day this guy gets more and more pretty to look at.

He winks at me and heat spreads up my neck so I quickly focus back on Liv.

Thank God I added the scarf this morning.

"Don't worry, Lolli. Now that Nate's done with you," she looks me up and down, pursing her lips, "I won't be wasting any more time on you."

I simply nod, attempting to hide my grin as Nate steps up next to us.

"Lookin' out for me, Liv?" he asks in a playful manner, but I see the mischief in his eyes.

She shifts, placing her slimy hand on his left bicep, and my eyes are frozen to where her skin is touching his.

"Always, Nate."

Bitch.

I catch her smirk before my eyes drop again.

Why is she still touching him?

"Thank you," he says in a low, computed tone and I think she might faint. "Class is about to start," he continues, not taking his eyes off hers.

"Yeah," she breathes, tilting her head and that skeezy hand starts to slide down his arm, making its way toward his hand.

His eyes still on her, he holds his hand out for me. In one swift movement, he pulls me in front of him, wraps his massive arms around me, and drops his chin to my shoulder.

Liv's brows jump as her eyes widen.

"Better get a move on, Olivia. Don't want to ruin your perfect record or anything," he tells her coldly.

She stares at his arm around my waist. When her eyes finally come back to mine, she glares and stomps off.

Nate laughs, spins me in his arms and slides his hands into my back pockets. "That was fun."

I laugh too, glancing at Liv's retreating figure. "I wouldn't be surprised if she has a shrine of you on her wall."

He nods, not at all listening to me, his eyes zeroing in on my mouth as he licks across his bottom lip, from one corner of his mouth to the other. My traitorous body shudders in his arms, from a damn look, making him chuckle lightly.

I pull away from him to head to Chem. "Class, Handsome."

When I hear him laugh, I lift my finger over my head and I flip him off. His laughter only grows.

It's deep and rich, and my hand flies to my chest bone, attempting to soothe the sudden pang. I try massaging it with my fingertips, but the pressure-like feeling doesn't dissipate.

My skin starts to heat as I continue forward, Nate hot on my heels.

I glance at him over my shoulder, earning a wink and a genuine smile. No teasing. No added sex appeal. Just a simple, easy smile directed right at me - hitting hard.

Facing forward, my brows pull in and my steps falter. Before I can stop it, I trip over my boot. Right as I prepare myself for the hit, a solid arm wraps around my middle and pulls me in tight. The impact of my back hitting his chest causes my head to fall back slightly, leaving my neck semi-exposed.

Nate dips his head, caressing my skin with his soft words. "You didn't think I'd let you fall, did you?" he whispers.

I peer up at him and my cheeks starts to heat as moisture forms above my brows.

He holds my gaze for a moment before stepping back and squeezing by me to enter the classroom. As he passes, his lips skim my temple. It's a small, probably unnoticeable, move. Simple, stupid, and maybe even by accident, but I feel it in my toes. A tingling, heated sensation spreads through me, warming more than just my core.

My body roots itself in place.

What the hell is happening to me?

He turns back to me, his tousled hair perfect, those dark eyes open and bright, happy. "You coming?" He smiles. The gentle one that turns his features soft and tender, and I'm officially about to freak.

"I, uh, I think I need some air." I go to turn, but his voice wraps around me, holding me, before my feet move.

"Kalani..."

Ever so slowly, I raise my gaze back to his.

His eyes are amazing. They're not the deep espresso color they normally are when he's looking at me. They're lighter. More milk chocolate than dark.

He gives me a subtle nod, asking me not to go...not to freak out, and I have no idea what to make of it. No idea how he always seems to know when I'm on the verge of running, metaphorically speaking. I think.

He does that a lot. Reads me, speaks to me without words, like he can see all the things others can't. Or maybe, when I'm near him, the clear, bullet-proof glass window that shields me from all prying eyes, opens.

That's fucking ridiculous.

Completely out of my element, I pull a classic Kalani move; roll my eyes to cover my discomfort, walk past him to take my seat, and refuse to think about it.

Of course, he had to go and make it worse by giving me the

space I needed to chill out, choosing a desk a few spaces away, further proving me right when I kind of wanted to be wrong – Nate understands what I need.

Clever bastard.

As the day goes on, I avoid eye contact with everyone, ignore when my name is called in the halls, and skip out on lunch –God knows how that would have gone.

When PE rolls around, I'm thankful for the reprieve.

The first one on the field, I skip stretches altogether, which of course means I'm able to skip any real interaction. But halfway through my run, I feel him fall in place behind me where he stays the remainder of the class period. It's equally agitating as it is calming, and I'm not sure what annoys me more.

When the longest day ever finally comes to an end, I'm beyond grateful practice is no more.

I kick the door shut behind me, drop my bag, and walk to my room. Throwing my hair up, I strip my bed bare, and head for the garage. Adding two detergent pods, just to be safe, I shove my Nate-infused duvet cover, sheets, and pillowcases into the wash.

I skip homework, skip a shower, skip dinner. I'm not even sure if I fed Nauni. All I know is my body is heavy and my mind is done.

Laying on the couch with a throw blanket, I smile when I feel sleep take over and everything begins to fade away.

Chapter Twenty-Six

K ALANI

"So, what are we doing over break?" Mia asks, as she swipes lip gloss over her lips.

I shrug, holding the door open for her. "I'm not sure. I was thinking about heading out."

"Yeah?" She cuts a weary glance at me.

I nod and stop next at her locker so she can swap out books.

"Anywhere specific?" she asks, her eyes focused on putting in her combination code.

"Mia..." I tilt my head and wait.

Her shoulders drop, and she releases a deep sigh before turning to me.

"I just need a good old-fashioned drive. Clear my head a bit. Maybe visit the stadium, I don't really know yet." I shrug, giving her a reassuring smile.

She chews the inside of her cheek, but nods in understanding. "So, all's good?" she asks, squinting.

"Peachy." I wink.

"Good," she smirks, shifting to lean against her locker, and jerks her chin. "'Cause it looks like someone's coming for you, Lolls."

"Trust me, Meems..." I turn, my eyes scanning over Nate's approaching body. "He always comes for me."

I glance back at her and we both start busting up laughing.

"What's so funny, ladies?" Austin asks as he, Parker, and Nate step up next to us.

She takes a deep breath and stands, red-faced. "Lolli was just telling me she has no issues pleasing a man." She just gets the last word out before we're cracking up again.

Austin and Parker laugh while Nate groans.

I glance at him, dabbing the corners of my eye with my sleeve.

He raises a dark eyebrow in question.

When I give him nothing but an all teeth smile, he crowds my space and backs me against the locker, his eyes narrowing in on me.

Too bad for him it's more on the sexy side than it is scary or intimidating.

"You do realize I like you like this, right?" I run my tongue over my teeth playfully.

"Like what?" His dark eyes drop to my lips, leading him to lick his own.

I kick off the locker so I'm flush against him, craning my neck to look in his eyes. "All demanding and tough guy." I lower my voice. "It's quite sexy."

One side of his mouth lifts. "I'm always like that."

"Then maybe I always like you..." I tease with a grin.

"You do."

"Yeah?" I raise an eyebrow, semi-surprised by his resolute tone.

"Yep."

"You guys are like the script before the sex in a porno, only better."

All our gazes fly to Mia, who shrugs. "What? You two are hot as hell just standing next to each other." She flails her hands around. "Add in Nate's sexy voice and Lolli's smooth, sultry rasp, you got a real wet money maker."

"You are so bizarre," Austin grins, bending to kiss her hair. "I like it."

"I gotta talk to Mr. Blan before class, I'll catch you guys later." Parker gives us a wave and walks off.

Nate turns back to me, looking a little hesitant and maybe... nervous? Which is strange for the Alpha.

"Talk to me, Handsome," Grinning, I grab ahold of the sides of his letterman jacket, swaying slightly.

He nods, standing tall. "The dance is on Saturday."

My brows pinch. "Uh-huh...?"

"Go with me."

"Why?" A laugh bubbles out of me.

"Because I want you to." The way his steady gaze is anchoring mine has me swallowing hard and unable to look away.

I nod lightly. "Okay."

He tips his chin down, his eyes flicking back and forth between mine. "Okay?"

"Yeah."

"Yeah?" He grins and it's so adorable, I have to reach out and touch him.

"Yeah, Handsome." I keep my eyes locked on his. "I'll go with you."

The smile that spreads across his face is the best I've seen yet, and equally infectious.

He nods several times, clearing his throat in an attempt to play it cool, but it doesn't work and he smiles wide again. He begins walking away, but stops, looks back at me for a long moment, takes a few backward steps, then walks off with more swagger than usual in his sexy strut.

"Did he-" Mia points after him.

"Yep." Austin laughs and walks off.

Her brows jump. "Wow. Okay." Then she turns to me and a grin takes over. "Bitch, we're going shopping!"

I laugh and head toward my locker, unable to wipe the smile off my face, ignoring the fluttering going on in my stomach.

On my bed, I cross my legs Indian-style and hand Nate a set of chopsticks.

"You're really gonna make me use these?" he groans, moving his fingers like some kind of alligator chomp.

I laugh, dropping a noodle into my mouth. "Uh-huh...no chopsticks, no Chinese food. It's a law."

"Where?" he scoffs. "China?"

I shrug, smiling and he pushes my shoulder playfully.

"Fine, but if I get shit all over your bed, you can't be mad at me."

"Deal."

He sighs and does his best to eat, only succeeding in getting a noodle or single piece of meat at a time.

"So, you went shopping with Mia after school today?"

I nod, taking a quick drink of my Dr. Pepper. "I did. Dress, shoes, check."

His brows jump, and he gives me a dumbfounded expression. "Really?"

"Yeah?"

"Don't girls normally, I don't know...cry and shit before they find the dress they want?"

"How do you know I didn't cry?"

When all he does is raise a brow, I start laughing.

"When are you gonna realize, Nathaniel?" I grin, taking a bite of my egg roll.

"Realize what?" The single piece of meat he managed to pick up slips from his utensils and he scowls down at our takeout.

My bottom lip pokes out as I shift onto my knees. Grabbing a decent size bite with my own chopsticks and hold it out for him, dropping it into his mouth as he stares at me.

"I'm not like most girls. I found one I liked. It fit. I bought it." I shrug and sit back on my heels. "It doesn't have to be complicated."

He nods, his eyes roaming my face as he chews.

The previews end, so I reach over and press play on the DVD.

"So, what are we watching?" he asks, turning back to his food.

I twist my shoulders back and forth, winking at him. "Switching things up a bit."

"You gonna tell me or do I have to guess?"

Straightening my spine, I give him my best Jafar voice. "Patience, Iago."

He puts food in his mouth to cover his grin and turns to the TV right when the opening credits begin. With a groan, he throws himself back on the bed, shielding his eyes with his right arm while I laugh at him, and move the food to the floor.

"Don't do this to me," he whines.

"You know what they say..." I sing song, dropping next to him. "Life is like a box of chock-o-lits-" I'm cut off when Nate reaches over, quickly pulling me onto his chest.

Laughing, I let my forehead fall against his pecs.

He's quiet for a few minutes before his fingertips start running up and down my forearms. I lift my head, resting my chin on my hands to look up at him.

"I learned a long time ago, by the way," he tells me, his gaze dropping to my mouth as he lazily runs his middle finger over my bottom lip.

When my brows pull in slightly, he continues. "That you were different." His eyes come back to mine. "Rare. Better."

I let out a shaky breath, unable to comprehend what's going on with my body. While my chest seems to relax more into his, my pulse starts to race, and my face pinches. When I try to push off him, his hands wrap around my lower back, holding me in place.

We lay there, unmoving, for a few minutes. His eyes burn into the top of my head while I face the wall, unable to look at him, and irritated because I can't figure out why. Once he's confident I won't move, he starts to massage me.

His hands make their way under my shirt. Lying his palms against my skin, he inches them to my shoulders, the pressure becoming firmer on their descend.

The second time they slide up, he unclasps my bra, and rubs back down, and this time, rough palms slide over my ass. The pads of his fingers lightly scratch where my skin meets my spandex shorts, sending a shiver down my spine, but his hands don't stop there.

His grip finds the back of my thighs, those rough hands sliding down to pull my legs up over his, my knees on either side of him.

I squirm a little and feel him start to swell underneath me.

Nate's right hand grips my chin, forcing me to look at him.

His dark eyes roam my face, reveling in what his simple touch does to me.

I'm hot all over, and the only thing on my mind now is the feeling of his skin against mine.

I push off his chest, pulling my shirt over my head. Allowing my bra to slide down my arms, I toss it to the side. When I tug on the end of his shirt, he lifts just enough to tug it off, then drops back on the pillow.

My eyes on his, I lean down, kissing his chest lightly. His breathing turns heavy, his chest rising and falling rapidly under my hands.

His right-hand slides into my hair, pulling my lips to his.

"You want me," he whispers against my mouth.

He's not asking, but I answer with a nod anyway. Pressing my lips into his, I kiss him hard and deep.

His left hand grips my ass, pushing my body down, grinding me into him.

When a deep moan leaves me, he reaches for the side table, grabbing a condom from his wallet.

I sit back and pull his shorts and briefs down to his knees, then scoot back up.

Taking his dick in my palm, I run my hand up the length of him, then back down, grinning when his leg twitches beneath me.

Staring at him, hard and ready, my mouth starts to water. My eyes slice to Nate's.

His heavy lids drop to my exposed chest then back to my face. He shakes his head. "Not tonight. I want inside you," he rasps, taking the condom from my free hand.

I nod and stand above him, pulling my shorts off.

"Leave the panties on."

"On?"

He rolls the condom on, nodding.

I drop back down, once again straddling him. He pulls my hands until I'm leaning over him, my hard nipples brushing his chest, our hands behind his head.

His fingers abandon mine to skim down the length of my arm, following the shape of my body until he reaches the hem of my underwear. He reaches between my legs with one hand, pushing them to the side, and runs his fingers over me, feeling how wet and ready I am for him, before positioning himself, then slowly guiding me down. His eyes close.

It doesn't take long for us to lose it, our moans blending together in satisfaction.

I drop to his chest and his hands fall to our sides.

Once our breathing has slowed, he kisses my head and I lift off of him, throwing myself on the bed beside him. He rolls up the condom and drops it next to the bed.

"Well," he begins, still out of breath, his eyes on the TV screen. "If I'm ever forced to watch this movie again, I don't think I'll complain."

"Yeah?" I laugh, turning to look at him with a brow raised. "What'll you tell your parents when you're suddenly sporting wood while watching Forrest Gump?"

His brows pinch. "Yeah, didn't think about that." He looks over at me, grinning. "But I'll watch it with you anytime if it starts out the same."

With a playful eyeroll, I stand and drop my ruined undies, pulling a San Diego State t-shirt over my head.

He eyes it curiously. "California, huh?"

I nod and turn to my dresser, setting some clothes for tomorrow on top.

"Is that where you want to go to college?"

I laugh with little humor. "No, Handsome. I'm not going to college there." I crawl back onto the bed, lying on my side to face him.

He pulls his shorts up without standing. "Where do you want to go?"

"I'm not going to college."

His brows jump. "Seriously?"

"Yep."

"Why?"

"I have other plans. Responsibilities," I tell him, hoping he'll drop it.

He doesn't.

"Is it because..." he swallows, seemingly unsure. "You know... money?"

A laugh bubbles out of me, and I shake my head. "No, Nate. It's not about money."

He nods, but the pull in his brows tells me he's not sure if he believes me, which is fine.

"Do you want to go to college?"

"No."

"No?"

"No." Biting my lip, I decide to give him a bit more, "I did take some online business classes at the community college near my house last summer."

"Business classes?"

Lips pursed; I look at the wall behind him. "Um... yeah, just to help me understand decisions I had to make about some stuff after my parents and grandpa died. There weren't many available for a high school student, but I learned what I needed to." Picking at some invisible lint on my t-shirt, I aim for a subject shift. "Anyway, college isn't necessary for me, so why deal with the drama, stress of school, and grades, if I don't have to?"

He nods politely, but I can tell he's confused, and I can understand why.

Most kids - athletes especially - are drilled about the importance of college growing up. For athletes, it's the beginning of everything. A make-or-break experience only a select few have the opportunity to participate in. But for me, it was different growing up. Everything I did, all the places I went as kid, were passion driven. Even if it wasn't expected of me, if an empire hadn't landed in my lap, I would still choose to live that lifestyle. I couldn't imagine a better life than one that revolved around football and photos – and photos of football. It's in my blood and I'm happy with that. I don't think I necessarily want to be the one taking the pictures, but fully involved for sure.

When Nate's hand gently rubs across my cheek, I blink away my thoughts, grinning at him as he tucks my hair behind my ear.

Tonight, his brown eyes are softer than normal, brighter somehow, and I can't look away.

I have to admit, he's not what I expected him to be. While he's arrogant and conceited, he's also... more.

"What are you thinking?" he whispers, his thumb caressing my cheekbone with soft, feathery strokes.

"You should go," I tell him quietly, looking down at my comforter, avoiding the crestfallen, confused look he gives me every time I tell him to leave. "We have school tomorrow."

When he doesn't move, I peek at him through my lashes, allowing his eyes to flick back and forth between mine.

With a sigh, he pulls himself off the bed, bending to pick up our garbage. "Yeah, I guess you're right."

Once he reaches the door, he looks back at me over his shoulder.

"I'll see you tomorrow?"

"Yeah, Handsome. I'll see you tomorrow."

He smiles and walks out of my room. I hear him lock my door before shutting it, get into his truck, and drive away.

I pull out my camera from the bedside drawer, gently setting it on Nate's pillow.

It takes me hours to fall asleep.

Chapter Twenty-Seven

K ALANI

By the time Friday rolls around, everyone's bouncing about the halls. Some eager for Christmas break, others excited for tomorrow night's dance, and some - like me - just needing to get the heck out of dodge.

The dance will be fun, I know that. Hangin' out with my friends always seems to be. But I'm tired. Maybe a bit anxious.

My mind seems a little overworked and I'm not sure I'm okay with that.

I really need a break from, well, everything.

I mean, I have spent the better part of four years virtually alone, which I didn't necessarily mind. I like being independent, making my own decisions. Shit, even as a little kid, I was on my own more often than not, what, with my parents' crazy schedules and our constant traveling, following the Tomahawks from state to state. While I loved it, enjoying all the things I got to see and experience, it wasn't exactly what most people would call a healthy lifestyle for a child.

My parents weren't there for moments like when I first learned how to swing or when I chipped my front tooth learning how to skate. I didn't ask my dad before going out with a boy and I didn't call my mom when I thought my heart got broken because of him.

We did, however, go to countless games and events; tasted the difference in southern versus city foods together. I loved them and they loved me, so we were good. Our life made sense to us, and it worked. Throw in my grandpa as much as he was able, and life was fun. Our own normal.

The shrinks I was forced to see when my aunt tried to have my emancipation revoked by the courts didn't agree. They said something about it teaching a child that emotional connections are of non-value and perceived to be a negative element in our lives rather than a positive. I understood their theory, but for me, having lived that particular lifestyle made the last two years simpler. Bearable.

Had I been raised in a home where we sat around talking about the ups and downs of our day, ending with a bedtime story and a kiss goodnight, I don't think I'd be standing today, let alone breathing.

While I was used to being alone, these last two years have been very different. I not only flew completely solo, but I was freely numb and taken at face value. Nothing more, nothing less. Just...existing.

Eat, sleep, run, repeat.

So, yeah, these past two months have been a little draining on my body, on me. I've been running more than normal, longer. Harder. And my body is feeling the repercussions of it.

This whole 'school and friends' thing is exhausting.

Add Nate to the mix, and...

I'm just not quite sure how to process all the things happening around me - within me. I've been a shell of a person for so long now that this stimulation, mind and body, is fucking hard to process.

To say my brain is ready to crash is an understatement.

"Lolli Bear," I hear Parker shout from the left of the parking lot, turning to search the masses for my blond-haired, blue-eyed friend.

"What's up, Hero?" I smile at him as he approaches, hugging him back when he reaches for me.

"Nothing," he says, releasing me with one arm, draping his other across my shoulder, steering me in the opposite direction of Mia's Jeep, aka my ride.

"Hang out with me today. I miss you." He squeezes my shoulder.

I wrap my hand around his waist. "It just so happens I have no plans till later." I smile up at him. "Whatcha got in mind?"

"Pizza and arcade games sound good? That way we can still make the party tonight."

"Sounds fantastic, but you'll have to take me home to change before the party, yeah?"

He opens the door to his truck for me. "Anything for you, Lolli Bear." He winks and runs around the truck to the driver's side.

As we exit the parking lot, I send Mia a quick text, letting her know I'll see her at the party, then drop my phone in my backpack.

"Let's have some fun, Hero."

He grins, turning up the radio, and we sing along to Florida Georgia Line's "This is How We Roll."

After pissing away a good fifty bucks in coins, and two trips back to the buffet line, we're finally pulling up to my house.

"You coming in?"

"Yeah, I need to get cleaned up, too."

"You keep spare party clothes in your truck?" I tease, unlocking my door.

He grins, winking at me. "I had all this planned, Lolli Bear."

"I bet you did." I roll my eyes. "Should we have a shot before we change, then another before we head out? At least attempt to be on everyone else's level?" I laugh, heading into the kitchen.

"Hell yeah." He walks in behind me. "By the way, Nate's lookin' for you."

When I turn to him with an eyebrow raised, he waves his phone in the air.

"He texted you looking for me?" I ask, frowning at the shot glasses as I pour in the dark liquor.

"Nope," he laughs, taking his glass from my hand. "Mia texted me, asking if you were with me because Nate texted her, asking if she knew where you were."

I gape at him.

He throws his head back, laughing.

"Seriously?"

Parker nods, then takes his shot and heads down the hall to get ready.

After taking mine, I fish my phone out of my bag, finding a missed call and text from both Nate and Mia.

Instead of reading through their messages, I simply open the thread and send them both the same response.

Me: getting ready. Be at party soon.

Thirty minutes and three shots later, Parker and I are walking up the driveway of Shawna's house.

"Drinks first?" he asks, holding his arm out for me to take once we've walked through the door.

"Yep, yep," I answer, glancing around. As usual, half the senior class is here, lettin' loose.

"Alright, Lolli Bear." Parker plants his feet in front of me, a can of Coke in one hand, shot in the other. "Open up." He wiggles his eyebrows.

Time to get the party started.

NATE

When Kalani didn't respond to my texts earlier, I was a little irritated, but I knew how she worked, and to push was to get pushed, so I figured I'd wait it out until it was about party time. But when she didn't answer my calls, I got a little pissed and figured she was trying to get out of the party she already agreed to come to. Not that I would have minded had she told me. I like having her to myself. Prefer it actually, even if it makes me sound like a pussy.

However, showing up at her house and her not being there threw me for a loop, and I decided I was pissed she didn't answer my calls or text. Pissed I didn't know where she was and pissed she didn't call me to tell me.

Then, when I tracked Mia down, who then tracked Parker down, finding out Kalani was with him, I went from pissed to fuckin' fumin'.

But leaning against the wall in the corner of Shawna's living room, watching her and Parker get ready to take shots together, standing far too fucking close for me, I'm about to lose my shit and rip someone's head off. Preferably Parker's.

I've never been jealous in my life, never cared what a girl did when I wasn't with her, but Kalani has a way of bringing out a few different sides of myself I knew nothing about - like the side that wants to physically disfigure one of his own friends.

If I wasn't so curious and admittedly a bit paranoid about how their interaction was going to play out, I'd be standing in front of her already, kissing her, if I had my way. Guess I'm an asshole because my eyes won't allow my body to move, too desperate to watch.

Parker's standing directly in front of her. Whatever he's saying has her covering her mouth with her fingers, bending slightly as she laughs. The move makes her fitted white long-sleeved shirt rise a bit, giving me, and everyone else, a tiny view of her soft, creamy skin underneath.

I can tell they've already had a few drinks. Obviously before they showed up here.

Together.

I groan and cross my arms in front of me, my eyes narrowing further.

When Parker holds her shot glass up, a Coke in his opposite hand, I almost kick off the wall. No way in hell is he pouring that down her throat, watching as her exposed neck swallows the liquid.

But before I can move, Kalani shakes her head, grins at him, then pulls the shot from his raised hand.

"That's right motherfucker," I mutter to myself, smirking in their directions.

Only me.

My brows jump when that thought hits.

The more I think about why I'm pissed at her, the more I realize it's my own damn fault.

Of course, Kalani didn't care to call me to see what I was up to or tell me what she had planned, and I was a fool to assume she knew I was coming over. Or that I planned to pick her up. Or that I was who she was supposed to show up with. How would she know that's what I wanted - what I want - when I haven't told her?

Kalani is simple. While most girls would read into every encounter they have with me or any other guy and try to analyze it, Kalani takes it as it comes.

I need to let her know what's going on in my head. Find out what's going on in hers.

My shoulder is bumped from my right.

Reluctantly tearing my eyes off my girl and the asshole next to her, I look to find Austin next to me, empty beer in hand.

"Come on, I need another."

I glance back at Kalani, finding she's shifted a little further away from Parker.

With a smirk, I turn to Austin, "Lead the way, my man."

As we step into the garage, where the beer pong table is set up and the ice chests are lined against the wall, I freeze when I catch the eye of the blonde-headed devil who can't take no for an answer.

"Fuck," I curse under my breath, preparing to step back through the door.

Austin laughs, clasping my shoulder. "No point in retreating now," he whispers. "The chick's a hunter. Now that she knows you're here, she'll track your man scent."

"Let's make this quick."

"I do love a good quickie."

"Idiot." Laughing, I shove him away from me.

Right when we grab our beers, a few guys from the team walk in and start talking stats from last week's championship game. We drop back into the folding chairs sprawled around the room and get lost in conversation.

I'm not sure how much time has passed, but know it's been too long, when a bony ass drops into my lap.

My hands immediately lift midair and freeze there; clearly even they want nothing from this girl.

"Hi, Nate." Her warm beer breath washes over my face.

In attempt to avoid her stench, I turn my head. "Get off me, Olivia, before I move you off myself."

She wiggles on me, failing at her attempt to arouse me. "You'd have to touch me to move me, Nate," she whispers, wrapping her hands around my neck.

With her wrists in my grip, I fly off the chair, but the girl doesn't drop like I thought she would. Nope. She wraps her legs around my waist, pulling her body closer to mine.

Right then the garage door opens, and I look up finding Kalani and Parker walking in.

Parker's eyes are shifting back and forth between Kalani's and mine, while Kalani's eyes are on Olivia. To make it worse, Mia walks in behind her, followed by Ashley and Alyssa.

And I'm still frozen, standing in the middle of the room, with this broad's legs wrapped around me.

Fuck.

Kicking into action, I yank her hands off me, so she's left with no option but to drop her legs, then push her to the side.

I walk right up to Kalani, who shifts her gaze to me, smiling instantly.

"Hey, Handsome." She takes a step closer.

"That wasn't what it looked like," I rush out, pleading for her understanding. "I swear, I was sitting there talking to my buddies, and she sat on me. I stood up to push her off and that's when you walked in." I'm breathing so heavy I might pass out, but I don't care. I need her to believe what I'm saying. To trust me.

I take a deep breath and allow myself to search her eyes, finding they're shining with... humor?

The fuck?

When I scowl at her, she pats my chest and pushes past me, grabbing a beer for herself out of one of the ice chests.

"I'm serious," I tell her, glancing at each of our friends briefly, finding the same confusion I'm feeling on their uncertain faces.

"Okay," Kalani says, smiling, shifting her eyes to watch the beer pong game, and now I'm getting pissed all over again.

"Wait." I hold my hands out, squeezing my eyes shut for a few seconds, so I don't go completely off the fucking wall and make an ass out of myself. "So, you're not upset you came in here and found Olivia wrapped around me?"

Kalani's beer freezes at her lips, her eyes bouncing to the wall then back to me. "No?" Her nose scrunches.

I drop my hands and stand straight. "You're serious?" I ask her, my voice laced with irritation.

"Uh," she blinks at me. "Are you serious? 'Cause I have no idea what's happening right now."

This fucking girl, who has me twisted in knots, walks in to find some chick straddling my waist, and she doesn't bat a fucking eyelash?

I step toward her, blood boiling. "Do you have any idea what it does to me when I see another guy even look at you?" I growl, desperate for her to hear me. "Or when Parker-" cut myself off, shaking my head at her slack-jawed expression and try again.

"Put you and any other guy in any possible equation," I raise both my brows, "and it all ends the same for me. Jealous as fuck. No matter what you're doing. Talking, walking, fucking sitting next to each other without even looking in each other's direction, and I fucking see red, Kalani."

She looks at our friends, who are trying, and failing, to act like they're not listening to everything we're saying.

"Wait." She jerks her head back a few inches, her long dark hair bouncing with the movement. "Are you seriously mad at me for not being mad at you about something that's none of my business?"

Not her business?

Not her fucking business?

What kills me is her blue eyes are telling me she believes that statement; that what I do is my business, and she has no say or right to care.

At a complete loss, I shake my head.

"Forget it," I mumble and storm out the side door leading to the front yard, hearing her ask the onlookers, "What just happened?" as I slam the door shut.

KALANI

My eyes must look like I'm on a good one, because what the fuck just happened here?

Seriously, the fuck?

"Lolli, think about it," Mia says softly, approaching me with caution. "You've been hanging out with Nate for a while now. I don't think it's wrong for him to assume it might be a little more than...casual."

I narrow my eyes at her. "It is casual. That's what he does. That's what we're doing."

"You guys agreed to be exclusive, Lolli."

"Sure, we agreed not to fuck around with other people, but that doesn't mean anything. We're not dating. Why is everyone looking at me?" I snap.

She crosses her arms, narrowing her eyes this time. "Casual," she mocks. "Right. So, if it stopped tomorrow? No more playtime, no more Nate. You'd be okay with that?"

I scowl at her and she smirks.

"Fuck off, Mia," I grumble, handing off my beer bottle to Austin, and make my way toward the door Nate just exited.

"Love you, too, Lollipop," she yells after me.

Once in the dead center of the street, I look around, finding Nate a few houses down, standing there with his hands folded over his head.

"Hey!" I shout, marching toward him.

He whips around, surprised, dropping his hands to his side, his shock turning into a frown of his own.

Good. We're on the same page.

"What the hell was that?" I snap, flicking my wrist in his direction, taking the stance of a bratty teenager: hip cocked, one leg extended, resting bitch face.

His frown deepens. "I want you."

"So!?" I shout, throwing my arms out.

"So, why can't you just admit you want me, too?"

"I'm fucking you, aren't I?" I raise both my brows in challenge. "I'd say it's pretty damn obvious I want you."

He levels me with a stern look. "You know damn well that's not what I meant." He stares at me for beat, his eyes softening by the second, making me grow uneasy. "I want to be with you Kalani. Me and you, and no one else," he tells me gently.

"Look around you, Nate. Life is bigger than this place. You may get everything you want here, but that's not the real world." I shake my head at him. "You can't just say you want something and get it. That's not how it goes. That's a fucked-up fantasyland." My chest is heaving, I'm so pissed off and confused, and pissed off that I'm confused.

Nate takes a step toward me, completely disregarding everything I just said. "I want you. All of you. Every stubborn and determined inch of you. I think you want me the same way."

He reaches out and grabs both of my hands in his.

"I don't care what you think." My voice loses some of its bite.

He smiles, a big beautiful one. "I know you want me like that, too."

"You don't know shit," I argue, my voice just above a whisper.

He stares at me, into me, and his hold grows a little tighter. My breath hitches in my throat, my gaze dropping to his hands.

How does he... why is he doing that?

He steps closer. Once my eyes find his again, he whispers gently, "Let me wake you up, Kalani."

My eyes flutter closed as the soft words I'd spoken to my grandfather flow through me.

"You can go to sleep... I'll wake up for you."

Opening my eyes, I look up at Nate.

The longer my gaze searches his features, the further his smile grows.

"I want you?" I whisper, my brows pulling in slightly.

"Yeah, baby." He nods, lifting his hand to tuck my hair behind my ear, resting his palm in the spot he's claimed. "You do."

I nod, letting him pull me into his arms.

His lips drop to mine slowly, giving me a sweet, silky kiss.

"So," I pull back, looking up at him again. "Just so we're clear. You're mine, as in only mine?"

He nods.

I nod as well, before turning to head back to the house.

"Whoa." He jumps, snagging my retreating hand. "Where you going?" he questions, his brows furrowed.

"I don't share, Handsome." I shrug, jerking my head in the direction of the party. "Figured it best to let Olivia know that now."

I watch as Nate's dark eyes grow darker, lowering with intent as he pulls me flush against him.

My pulse spikes.

He slides his left hand in my hair, gripping it tight, while the other hand grips my ass. Pulling, he tilts my head back, dipping his tongue down to lick up my throat.

"You gonna fight for me, baby?" he rasps, nipping at my jaw teasingly.

"Mmm..." My eyes close, and I lean my head back further.

He groans, trailing his nose up my cheekbone, bringing his lips to my ear. "Tell me..." he whispers.

My fingernails dig into his forearms. "If you're mine..."

"I am." He squeezes my ass, pulling me even closer.

"Then I'll always fight for you."

He pulls back and looks into my eyes, revealing the truth in his as well.

He nods.

I nod.

We're on the same page.

Chapter Twenty-Eight

K ALANI

"Crisis averted!" I hear Mia yell from the kitchen.

"Didn't realize there was a crisis?" I semi-shout, stepping out of the hallway and perching on the back of the couch to slip my heels on.

"Well," she slams the cupboard shut, "there was. The flasks wouldn't fit in my bag, so I – holy, God damn!"

With a frown, I look to her, wondering what the problem is now, but when I see her brows have disappeared under her side-swiped bangs and her wide-eyed gaze traveling down my body, I stand tall, giving her a slow spin.

She squeals, her red curls bouncing as she runs over to me, pulling me in for a quick hug.

"Man, Meems…" I pull back. "This color looks killer on you. Your skin looks flawless."

She steps away and flutters her eyelashes, giving me a spin of her own. And she looks amazing. Her long red hair is curled in tight spirals, laying against her right shoulder. Her eyelids are covered in a gold eyeshadow, a darker brown in the crease, giving her natural-looking smoky eyes.

Her dress is badass. The rose pink, slinky, strapless number reaches her mid-thigh. The top is lined with thin, gold rhinestones that wrap all the way around, following the line of her zipper and stopping right where the curve of her ass begins. In the front, the center of the dress has the same design, only the stones shoot out from the center, each getting smaller as they ascend, then blending into the dress before reaching the curve of her breasts. Paired with gold studs and pumps, she looks like a damn goddess.

"Thanks, Lolls, but know you look 'like, whoa', too!" She smiles, bouncing back into the kitchen. "So, the crisis. The flasks wouldn't fit in my purse." She stares at me.

My brows pull in. "Okay..."

"So, get over here and help me drink this!" She hits the countertop several times dramatically.

Laughing, I slide onto one of the barstools. Flattening my palms on the top, I lean in. "Let's get the party started."

By the time the boys show up, about three... or was it four, shots of Patron later, we're feelin' good and ready to get our groove on.

"Lolli!" Mia drunkenly whispers, peeking out the peephole on the door.

Giggling, I step up next to her. "What?" I whisper back, smiling.

"I can't see Austin, 'cause Nate's big ol' body is in the way, but right now," she switches eyes, "I don't even mind because he looks so good!"

"Yeah?" I grin and try squeezing in next to her to look out the tiny dime-size hole.

"You guys know we can hear you, right?" We both jump back

when Austin's humor-filled voice booms from the other side of the door.

We look at each other and start laughing.

"Kalani!" Nate shouts, and I launch forward, trying to swallow my laughter.

With my hand on my hip, I swing the door open and cock my head to the side. "Hello, boys."

Nate laughs at something Austin says, turning back toward me when he hears my voice, his excited smile slowly dropping from his lips as his eyes lock onto mine.

We stand there for a few seconds, holding each other's gazes, until Mia pushes my hand from the door and runs, jumping into Austin's arms, effectively breaking the staring contest Nate and I had going.

I glance over his shoulder, smiling, and he turns his gaze to the two behind him.

Mia slides down and grabs Austin's hand, dragging him across the lawn. "Come on. My mom wants to see your face."

Nate turns back to me and steps into the house, forcing me to step back, then closes the door behind him.

"Hi." I give him a one-sided smile that he returns.

"Hey." His hands reach out, tracing the tight fabric that stretches across my shoulders, following it down my ribs and thighs as it clings to me like a second skin.

My dress is long and tight in all the right places, accentuating each and every curve of my body. The royal blue gown has a few inch-thick straps that lay over the curve of my shoulder, the front dipping down just enough to follow the arch of my breasts. There is rouging on the sides against my ribs, allowing the stretchy material to form to me flawlessly. The dress loosens just enough below the curve of my ass to drop evenly to the floor, giving me some wiggle room. Like Mia, I went with the smoky eyes, but opted for a dark charcoal color to contrast my light eyes, and my hair has a deep side part, with big barrel curls laying against my back.

His eyes finally come back to mine, but when he opens his mouth to speak, I turn, sweeping my hair to the side, and give him the view from behind.

I hear a whoosh of a breath leave him, before his hands find my hips, and he pulls my backside into him.

His right hand leaves my hip and traces the drop of the open back that stops an inch above my panty line. If I were wearing any, that is.

The alcohol in my body has my blood warm already, but Nate's quickly setting me on fire with his heated breath on my neck and rough hands on my skin.

"Kalani..." He breathes into my ear and I bite my lip. "You're so fucking beautiful.'" He kisses my exposed back. "Perfect." Another kiss. "Mine."

That does it.

I spin in his arms and smash my lips against his.

Nate responds instantly, growling into my mouth.

The second my back hits the wall, the front door swings open.

We both turn to scowl at a smirking Mia.

She winks and walks into the kitchen. "Told you two minutes was too long to leave them alone, Austin. They fuck like rabbits."

Austin laughs and hops up to sit on the countertop. "Oh, I had no doubt." He grins. "Looking good, Lolli."

"Thanks." My eyes drop to his chest when I see his rose-gold tie shining.

That's when I realize I haven't even looked Nate over yet. I was too busy getting turned on watching his reaction to me.

When I shove him back some, his brows crease, but I see the smirk take over as my eyes travel down his frame.

His suit is tailored and expensive; has to be, because no one fills out a cheap department store rental like this.

The black slacks fit him to a T, laying perfectly over his dress shoes. A black button-up peeks out from underneath his tux jacket, also black. Not a splash of color anywhere on him. I guarantee every dude at this thing will have a vest, tie or something matching their date's dress. Just another thing to add to the list that makes Nathaniel Monroe stand out over everyone else. And he'll definitely stand out tonight...

This black on black thing is sexy as fuck.

"Oh, my God, stop!" I hear Mia roll her eyes and roll mine in response.

After the boys take a few shots to catch up, we head for the door, but something stops me, and my eyes fly to Mia's.

The second our gazes connect; her smile slowly fades. Dropping Austin's hand, she steps up to me, her pretty green eyes flitting back and forth between mine.

I give her a small smile and she wraps her arms around me, hugging me tight. I allow myself to picture my mother's face for a moment, but unlike the time before, I can hear the honey in her voice.

My eyes fly open and I step back.

Both Nate and Mia take a half a step toward me, but I stop them with a raised palm.

"Kalani..." Nate's voice is tense.

"I'm fine." I look between the two of them. "I promise, but give me just a sec." I don't give them a chance to respond and hustle down the hall.

Once in my room, I pull the top drawer of my nightstand open. Picking up the camera my parents gave me, I release a heavy sigh and a smile takes over my lips.

I told them I was okay and I am.

I haven't been able to hear my mother's voice since my aunt showed up at my door two days after her death. Maybe I blocked it out, or maybe it was the fact that my mom and aunt share the same face, but whatever the reason, it was gone in an instant. But I can hear it right now.

Closing my eyes, I hear the flowery voice she used at the end of every night's phone call. The soft, kind, and questioning voice that always reminded me how much she loved and missed me, and wished I'd decide to travel with them.

I know she always wondered if what she was doing was right, if allowing her underage daughter to live alone while she traveled from state to state, living the dream life she and my father were lucky enough to earn, was the right thing to do. She felt like she was abandoning me, but to me, what she did was completely selfless and showed how strong she was.

She knew how badly I wanted to live as normal a teenage life as possible, and she loved and trusted me enough to let it happen. And I never let her down. Nothing above the normal teenage crap anyway.

With a smile on my face and camera in hand, I march past the troubled gazes and head out the front door, but when the tip of my shoe hits the grass, I hesitate.

My eyes instinctively latch onto Nate's.

As expected, he knows what I need, even when I don't.

He holds my gaze as he walks to me. Nodding subtly, and taking my free hand in his right, his left hand on my lower back, he guides me forward. Suddenly, all my reservations are gone, disappearing from the touch of this unexpected man-boy.

"Lolli..." Mia's voice is a weak whisper. "What...what are you doing?"

We step onto Mia's porch, and I turn to her. "Wanna go get Aunt Kara and Uncle Ben?" I give her a small smile. "Thought maybe they'd like a picture with us."

Her head shakes lightly, her gaze dropping to the camera in my hand before finding its way back to mine. Her eyes fill with tears as she nods and runs past me into her house, Austin following leisurely behind her.

Nate's hand grips my arm gently, wheeling me around to face him.

His eyes are worried, pinched at the edges, and unsure, searching my face for signs of anxiety or fear or whatever it is he normally sees. I've been blocking everything out for so long, I'm not sure what to feel or when, but Nate seems to.

He slides forward, bringing his body closer to mine, and tucks my hair behind my ear for the first time tonight. The fact that I noticed that should freak me out. Apparently, it doesn't, because my head decides to press into his hand, my eyes feel the need to close, and my lips lift slowly, demanding to meet his.

The kiss is soft and slow and closed mouthed, yet it's powerful and pure and full.

His forehead finds mine and he releases a deep breath. "You don't have to do this, you know," he whispers, his eyes shifting from the camera to Mia's front door, and back to me.

I smile and take a step back. "I know, but I want to." I turn, placing my back against his chest and raise the never before used camera that's sat in a dark drawer since the day I got it. "Smile, Nathaniel." My voice is light and airy and maybe a little…sad.

I'm not sure what it is exactly, but when his lips find my temple and the flash blinds me for a split second, my body feels the strangest featherweight feeling. It's heavy and pressure-filled, but light and revealing.

The photo prints instantly and I shake it around, helping the picture come into view. And when it does, my chest aches.

I look beautiful, pressed into Nate's body, his arms protectively around me, my free hand clutching his forearm - needing to touch him. My smile is bright and real, my eyes open and shining. But it's Nate's expression that has my breathing grow deeper.

His head is dipped ever so slightly, his lips resting on my temple, nose in my hair. His dark eyes are closed, almost squeezed shut, as he breathes me in.

He looks completely serene.

He kisses my cheek. "I like it." Turning me, he pulls me closer, so we're chest to chest, and gently takes the camera from my hand. "This one's mine." He dips down the few inches shy my heels leave me, kisses my cheek once more, then turns to face the camera. "Smile, baby."

His fingers tickle my ribs, making me laugh, then the flash goes off.

Chuckling, he steps back right as the door opens.

My body freezes and my eyes dart to his.

He stares at me, transferring courage without words.

I nod and turn around, watching as a smiling Uncle Ben and hesitant Aunt Kara follow Mia and Austin out the front door.

Uncle Ben walks right up to me with a smile. "My, Lolli. You look beautiful."

"Thanks." I smile, glancing past him as my aunt takes another step.

She really is stunning.

"Aunt Kara." I clear my scratchy throat, taking a single step forward, watching as her hands clench and release the hem of her cardigan. "Would you mind taking a picture?"

She doesn't speak but gives a trembling smile and reaches for the camera, flinching when I pull it back.

"No," I shake my head. "I'd like to take a picture with you, Uncle Ben, and Mia." I hold her blue eyes with mine. "A family picture."

Her face tightens and her nose turns red as she hastily nods her head, a small sob escaping before she can force it away.

Reaching my hand behind me, Nate's large fingers find mine, and I pull him forward. "You've met Nate."

Her eyes stay on me for a few more seconds before she allows herself to look his way. The moment her eyes find his, her shoulders relax and tears roll down her face. She nods, just once, and I see him do the same out of the corner of my eye.

Uncle Ben steps up and rubs her back. "How about that picture, ladies?"

I turn, reaching a hand out to Mia.

She takes mine in one, her mom's in the other, and walks us back into the grass.

Nate takes the camera and gets into position to take the shot.

Mia and I wrap our arms around each other, her mom and dad on either side of us.

"Smile."

And we do.

With a backward wave, we stumble out the school gym, heels in my hand, a crown in Nate's, a flask in Austin's, and a bra in Mia's.

"What now, y'all?" Mia hiccups, stumbling into Austin as she walks.

"Now we go to the hotel party."

"I wonder why Parker never showed. He said he'd meet us there."

Mia tenses, then shrugs. "Guess he decided not to come since he no longer had a date."

My brows pull in. "But, I thought he was bringing Ashley?"

Her gaze slides to the gym and she shakes her head. "She told him last week her parents decided to leave Friday after school for vacay instead of waiting till after the dance. Alyssa had to cancel on her date, too."

"That fucking sucks. Why didn't he just come with us?"

Her eyes shoot wide and she gets a bit defensive. "How should I know? Maybe he didn't want to come? Who knows?" She throws her hands up and stumbles toward the parking lot.

My brows shoot up and I look at Austin.

With a shrug, he stuffs his hands in his pockets, heading off in her direction.

"Whatever," I mutter and follow the two of them, looking over my shoulder when I realize Nate's not following.

He stares at me for a second, his face unreadable, before his feet

MEAGAN BRANDY

start moving again, leading me to his truck so we can grab our bags.

The rest of the night goes by in a flash. Dozens of drunk seniors mill around, hopping from room to room in the wing of the local Millow Inn reserved specifically for those attending the dance tonight.

Being only a block up from the high school, it was the safest plan of action. Apparently, the hotel owners, school faculty, and town sheriffs turn a blind eye on dance nights, so long as it stays semi under control, and all vehicles are left in the school parking lot.

I grab Mia's hand and pull her off the sofa we're sitting on. "Come on, Meems, let's get these dresses off."

"No!" Nate turns from his conversation with his friend, saying it too quick and too loud, earning a few chuckles around the room, and a raised brow and a smirk from me.

He smirks right back and I could kiss him.

Mia laughs and drops back down. "Once this baby comes off," she winks at Austin, "I have no need for clothes, so you go ahead. Looks like Nate may wanna help you out of that dress himself, though." Her gaze drops to his crotch then back to mine with a wink.

My eyes narrow on her and she throws herself back, laughing. "And so it begins, Lollipop. And soo it begins." Her smile is bright and fueled by tequila.

I flip her off, not quite understanding her nonsense. "You comin', Handsome?"

He holds a hand up to number Thirty-five, second string wide receiver, as he responds. "Two minutes." He gives me a look that says, 'your ass better stay right there'.

I walk out of the room and head toward mine.

As I round the corner, I bump into someone exiting their room.

278

"Shit." I stumble back a bit, grabbing ahold of the wall to steady myself.

A hand comes out and latches onto my waist, even though I'm already standing straight. Looking up, I find Jarrod smiling down at me.

My hand reaches out and presses onto his chest.

The initial thought was to push him back, but when I feel overheated, wet skin against my palm, my eyes drop to where my hand lies.

Right in the center of his chest...his sweaty, shirtless chest.

He chuckles and my gaze lifts to his. "You like what you see, Lolli?"

I drop my hand and step back, removing his hand from my waist.

His green eyes darken slightly, but he tries to keep his smirk in place.

"Enjoying yourself?"

His smirk grows. "You wondering what I did in there?" He takes a step toward me, erasing the distance I put between us. "I could show you?" he whispers and reaches up to rub my cheek.

I jerk my head away and quickly step around him. "I got my own party going on tonight, Jarrod, but thanks."

His jaw clenches and his eyes narrow, but only for a second before he forces a playful grin. "Guess I'll see you some other time."

I shrug and turn away from his eerie eyes, throwing an, "Or not," over my shoulder, before stepping into my room.

A few minutes later, the soft knock at the door has my body warming. I've got alcohol, adrenaline, excitement, and so many other emotions I can't even name running through my veins right now. I want nothing more than to spend a few hours working them out with Nate. Naked.

But when I open the door, I don't find Nate, but a disheveled-looking Parker instead. He gives me a wry grin and I reach out, bringing him inside and shutting the door. I pull him to the bed to set him down. He stumbles a bit, but eventually lands his ass on the mattress.

"What's going on, Hero?" I rub his hand and he drops his chin to his chest.

He shakes his head but doesn't lift it. "I don't know, Lolli Bear." I can tell he's far from sober.

"You didn't come to the dance."

He shakes his head again.

My brows pull in and I use my other hand to rub circles across his back. "Is it... Ashley?" I ask, my eyes pinching at the sides, trying to understand. "You upset you didn't get to take her to the dance or something?"

He laughs bitterly and throws himself back, squeezing his eyes shut. "No, it's not Ashley. I was only taking her to help her out."

"What do you mean?" I drop down next to him, propping myself up on my elbow.

"She's in love with an asshole and, apparently, that asshole asked her to come to the dance, but she knew it was a bad idea to go with him, so she told him she had a date. I just so happened to be the first guy to walk by after the fact," he chuckles.

"Aww," I coo. "You really are a hero." I laugh, dropping my forehead onto his chest briefly.

"Why do you call me that? Hero?"

"You don't like it?"

He smiles, his eyes closed. "I like it, just wondering."

I hesitate for a moment, unsure of what I wish to share. But looking at Parker, I decide I can give my best friend something, even if it's a small something.

"Because you remind me of my OG, Hero," I joke, doing my best to take the seriousness away.

He laughs lightly, his eyes roaming my face, waiting for more.

I smile slightly. "When I first saw you, your eyes stood out instantly, such a clear, light blue. It was more than just the color. It was the kindness behind them, the soft air around you. I knew you were a happy-go-lucky, all-around good guy. You gave me this familiar feeling of comfort I had lost."

The grin on his face smooths out and he gazes at me, making me a bit nervous, but I keep going. "My grandpa was like you. Happy and fun, the peacekeeper between others. Kinda like you are with your parents." He swallows. "You're dedicated and eager, confident, but in a respectful way. And you get me." I laugh and he raises a blond brow in question. "You're like the epitome of the guy you 'bring home to mama' or maybe it's daddy, since I'm a girl."

"They always say little girls grow up to marry men like their daddies." He grins.

"You're an idiot." I laugh.

"So, what you're saying is I'm perfect?"

"Yeah, Parker," I smile down at him. "You kinda are."

He nods, then looks away, turning back with a smile. "I knew you loved me."

I bust up laughing and he shakes his head at me, but the look in his eyes tells me how much he needed to hear my words.

When I lift myself up, and he stares at me, unblinking.

"What?" I grin.

A soft smile forms on his lips as his eyes roam my face. They lower, following the shape of my body, slowly rising back to meet mine.

"I can't believe I didn't notice when you opened the door." He licks his lips and nods. "You look amazing, Lolli Bear," he whispers and my brows pull in. "Your eyes, they're really blue tonight."

"It's the dress." I search his face. "The contrast and shit."

He chuckles lightly, his hand coming up to trace the line of my left eyebrow. "Nah, it's you." He smiles, another sad one. "You're here right now, Lolli. All of you."

"I don't understand," I place my palm on his hand that splays across his stomach.

"You told me what you see in my eyes. Well, I see things in yours, too. They always have a shadow, a little something in them, hiding a part of you." His hand lifts from under mine, coming back down to cover it. "But it's gone tonight. Your eyes; they're big and bright and beautiful." His eyes skim me one more time. "You're beautiful."

He sounds so sad, so lost.

"And you're happy," he says, his face pinching slightly. "Right? You're happy?"

I nod, searching his face to try and figure out what's going on with my friend, but I come up empty. While I see pain and confusion laced in his features, I can't figure out why.

He chuckles again, scrubbing his hands down his face. "I'm kind of drunk, Lolli Bear." He drops his hands and sighs. "I'm sorry. I should go."

"You don't have to. You can stay if you want."

He hops off the bed and makes his way to the door. Turning back to me, he smiles, but it doesn't meet his eyes. "Come on, Lolli. Look at you." He gestures to my body with his hand. "You in that dress?" He raises a brow playfully. "You and I both know how tonight ends for you." He waves and opens the door, revealing Nate on the other side.

Nate's head snaps up, his hand frozen mid-air, as if he were about to reach for the handle. His eyes narrow and he looks from Parker to his keycard, to the number on the door, then back to Parker.

When I push up off my elbow to rest my weight against my palm, the movement catches Nate's eye and his gaze darts to mine, dropping to my dress, the bed, and back to my eyes.

His dark eyes are blazing, so I don't say anything. I know him and I know he needs to go through his entire thought process before anything. If not, well, the whole 'thought' part never catches up and he acts like a crazy person.

His eyes shift back to Parker and narrow in a way I don't like.

He looks crazed and ready to kill, but I can read what his body language isn't saying, and he's a little unsure of what to think at the moment.

I stand.

"Hey, man." Parker nods, pulling the door open wider.

"What's up?" Nate's feet widen slightly, his body not budging an inch.

Parker shrugs. "Just came by to hang with Lolli for a bit. I'm down the hall." He jerks his head to the left. "Room 11."

"This is Room 54." Nate's brows drop even more.

Parker scoffs and shoulders past him. "I'm aware, man. Like I said," he gives Nate a hard look, "I came by to hang with Lolli." He turns to me, his features relaxing instantly. "Night, Lolli."

I nod, rushing forward when he's gone from my view.

Nate's eyes narrow and his nostrils flare, but I place a hand on his chest, offering him the only comfort I can right then, and peek out the door around him. "Hero!"

He turns around, a brow raised. His eyes are glazed from the alcohol, but it's more than that. They look a little empty, which is not normal for my spunky, easygoing friend.

"You okay?"

He nods, waves, and walks away. I know he's lying, but now's not the time.

Nate shifts away from my hand and hastily storms into the room, quickly locking himself in the bathroom.

After closing the door, I walk to the sofa chair and sit down to wait, hearing the sink water turn on. I picture him scrubbing his hands down his face, maybe pulling on that hair of his a little bit.

I'm an asshole for thinking about how sexy he probably looks right now, when I know he's upset, but I can't help it.

Everything he does is sexy.

The water turns off and the bathroom door opens. Nate walks out with his eyes to the ground, tosses his wallet and keys on the table, then pulls out the shot glasses and second bottle of Patron we bought for tonight.

Harder than necessary, he sets the mini glasses on the table, opens the bottle, pours a shot and downs it, then pours another. After taking the second one, his head drops back to scowl at the ceiling.

When I stand, his gaze snaps down and he pours another.

I reach into his bag and grab the Ziploc full of pre-cut limes, and the small saltshaker.

His greedy eyes can't take it, and they watch my tongue as it licks the skin between my thumb and pointer finger, sprinkling some salt over the wet spot. His follow my other hand as it reaches into the lime bag and places the thin cut citrus between my lips.

His breathing gets louder and he licks his while staring at mine.

Wildly tossing back the shot, he lifts my hand to his mouth, his tongue angrily licking the salt off me.

His eyes dart to the lime and he pushes forward, gripping my forearms firmly. When I tilt my head, offering him the lime, his eyes finally connect with mine. They narrow a little more, his brows dropping lower. His hands come up to case around my neck as he brings his mouth to mine, biting into the lime and tearing it from my lips. He spits it to the side.

"Why was he in here?" he growls, fury burning in his dark eyes.

"Because I let him in." My voice is calm.

His nostrils flare. "Why?"

"Because he wanted to talk."

He scoffs and scrubs his hands down his face. "Talk. Right." He scoffs again. "So, you had to lay down on the bed to chat?"

My head rears back, and my hands find my hips. "Say whatcha gotta say, Handsome. Don't be a pussy about it. No games, remember?"

"Fine." He steps up to me, bringing my body flush against his. "Here it is. Knowing he was in here with you makes me feel sick," he grits out. "Literally. I almost puked in the bathroom just now."

His hands are flying around as he bends at the knee to bring himself eye level. "No other guy should be in a hotel room with you, or any fucking room with you alone, for that matter! Never!"

"Do you not trust me?" I ask as calmly as I can, when really, I'm thinking about smacking him upside his head. But I get it.

Kind of...

He stands tall and tilts his head. "Trust?" His brows raise. "Trust. Kalani, this has nothing to do with trust, and everything to do with how fucking fine you are, and the fact that every guy in this place, at our school; basically, anyone who sees you wants to fuck you, and has thought about it at least once!"

I don't even know how to respond to that.

He stares at me for a few seconds, his chest heaving with each exasperated breath he takes.

His knuckles come up and tap against the side of his head. "The images in my head right now..." His eyes widen. "You lying on the bed in that dress with your hair draped over your shoulder," He pauses and I don't think he notices the way his voice grows quieter with each word spoken. "The ends touching the blanket, and your head tilted up showing the line of your sleek, soft neck..." He swallows hard, his brows pulling in slightly as he focusses on something over my shoulder.

I place my palms on his chest, realizing when his uncertain eyes find mine, he's not mad Parker was in here. Not really.

He's scared. Or maybe threatened is a better word for a guy like him, but whichever it is, both leave him seeking the same thing. Reassurance.

"Parker's my friend, and I'm his." Nate doesn't say a word. "He'll be around awhile, probably forever, and I won't deny him when he needs me." I pause on purpose, making sure he's hearing me. The tick in his jaw tells me he is. "Unless you needed me more."

He swings his guarded eyes to mine.

Stepping out of his embrace, I walk around the bed, his eyes

285

tracking my every move, and pull my phone out of my overnight bag. Turning on my playlist, I set it at random, then climb on top, laying exactly the way his mind imagined. The way he wants me.

When I lift my head to look at him, his tongue peeks out and skims across his lower lip, his eyes dropping to travel the length of my body. When they come back to mine, they're black in color.

Slowly, I allow my elbow to slide across the cheap hotel blanket and drop onto my back.

Nate steps up to the edge of the bed, eyes blazing. He reaches out, feeling the soft material of my dress between his fingers.

He then crawls up me, dipping his head to lick the curve of each breast, then my throat, earning a soft moan from me. His mouth finds my ear, where he bites, then kisses, apologizing wordlessly. "I need you."

"You have me."

His body tenses slightly, his eyes flying to mine and I can't help the laugh that bubbles out of me.

My arms find their way around his neck, and I bring his forehead down to mine. "Did we not go over this, Handsome?"

He gives a terse nod.

"Yeah," I nod in return. "We did. I'm yours. You're mine." I pepper kisses on his lips, whispering, "It's a done deal."

"You're mine," he growls, his fist tightening in my hair.

"Yeah." I grin.

His eyes narrow. "You do realize, when I say you're mine, that doesn't just mean you only fuck me and I only fuck you, right?" He raises a brow. "It means your everything is mine, Kalani. All of it..." he says, his finger tracing my bottom lip, "is mine. All of you."

I nod again, feeling even more breathless.

His eyes penetrate mine. "This is more than just sex."

Excitement and fear - two emotions my body is trying to figure out how to process - flit through me at the possessive and assured tone he uses, but I push everything aside and allow myself to enjoy the now.

I run my hands down his chest, pushing them back into the hair at the base of his skull. "So, tell me... what are you gonna do with me?" I whisper, letting the tip of my tongue tease his full lips.

He lifts slightly and reaches for my phone, choosing a not so random song that makes my heart beat even faster, then lowers back down to me.

"I'm gonna fuck you long and hard." His hands case mine behind my head. "Then soft, and slow," he whispers into my skin. "All night long, that way you can't make me leave."

And when The Weeknd's "Acquainted" starts playing through my tiny phone speaker, he does. All night long, only leaving when my eyes refuse to stay open in the early hours of the morning.

Chapter Twenty-Nine

K ALANI

Winter break came and went in a whirlwind of bliss.

I spent the two-week vacation in California, allowing myself a small trip down memory lane for the first time since my family passed.

I mean, I didn't go home. I couldn't. Not with the way I've been having a harder time shutting down my thoughts lately - that's too much. But I did go to the stadium and watch the AFC Wild Card game the Tomahawks were playing in.

While they weren't horrible, they did have a tough year. In reality, they've been having a tough 'year' since my Grandpa retired as their coach and took on the partial owner role three seasons ago.

They could use a new safety - he gets dipped on the regular, and that's not okay- maybe even a new QB. Maiven Walkins, first round pick from Indiana, got sacked during the second preseason game against Dallas, one he never should have been playing in the first place, taking him out for the season. The second string is good, but far from great. They need an arm like Nate's – fluent and precise. Too bad he's still got a few years of college ball before he's eligible.

Pressure builds in my chest and I do my best to take a deep breath.

Nate.

That boy crept up on me like the fourth shot of Patron, warming my body from the inside out, leaving me feeling weightless and capable. Completely knocking me off my feet.

It's not like I thought it would be, caring about someone. I kind of like it. It's fresh and new, and making me realize that sometimes it's okay to allow yourself to feel things, not that Nate ever gave me a choice. I tried so hard to keep him at arm's length, keep it skin deep, but when all I want to do is pull him in and keep him there, feel his warmth against mine, that's kind of hard to do.

It was a wasted effort from the start. I should have known the minute he pissed me off the night he knocked on my door, refusing to believe we hadn't slept together. I hadn't let anyone get under my skin in a long, long time, and he managed to within seconds on day one, making me think of him on day two.

Truth be told, I missed him while I was gone. I kept thinking about him during the game, wanting to turn my head and argue play calls with him, but as soon as the thoughts would come, I told myself I was being a stupid teenage girl and made myself stop. Then, when I went to the beach, I kept thinking about how nice it would be if he were there to wrap his arms around me; help keep me warm. Again, I told myself to shut up. But the following day, I was running along the shoreline, my legs beat and ready to give out, when the raspy draw of Evanescence blared through my Dre's, momentarily stopping me in my tracks. It had been a while since I'd allowed myself to listen to "Bring Me To Life" but from the first chord of the song, it was as if my body got a second wind, feeling lighter with every stride taken.

Nate woke me up from the empty life I'd forced myself into, filled the hollow parts I created with wonder and anticipation. He did that. He's been showing me that life is more than movements and motions, more than processes and requirements. He's waking me up and he doesn't even know it. Or maybe he does, I don't know.

I thought about calling him when I drove in late last night but decided against it. Then, this morning he texted that he had an early meeting with his coach and he'd meet me at school. So, yeah, I'm a little antsy and excited to see him after being gone for two weeks, and I think I'm okay with that.

Smiling to myself, I wrap my skull-covered scarf around my neck and head out the door, finding a shining Parker waiting in my driveway for me.

He hops out and jogs over, encasing me in a big bear hug.

"What are you doing here?" I pull back, looking up at his bright blue eyes with a smile.

He shrugs and takes my bag from my shoulder. "I didn't want to wait until school to see your pretty face." He winks, tossing my bag on the middle seat of his truck. "I missed ya, Lolli Bear."

Once I hop in, I turn to peck his cheek before he shuts the door, and jogs around to climb in the driver's seat.

"I missed you, too, Hero." I buckle my seatbelt and shift toward him. "Did you get the pics I sent you?"

He nods, placing his arm behind my seat as he reverses out of the driveway. "All fifty-seven of them."

He laughs when I smack his shoulder with the back of my hand.

"You mean the Californian ass didn't pique your interest?" I tease and settle back into the seat.

"Why did you send me a bunch of random ass shots?"

"So you could see all the options California has to offer."

"And why would I need to know this?"

Biting the inside of my lip, I take a deep breath.

While I was on vacation, I'd thought about what I really wanted. While I don't plan to go to college, I do plan on leaving here and heading back to California. I know everything I want to know about being part-owner of a professional football team and complete owner of the NFL's largest outside contracted photography team, Embers Elite Exposures. From the age of twelve, I was brought into all the decisions - Papa said I had to be since it'd be mine one day - before they were made, so I've been through the processes ten times over. But I was thinking it would be nice to build a team of my own for when I take on more responsibility in both matters.

I also happen to know Parker isn't wanting to play college ball, and plans to major in Business and Accounting, so I decided maybe I could share a bit with him, in hopes of getting him to join me.

"Well..." My forehead wrinkles as I stare out the front windshield. "Shit," I mutter, dropping my face into my hands. "Pull over, Hero." My voice is muffled by my hands.

"Hang on, Lolli Bear. We're pullin' into the school lot anyhow."

When I drop my hands, I see he's turned into the first lot, furthest from the entrance.

He kills the engine, undoes his seatbelt and turns toward me.

"Okay." I place my palms up. "Hear me out, alright?"

His brows drop in concern, but he nods.

"So, when the year's up, I'm going home." He nods again, letting me know he's following. "Right, so..." I wrinkle my nose. "Home is in California."

He grins. "I know."

"You know?" My head draws back.

He chuckles. "I pay attention, Lolli Bear. You're a weird combination of hippie, social outcast, and surfer chick. Your coffee is over-complicated, burritos are its own food group to you, and you say 'awesome' and 'hella' in every conversation. You're all California, honey."

I purse my lips and cross my arms over my chest. "I don't surf."

He throws his head back, laughing, and reaches over to tug a piece of my hair. "Don't be mad. It's cute."

"Whatever." Smiling, I roll my eyes and get us back on track. "Anyway," I hold his gaze for a moment. "I was thinking, maybe you'd want to come with me?"

Parker's face tightens as he searches my eyes.

"I mean, you could finish school wherever you want, but if you decided to move to California, now or after college, you could stay with me...or I have a few properties you could move into."

He stares at me.

Fuck it. I lay it all out there. "I'd like you to come work for me." His brows drop even lower. "I kind of own some big... uh... stuff. Important, high-functioning, crazy competitive things and, well, I'm gonna need someone business savvy to help me out. It'd be a full CEO, top-tier position. Highest paid. The only person you'd answer to is me, but really, you'd make the majority of the decisions, have a few dozen people beneath you. I'm not interested in that side of the business, but I'll need to be in the loop about everything."

I watch as Parker continues to blink at me.

"My current CEO is retiring in two years, so you could intern with him after your first year of college, maybe even travel with him this summer, if you want. He'd show you everything you need to know; help you build your class schedule based on what you'll need to take first. Once he's gone, I'll figure it out until you're ready, not that Mr. Marshall would up and leave me hangin'. But I could use you, Parker. I need someone I can trust. Plus, it'd be nice to have a friend around." I hold his gaze so he knows I'm not joking.

He scrubs his hands down his face and shakes his head to clear whatever it is he's thinking.

"So..." he draws out slowly, looking out the windshield. "You want me to come to California so I can work for you once I have my business degree?"

I nod, working the inside of my lip with my teeth. "And to hang with me, yeah."

"Lolli, you do realize I have no idea what the fuck you're talking about, right?" A smile breaks over his face, and I release the breath I didn't know I was holding.

With a chuckle, I sink against the door. "I know." I continue to laugh. "Baby steps, Parker, baby steps." I smile at him.

He nods. "California?"

"California. I'll tell you more after you mull over the idea of going with me. Even if you don't want to work with me, I'd still like for you to come. Like I said, I have a place for you to stay for free. No dorm rules," I add hopefully.

"Man, Lolli..."

My phone beeps and I look at the screen.

Nate: ready or not, here I come...

My brows pull in, right when my door flies open.

I scream, thinking I'm about to hit the concrete, but I land in a pair of warm, firm arms. Looking up, my breath catches in my throat as my eyes lock onto a dark pair of brown ones I've been dying to see.

He smiles down at me, his fingers sliding against my sides, where his arms hold me. "Hi, baby," he whispers.

My chest feels like I just took a hit, and my eyelids lower. "Hi,

Handsome," I breathe, reaching up with my hand to skim my fingers across his jaw.

He adjusts his arms so he can swing my body upright, and I wrap myself around him, his palms coming down to cup my ass. His lips skim my temple, then he drops his forehead to mine.

I hear Parker's door open and close, then footsteps carrying him away, but I don't take my eyes off Nate as he turns my body, pressing my back against the passenger side door.

He runs his nose along mine. "I missed you."

"I kinda, maybe, missed you, too." I smile and press a light kiss to his lips.

One side of his mouth lifts and a mischievous glint takes over his brown gaze. "Oh, you missed me alright." He presses his body firmly against mine, squeezing my ass harder.

I lick my lips.

He leans in, running his nose down my cheek, across my jaw, then up to my ear. "And not just my body, Kalani," he whispers, his tongue flicking out to tease my skin. "Though, you missed that too, didn't you?"

My head falls against the window, a soft moan sliding past my lips.

Slowly, he pulls my scarf off, and kisses my neck, his warm breath bringing goosebumps to my skin. "Tell me..." he murmurs.

"Take me home..." I breathe, gripping his shoulders tighter, "and I'll do you one better."

He chuckles, bringing his forehead back to mine. "I wish, but I have to meet with the counselors today for some college stuff, but I will be taking you home later." He sucks my bottom lip into his mouth briefly. "Believe that."

"Fine." I drop my legs from around him, squeezing them together slightly to try and settle myself down, but all it does is create more friction and I slink against the truck.

He notices, like he always does, and a sexy smirk comes out to play. "You need me to take care of you, baby?" he asks, in a low, husky voice, stepping into my space again.

I lick my lips, nodding, because I do. I don't know why, but I need something... him, like right now.

He peeks over his shoulder while nudging my legs open. The parking lot is mostly deserted now; that, or everyone's closer to the front of the school, since Parker parked in the back of the lot.

His warm hands tease up my sides, my leggings doing nothing to mask the feeling of his rough touch against me. Then his fingers dip into the front of my yoga pants and panties.

I shake my head, and he frowns.

Fisting his letterman jacket, I pull his body against mine, and crash my lips into his. We both groan on contact. Our overheated, overeager mouths smashing together, tongues tangling and teasing in a way that shows how much our lips have missed each other.

I pull back and whisper a heady, "You," then kiss him hard again. "I want you."

He tries to stand his ground, shaking his head at me, but when I reach between us and squeeze his junk, he lifts and carries me to the back of Parker's truck.

As if I weigh nothing, Nate tosses me over the tailgate, hops inside and sits himself against the back so his head is lying against the cab window. He pulls off his jacket and motions for me to sit, turning me so my back is against his front, my thighs on top of his. Placing his jacket over my lap, he slides my pants and panties to my knees, freeing himself at the same time. I hear a packet tear, then my hips are lifted, and he's pulling me down on top of him in one, quick, thank-fucking-god movement.

When I attempt to lift, his hands clamp onto my hips, steeling me in place.

"No," he breathes into my ear. "I don't want anyone to see you."

I look around, seeing not a soul in sight, and try again.

His fingertips dig into my skin, and my heart rate spikes even higher.

His warm laughter heats my neck as he whispers, "Anyone could walk by, and I'll be damned if they get to see what your face looks like when you're riding me."

"Mmm." My hands come down to cover his, and I squeeze him with my walls, needing some kind of something, and needing it now.

He senses it, knows that I'm seconds away from demanding, so he gives me what I need.

Dropping himself down on a slant, he pulls me back so my ass is sitting on his pelvic bone, giving himself just enough room to lift his hips, sliding in and out only a few inches with each motion, but it's enough right now. Perfect, really.

When he lifts, pressing into me as far as he can, he rolls his hips, using his hands to grind me against him the way he wants it.

My head drops back to rest on his shoulder, my pants visible above me in the cold January air. It's erotic, the way my deep breaths turn into smoke above me, fanning out into the air like the heat that's spreading through my body.

My right hand reaches up behind me to cup Nate's cheek, and his lips drop to my neck. Licking, biting, kissing, he sends a tremble through my entire body.

Again, he senses what I want...what I need, and he lifts his right hand to his lips, where he coats his pointer and middle finger with spit. Dropping his hand back beneath the jacket, he rubs his warm fingers over my clit. Applying slight pressure, he begins making small circles while increasing the speed of his hips.

I press myself further into him and within seconds, he's gripping my chin, catching my whimpers in his mouth as I come apart in his arms, my sex gripping him in uncontrollable spasms.

Both his hands find my hips again. Keeping my mouth locked on his, he grinds my ass into him, letting out a deep, guttural groan, when my teeth find his bottom lip.

My body goes lax against him, and I seriously think I might need to go to bed after that.

So fucking good.

Nate kisses my temple. "So fucking good."

I grin, even though he can't see me.

His arms wrap lazily around me, his chin resting on my shoulder. After a few minutes, he speaks. "You know I missed you, right? Not just this."

My body grows warm and not from arousal. My head dips slightly, in an attempt to cover the crimson color burning across my skin, and a low, strange, "Yes," leaves my lips.

Nate's chest swell underneath me.

I close my eyes and allow myself to fall further into him.

I'm placing my Government book in my locker when I feel him.

Peeking over my right shoulder, my body feels like I just did a dozen somersaults.

His smile is bright and beautiful, and on me.

Eyes still locked on his, I slowly turn to lean against my open locker, ignoring the metal that digs into my back, because I don't wanna miss the show in front of me.

Nate's walking toward me and, if I didn't know better, I'd say it was just the two of us in the hall. It kinda feels that way when he steps in front of me.

He doesn't speak.

Neither do I.

His eyes roam my face; mine stay trained on his.

When his hand comes up, pushing my hair behind my ear, we sigh in unison, like we were both waiting for this - the innocent touch of his skin against mine. His hand glides down my body, until he can catch my fingers with his, his touch never once leaving my skin. Raising my hand to his mouth, he skims his lips across my knuckles. It's light but speaks volumes.

He looks into my eyes.

I look into his.

He nods.

I nod.

We're on the same page.

This is more than just sex.

Chapter Thirty

K ALANI

Mia skips into the house, a bright pink binder in hand, making a show of taking her seat next to Austin at my table.

"Nice of you to join us, Meems." I cross my arms and glare at her.

She rolls her eyes and folds her hands on top of her binder. "Relax, Lollipop. It was important."

"Yeah?" My brows jump. "Well, next time you plan to make us wait an extra twenty minutes, after making me get up early on a Sunday to cook you fuckers breakfast, don't."

Nate squeezes my knee and I turn my glare on him, making him chuckle and raise his palms in surrender.

"Come on, guys," Parker grins, placing a brand new steaming cup of coffee in front of me. "You don't mess with Lolli and her sleep. Or her French toast." He winks and takes the spot to my left. "Or before she's had her coffee."

"We get it, man," Nate grumbles.

Grinning, I bump my shoulder into Parker, making him smile into his cup.

Mia's eyes pinch, but she drops her gaze to her binder, opening it slowly. "Anyway," she looks up and locks eyes with me. "Spring Break-"

"No." It comes out fast and harder than I would have liked, making all eyes turn to me, but I keep mine locked on Mia's, kind of wishing I could smack her for making this a group conversation.

"Mexico. One week. Us and a good two dozen others or so from school. We'll celebrate your birthday..." She trails off, sinking into her shoulders slightly.

I can see the nods and grins around me, but again, my eyes stay trained on Mia's green ones. "No."

She sits back slowly, giving me a sad smile, and my chest starts to rise and fall rapidly. My nostrils flare as my lungs fight for air that my stupid body won't allow. My legs bounce uncontrollably, and my mind fights to stay in the now.

I drop my gaze to my lap and count the shields on my Captain America pajama pants.

One, two, three...

Nate's hand finds my limp one that has dropped alongside my chair, and his fingers lace through mine. He waits for my gaze to shift. Waits for my fingers to close around his. Then, he squeezes. Gently.

My eyes fly to him and his chin drops a fraction of an inch.

A message.

I'm here...

He's here.

Nate leans over, slowly placing his lips just behind and slightly below my ear, in his spot. My head leans into him as he places a slow, closed-mouth kiss to my skin, lingering there for a moment, and my body decompresses instantly.

He's... got me.

And I think he does.

"Does... what?" Austin drawl, and my eyes - that I didn't realize had closed - fly open and shift around the table.

Parker's staring into his coffee mug, Mia's eyes are flitting back and forth between Nate and me, and Austin looks thoroughly confused.

Nate chuckles beside me, giving my hand another quick squeeze before being the first one to reach for the food in front of us – cold food, I might add.

Once we all have our plates piled high, and warmed back up, we settle into a nice Sunday breakfast.

I glance at Mia, finding her pushing her eggs around her plate, one shoulder dropped completely so her forearm can rest on the wooden table. I peek at Nate who, shocker, is looking at me. He sees the question in my eyes, the one I haven't even figured out myself, and gives me a one-sided grin, his gaze sliding to Mia, then coming back to me, before focusing on the ridiculous amount of bacon piled on his plate.

"So, where are we staying, Meems?" I ask, taking a quick drink of coffee before meeting her eyes. "In Mexico?"

Her eyes glaze over, but she holds it in and a big beautiful smile shows off her perfect teeth. That's all she needed because she launches into a good hour-long speech, explaining each and every detail of the trip she's apparently already planned.

Sneaky bitch.

After we eat and clean up as a group, I hand her my credit card and tell her to pay for both our rooms.

"You mean you don't want to share?" She lifts a brow, a smirk on her lips.

Happy that she doesn't fight me about the money thing, I smile. "Hell no," I tell her, wiggling my eyebrows.

She winks, bouncing over to where my laptop sits on the coffee table. Austin and Nate plop down next to her.

In the kitchen, I find Parker lingering against the counter.

"Hey." I sidle up next to him.

He grins down at me, but it doesn't meet his eyes. "Hey."

He must see my worry – another new emotion - because he reaches out and jostles me, chuckling lowly. "I'm good, Lolli Bear."

"You're a liar, but okay." I grin at him, leaning against the countertop next to him. "You thought anymore about California?"

He doesn't miss the way my voice lowered at the questions and cuts a glance toward the others – toward Nate. He looks back at me, his eyes shifting back and forth between mine before a wide smile breaks out across his face.

"Shut the fuck up?" My heart rate spikes.

He laughs and opens his arms.

With a quiet squeal, I jump into Parker's arms, squeezing him tight, only to pull back seconds later and look up at him. "Seriously?"

He grins down at me, running his hands up and down my forearms. "Really. Give me the details later, but I need the general area now, so I can see what college options are around. But, yeah, Lolli Bear. I'm ready to get out of here. Text me the info later."

"You won't regret this." I squeeze his shoulders.

His smile falters slightly, but he shakes it off, pats my arm, and walks into the living room.

When I turn to follow, I find Mia staring at me with questioning eyes. I playfully stick my tongue out at her and she turns back to the computer screen.

"Okay, Lolli, we're all booked and they're holding a dozen other rooms in the same wing for whoever." She turns to the boys. "So, you guys better get on it before word gets out or you'll be on the opposite side of the resort."

I plop down next to Nate, who pulls me onto his lap. "Austin, when did you say you turn eighteen?"

He smirks. "Last October, according to the ID I just bought." He wiggles his eyebrows.

"I should have known," I laugh, dropping my head to Nate's shoulder.

For the next twenty minutes, Mia shows us all the things we 'have' to do while there, then shuts the laptop and sits back. "This is going to be fun! I'm excited!"

I roll my eyes. "Okay, guys. You're fed, vacay's set, now beat it. I got shiz to do, followed by doing absolutely nothing." I let out an overexaggerated sigh, pulling myself to my feet, and they all follow suit.

Mia laughs and pulls Austin to the door, who waves over his head on their way through it. "Thanks again, Lolli. Later."

Parker wraps me in a half-hug, kissing my temple lightly. "Bye, Lolli Bear."

"Later, Hero." I smile at him, reaching to my right to capture Nate's large hand in mine as Parker makes his way out the door.

"Guess I'll talk to you later." Nate sighs.

"You leaving?" I tilt my head, looking up at him.

His brows pinch slightly, and he wraps his hands around my lower back. "Am I not?"

I shrug and run my hands up his chest. "If you have stuff to do or whatever, that's fine."

The corner of his mouth twitches slightly. "I don't, but did you not just tell everyone to go?"

"Everyone? Yeah." I look at him. "You? No."

His arms tighten around me, bringing me even closer to him.

"You feel like running around doing boring shit with me, then watching a movie or something?"

He eyes me for a few minutes, then nods.

"I was going to borrow Mia's car..."

"No need." His eyes drop to my lips.

I lick mine. "Okay."

Then all hell breaks loose and before I know it, we're both naked and sweaty, laying on the living room carpet.

Hours later, the sun has set and we're in my bed, listening to music, partially dressed, him feeding me cookie dough ice cream.

We didn't get shit done.

"You know, for a girl who loves football, it's kinda strange that you don't have cable. We could be watching a game right now."

"I needed a break this season." I give him a tight smile.

"I could," he hesitates, "you know, pay for it, if you want it or whatever."

I lean over him and kiss his lips, licking the drop of vanilla he left behind. "It has nothing to do with money, Handsome. But thank you." I smile.

When I go to pull back, he shoves the carton and spoon aside quickly, and pulls my left leg over so I'm straddling him.

He looks up at me, his eyes searching mine for a few moments, and I watch as his lids lower, but not from arousal.

"Kalani..." My name leaves his lips on a breath and my insides tighten.

His tone is raw and divulging, and panic fills me.

He sees it and a dejected, almost tired, expression takes over his perfect face.

With semi-shaky hands, I run my fingers from his thick hair, down his neck and back up, watching as he blinks slowly up at me, his long lashes scratching at his skin.

One of his hands leaves my thigh and slides across my cheek, where it pauses briefly before tucking my hair behind my ear.

"I like when you do that." My voice is thick and extra raspy.

"I know." He smiles softly up at me.

"How do you know?"

"Because, you hold your breath every time I do."

My chest cramps. "Is that why you do it? Because I like it?"

Say no...

"No." He grins. "I started to because it was the only gentle thing you'd allow. Then," his eyes roam around my face, "I had to keep doing it because I needed to feel your skin against mine. And now..." He runs his fingers down the length of my hair, letting the curl fall from his fingertips when he reaches the end. "Now I do it because my body craves the look you give me when I do."

"What look?" I breathe, my body growing heavier, more relaxed.

"The one you're giving me right now." His hands glide across my collarbone. "While your eyes are low and aroused, they're also full of fear and wonder. You're scared of what you're feeling when I'm touching you, but you're dying for me to do it again." He leans forward and kisses my neck, his hands sliding down my back to rest on my ass. "But you don't understand any of it, so you put up that wall of yours." His nose feathers across my jawline and my eyes flutter closed. "You're not used to wanting something." His teeth scrape down my earlobe and my body shudders. His breath warms my ear. "But more than that, you're not used to needing something." When I feel him pull back, I open my eyes to meet his, searching.

My breathing speeds up and everything starts to ache, my head, the sensitive spots between my legs, my chest.

"What do I need?" It's a desperate whisper – a plea, begging him to tell me.

His body, his heart... a Xanax?

I have no idea.

His shoulders drop a little, and when he blinks, he keeps his eyes shut a second longer than necessary. "I think I know, but you have to figure it out on your own, Kalani."

"How?"

He shrugs.

"What if I don't? Figure it out, I mean."

His hands slide under my ass, gripping me as he stands. He sets me on the bed and leans down, his lips hovering over mine. "Then it'll be me who's numb."

He kisses me.

It's soft and slow and far too short.

He tugs on his track pants and reaches for my hand, pulling me off the bed and walking beside me until we reach the front door where he grabs his keys and slips on his shoes.

I start to pull his shirt over my head but he squeezes my hand, shaking his head.

He pulls his sweater on, kisses my cheek, then drops his forehead to mine. "I'll see you tomorrow?" he whispers, running his hands up and down my arms.

Not trusting my voice, I nod, tilting my head slightly to feather his lips with a kiss.

"Goodnight, Kalani," he says softly, and walks out the door.

When I close the door behind him, my body sinks against it, my mind at a total loss to understand what's happening.

"Goodnight, Nate," I whisper in the nothingness that surrounds me. And for the first time, in as long as I can remember... I feel alone.

XOXOXOXOXOXOXOXOXOXOXO

"Alright." Mia spits her gum into a napkin. "Valentine's Day is next week and I need your help. I want to keep it light and simple. Not an 'I love you', but an 'I love your body and you're cool'."

After thanking the hostess who sets down our waters, I scowl at Mia. "You're asking the wrong person."

"You have had boyfriends, Lolli... in the past." She shrugs her sweatshirt off. "What did you do for them?"

"I don't know, Candy Grams at school. Maybe some chocolate and makin' out behind the bleachers."

She gapes at me. "Seriously?"

"What?" I laugh, shrugging. "I was like thirteen, fourteen, last time I worried about that." Her shoulders droop and she puffs her lips out. "Just do whatever and end it naked. Win-win."

She purses her lips while shaking her head. Eventually, she gives up and laughs. "God, you are such a guy."

I grin with my straw in my mouth. "Nothing wrong with closing out the day with a happy ending."

"Considering I've heard Nate leaving your place every night for the last few weeks, I'd have to say I'm aware." She smiles, then averts her eyes from mine.

"Talk to me, Mia." Setting my cup down, I cross my arms and tilt my head at her. "You know I don't like this pussy-footin' around kind of stuff."

"Nothing, really." She nibbles on the inside of her lip. "I was just wondering if, you know..." She finally meets my eyes. "Is it serious, or...?"

My brows pinch and I look past her shoulder, thinking about her question. "I like him. I know that much. And I don't like the thought of him with anyone else. It's good the way it is, just day to day, no pressure, ya know?" I look back at her and she nods, her red hair falling over her shoulder.

"You both seem really into each other." She smiles and leans back in her chair. "I've never seen Nate like this and I've known him since Kinder."

I smile and look down at my hands.

She gasps and my gaze flies to hers, finding her mouth and eyes open wide, and her finger pointing at me.

"What?"

"You're freaking blushing!" She claps excitedly.

"Shut up, Mia."

"The stone-cold Kalani Lee Embers is blushing," she sing-songs.

I kick her under the table. "Shut up, bitch."

She only laughs harder and I join in, my gaze dancing to my left. My laughter dies on my lips when I see Jarrod and Olivia in the booth a space over from us, having heard our entire conversation.

Mia notices my glare and follows my gaze.

Olivia smirks and leans back against the booth. "Wow, Lolli. Every night, huh? Hope you're on birth control."

"Why?" Mia asks in a sugary sweet voice. "They'd have the cutest little bambinos. Don't you think, Lolli?"

But I'm not looking at her.

My eyes are locked on Jarrod as he taps on the screen of his phone, looking from it to me in jerky movements.

My eyes pinch at the sides as I replay mine and Mia's conversation in my head, and my body freezes.

Mia used my full name and Jarrod is a football fan. There's no way he didn't put it together. It's confirmed when he meets my gaze and holds it.

His face is laced with malice. Slowly, one side of his mouth lifts into a cynical smirk, and I know he's figured it out.

It's not that I'm ashamed or embarrassed about who I am and who my family is – was. I loved my parents, my grandpa, and the life I lived. However, that doesn't mean I want everyone to know I literally have millions sitting in my bank account. Or that my family is dead. I don't want whispers or pity, or questions, and I sure as shit don't need the fake friendships money brings.

In my peripheral vision, I see Mia shift in her seat when she realizes the fun is over.

Along with my heart rate, Jarrod's smirk grows when he holds his phone out for Liv, but his eyes stay glued to mine. I can see him gauging me, trying to decide which reaction would benefit him the most.

Dick.

Liv, however, couldn't hide her response.

All eyes shift to her when she gasps, her pink nails lifting to her lips briefly, before she realizes her mistake and zeros in on me. Her gaze is more calculating and confused than Jarrod's. Her pathetic ass doesn't get it, I can see it in her icy blue eyes. She's wondering why I didn't waltz into school that very first day shouting to the rooftops, "I'm Lee Ember's granddaughter! Look at me! Love me!"

Bitch.

She stands slowly, reaching for her purse without taking her eyes off me. "I've lost my appetite. Let's go." Her gaze cuts to Jarrod quickly, who tosses cash on the table while standing.

With that, they make their way out the front door.

"Shit, Lolli," Mia's face contorts. "I'm sorry, I didn't see them there."

My shaky hand finds my temple, and I inhale deeply. "It's fine, Meems. I know." I look to the ceiling.

"You think they're planning on spreading the word?"

"Honestly?" Pinching the bridge of my nose, I shake my head. "No. I don't."

When Mia's brows jump, I explain.

"She's shocked right now. She's all about self-image and anything that will take her a few steps up the invisible social ladder she's created in her head. She knows if she goes around telling people, it'll gain me more attention, and that's the last thing she wants." I take a drink of water.

"She ran her mouth awhile back, saying I didn't belong in Nate's world. Basically, calling me a poser, more or less..." I tilt my head in thought. "This is the last thing she wants people to find out."

"Yeah, maybe. And Jarrod?"

I frown as I stir the ice in my cup with my straw. "I have no idea..." I look up to find Mia's worried eyes on me. "But they will use it for something."

She drops back against her chair. "Yeah."

"Yeah."

Chapter Thirty-One

K ALANI

I'm just stepping out of the girls' locker room when Nate wraps his arms around my thighs and lifts me.

My backpack falls to the floor as I laugh and lean forward to connect my lips with his.

He smiles against my mouth and gives me a hard peck, before pulling back to look at me. "Hi."

"Hi." My tone is laced with amusement. Here he is, lifting me off the ground just to kiss me and say 'hi', when we both just got out of gym - a class we have together.

"I'm gonna need you to wear some tight-ass jeans, your sexy black boots, and matching jacket tomorrow night. I'll let you pick the shirt." He winks.

My brows lift teasingly. "Oh, really?" I run my fingers through his dark hair.

Dropping me to my feet, he nods, seeming mighty pleased

with himself. "Really. I'm picking you up at seven." He bends and grabs my bag off the ground, swinging it over his shoulder.

"And where, might I ask, are we going?"

"It's a surprise." He laces his hand with mine, bringing it to his lips for a quick kiss as we make our way toward his truck.

"Alright. As long as it ends the same way every other night has, then I'm game."

He pushes me against the rock wall of the building quickly, his dark eyes searing through me, waking up every nerve-ending in my body.

"It'll be better."

It's a promise, one I'm okay accepting.

"Okay."

His eyes shift back and forth between mine, then his sexy smirk graces his perfect lips and he pulls me off the wall.

"Mia's waiting for you out front. I have a few things to finish up before tomorrow, so I can't come over tonight."

Apparently, I'm pouting because he laughs and pinches my bottom lip between his fingers. "Stop it." He smiles down at me. "If I can make it by, I will."

I smash my lips to the side to keep from smiling. "Sorry. I just kinda like having you around."

His smile grows. "I know."

I search his eyes. He's not being cocky or conceited. His smile's genuine and just for me. He drops a quick kiss to my lips. "See you tomorrow. Seven on the dot." He steps back, only letting go of my hand when the distance forces him to.

I nod, watching as he jogs backward toward his truck.

"Looks like it's just me and you tonight, kid," Mia teases as I hop into her Jeep.

I can't wipe the smile off my lips if I tried. "Looks like it."

NATE

Two at a time, I all but run down the stairs, laughing when I almost fall on my ass at the bottom.

"Whoa, son." Smirking, my dad saunters toward me, smoothing his hands down his dress shirt. "Where's the fire?"

I look from him to me, realizing we're practically wearing the same thing: dark jeans, a long-sleeved button up with the arms rolled up to our elbows, only mine's a dark navy-blue and his is black, and black boots.

"Just excited to pick up Kalani, I guess." I shrug and pick up my wallet from the entrance table, sliding it into my back pocket.

Dad nods, giving me a probing look. "You tell her where we're headed?"

My smile grows and I shake my head.

A deep sigh leaves him, and he chuckles. "Oh, lord. She has no idea we'll be around tonight, does she?" He raises a thick brow at me.

"Nope." I smile.

He shakes his head in amusement. "I hope you know what you're doing, son."

"Honestly?" I laugh, dropping down to tie my boot. "I haven't a clue. All I know is I want to keep her by me." I stand again to meet his gaze.

"Yeah?" he asks, his face neutral.

"Yeah."

After a few moments, he asks, "For how long?"

"As long as she'll allow."

Eyes pinched around the edges, he nods and scratches at his chin. "You using protection?"

I think about lying, but I don't keep secrets from my parents; that's why I have the freedom I do. "Ninety-five percent of the time, yeah."

Both brows raise this time.

I clear my throat, my hands finding my hips. "Sometimes we don't really, uh...plan it?"

Dad tries, but fails, to keep his laugh in. Clasping one of my shoulders, he gives me a small shake. "I guess that's to be expected. Just be careful." He stabs a finger into my chest. "Your mama said no grandbabies till after college."

I shrug him off, smoothing out my shirt. "Yeah, yeah. I know. I'm in no hurry."

Not that it would be a bad thing if she did accidentally get pregnant. I bet she'd be as gorgeous as ever.

"Oh, hell."

My gaze flies to my dad's, finding him running both hands down his face, his fingers pausing over his lips, "You just seen it, didn't you?"

Shrugging, I look to my left.

"Seen what?" We both jolt when we hear my mother's soft voice.

"Nothing," leaves both our mouths at the same time, making my mother laugh.

"Uh-huh." She makes her way down the stairs.

My father turns toward her, and when her eyes shift to him, I see her chest fall with a deep sigh, and a light pink brightens up her fair skin.

I slip onto the porch to give them a few moments of privacy.

On the way to Kalani's, I figure it's as good a time as any to fill my parents in on a decision I made.

"So." I clear my throat and lean forward, placing my elbows on the back of both their seats. "I wanted to let you guys know I made a decision about college."

I watch dad's hand tighten nervously around the steering wheel, but I gotta give the gold to my mother for her attempt at a very nonchalant, "Oh?"

"Yeah." I nod. "I'm going to take Coach Jeffery's offer to play for UCLA."

Dad nods at the road, and mom pulls her pink cardigan closer to her chest. "California?"

"Yeah."

"That's great, honey. We're very proud of you." My mother smiles at me over her shoulder, her left hand coming to clamp over my mine. She gives it a small squeeze.

"You make this decision for yourself, son?"

When I look at my dad, I see the lines at the corners of his eyes are a bit deeper than normal. Patting him on the shoulder, I put his mind at ease.

"Aside from my counselor, you two are the only ones who know if that helps. I haven't discussed this with, uh, anyone. I looked into the housing, the team's rep, and history. Everything down to the weather and local surrounding area. Shops, fun, all of it. I already talked to Mase and Ari, and they're both headed to Avix, so they'll be around, too." I nod, even though they can't see me. "I want this."

No need to tell them Kalani played a huge part in my decision and is the entire reason I looked west in the first place. I don't know exactly where she's headed, but I have a feeling it's back that way. I've paid attention to signs she gives or lets slip. I know the beach she and her parents frequented the most was in Capitola, which is near more Northern California, and her favorite French toast - other than her dad's - was at a place called 101 Cafe. I looked it up. It's a hole-in-the-wall diner, in a beachy town called Ocean-side, in Southern California.

UCLA is the safest bet. And if, for some reason in the end - God forbid - she doesn't want me, want us, I'll still be happy living there. Not that I plan on letting her slip by in the first place, but still.

"Well, then I'm happy you found a place you're excited about, son."

We pull up at Kalani's and I'm about to jump out the still rolling truck, when my mom grabs my hand, halting my movement. "We really are proud of you, Nathaniel." My mother's voice is soft and low. "You've grown so much in the last few months, and..." Her eyes glaze over and my dad places his hand on her knee. "We're just really proud."

I smile and lean forward, kissing her cheek. "I know, Ma. And I feel better. More... me, I guess." I laugh lightly, shaking off the seriousness of this conversation.

I step out.

As I walk toward Kalani's door, my palms start to sweat and my breathing gets a bit heavier.

I glance back at my parents.

My mom sits in her seat with her head resting against the back, smiling knowingly at me. Her eyes shining and soft, she tilts her chin toward the door.

I knock.

When the handle starts to turn, I inhale deeply.

Every single ounce of air escapes me, leaving my lungs starving and desperate when Kalani pulls the door open and leans her tiny little body against it, looking up at me through dark lashes, her eyes bright and clear.

She's so beautiful.

Subconsciously, my feet find their way directly in front of her.

Her head tilts back, allowing her to look up at me, and her arm drops from the door.

My right-hand lifts to her face and I run my knuckles across her soft, flawless skin. I can't tell if she's wearing more makeup on her cheeks than normal, but they look a little pinker, her eyes a little bluer.

My hand continues upward.

Already anticipating it, I look to her lips, watching the slight twitch that always graces the left side of her mouth when my

315

fingers skim above her ear and curve around, securing her hair behind it.

My left hand comes up to cup her cheek, my thumb stroking her skin softly, watching as she closes her eyes on a tranquil, slow blink, her eyes opening even brighter. More vibrant.

Her right hand covers mine, while her left sprawls across the center of my chest, giving her a base to support herself on as she lifts onto her toes to kiss me.

As if I would let her fall.

Her deep sigh fans across my mouth when her bright red lips press against mine.

I step further into her, threading my hands deeper into her hair, kissing her back a little harder.

A loud horn sounds instantly and we're jolted back to reality.

Kalani's eyes turn wary as she lowers herself slowly.

"Handsome?"

I grin. "Hi, baby."

Her eyes narrow slightly, but she's not upset. "Is that your dad's truck behind you?"

She tries to hide her small frame behind mine, but I move out of the way, giving her a complete view of both my parents leaning toward the window, arms waving at her.

Now I know it's a blush that creeps up her chest, neck, and cheeks.

She lifts a hand to wave. "You are so dead," she says through a big, fake smile.

Laughing, I grab her hand, and place a quick kiss to her knuckles. "Sorry, but I knew you'd try and back out if I told you and, I promise you, tonight will be a good time."

She eyes me for a minute, then smiles at the ground, letting me lead her to the truck. "I know it will be."

This time, she squeezes my hand.

Funny thing is, I don't even think she realized it.

Chapter Thirty-Two

N ATE

She's leaning against the metal slab of a concession booth, one hip cocked out. Her right hand holds a tube filled with red Slurpee that's about as tall as she is, her left holding the neon green straw she keeps pulling to her lips. She throws her head back, laughing as my slightly inebriated mother tells her some story about who the hell knows what. It's a simple thing, yet she's never looked so gorgeous.

It's a cold night, but the body heat from the hundreds of others around, and the few shots of Patron we snuck into our drinks, has her skin flushed and alive.

My eyes zone in on her lips again when her mouth closes around the piece of plastic for the dozenth time.

A deep chuckle from my left has my attention snapping in that direction.

My dad's leaning up against the side of the building where we're waiting for the girls to come back with drinks, a dickhead smile in place.

"What?" I groan, crossing my own arms and he laughs harder, grabbing at his stomach in the process.

With a shake of his head, he reaches around and scratches at the back of his neck, jerking his head toward our women. "You look 'bout ready to murder that there piece of plastic, son." He grins even wider. "You jealous of a straw?"

I try to scowl at him, but it doesn't work and I start laughing with him.

On an inhale, I nod, my eyes on my girl. "Yeah, Pops. I think I am." I swing my head back toward him and he kicks off the wall, coming to stand next to me.

"You told her yet?" He looks from me to her and my eyes follow his.

The second my gaze lands on her, she looks up, having sensed it, locking her eyes with mine. The smile that takes over her face nearly knocks me on my ass. It's then I know.

Finishing off my 'Slurpee', I hand it to my dad without looking at him. Nothing could make me take my eyes off hers right now. "Come stand with your wife," I tell him as my feet start moving. "I'm taking my girl for a while."

The closer I get to her, the taller she stands, and the more her eyes wrinkle in excitement. Not caring who's around or watching, I cup the back of her neck and smash her lips into mine. It's not open and heated, but it's strong and meaningful.

When my lips are simply pressed against hers, and that uncontrollable heat builds deep inside me, spreading across my body, that has to mean something. This girl was made for me. She's everything.

Perfect.

A raspy giggle leaves her and she pulls back slightly, but she doesn't take her hands off me. "Guess I'm not the only one whose internal monologue is kinda broken." She smiles, earning one from me.

I stare at her, slide my hands down her arms until I reach her fingers, then thread mine through hers.

And, as if I planned this exact moment for the perfect time, the band steps back onto the stage, the lead singer asking us to give a round of applause to the guest performer, then announces their next song.

With a quick kiss to her lips, I tug on her hands, and together we run into the mob of people, stopping when we've reached a nice, crowded, lively spot.

She throws her arms around my neck, kissing my lips, right as the opening cord and soft melody I've been waiting for –was hoping to hear- streams through the arena speakers.

Nickelback begins to perform their throwback of the night, "Never Gonna Be Alone."

I wrap my arms around her and hers come down to wrap underneath, so her palms rest on my shoulder blades, then slide across my back.

I pull her in, my fingers trailing across the exposed skin at her waistline, wanting her to feel the promise of the song.

The year's coming to an end, with only a few months of school left, and I still don't know for sure where her mind is. I do know she's never been the happy Kalani she is now. At least, not in a long time.

This Kalani, while still true and honest, is open and unsure. She's beauty and pain, light and dark. She's brave. She knows better than anyone that today might be it, but instead of assuming it will be and cruising through, she's smiling and laughing and living. And not just on the surface anymore.

At first it was just around me, but I see her opening up with others now, and I couldn't be prouder of her.

She's alive. I can feel it in the way she touches me, see it in the way she looks at me, and I need her to know...

"Never gonna be alone..." I sing my promise in time with Chad Kroeger and her body tenses, sending my heart into overdrive, fueled by pure fear. But it's only for the briefest of moment before she pulls me tighter against her. Securing my place next to her.

I'll take it.

Kalani passed out on the forty-five-minute ride home and is laying her tiny body across mine. I brush her hair out of her face, preparing to wake her when my mom clears her throat, soft and quiet, careful not to wake my sleeping beauty.

When I look up at her, her eyes appear a little moist as she smiles at me. "Do you have to wake her?" She tilts her head slightly. "She could stay, if you'd like."

I grin, wishing this were an option, but knowing Kalani wouldn't go for that. "Thanks, Ma, but I'm gonna take her home."

Mom smashes her lips together in a smile, nodding at me.

When I lift Kalani and step out of the truck, she stirs slightly and wraps her hands around my neck, her face tucking into my chest.

Each step I take, her lips brush across my collarbone, and my grip on her tightens.

She feels it, the heat coming off my body and her eyelashes flit across my skin, sending an electric shock straight to my groin.

Her tongue peeks out, tasting the salty sweat of my skin, while her fingers skim up the line of my hair.

"Handsome." Her voice is raspy with sleep and desperate with need.

"I know, baby." I pull the door open and set her on the seat, but she catches my face before I can move and pulls my lips to hers.

Her kiss is soft, lazy, her silk tongue slipping past my lips. "I want you," she whispers.

"I know." I run my palms up her jean-covered thighs.

"I need you."

My blood flows faster as I slowly pull back to look at her.

Her hand comes up, and she runs her fingertips across my jaw. "Take me home, Handsome." It's barely audible, barely a breath that escapes her lips, but it roars through my body like a stadium speaker announcement. Loud, and clear, and booming. Or maybe that's my heart hitting my ribs.

She needs me.

I need her.

I've never driven so fast...

We've been lying in her bed for a few minutes, her wrapped in my arms, me wishing she'd allow herself to stay there. But as much as I hate this part, hate leaving her, the last thing I want to do is push when I know tonight was heavy. So, I kiss her forehead and shift out from under her, making my way into the bathroom to toss the condom.

I pull my boxers on and am reaching for my jeans when her hesitant hand catches mine.

When my pinched gaze finds hers, she averts her eyes to the floor.

"Kalani..." I whisper and she drops my hand.

With a shake of her head, she lets out a small laugh and walks past me to throw on a shirt.

At her door, I tell her good night, placing a soft kiss to her lips, her cheek, her forehead, then step out into the cold night air, making my way to my truck.

"Nate!" Her voice is urgent and heavy.

With my brows pulled in, I turn to her.

Something in her eyes tells me not to move, so I keep my feet planted the few steps they've carried me from her door.

Her gaze is, again, on the floor, and her right foot is bouncing against the cold tile floor.

Finally, she laughs and looks up.

She takes a single step, extending her arm out for me, and my chest tightens.

Afraid to misread this, I place my palm in hers blindly.

Her eyes flit back and forth between mine, and that's when I hear the words flowing through the speakers in the house.

Could be the song, could be something else, but whatever it is, I stop breathing when she whispers, "Stay."

Needing to know if I heard her right, or if my desire to do so fucked with my head, I dip down so we're eye level, gripping her flushed cheeks tight in my palms. "What'd you say, baby?"

Her hands fly to mine and she pulls, trying to remove them. An attempt to duck and run, I'm sure.

I won't allow that.

"Nuh-uh." I shake my head, scraping her bottom lip with my teeth. "Say it again." My voice is rough and demanding, but that's what she needs right now.

Proving me right, her chest pushes out and fire sparks behind her blue eyes, while her hands drop to my chest. "Fine. I said stay, Handsome," she snaps, her brows pulling in, daring me to deny her.

I could never.

A grin splits across my lips and hers follows. She rolls her eyes and tucks herself into my embrace to try and make light of the mood, but there's nothing light about it. This is big. Especially for her. While I've been wanting to stay since I dragged her out of her date with Jarrod, Kalani has been doing her best to keep things simple.

So, yeah, this is big.

I'm gonna make it better.

With a ridiculous smile on my face, I pull back, grasping her shoulders. "Get some sweats on, and some shoes. I have an idea."

With a light laugh, she agrees and runs back into the house, emerging not a minute later, ready for me to lead her wherever I wish.

I kill the lights and turn down the dirt road.

"Uh... Handsome?"

I grin, ignoring her as I pull my truck next to my dad's. Turning off the engine, I shift toward her in my seat, my forearms resting on the steering wheel and back of the seat. "Watch for a light, then get out. 'Kay?"

Her brows lower, but she's grinning.

I take that as a yes and dash toward my house, sneaking inside as quietly as a six-foot-two, one-hundred-and-eighty-pound guy is capable of, and head into my room, locking the door behind me.

Grabbing the flashlight from the top of my dresser, I head to my window and throw it open, shining the light onto the hood of my Hummer.

Slowly, she emerges, shutting the door gently behind her, her eyes squinting at me. It's not pitch black out, and the stars are shining brightly, so she can see me fairly good.

Her eyes take in everything around and return to me.

I grin and lean against my windowsill. Cupping my mouth with my hands, I shout in a whisper, "Come to me, Jenny."

Her face pinches slightly, then her fingers lift to her mouth. Finally, she squeals and stomps her feet before running to the side of the house on the tips of her toes.

I watch, my eyes glued on her, as she makes her way up and over the balcony... making her way to me.

Her breath is a bit heavy from the climb, mixed with excitement, but her smile is wide and real, and her eyes... Her eyes are bright and loving.

"Hi, Forrest."

I smile. "Hi, Jenny."

When I reach for her, she blushes, slips her hand in mine and steps through the window. The moment her feet meet my floor, she wraps herself around me, pressing her cheek into my chest, and my arms envelop her.

"Tonight was perfect," she mumbles into my shirt.

"Almost," I whisper into her hair, and pull back to toss my shirt to the floor, kicking my shoes off in the process.

Her arms lift, allowing me to slide off her sweater, then her feet for me to pull off her shoes, leaving her in sweatpants and a t-shirt.

I bite the inside of my cheek to keep from smiling when she takes the initiative to pull the covers back and slides in first. She faces the wall so I tuck in behind her, pulling her as close as our bodies will allow. She lifts her head, allowing my arm to slide under the pillow, then drops back down.

Small sighs keep leaving her and my chest tightens, along with my arm that's wrapped around her. Every time her chest inflates, mine pinches.

"Now it's perfect." Kissing the back of her head, I dig my face into her hair to breathe her in.

My grip loosens when she props onto her elbow, shifting to look at me over her shoulder. Her eyes roam my face for a few moments, like she's trying to memorize everything about me, and this glossy look I've never seen, but instantly love, takes over.

With a small tug, I pull the hairband from her hair, watching as it falls over her shoulders. When my hand comes up to tuck her thick locks behind her ear, she leans into my palm, closing her eyes. She turns until her lips graze across my skin, then brings her pretty blues back to me.

"Happy Valentine's Day, Nathaniel," she whispers, unblinking.

Gently guiding her mouth to mine, I kiss her lips soft and slow.

"Happy Valentine's Day, Kalani."

She tucks her body back into me, and we fall asleep, together.

Chapter Thirty-Three

K ALANI

Blankets in hand, Mia and I make our way to the gate. The Knights were invited to play in a spring, end of the year, farewell game against the Crenshaw Tigers from the next town over. According to Coach, it's the seniors' last hoorah before real life begins.

For some of these boys, tonight will be their last night suiting up and stepping under the lights. For others, like Nate, it's a goodbye tribute to the coach that allotted them the opportunity to look forward to the future that's impending; the chance to play in a bigger stadium under bigger lights. Emotions are going to run high tonight.

After paying the five-dollar student fee, we walk inside and make our way to the first row, front and center, and right on the fifty-yard line. Perfect view of the boys. Of my man. Unfortunately, that also means the cheerleaders are in sight. And by cheer-leaders, I mean Liv.

Yay.

"Mr. and Mrs. Monroe coming?" Mia asks, as she wraps her black and red blanket around her shoulders.

"Yeah. Sara texted me a little bit ago. She said they'd be here."

Mia bumps my shoulder, so I turn to look at her.

"Sara, huh?" she teases.

To hide my smile, I breathe into my hands, rubbing them back and forth for warmth. It's cold as shit here for early spring. "She says she's young and doesn't like being called missus, that's all."

Mia nods, a grin on her lips. "Yeah, that's a bunch of shit."

My mouth drops open and now it's me bumping her.

"What?" she laughs, pulling her blanket up higher. "It's true! I've been hearing Liv call her Mrs. Monroe at all the barbecues for years. Never once has she said, 'Please, call me Sara'." She smiles widely at me.

"Yeah, well." I bite the inside of my cheek. "She kinda likes me, I guess."

Thankfully, a scoff is all I get and she buries her face in her phone.

The boys' jog onto the field and start their pregame warmups, so I stand and lean against the railing, watching Nate as he commands his team with simple stretch calls.

It's all routine and they know it by heart, but they wait for his order before manipulating their bodies as needed.

His head shifts toward me, and while I can't see his eyes from here, I know they're on me. I can feel them, burning straight through my chest.

Since Valentine's Day last month, Nate has spent at least four nights out of the week at my house, and to be honest, I kinda wish he'd stay more. I like him being there, like waking up to him. I hadn't realized how much I missed having someone around.

As a child, someone was usually there, but as a teenager, other than those last couple months when my gramps finally moved in, everyone was sporadic. I never stopped to consider what it would feel like to have someone like this. Just to eat and watch movies with. It's nice and it's bringing back simple memories I'd lost. He's bringing them back.

Nate's unknowingly healing pieces of me I didn't know needed mending, helping memories and feelings I forced my brain to forget to resurface. I hadn't realized, when I shut down my psyche, I'd also lost all the good moments in my life. But when you don't allow your mind to sit idle, when you force it into the here and now only, I guess it's inevitable. It's also tiring. And I'm tired of being tired.

"Hey!"

Peeking over my shoulder, I smile, giving a little wave to Nate's parents as they shimmy down the aisle toward us.

The second she sets her bag down, Sara wraps me in a quick one-armed hug, then mimics my position. She smiles, letting her eyes roam the football field, then looks down over the railing at the cheerleaders who are four or five feet below, warming up on the track.

"Oh!" She claps her hands, whirling back to her bag. "I brought you something!"

Releasing one hand from the bar, I turn slowly, and lean my back against it. Sliding my eyes to Mr. Monroe - Ian - I quirk a brow.

He shrugs like he has no clue, but the tip of his lips tells me he does. He always knows when it comes to his wife. It's as if they're two people sharing one soul. What they have, it's something to strive for.

My eyes shoot wide when she turns back to me with Nate's away jersey in her arms. It's red with the number twenty-one embroidered on the chest in big, black letters - opposite of his home jersey. She turns it in her hands, showing me the Monroe nameplate across the back.

"What do you want me to do with that?" I smash my lips to the side.

With a huff, she shakes her head and thrusts the jersey to my chest. "Wipe that scowl off your beautiful little face and put the damn thing on, Kalani Embers."

When Ian and Mia laugh from behind her, I narrow my eyes at both of them.

Traitors.

"Yeah, Lolli," Mia singsongs. "Wear it."

"I don't need to prove anything to anyone." I cross my arms and stand up straight. "He knows and I know. That's all that matters."

When I lock eyes with Ian, he tips his head slightly, his eyes soft, reminding me of his son, but Sara looks about ready to cry.

Shit, wrong thing to say?

She steps up to me, gripping my shoulders, and my brows pull together.

"We know that sweetheart," she whispers lightly, the gentleness of her voice making me hold my breath. "I didn't bring you this so you could show it off to the world. I know that's not you. Though," she laughs slightly, "I have to say, I wouldn't mind if you did, because you're you. But, I brought this for you because I know what it would mean to him." Her eyes shine with unshed tears, and my ribs start to ache. "You sitting here, under the lights on his last night as a high school football player, with his name and number proudly displayed on your cute little body." She squeezes my shoulders again, and out of the corner of my eye, I see Ian's hand come to rest on her lower back. "He'll never forget it," she whispers.

Heat spreads up and across my neck and cheeks, but more importantly, warmth takes over my body in a way I've never experienced and can't explain.

After a glance between the two, I nod, then reach for the jersey.

She smiles brightly and sits down on the bench, digging in her bag like she didn't just tell me Nate would carry a piece of me with him, no matter where life took him. Like she didn't just say she knows and understands the person I am, and she wouldn't have me any other way.

My chest starts to tighten, my eyes pinching at the sides, and I feel the sudden need to run.

My body turns on its own accord, and my eyes find their harbor immediately.

He senses me.

Nate's head turns in my direction, the ball he's been tossing around to warm up his muscles freezing in his hands. He angles his body toward mine, silently asking if he needs to come to me.

He's got me.

Air makes its way into my lungs and the pounding in my head lessens.

His helmet tips slightly and a smile breaks across my lips.

I can picture the scowl on his handsome face right now, the drop in his brows, the challenge in his dark eyes.

Fuck it.

In one quick motion, I yank his jersey over my head, then grab the railing with both hands.

When the ball falls from his grip, I can't help the laugh that escapes me. He takes two steps toward me, then prepares to jog, but Mr. P. is quick with his interception and a deflated Nate turns back to his partner, snatching the ball off the ground in a pissy motion I find sexy as hell.

"Told ya."

I turn back, finding both of Nate's parents smirking, Sara nestled between her husband's legs as he sits one bleacher up, his arms wrapped tightly around his wife.

Laughing, I take my seat between Mia and Sara. "Let's watch some football."

The buzzer sounds and we all get sucked into the lights, whistles, and exhilaration a Friday night game brings.

The boys play their hearts out as the realization of the night sets it for both teams. It's all sweat, blood, and dedication on the field, making for one hell of a game.

On the last play, the crowd stands.

Nate calls his play, pointing in both directions, adjusting his guys as needed and gets set. Holding the ball, he searches for an opening, but finds no one free. His only option is to make a run for it.

With the ball tucked tight, he books it, stiff-arming the safety as he makes a dive for him, and from there, it's open field.

We jump up and down, screaming together as Nate crosses into the end zone, scoring the winning touchdown with only seconds left on the clock. Sara and Mia hug me, then hug each other, a trend that flows through the crowd.

I lean over the railing, yelling out to the boys, watching as Nate jogs back, his teammates hitting his shoulder pads, and slapping his helmet along the way, but he doesn't stop when he reaches the sidelines. He tosses his helmet and keeps running. Headed right for me.

He picks up speed right before he reaches me, leaping up to latch himself onto the railing, smashing his lips into mine in the same motion.

With a smile, I pull back, allowing him enough room to throw his legs over the side.

His smile is wide and elated. He pulls my body against his, his brown eyes dropping to his jersey I'm wearing, then swinging to his parents.

"Ma?"

I turn to see her watery eyes as she nods.

He looks back to me, dropping his sweaty forehead against mine. "Thank you for wearing it."

"I almost didn't." I reach up, brushing his sweat-soaked hair back.

He catches my hand on its descent, and brings my wrist to his lips, placing a soft kiss there. "I know."

When my eyes pinch, he cups my cheeks, his dark eyes reaching deep inside me, pulling strings I didn't know existed.

His grip tightens in warning, so I raise my hands to cover his and hold my breath. I can feel the accelerated rhythm of his heart beating through his palms.

Those chocolate eyes implore mine. "I love you."

I'm shaking my head before he even finishes.

"Yeah, Kalani." He nods, sureness carrying his voice. "I do. I'm in love with you."

"No. You're not," I shoot back, my body turning to cement.

He smiles and I don't miss the chuckles around us. "Yes, I am. And you're in love with me, too."

"No, I'm not."

He steps into me. "Yes. You are. I know you are."

"You don't know shit," I whisper, unable to catch my breath, my eyes darting across his face, searching for a sign of... something.

He brushes my hair out of the way. "How do you feel when I touch you?"

"Warm."

"And when I hold you?" His arms wrap around me, his pads making him even larger.

My hands drop to his chest, the fight in me slowly dissolving. "Safe," I mutter.

He brings his mouth to my ear, whispering, "And when I fuck you?" He pulls back, locking our gazes once more, dipping his chin slightly.

I don't answer right away, but after a few moments, "Everything... loved," squeezes its way past my lips.

He nods and that perfect smile lights up his entire face.

"Oh, my God..." I think I say out loud. "When did this happen?"

His forehead drops to mine again. "It doesn't matter, baby."

I bring my hands to his waist, pulling back again. "I'm in love with you?"

He laughs, nodding his head.

My chest tightens and expands at the same time. Closing my eyes, a sense of belonging, of need and want, settle inside me and suddenly, while nothing makes sense, everything feels right. Him here. With me. Opening my eyes, I zone in on his.

"I'm in love with you."

With that, he pulls me into his arms and kisses me, not caring about the hundreds of fans around. Not caring that his parents and my cousin just witnessed this moment, he kisses me with everything he has, making sure I know exactly how much he loves me.

And I do the same.

Later that night, Nate and I are sitting on the lawn in Parker's backyard, me nestled between his legs, my back to his front, taking a break from the chaos that is an Alrick High senior bash.

This party reminds me of that first one I was dragged to back in November. People are crazy drunk and high on adrenaline and – let's be real - some other shit, too. Even though it's cold out, there is less clothing here than a strip club, and I'm pretty sure I saw a few getting down and dirty on the makeshift dance floor.

Spring break is in two days. I guess they're prepping for the massive hangovers they're bound to be in.

Nate's arms tighten around me, his face burrowing deeper into my hair, and I turn into him, bringing my cheek against his, enjoying the feeling of simply being near him. Feeling him.

It's crazy that just a few hours ago, I realized I loved him, because right now, sitting here with him, it feels like it has always been this way. Like there hasn't been a time where I didn't love him. He pulled some kind of quarterback sneak on me and found his opening, capitalizing on it.

Dirty jokes aside, I knew he had gotten inside me. I knew he burned himself deep into my being. There was no way a guy like him could make my body feel alive the way he does, bringing me back from the edge of a panic attack and give me the courage to make the first move with my aunt, without having left a mark on me.

He's become my everything in this short time and while it scares the shit out of me, it offers me a calmness I've never known and can't explain.

"Nate?" I whisper into the night, gazing up at all the stars.

"Hmm?" He takes a deep breath, inhaling me, his thighs tightening against mine. When my body trembles, I feel his mouth morph into a smile against my skin, and my heart beats out of my chest.

"There are things you still don't know about me." My voice is low and hesitant, not because I don't want him to know, but because I'm nervous. I don't want him to look at me and see an opportunity, not that he needs one. He's a badass on his own and will have no problem in college ball or after, but still. I guess maybe I'm afraid of being needed versus him needing me.

"I know everything I need to know, baby." He kisses my temple. "And everything else, I'll learn along the way."

I nod, my brows pinched. "Yeah, but my family-"

"There you guys are!" Mia slurs from the sliding door, gaining both our attention. "Austin is in need of your assistance, Mr. Monroe." She hobbles out the door, two unopened beers in hand, and plops down on the ground next to me.

Laughing, I grab onto her arm to stabilize her.

"I'll keep your girl company." She shoos him away. "Go on now."

Nate shakes his head with a smile, drops a quick kiss to my lips, and makes his way into the house.

Mia twists off the top to a beer and hands it to me before opening her own. "Cheers." She thrusts her bottle out and instead of clinking ours together, the bitch hits the top of my bottle with the bottom of hers, making mine overflow, forcing me to down about half of it in one drink.

Her body tips to the side when she laughs, but she sticks an arm out, righting herself.

"Bitch." I nudge her, throwing her off balance again.

"You love me." She lays her head on my shoulder.

"I do."

"Aaand you love Nate?"

I nod, looking off to the side.

She's quiet for a few seconds, then whispers, "That's really good, Lollipop."

While I know she's happy for me, her tone has an underlying sadness to it. It's more of a plea than a whisper. I have to ask her what's going on with her. She's been acting weird the last few weeks, and I can't figure it out. "Mia-"

"Okay, so," she cuts me off and I bite my inner cheek to keep quiet.

Clearly, she doesn't want to talk about it, and if anyone gets not wanting others to pry, it's me.

"I think we've got everything we need for the trip. All I need is a couple new swimsuits. How 'bout you?" Mia slurs, lifting her head to peek at me.

I wink and watch her shoulders relax. "I think I'm good, other than travel shower shit."

"That's easy enough." She nods, slamming back the rest of her beer. She's about to speak when something catches her attention over her shoulder.

I glance back, seeing Liv's silhouette through the door. Following her line of sight, I see Parker, Austin and Nate laughing and taking shots.

A smile crosses my lips. Shifting my eyes back to Liv, her posture stiffens.

The chick must have a bitch-o-meter or something because she lifts her plastic head and spots me in the yard.

She smirks and stands up taller, flipping her fake blonde hair over her proper little shoulder, opens the door, and steps out quietly.

"Bitch," Mia mumbles under her breath.

I narrow my gaze at her, hoping she'll get the hint and go the fuck away.

"So, Lolli." No such luck. "How's it feel?"

Releasing a huff, I indulge her. "How's what feel, Liv?" I lift my bottle to my lips.

"Living on someone else's fortune?"

My hand freezes midair, my head turning slowly to look her in the eye.

Her smirk deepens.

Oh, okay. We're doin' this...

I hop to my feet.

No way will this bitch look down on me.

NATE

Head tipped back, I let the liquor burn its way down my throat and slam my shot glass on the countertop-turned-bar in front of me.

"Shit's nasty, isn't it?" Parker squints his eyes, pulling the cheap whiskey bottle closer to read the label.

"Hell, yeah." I cough, wiping my mouth with the back of my hand.

"Freshman must have brought it." Parker's body shakes, the aftertaste hitting him.

"Oh, shit!" Austin's slur grabs our attention.

Following his line of sight, I see Liv with her hands on her hips, yapping something at my girl and Mia, who are sitting in the same spot I left them, but Kalani is quick to pop to her feet.

"The fuck's she doing?" My gaze narrows, but I can't see around Liv's body.

"Probably spittin' some shit about you." All our heads swivel around, finding Jarrod leaning against the nearby wall, his arms crossed over his chest, looking like a privileged asshole. "Hope it's false."

I'm quick to step up to him. "Something on your mind, Hollins?"

The bastard smirks, kicks off the wall and raises his beer to us, before disappearing into the next room.

When I turn back to the girls, I see Mia has stepped a few feet away, giving them some privacy. I look over at Kalani, who is now inches from Liv's face. "Damn it." I sidestep the barstool and place my hand on the sliding door's handle.

"Don't." Parker shoves in front of me, blocking my path.

My breathing picks up and I clench my jaw. Parker's big, but I'm bigger. "Get the fuck out of my way, Baylor. This don't concern you."

He rolls his eyes. "Sure. Fine." He throws his hands up, tilting his head slightly. "Go ahead, big man. Walk out there in the middle of a female version of dick measuring. Let's see who tells you to fuck off first." The smug bastard folds his hands in front of him, like he's preparing for a show.

Dick.

I look back at Kalani, fighting the smile that tugs at my lips when I see her little finger jabbing into Liv's chest. When I turn back to Parker, he smirks and raises a bottle of the good stuff, pouring us each a fresh shot.

Me and the boys prepare for another shot, all the while I'm

watching Kalani out of the corner of my eye. Austin's obnoxious laugh tells me I'm not fooling anybody.

"So, that was it boys, the final go. We'll never play on a field together again," Austin announces, raising his glass and we follow suit.

My face pinches when the liquor hits my throat. "You don't know that. There's always college ball," I tell them with a shrug.

Austin nods, tossing peanuts into his mouth. "Yeah." He chews while he speaks. "What's everyone doing for college? We've haven't talked about it since winter break."

With my body leaning against the edge of the counter, I pull out my phone to look at the screen I know shows nothing, but it makes me look busy so I can try to avoid the question. I want to tell Kalani before I tell my boys.

"I'm headed to Michigan," Matt Wicker says. "Heard Hollins is headed there, too."

Austin nods. "Yeah, I heard. How 'bout you, Baylor?"

Glancing out the window at the girls, I hear Parker clear his throat.

"San Diego State."

My head jerks so fast I feel a crick in my neck, but I ignore the pinch. "California, huh?" I make no attempt to hide the accusation in my voice.

He holds my gaze, nodding.

"When-"

The back door slams shut, cutting me off, and a pissed off Kalani and Mia stomp past us to the bar.

No one says anything as Kalani pulls the bottle from Austin's hand and tips it back against her lips, taking a nice size swig.

She coughs, wipes her mouth and goes for another, but before she can bring it to her mouth, Parker sticks his shot glass out, waving it back and forth in front of her with a smile on his pretty boy fucking face.

The bottle freezes at her lips. She looks at the glass in his hands, back at the bottle, then at the dishes on countertop. Shoving his hand away, she sets the liquor down and snatches a lime.

She steps in front of me with fury in her eyes. Roughly shoving the slice of lime in my mouth, she tips the bottle back, then smashes her lips into mine, biting both the lime and my lip in the process.

It's sexy as hell.

But she doesn't stop there. Spitting the lime out, she wraps her arms around my neck and jumps up, locking her legs around me.

When people around us start to hoot and holler, I pull back, bringing my mouth to her ear. "These fuckers don't get to watch you like this." She licks my neck and a lightning bolt shoots through me. My hands tighten on her ass. "Stop."

She pulls back and gone is the fury. It's replaced with a dirty, mischievous gleam that makes the hairs on the back of my neck stand up in anticipation. She opens her mouth to speak, but Mia beats her to it.

"Heads up, Lolls."

Kalani tenses for a moment, her eyes narrowing and slicing to the back door that's being pulled open by a distraught-looking Liv.

My brows pull in as I watch this chick I've known most my life, and never seen any true emotions from, look like she's about to cry as she shakes her head at my girl, a dubious expression on her made-up face.

Kalani drops from around me. She stays in my arms but turns her head to Liv.

Liv looks from her to me and back. "You won't get away with this, Lolli. The truth will come out." She doesn't have her normal 'girl on a power trip' tone. She sounds kind of concerning.

Kalani just rolls her eyes at her. "Whatever you say, Olivia. The conversation's over."

Liv looks to me with a strange plea in her eyes, but she doesn't speak, instead running off.

Kalani looks back at me, her blue eyes now tired.

"You ready?" I tilt my head, sliding my fingers into the back pocket of her jeans.

She nods, leaning into me.

"You coming with me to get swimsuits tomorrow, Lolli?" Mia slurs, stumbling against Austin's unsteady body.

"Yeah." She brings her hand up to cover her yawn. "Sure."

"Cool. So, everyone be at Lolli's house by nine am sharp on Sunday. Plane leaves at noon." She squeals, clapping her hands together. "I'll send out a text."

"Goodnight, Meems," Kalani calls over her shoulder as we make our way to the door.

"Use protection, Lolli!"

Kalani flips her off over her head, earning a round of laughs.

She's quiet and lost in her own world on the walk to her house. I can't help but wonder what all that shit with Liv was about, but I don't ask. Clearly it pissed her off and if she wanted to share, she would. So, I don't push. With Kalani, it's a pick and choose your battle kind of thing, and this one is not important enough to poke at.

"You hungry?" she asks once we're inside slipping our shoes off.

"Starvin', baby."

She turns, giving me a flirtatious smile over her shoulder. She reads the intent in my voice. I am starving. For her.

"Sit on the couch, Nathaniel." Her lips barely move, and her tone is so low, her sexy little rasp more profound. "I'll be right back."

With that, she heads down the hall and like a good boy, I do what I'm told, losing my shirt in the process.

A minute or two later, soft music plays through her house speakers, and she rounds the couch, coming to stand in front of me.

My breath is stolen from me like a hit to the stomach.

Kalani is in nothing but my high school jersey. The one I'll never wear again, but I'll make damn sure she gets plenty of use out of.

A condom package drops from her fingers, falling next to me on the couch, and she kneels in front of me.

Her fingers find my belt, pulling it from my jeans, her blue eyes locked on mine.

When she tugs, I lift my hips so she can pull them down, taking my briefs with 'em, and my hard-on springs free.

My hands skim up her arms, my fingertips scratching across her collarbone lightly. I grin when her body trembles.

When I reach her neck, her palm closes around my dick and she squeezes, making me involuntarily flex in her grasp.

She smirks and her eyes leave mine to watch as she works me with smooth, firm strokes.

She starts off slow, gliding her soft little hand up and over the head, then all the way back down and I grow impossibly harder in her hold. Her other hand slides up my thigh, her nails scratching lightly as it makes its way up my chest, where she gives me a gentle nudge.

My body collapses against the couch cushions willingly, my legs relaxing into the seat. Eyes on her, I watch her hungry gaze roam over my naked form. Her lips part slightly and her hand picks up speed. Dipping her head, her tongue sneaks out to lick the precum that's shining on the tip of my dick.

A deep grumble escapes, and my hand finds her hair, right as her mouth opens for me.

Her lips don't touch my skin until she has as much of me in her mouth as she can manage, then she seals them around my shaft, sliding them up while sucking lightly, her tongue rolling against me.

She does it again and again, sucking harder and faster each time, and my head falls back against the couch.

"Damn, baby... mmm." My grip tightens.

She likes it, the feeling of me pulling on her hair, because her speed picks up, her grip tightening around me, and my hips buck.

Quickly and as gently as I can muster, I push her off me. Reaching down, I squeeze my dick, trying to ease the ache I've just created by making her stop.

When her bottom lip pushes out in a fake pout, I launch forward, pulling it between my teeth. I suck it hard, then bite it gently, watching her eyes close from the feeling, a small whimper making its way out of her as she opens for me, begging my tongue to play with hers.

As I lean back, she follows, climbing up to straddle my waist.

My hands slide up her thighs, coming around to squeeze her ass.

She moans into my mouth, grinding her pussy against me. She lifts slightly, waiting for me to enter her, but I don't just yet.

I reach between us and grab ahold of myself, using the tip of my dick to rub circles against her clit. She's so ready, her thighs tighten around mine from the simple contact, so I tease her, my head pushing at her opening, then slide it back up to circle her clit again, and her head falls to my shoulder.

She kisses my collarbone, then fists my hair and pulls my head back roughly, taking control of my mouth.

I tease her again, but she was ready for it this time, and drops down with all her might, forcing me all the way inside her.

"Fuck…" I groan, my hand flying to her ass, pushing her down more, harder.

She nods and brings her forehead to rest against mine, her teeth sinking into her bottom lip, her moan coming out as a harsh breath through her nose.

I hold her there, pushing up into her as far as I can go.

"Condom, baby," I whisper against her lips. "Condom."

I shift slightly and her eyes squeeze shut, her hold on my shoulder tightening.

"Just pull out."

Oh, thank fuck.

I nod and move her ass back and forth against me.

She lets out a deep breath and starts riding me, slow and steady, grinding into me, her clit rubbing against my skin.

We're so close.

My hands slide up under the jersey and I grip her tits in my palms, squeezing them while my thumbs and pointer fingers pinch her nipples, rolling them around.

"Mmm... " Her head falls back as her speed picks up.

I grab the hem of the jersey. "Up."

Her arms lift above her head and I whip the jersey off, my mouth immediately closing over her right nipple.

"Oh... fuuuck," She slides her fingers up my neck, holding my head on her as her hips begin to circle against me.

When I release the right nipple and move to the left, her hands fly to the back of the couch, her insides tightening.

She explodes, a long, deep moan coming from within her chest, and her body twitches against mine, but I don't stop. I reach between us, rubbing her clit, grinding her against me. Within seconds, she's panting again. Her moans turn into desperate pants and I feel my own release teetering. I quickly pull her off me and lay her on the couch, roll a condom on and push back into her. Her legs lift and wrap around me, her nails leaving marks on my back.

And I'm done.

Groaning, I squeeze her ass hard and push myself inside her to the hilt, my hips twitching and she's right there with me. Her eyes roll back, her sex squeezing every drop out of me, and I collapse onto her.

Once our breathing has settled, I pull back to look at her.

She gives me the softest smile and traces my jaw with her finger. Lifting her mouth, her lips brush mine gently, and she drops back down. "I love you," she whispers, a beautiful flush covering her skin.

I run my fingers through her hair, looking deep into her eyes. "I love you, too, baby."

When I go to stand, she shakes her head, pulls the condom off me and tosses it carelessly to the floor. Both our bodies are slick with sweat, but I couldn't care less. We can clean up later. My girl wants me to hold her, so that's what I'm gonna do.

I'll hold her forever if she lets me.

Chapter Thirty-Four

K ALANI

After setting my bag onto the porch, I run back inside to close the kitchen window.

"Ready, Freddy?" Mia bounces in.

"Yeah, I think so." I toss my keys into my purse, making sure my charger is in there as well. "Did you give your mom my house key?"

She rolls her eyes. "Yes, Lolli. She's got the cat, mail, and plants covered for the week."

"Okay then, I think... Wait!" I turn and dash to my room.

Pulling my bedside drawer open, I grab my camera. Running my fingers over the top, a smile graces my lips.

This camera was supposed to be used for happy memories on my birthday the year my parents gave it to me. My grandpa was there; my parents were going to be there.

"I'd say it's time, huh?" I whisper, looking over my shoulder at Nate.

He's leaning against the door frame, arms crossed over his chest, his soft brown eyes on me. Kicking off the door, he walks over and wraps his strong arms around me. He pulls the camera from my hand and lifts it in the air before dropping his lush lips to mine, kissing me slow and gentle.

A flash goes off and he pulls back, winking at me.

He's quick to snag the Polaroid before I can, pulling it into his chest. "This one's for me." He winks again, nodding his head toward the door. "It's time to go. We'll bring the camera."

With a nod, I loop my arm through his.

The flight is smooth sailing and by nightfall, we're checked into our rooms and dressing for dinner.

It's March thirtieth. My birthday's in two days and I'm okay. I don't have a constant headache, I can breathe easy, and I don't have the urge to jump ship. I'm calm and collected, happy even. And I have Nate to thank for it.

Speak of the devil.

His soft knock sounds at the door, and I hustle out of the bathroom to open it.

Nate rushes in, picking me up swiftly, and spins me around.

Laughing, I lay my arms over his shoulders.

He peppers my lips with kisses. "Tell me again why we even bothered with separate rooms?"

"Because when we booked, your ass was getting sent home to sleep."

He smiles and kisses me one more time before setting me on my feet. "Yeah." He smacks my ass as he walks backward onto my balcony. "Now you beg me to stay." His smirk is cocky. "See how that worked out in my favor?"

I slink up next to him.

"Man, your view is killer."

I nod, looking out over the resort. The moon is shining against the ocean, creating a silver glow in the sky. "You act like you can't see the same thing." I nudge him playfully and his arm wraps around me.

"Yeah, well. Yours looks better somehow."

"You're, like, what? Four doors down or something?" I laugh, walking back into the room.

He grins, spinning to lean his arms and back against the railing. "Yep. How you like the colors?" He raises an eyebrow.

I look around the room, taking in the cast-iron, renaissance theme. The walls have a golden crown molding that blends into a pale pink color, with wrought iron crafting hanging sporadically along the walls. The bed is large with iron posts that climb to the ceiling and a golden satin lay across the tops, tying around each beam.

There's an antique-looking dresser with fancy knobs that match the curves of the plush chairs that surround the small table in the corner. An identical set of table and chairs sits on the balcony.

My eyes find Nate's and my chest swells. "You made sure my room was colorful, didn't you?"

He nods, his brown eyes roaming my face, and any piece of me I may have still owned just became his. "I love you."

He smirks and saunters his strong body toward mine.

He's dressed for dinner. His dark jeans stretch nicely across his thighs, laying a little loose down his legs. He has his long-sleeved, gray button-up untucked, with the arms folded to his elbows, and he's wearing a pair of black boots. His hair is mussed perfectly in an unkempt, clean and sexy kind of way.

When he reaches me, he holds my eyes captive while his hands skim up my thighs, lifting my dress up and over my hips. He bends his head and peeks down, a groan leaving him. He backs me into the edge of the table. "I knew you couldn't possibly be wearing any panties in this thing." He runs his fingers under the cups of my bra.

"I didn't want the panty lines."

"You know how much I like to push 'em to the side." He pretends to pout, dipping his head to kiss on my neck.

"Yeah, well." I grip his shoulders tight, squirming as he slips a finger inside me. "One less... step."

"Mmm... " He bites at my shoulder, adding a second finger, while bringing his thumb to my clit. "I wanna hear you, baby."

My eyes squeeze shut. "Everyone's waiting for us."

"Let them wait."

"Our food will be cold."

"We'll ask them to warm it up."

"But-"

His hands slip from me and he chuckles when I protest.

"Okay, fine." He walks to the bed and drops down. "Put your shoes on and we'll go." The asshole reaches into his pocket, pulling out his phone.

I see the laughter in his eyes; he knows damn well what he's trying to do. And it's working.

I cross my arms and frown.

His head falls back and deep, rich laughter flows from him.

Pissed off, I turn to grab my shoes off the floor, but he's quick and has me on my back on the bed before I even get them in my hand.

His hand is between my legs again in an instant, his erection pushing against my hip.

His fingers sink into me slowly, and his mouth comes to my ear. He blows warm breath across my neck, working me slowly at first. Then, he adds more speed, pushing down on my clit with his thumb.

When my breathing speeds up, he bites my earlobe, then sucks away the sting.

My fingers clutch at his skin, holding him tight as my orgasm builds.

He pushes in deep and freezes.

I try to roll my hips into his hand, but he pushes his pelvis into me, forcing me still.

"Nate-"

"Are you gonna stop me next time?"

I squeeze my eyes shut, pushing down on his fingers as much as I can, squeezing him from the inside.

"Tell me," he growls. "Tell me I can touch you, please you, whenever and wherever I want." He licks my neck. "Tell me..."

"You can do whatever you want to me, Handsome." I look over at him. "I'm yours."

His lips crash into mine and I ride his hand like I'm at the damn rodeo.

"Fuck me," I beg between kisses. "Please."

"Fuck," he adds another finger. "Then we'll really be late."

"So what, this is our vacation, too."

"Shh," he chuckles against my mouth, working me into frenzy until I come on his fingers.

When he pulls out, I relax into the comforter, watching as he kneels in front of me, running the warm rag over my sex. It's gentle and meant to clean me, but my eyes close and I moan into the pillow.

"Damn," he rasps, his fingers replacing the cloth. He runs them up and down slowly, and the bed dips. "You need more, baby?"

I don't know what's wrong with me, but, yeah, I do. But I don't have to say it, he already knows.

Right when his warm breath hits my thigh, someone starts pounding on the door.

Nate groans and drops his forehead on my leg.

"Would you stop cock-blocking them all the damn time!" We hear Austin's laughter.

Mia grumbles and I can picture her stomping her foot in a fit. "No! I won't! Not when we're waiting on their asses." She pounds on the door again. "Bitch, I know you hear me. Let's go!"

Laughing, I pull myself into a sitting position.

Nate rolls his eyes and steps off the bed. He pulls me up and kisses my forehead. "I'll take care of you tonight."

I stand on my tiptoes and kiss him gently. "I know."

We don't bother opening the door until my tan wedges are buckled and my hair is smoothed down.

I'm wearing a coral, spandex-like dress that's tight and slinky with two thin straps. I paired it with gold hoops, my hair is down and straight, and I put on some nude shadow, mascara, and a soft pink lipstick.

"Finally, assholes." Mia loops her arm through mine. "No one wanted to order until everyone was here. Guess who was last to arrive?" She pins me with a glare.

I shrug, and peek over my shoulder.

Nate winks at me, so I turn back and let Mia drag me along.

Once we're all seated, everyone says hello and starts on their drinks.

Turns out Mia's a damn liar because the hotel is buffet-style and on twenty-four seven as part of our all-inclusive packages. I don't mind though, because it's kind of fun to have such a large group eating, laughing, and drinking together.

The room is a large open area with different foods lining the right wall, a kitchen tucked behind them. The center of the room is nothing but cherrywood tables and chairs scattered everywhere, while the left side is an open dance floor with a DJ booth in the corner. There are large open panels along the whole left wall, allowing you to look out at the ocean, letting the night air flow through the area.

There are at least eighty other students from Alrick that booked, all from different crowds, and staying in different areas in

350

the hotel. Our floor though, is full of rough and rowdy football players and their groupies.

Out of the corner of my eye, I can see Jarrod staring at me, so I shift my body toward Nate's.

His hand squeezes my thigh in acknowledgment, and he continues talking to a guy I recognize but don't know his name.

"Lolli Bear!"

I turn, searching for Parker in the masses on the dance floor.

He waves me over.

I throw back another shot and stand. Nate catches my movement and nods his chin in question. I kiss his cheek quickly. "Going to dance," I tell him and hustle away.

Parker holds a hand out to me, shifting his shoulders to the music. I slide my hand into his and he pulls me in.

We dance along to the beat of the high tempo music. A few minutes later, a bunch of others join us on the dance floor. Parker turns and starts dancing with both Ashley and Alyssa, who have pancaked him between them, not that he's complaining.

I close my eyes and let my body flow. When I open them, a few verses later, Jarrod is standing in front of me and for once, he has his old playful smile on his face.

Cautiously, I keep a good distance, but when I realize he's laughing and smiling at everyone around us, just trying to have fun like I am, I loosen up and allow him to step in closer as we dance.

Right then, the lights dim and colors slide across the rooftop of the dance floor, and a sultry song I've never heard before comes on, so I take a half of a step back, but Jarrod's quick. He grabs my hips gently and starts to move his along with mine. When he doesn't try anything else, I keep dancing.

Mia bounces up with a tray in her hands. "Shots, bitches!" Jarrod raises a brow and holds his out.

We clink glasses and down the cheap tequila.

"Ugh," Jarrod cringes. "That's disgusting."

I laugh. "Maybe, but it was free, right?"

Laughing, he steps to me again and we keep dancing.

My eyes shift to Nate, and I see Liv has taken my empty seat. I almost laugh when I see the irritated expression on his face. She catches my eye and I flip her off.

"I'd watch out for her," Jarrod whispers into my ear.

My head pulls back slightly, and I look up at him. "What do you mean?"

He shrugs and tries to keep dancing, but I halt his movements, grabbing onto his arms. "Seriously, Jarrod. Talk."

He releases a deep sigh, leaning his body toward mine.

I pull back and narrow my eyes at him, but he grins, shaking his head. "I didn't want to shout, that's all."

When my face smooths out, he leans in again. "I don't know exactly," he whispers, his hand finding my lower back. "I don't trust her, that's all. She's always wanted Nate. She'll probably try to make a play for him."

I laugh when I hear his explanation. "I'm aware, trust me. She can try, but it won't work."

He pulls back and looks down at me. "How do you know, Lolli?"

"Trust me, Jarrod." I smirk. "I know." I look back at Nate, finding his eyes narrowed in my direction.

He pushes out of his chair, shaking off Liv's hand as she protests and stalks toward me, his eyes dropping. I follow his gaze, realizing I'm still holding on to Jarrod's arm, and his hand is still on my back.

I quickly let go of him and step back.

He laughs like he's been waiting for this and lifts his hands in surrender when Nate steps in front of me. "Get the fuck outta here, Hollins."

Jarrod winks and walks a few feet away to dance with some others from our school.

He turns toward me. "What was that all about?"

"Just dancing."

"Did he hit on you?" He clenches and unclenches his fists at his sides.

I smirk and lean into his chest. "No. He acted normal for once." I shrug a shoulder. "I think he's over it."

"Over you, you mean?" he scoffs, raising a brow. "'Cause I highly doubt that." His eyes run down my body, his tongue sliding across his bottom lip on their way back up.

"You jealous, Handsome?"

His jaw ticks, but he says nothing. He grabs ahold of my biceps, kissing me before spinning me around, gripping my hips tight and moving to the music.

After a few minutes, he leans in, his words a low growl in my ear. "Don't let anyone touch, Kalani. I can't handle it."

I nod and push my ass into him, feeling as he starts to grow hard.

"I'm serious."

I nod again and he chuckles, knowing damn well having his body against mine is doing bad things to me. The good kind of bad things.

We dance and drink the night away and, before we know it, we're all creeping up to our beds just before the sun is set to rise.

Mia yawns, leaning up against the elevator wall, her black wedges dangling from her fingers, red hair sticking out of her forgotten ponytail. "Hangin' by the pool tomorrow?"

We all groan our agreeance and shuffle out into the hall.

"Don't call me, Mia. I'll have my ass there when I'm good and ready."

"Whatever." Bringing her hand to cover her mouth, she yawns again, scrunching her face when she gets a whiff of her sweaty shoes. "Have your morning, but be ready to party tomorrow night, birthday girl."

I flip her off and step into my room.

Nate and I drop onto the bed at the same time, laughing when the impact bounces us to the center.

He hooks his arm around my waist and pulls me closer, tucking my head into his chest.

"I still need to take care of you." His voice is thick with exhaustion.

I grin, using the little bit of energy I have left to tilt my head and kiss his neck. "I can't even undress, let alone get freaky," I tell him, making us both laugh. "Tomorrow."

He pulls me in impossibly tighter and kisses my forehead.

"I love you, Kalani." It's the last thing I hear him whisper before sleep takes over.

Chapter Thirty-Five

K ALANI

The sun is warm and shining bright over the resort. Hundreds of people mill around, some swimming in the turquoise waters, some lounging, like me, and others having drinks at one of the many surrounding bars.

Mia chose the Grand Park Royal resort specifically because, from the lounge area of the hotel pool, you can look out over the Mexican Caribbean that's only a good fifteen to twenty feet further, so we have a killer view of miles of open sea and clear blue skies.

Though we woke around ten, Nate and I didn't make it down until around noon. Once showered, we decided on room service for brunch instead of going to the dining area with everyone.

After we ate, we dressed in our swimsuits which, naturally, distracted the both of us. So, we had some fun with the balcony doors open before redressing and joining the group.

Alyssa plops down in the lounger next to me, covering her face with a large sun hat. "Ugh...hangover from hell," she grumbles.

"Nate fed me Excedrin and a Bloody Mary for breakfast."

"You know, you came along at the perfect time for him. He needed someone to straighten him out before he headed to college. If not, he'd have a baby and Chlamydia by the first semester."

I pop one eye open, laughing, finding her grinning at me with the hat still lying over her eyes.

I shift my seat so my back is inclined and my legs are stretched in front of me. My eyes find Nate across the pool. His hat is turned backward and his trunks hang enticingly low. He's laughing with the guys, a beer in his left hand while using his right to tell a story.

"You love him."

I turn back to Alyssa. "Yeah, I do."

She places her hat back on her head and mirrors my position on her lounger. Her eyes find the boys and she takes her time ogling each one. When her face turns sour, I turn to see Liv and her minions slink up to the bar where the boys are.

My lips purse. "It really is too bad she's such a bitch."

"Right."

"Her body is bangin'."

"Your tits are so much better, though."

Laughing, I swing my legs over the side of my chair. "But her legs...God damn. They're like half her body."

"True, but her face is only pretty with all that hooker makeup."

I stand, pulling the hair tie of my high ponytail tighter. "So, I win, then?" I grin.

She looks me over in my white bikini.

The bottoms are low, with the skinniest of strings that lays just below my hip bones, connecting the front fabric to the back. The double-D top cuts down to my breastbone with a small gold pendant in the center and wraps around, hooking like a bra would, while the triangle top ties around my neck. I've been tanning recently, so I knew the white would be a nice contrast against my skin.

"Girl…" she draws out slowly, licking her lips seductively, "I'd fuck you any day over her."

I laugh hard, bending down to snatch my sunglasses off the floor. "I'm ready for something strong. You want?"

She leans back, closing her eyes. "Nah, I'm good for now. I still haven't been able to eat." She brushes me away with a sweep of her hand.

I decide to walk to the bar closest to me. I hop onto the bar stool under the bungalow-style overhead and order a shot of Jack.

"Make that two."

I look to my left, finding Jarrod stepping up next to me.

I can't help but notice his body, him being shirtless and all.

He's hard and defined in the right places. Mix all that with his green eyes and blond hair, it's no wonder he's a popular piece of meat. It does nothing for me, though.

He smirks, knowing I was looking. "Hey, Lolli."

I roll my eyes behind my glasses and place my elbows on the countertop.

"How you feeling today?" He sits on the stool next to me.

"I'm good, actually." I turn to him. "You?"

He thanks the bartender when he sets our shots in front of us. "I'm good. Didn't drink much last night." He lifts his drink.

I hesitate for a moment, then lift mine, clinking glasses with his.

The dark liquor burns on the way down, but the sweet after-taste soothes it enough.

"You want another?" Jarrod tilts his head.

I nod.

He orders us both another round. "So, it's your birthday tomorrow, huh?"

I blow out a breath. "Yes, sir." I raise a brow at him. "How'd you know?"

"Mia has a big mouth." He grins and we both laugh.

"That she does." This time, I raise my glass to him.

His eyes freeze on me for a moment, then he turns and grabs his shot.

We cheers and throw 'em back.

I go to push off the counter but he reaches for me, gently wrapping his fingers around my elbow.

I look from his hand to his face.

He smiles softly. "Thanks for this, Lolli. I didn't mean for things to get weird between us."

I drop myself back into the seat and he releases my arm. "Don't worry about it."

"No really." He looks away, then turns back to me. "I shouldn't have gotten so upset about you and Nate. It's not like we'd been dating and then it happened. I guess I just didn't expect it, that's all."

Damn Nate and his bringing out my emotions because now I feel kind of bad, and I don't like it.

"Two more and a Jack and Coke, please," I order and shift toward Jarrod. "It was kind of shitty how it went down, though. Sorry about all that. I had no idea Nate was gonna go full on 'me Tarzan, you Jane' on me that day." We both laugh. "If I had, I would have suggested a different place to eat."

Jarrod stops laughing and looks over at me. I turn to my shot, realizing maybe I shouldn't have said that.

I can see his eyes rake over my body out of the corner of my eye, watching me as I down my shot.

When I turn to look at him, he grabs his, smirking into the glass before he tosses it back.

Spinning the chair around, I push my glasses onto my head, and look out over the water, laughing when I see Mia jump onto Parker's shoulders, a bright smile on her face as she tries her best to dunk him.

"Looks like they're having fun."

I nod, biting my nail.

I jump slightly when Jarrod's hand wraps around my wrist, pulling it from my mouth.

"Don't do that," he whispers, his eyes locking onto mine. He quickly looks away. "Man."

"What?"

He sighs and looks back at me. "Your eyes can really put a guy on his ass, that's all."

"Well, stay on your damn feet, Hollins," I disregard his comment with a laugh. "You're too damn heavy for me to pick back up."

He laughs too, but it doesn't sound all that genuine.

Hopping off the stool, I clutch the bar to keep from falling, the effects of the alcohol stalling my reflexes momentarily.

Jarrod's hand grabs my hip to steady me and I quickly pull away.

"Catch you later, Hollins." Picking up my drink, I wave it at him.

He watches me the whole time, probably even after I turn around and walk off.

Nate spots me from across the water and winks, turning back to the conversation with his boys.

Once in the warm pool, I dip down to my shoulders, careful to keep my drink high above the water, and walk toward Parker and Mia.

He spots me instantly and smiles, wrestling free of Mia's grasp. "Hey."

"Getting the party started?" He grabs my wrist and brings my straw to his mouth for a quick drink.

"Yep." I laugh, offering Mia some.

"No thanks. I'm gonna go get something. Catch you guys later," she says, making her way out of the pool.

"So, what's the plan for tonight, Lolli Bear?" Parker asks, lifting me into a cradle position in his arms and spinning in circles.

I lay my head back and throw my hand out, letting the water create a wave over my palm. "Not sure exactly. Dinner, drinking, and dancing, I think. Per Mia, it doesn't matter what we do as long as we're out when the clock strikes midnight."

"Well, anything special you want to do today?" he asks, setting me on my feet, a big smile on his boy next door face. "I could take you on a hike or something?"

I smile at my friend. "I ever tell you; you look like Paul Walker?"

He laughs, dipping his head back to wet his hair, then runs his fingers through the thick blond tufts. "I thought I looked like your grandpa?" he teases.

"I said you remind me of my grandpa, ass, not that you looked like him." I hit him in the chest. "Seriously, though, you look like you just stepped out of Fast and the Furious, ready to take a ride."

"You want to go for a ride, Lolli Bear?" There's a wicked gleam in his eyes, so I jump back, thrusting my hand out.

"Oh, no you don't." I wiggle my cup. "I have a drink in my hand."

He steps closer, so my palm is flat against his pecs. "You better down that thing then."

I narrow my eyes and his grin grows.

Groaning, I down the drink, tossing the plastic cup to the side, and try to dodge him, but he's quicker and has me spun around and over his shoulder in seconds.

I kick my feet, laughing hysterically, trying to get free. When he makes it to the steps of the pool, he clasps my thighs tight so I can't wiggle.

"Don't try to get free or you might fall and get hurt," he laughs and starts jogging away from the resort pool.

"You are so dead!" I shout, still trying to control my laughter.

Nate catches my eye on our way past, and stands, but we're out of sight before I can see anything else.

I see the sand, then the water, where Parker's dunking us both into the warm Caribbean. He doesn't let go when we come up for air; just walks further into the water, laughing.

He shifts my body, holding it in a cradle position so I sprawl out like I did in the pool, and he takes the cue, spinning me around, only slower this time.

"Man, Hero," I gaze up at the orange-streaked sky. "This is nice."

"Yeah," he rasps. "It is."

I glance at him, finding him looking down at me.

He smiles.

"Can I have my girl back now, Baylor?"

Parker spins around to see Nate making his way into the water, and the sight of him makes my mouth water.

Parker slowly sets me down until my feet hit the ground and kisses my temple. "See you guys in a bit."

I nod, sinking down to my shoulders, waiting for Nate to come to me.

He hands his drink off to Parker on his way, smacking his shoulder in thanks.

Nate smirks and dips all the way under the water, coming up once he has my legs wrapped in his arms.

He lifts me out of the water and I slide down his body until I wrap my legs around his waist, water beads rolling down his face.

"Hi."

"Hi." I lean forward, running my tongue across his lips.

"Whiskey?" he grins.

I nod, grinding into him in response.

"I thought it was the tequila that made your clothes come off," he teases, his hands rubbing up and down my thighs.

I shake my head. "Nope. It's you."

His eyes dilate. "Me, huh?" He slides his hands into my bottoms, cupping my ass roughly.

I nod.

He walks us further into the water, sliding me back and forth against his dick.

"Handsome," I roll my hips into him. "Take me to my room."

"No."

I pull back, raising a brow. "No?"

"Nuh-uh." He stops walking when his shoulders are submerged, his hand coming between us to pull himself from his trunks.

I gasp, clutching his neck tighter, and look around. While there isn't anyone around us, there are people on the shoreline.

"Someone will see."

"I would never let anyone see you." He kisses my shoulder, my neck, my ear.

"But the water is clear." I grin.

"We'll have to be discreet."

"But-"

He pulls back, narrowing his lust-filled eyes at me. "When I want, where I want...remember?" He raises a cocky eyebrow at me.

All I can do is nod. I love him like this, all bossy and sexy and shit.

His fingers slip under my suit and find their way inside me. He groans instantly, and my head tucks into the crook of his neck. "Damn, baby. I can feel how ready you are, even in the water." He teases me with his fingers and thumb, giving me no choice but to roll my body against his hand. "You ready for me?"

"Yes," I pant into his wet skin.

In one fluid motion, he slides into me, wrapping his arms around my back to pull me as close as possible.

I moan into his neck.

"There you go, baby," he coos into my ear, one hand coming down to guide my hips in slow, rotating movements. "Nice and slow."

"Mmm... " My hands leave his neck to rub on his biceps, loving the way they flex under my touch.

He lowers us further into the water, so only a sliver of our necks and heads are bobbing on top.

Apparently, Nate is no longer concerned with discreet, because he fists my hair and brings my mouth to his, kissing me hard and deep. Groaning, as he bruises my ass with his grip and bounces my body against his.

He swells inside me and I know he's about to burst like I am. He starts to lift my hips, but I lock my legs tighter around his back, grinding down hard, not letting him pull out.

We come together, moaning and biting at each other's mouths.

He pulls my bottom lip between his teeth, his body shuddering against mine. "You're so fucking perfect."

"Right back atcha." My legs fall from his and he catches my sated body in his arms.

Smiling, he kisses my forehead, and starts walking back to shore.

"That's what vacations are made of." I grin, winking up at him.

"Just wait. After midnight tonight," he kisses my lips quickly, "I'll show you what birthdays are made of."

"After midnight," I muse, closing my eyes, letting him carry me through the water. "Sounds perfect."

Nate sits by the poolside bar, chatting with a few guys I don't know.

As soon as he sees me walking up, he gives me his goofy drunken grin.

"Hey."

"Hey," I laugh, saying hello to his new friends. "I'm gonna start getting ready. We leave in about two hours."

He nods, pulling me in for a quick kiss. "Alright. I'll head up in an hour or so. Meet me at my room and we'll walk down together?"

"Okay." I make a dash for it; happy he isn't insisting on walking me. This way, he won't distract me with his naked body in the shower, and we won't be late for once.

I bump into Mia on my way to the elevator.

"Hey!" She smiles brightly. "I put a new dress on hold at the little shop just outside the hotel. I'm running to grab it really quick. Wanna come?"

"I'm actually going to start getting ready before Nate comes up," I laugh. "Meet you downstairs at seven?"

"Yep!" She smiles and bounces away.

Right when I step into the elevator, a hand slips through to stop the doors from closing, and Jarrod stumbles in, laughing.

"Almost missed it." He smiles.

"Yep." I press the number twelve and the doors close again. "You on twelve too?"

"Yeah." He nods, pulling his phone from his pocket to check the time.

"You coming out with us tonight?" I ask him, leaning against the wall.

"Yeah, I'll be there, but a little later." He smiles. "Gotta sleep off this buzz and refresh for another one."

"Sleep sounds nice."

The door dings open and he motions for me to go first.

Neither of us speak as we make our way down the hall toward our rooms, but when I stop at my door, he grabs the door handle in one hand and places the other on my back. I look up at him, confused, and he smiles down at me.

"Just in case I miss the midnight mark." He leans down and places his lips to my jaw quickly. "Happy Birthday, Lolli."

I shrug him off and smile to be polite, mentally deciding Jarrod Hollins is trouble. "Thanks," I mumble, then squeeze inside, not looking back when I shut the door behind me.

Chapter Thirty-Six

N^{ATE}

"Alright, fellas." I toss a five on the bar top and stand, thanking the bartender. "I'm running out of time. Gotta go get ready for tonight." I tip my chin at Austin.

He downs his drink, motioning for another. "I'm headed that way in a few. Grabbing one for the road."

"Just be in the lobby by seven, yeah?" I raise a brow. "We're heading over to the next resort for dinner, then going to Coco Bongo for drinks and shit."

He nods, brushing me away with the back of his hand.

I don't even make it through the glass, wall-length sliding doors before I'm stopped.

When she walks right in front of me, my hands find my hips, my head dropping back to stare at the gold-flecked covered ceiling. "What, Olivia?"

"Got a minute?" She cuts her eyes around nervously.

"No. Actually, I don't." I step past her. "I'm running short on time already."

"It's about Lolli!" she shouts, desperation dripping off her tongue.

I keep moving for the elevator, pushing the little green arrow when I reach it.

"Look, Liv." I turn to her. "I get it. You don't like her, but that's too damn bad. We," I motion my hand between the two of us, "were never a thing. We hooked up a couple times. That's it."

She looks at her bare feet, then back up at me through sad eyes, hidden by heavy makeup. "I know, but this isn't about that. I'm just worried about you."

When I roll my eyes, she steps closer. "I'm serious." She looks up at me. "She's lying to you. Tricking you."

I throw my hands up and take a step back. "Okay." My brows jump, making my hat lift off my head slightly. "I've heard enough." The elevator door chimes at the perfect time and I step inside. "Go away, Olivia."

She doesn't, and she's quick to step in with me, making it a point to push her ass out a little further than necessary, rushing to push the button to close the doors before anyone else can join us. "I'm serious. She's using you!" she all but yells at me.

Running my hands down my face, I can't help but laugh. "Yeah, okay." I shake my head, praying someone else gets on along the way up.

They don't.

Olivia rambles on about how Kalani doesn't care about me, about how she's using me for status, and I tune her ass out the entire time, jumping out of the tiny silver box the second the doors open.

"Go away, Olivia!" I shout, not bothering to look behind me.

"Nate, please! How can you not see it?" she pleads, her feet padding the floor in her attempt to keep up with me.

Eyes on the white door in front of me, I slip my key card in.

"Have a nice night," I throw over my shoulder, stepping into my room.

"I have proof!" she rushes out, running each word together, her eyes darting down the hall, then back to me.

When the door freezes, half-closed in my hand, I think I see her lip twitch as she steps in front of me.

Her shaky hand lifts, waving her phone back in forth a few inches from my face.

When I don't slam the door on her, she steps even closer. "Let me come in," she whispers, "and I'll show you."

My eyes narrow.

She gives me a sad, side smile, tucking her long blonde hair behind her ear.

Against my better judgment, I demand, "Show me."

"Let me in and-"

"Show. Me. Olivia." I all but growl, determined to call her bluff. Needing to, really.

She sighs and looks at her phone. Pressing some buttons, she bites her lip, turning the screen to me.

It's Kalani and Jarrod, a picture from last night when they were dancing. He has his sloppy hands on her hips. Her head is tilted back as she laughs.

I shrug, cutting my eyes back to Liv. "Nice try. I'm well-aware they were dancing last night. You were the one that pointed it out to me." I raise a dark brow at her. "Remember?"

"That's not the only one." She pulls the phone back, swipes to the left, and thrusts it back in my face. "See. Today. They were drinking together."

This photo is of Kalani in her sinful white two-piece that shows off her sun-kissed skin, sitting next to a shirtless Jarrod. They're clinking shot glasses, smiling at each other.

My jaw ticks, but I shrug. "Already knew this too. Seen 'em."

My eyes still on the phone, I see Liv nod in my peripheral. She reaches around and swipes, not pulling the phone away.

Jarrod and Kalani laughing.

Jarrod and Kalani leaning toward each other.

Kalani lifting her glasses to look at the prick.

Jarrod's hand on Kalani's arm.

My eyes fly to Liv then back to her phone. "Why did you take all these? So, they hung out a little." My shoulder jerks up in a not so casual shrug. "Big deal. They're..." What? Friends? "Cordial."

She nods and steps closer. "I thought so too, until I came up here earlier to switch swimsuits and saw..." She turns her phone toward her, pulling up another set of pictures. "This."

This picture is Kalani walking into the elevator, Jarrod following close behind. The next one is him stepping in with her.

My pulse spikes, thumping against my neck. "Not a big deal."

Liv laughs lightly, hearing the tightness in my voice.

She nods, pulling up one more picture. "And this one."

It's a clear shot of Kalani standing in front of her room.

With Jarrod.

One of his hands is on her door that's cracked open slightly, the other holding her bicep. I can't see her face because his is tilted, blocking her, but it's as clear as a fucking blitz, his mouth is on her.

I lose balance slightly, having to take a half step back to right myself.

Olivia takes it as in invitation, stepping inside, closing the door behind her. "I'm really sorry, Nate."

I squeeze my eyes shut, shaking my head.

No. No.

"Get the fuck out of here, Olivia." I narrow my eyes. "I know that's all bullshit. You're just trying to cause problems."

My chest tightens. That's all it is...right?

"Seriously, Nate?" She gapes at me, her eyes glazing over. "I give you proof and you still believe in her?"

"Yeah." I step toward her. "I do."

With a shake of her head, she sits down on the edge of my bed.

When her gaze lowers to her phone once again, I hold my breath.

"I didn't want to have to do this," she mumbles, sounding not at all remorseful. "I thought the pictures would be enough, but clearly they're not. She's worked some serious magic on you, Nate."

When my brows pull up, Olivia rubs the silk comforter, motioning for me to sit beside her.

I sit in the chair across the room.

She sighs, crosses her long legs, and pushes a button on her phone, before setting it beside her and leaning back on her elbows.

Kalani's raspy voice fills the room, sounding a little muffled by distance.

"What is this?" I ask, my eyes locked on the lit screen.

"Shh..." Olivia answers.

"Olivia."

"A recording, Nate. You need to hear what your precious Kalani really thinks." When my eyes fly to hers, hers seem to soften around the edges. "She admitted everything, Nate," she tells me, then presses play on her and Kalani's conversation once more.

"What about him?" Kalani spews, irritation lacing her words.

"Why are you with Nate?"

"NFL pays high for recognizable talent," she states, matter-of-factly.

My brows grow close, my chest tightening slightly.

"So, that's all this is to you?" Olivia sobs. "What about Nate?"

"I don't care about Nate!" Kalani yells.

· · ·

It feels like my heart has stopped beating. Using the heels of my hands, I push into my eye sockets, not wanting, but needing to hear the rest.

"So, what is he to you?"

"Easy. Money, a title, and a ticket."

Kalani's voice is so calm and unaffected, I want to puke.

"So, you don't even love him?" Olivia whispers in a broken voice.

"Are you fucking kidding me right now?" Kalani's voice booms.

"You're going to hurt him!" Olivia shouts. "You're acting like money is everything!"

"Money is everything!" Kalani shouts right back.

"So, you don't love him. How could you say that?" Olivia yells.

"Because it's the truth!"

I fly off the chair and rush into the bathroom, doubling over, as the contents of my stomach splash into the toilet.

Money is everything? She doesn't love me?

What. The. Fuck.

More vomit makes its way up my throat.

A soft hand finds my bare back, rubbing small circles in attempt to comfort me, but all it does is make me feel sicker.

"Go, Olivia. I need a minute here," I grumble into the porcelain throne.

"I don't think you should be alone right now, Nate. I know this hurts you," she whispers in a somber tone. "I'm so sorry."

"Right," I scoff, reaching past her to flip on the shower.

"'Cause you're all tore up about it." I toss my hat on the counter-top, turning to face her. "You been waiting for this."

She smirks slightly, stepping closer to me. "Maybe I have." Her hand slides down my chest. "But that doesn't mean I wanted you to get hurt in the process." She leans into me. "Let me make you feel better," she murmurs, brushing her tits across my chest, making sure I feel her hardened nipples through her thin swim top.

I let my eyes rake over her nearly naked body, following her long shape in her hot pink bikini, and bring my eyes back to hers. I drop my trunks to the floor, watching her grow hungry, and maybe a little vindicated.

"Let yourself out." I step into the shower, slamming the glass door behind me.

It only takes a few seconds for the bathroom door to close behind her.

My head instantly drops to the tiled walls.

Kalani.

My beautiful, broken, blue-eyed girl...is a lying fucking bitch, caught red-handed.

What. The. Fuck.

KALANI

After stepping into my heels, I smooth my dress over my hips, and turn to look myself over in the mirror.

The dress is a fire engine red, with see through lace shoulders. The front is nice, the lace dropping down onto a V-neck cut, showing just enough cleavage to drive Nate crazy, but the back is my favorite. The lace lays from my shoulders to an inch above my ass, so my tan skin is visible through the material, making a bra impossible to wear. It's tight and slinky and ends a few inches down my thighs.

I paired it with some five-inch black heels and diamond studded earrings. My dark hair is down with big beach waves, and I winged my black eyeliner. The final touch is a long-lasting matte lipstick in the exact shade to match the dress, and bam. I'm ready to get tonight's party started.

Grabbing a granola bar off the counter, I toss pieces in my mouth, just in case my lipstick has yet to dry, and pick up my phone to text Mia, letting her know I'm grabbing Nate and we'll be in the lobby in five.

She texts right back.

Meems: uh-huh, we'll see about that. No hanky panky. We're already down here having a drink. Hurry up.

I toss my phone to the bed, deciding I don't want to bother with it tonight, grab my room key and cash, and head out the door.

Nate's room is only a few doors down the hall, so I'm knocking in seconds.

It takes a good minute, then the door flies open and a scowling Nate looks down at me.

"Hey." I see he's still wrapped in a towel, water dripping down his solid chest. When I reach to brush it off, his hand grips my wrist.

My gaze flies to his, hoping to find that dilated look his brown eyes get when I'm near, but instead I find a set of dark ones, hard around the edges, glaring down at me.

He tosses my wrist away from him with force.

"Uh..." I cut my eyes left, then back to his. "What's going on?" I frown. "You look pissed, and you're not ready to go. Everyone's waiting down-"

My voice cuts off when his smirk turns vile and predatory, his hand dropping from the door frame.

I take a step back and he lets his door fall open the rest of the way.

My eyes find her like a truck driver would at a pit spot.

She's laying on her stomach, her fake blond hair laying over her shoulder, while she kicks her feet in the air casually, her naked ass bouncing slightly with the movement.

Olivia rests her head on her propped elbow and uses her fingers to wave at me from Nate's bed.

And I just stand there, my eyes roaming her naked, perfect body, that's on top of my boyfriend's bed.

I force my gaze away from her, locking eyes with a Nate I haven't seen in a long time.

His stance is loose and comfortable. Confident. His face relaxed and collected. Arrogant and privileged.

This is Nate Monroe, the star quarterback, playboy extraordinaire.

A stranger.

I nod, my eyes never leaving his, a laugh bubbling out of me like vomit, because this is so beyond fucked up and I have no idea how to even begin to process this. I've never been let down by anyone based on choice, and the sudden hollowness in my chest gives me no help in deciding how I'm supposed to act.

"She must have come in here with a really good plan, considering I didn't see this coming." I shrug, tipping my head slightly. "But I guess that's the best kind of play, right?" My eyes flit between his. "The ones you never see coming. The ones you can't read." I laugh again. "Those are the ones that win a football game."

I take a step back, my eyes cutting to Liv's and that smirking face I want to ram my heel into. "I definitely didn't see this one coming. And I'm all about defense."

"Yeah, well," he seethes. "Never figured you for a scheming bitch, either. So, I guess we're on the same page, huh, Lolli?"

Lolli. Ouch.

A sad smile graces my lips and I hate myself for being unable to wipe it away. "What'd I tell you, Handsome?"

His entitled eyes and self-assured face morphs, tightening around the edges and pinching between his eyes at my question. Or maybe it's the broken tone the words left me in.

"In the beginning?" I stare at him. "I said, if there was ever something you needed to know, ask, and I wouldn't lie to you." His face falls.

"Yeah," I nod. "You remember."

My eyes shift back to the bimbo who, somewhere along the way, grew some self-respect and covered herself with a pillow.

The hole in my chest widens.

I look back to Nate. "I'm gonna go meet my friends and enjoy my night. You two do the same."

With that, I turn and walk away, rushing through the elevator doors at the end of the hall before my brain has a chance to process what the fuck just happened.

One thing is for sure.

I'm getting fucked up tonight.

Chapter Thirty-Seven

K ALANI

"About freaking time!" Mia shouts, throwing her hands in the air when I walk in to the lobby bar. "Wait. Where's Nate?" Her eyes search my face and she hops off the stool, rushing to stand in front of me.

"Lolli?" Her brows pinch.

I hold up my hand to silence her, startling Parker when I yank his drink from his hand and toss it back.

He looks me over, appreciating my ensemble, then attempts to lock eyes with me, but I turn to the bartender, signaling for another one of whatever I just drank.

Jarrod laughs from beside him, and my eyes cut to him.

"You made it, huh?" I ask, not giving a shit, but trying to get the attention off me.

He smirks, his covetous gaze raking over me. "I did."

I nod and pick up my new drink, downing it in seconds.

"Lolli Bear?" Parker's quiet words and soft touch against my arm have my iced-over heart thawing slightly and I force my eyes to his, feeling the emotions finally starting to catch up to me. "Where is Nate?" he asks sternly, somehow knowing he won't like the answer.

"Probably balls deep in Olivia by now."

His brows shoot into his hairline and Mia yanks me around.

"What?!" she shrieks, and Parker shoots out from behind me.

I run the few feet to catch up to him. "Hero, no!" When he doesn't stop, I jump in front of him, wrapping my arms around his stomach. "Parker, stop."

His chest is heaving, his fists clenching at his sides.

When I look up, he turns his face away from mine.

"Look at me."

He refuses.

"Hero," I say softly. "Look at me. Please."

Reluctantly, he turns his icy blues to me and I watch them chill as they roam my face. "Lolli Bear. Let me go," he begs, bringing his hands up to cup my face, his breathing heavy. "He doesn't get to do this to you."

I smile, squeezing him tighter. "Let's go eat and have some fun."

His face constricts, his eyes searching my face once more.

With a curt nod, he steps away and we walk back into the lounge.

"What the fuck is going on, Lolli?" Mia demands, but when I turn my vacant stare on her, she bites her lip and nods, tears making her green eyes gleam.

That's the end of this conversation.

By the time we make it back to the bar at our resort, we've lost half of our partygoers, so it's just Mia, Parker, Alyssa, me, and my best friend tonight, good old Jack Daniels.

"Shouldn't we be drinking," Alyssa hiccups, then laughs, "Captain Morgan or something, since we're on the sea or whatever."

Mia tosses back another shot. "We're not on a cruise, dumbass."

We all laugh at that because it's just so funny.

"Come on, Mia." Alyssa stands on wobbly pink heels, throwing her arm around Mia. "Let's go cuddle and go to bed."

"'Kay," Mia slurs and they walk off, not bothering to say good night.

I drop my head onto the countertop, watching people get down on the dance floor to the slow, wind-down music the bar's playing.

Parker rubs my lower back. "You 'bout ready, Lolli Bear?" he asks me gently.

I shake my head no.

The shock from tonight's events is starting to wear off as reality and unwelcome emotions fight their way to the surface. The last thing I want to do is go back to my empty room with the night closing in on me like a wave, spinning me round and round. Giving me a glimpse of the surface, only to drown me in the end. "You can go. If you want."

He shakes his head, his sad blue eyes on mine, and holds his hand out for me to take.

A sloppy smile forms on my lips and I place my hand in his, letting him walk us to the dance floor where we slow dance to a few songs.

With a deep sigh, Parker whispers into my ear, "Happy Birthday, Lolli Bear."

His tone is so soft and low, and I know he can feel it; my resolve, withering. My heart cracking open. It's coming, the break before the fall, before my body shuts down, freezing everything inside me.

And I can't wait for it, the numbness. Because right now, I feel like I'm dying.

As if the soul-crushing feeling isn't enough, Nate walks through the door, the blood-sucking blonde in his shadow.

He looks like shit. Rough and wrinkled. Probably from rolling around in the sheets with his whore.

He's such a handsome prick.

His eyes lock with mine and he has the decency to tense for a moment, then the nerve to scowl at Parker's hands around my waist.

Dick.

I pull Parker to the bar for more numbing juice.

This time, I ask the short, pudgy guy to leave the bottle.

Parker saw Nate. I know he did because he's doing his best to shield me from his view. It's a futile attempt because I can feel him. Feel his stare, his presence, his everything, as always.

The universe must really fucking hate me, because right then, Christina Aguilera's "Just a Fool" streams through the speakers. Listening to her words, I realize that's what I've been. A fool in the worst way. I should have known how it would all go down in the end the moment I laid eyes on the drunken playboy that very first night.

Thinking I could open up, love someone and be loved back. Have the little bit of normalcy in my life when I'm anything but a normal nineteen-year-old girl...it was a rookie move, for sure. I'm a multi-millionaire with her name on the most successful sports photography company, not to mention the co-owner of the San Diego Tomahawks.

A sad laugh escapes me and I take another swig from the bottle.

Parker looks at me, his eyes pinched, at loss of what to say, or do.

That makes two of us.

I go to step off the stool, but stumble, falling halfway to the floor before he catches me.

I laugh and lean into him, closing my eyes in attempt to block out the lyrics.

Just like in the song, I should have kept my mouth shut. I never should have opened up and allowed Nate to embed himself inside me, to wake me up and bring out all this cheesy, Lifetime movie shit. I should have stayed locked up tight, emotionless and empty. Life is so much easier that way.

"Lolli?" Parker whispers, his knuckle gently bringing my gaze to his when he feels my body start to quake. "You alright?"

I pull myself out of his arms, twisting to grab the bottle from the sticky countertop. Bringing it to my lips, I take another swig, watching Parker's brows drop in concern.

I push off the bar and take a few steps toward the dance floor but stumble again.

This time, four hands reach out to steady me, one set heating my skin despite the situation. I shove away from Nate and settle into Parker's tense arms.

Nate's head jerks back, shock flashing across his features before he erases it and scowls at Parker. "How much you let her drink?"

"None of your damn business!" I shout drunkenly, spitting on that stupid dress shirt that looks so good on him. "Don't fucking concern your piece-of-shit self with me, Nate."

His eyes fly to mine, and I think I see remorse in them, maybe a little confusion and hurt, but definitely a dash of uncertainty. Too bad my brain shuts that shit down real quick, and flashes a picture of Liv's perfect ass, naked on Nate's bed, in front of my eyes instead.

His gaze cuts to Parker. "She's trashed."

"You're the cause," he throws back, through clenched teeth.

"And I'm right here," I slur, bringing the bottle to my lips again.

"Give me that," Nate demands.

"Uh," I cut my glance to the side and back quickly, "no."

"Kalani," he growls. "Give me the bottle before I take the damn thing."

I tuck it into my chest, but Nate's quick, pulling it from my hands in seconds.

"I'll never let go, Jack..." I slur, laughing as he yanks the whiskey from my grip, the force sending me stumbling right back into Parker's arms.

"Come on," Nate grumbles, reaching for me. "I'll take you to your room to sleep this shit off."

A harsh laugh leaves me and I rip my arm from his, fire searing through my veins and threatening to set me aflame. "Get. The fuck. Away from me, you rat bastard." I shove him sloppily, as fruitless as it may be. "You have zero claim to me and zero right to worry about what I'm doing."

"Don't stand there and act like this is me!" he screams, his face inches from mine, his breathing out of control.

My foggy eyes roam his face, looking for nothing in particular, but finding the tick of his jaw, the vein at his temple protruding. His eyelids are even shaking.

He's pissed.

My hand twitches to reach out and comfort him, to wipe the frown away, but again, Liv's ass flashes in my head, along with the thoughts of what they probably did once I left, or before I got there.

The saddest part...that's not even what's killing me inside, him being with her.

Nate didn't trust in me. He didn't believe in me, at least not enough to stop and consider that maybe whatever the bitch threw at him was false. He could have – more than likely, did - fucked her repeatedly tonight, and it still wouldn't compare to the third-rate feeling slicing through me right now.

Focusing on each step, I turn away from Nate and head for the door.

As soon as the warm, salty air hits my face, I take a deep breath. Grabbing onto the railing a few feet in front of the club, I bend at the waist, trying my damndest to keep everything in.

"Come on, Lolli." Parker's hand closes gently around my forearm. "Let's-"

"I said, I had her!" Nate shouts, his voice growing closer.

I turn just in time to see him shove Parker away from me, but Parker's quick and in Nate's face just as fast.

"Had!" Parker shouts, pointing a finger into Nate's chest. "Key word, Nate!" Parker steps further into his space. "Had," he repeats, knocking noses with him.

"Don't fuck with me right now, Baylor." Nate's lip curls, his words leaving him in a deep, low rumble from within his chest. "I won't hesitate to lay you on your ass."

Parker scoffs, not moving an inch, and Nate's dark eyes narrow.

"I'm taking her to her room," he says like his words are law and we're supposed to bow-fucking-down and listen.

They both turn to me when a humorless, dead laugh passes my dry lips. I smirk, leaning my back against the metal beam, letting my eyes roam over Nate, from his black boots to his black eyes.

I tilt my head slightly, a sickening smile on my lips. "Look at him, Hero." Nate's teeth grind together. "Trying to be all noble." I spit out the last word, pushing off the railing, and step up to them, my chest brushing both their arms as they stay rooted in their standoff. "You're not a knight in shining fucking armor, asshole."

I take a step closer and Parker makes the right move by taking a step back, letting me run the show.

"You're a weak, insecure bastard who walks around pretending you're not." I cast my eyes down his form, trying my best to make him feel as disgusted with himself as I am in me at this moment. For believing in him. In us. "Not even man enough to ask your fucking," I lift my fingers to use air quotes like a bratty teenager, "'girlfriend' for the truth to whatever story was cooked up, but instead, deciding to believe the school slut, who's just looking for the first jock strap to drag her along." I shake my head, stumbling a bit as I step back.

His hand immediately shoots out to steady me, a reflex action I'm sure, but I smack it away.

His eyes narrow and his nostrils flare, but he says nothing.

"Why did you do this?" I shove him, my long hair falling into my face. "Huh? Why did you push me, make me feel... make me love you?" I palm my chest, my face pinching as the pain gets stronger. "I didn't want this," I shake my head furiously. "I didn't. But you had to have me."

Thick, dark brows pull in to frame muddled dark eyes; so low, they're almost touching in the center. He takes a step forward, but my hands fly up, freezing him and his designer jeans in place.

"Guess the joke's on me, though, huh?" I laugh lightly, looking up at the star-filled sky briefly, then back at Nate. "Thinking I could come back from all the shit life's thrown at me." I look past him. "Be happy."

I kick off my shoes, then bend down to pick them up. "Here I am, exactly two years later." I look back at Nate then, seeing the horror and recognition of what today really is written all over him.

"Kalani..." he whispers, his shoulders dropping as low as his massive frame will allow, his eyes pinched, lips tight.

I shrug a shoulder. "April fucking fools to me."

With that, I turn and walk away from his shocked, confused, handsome fucking face.

Chapter Thirty-Eight

K ALANI

Parker shuts the door to my room, his eyes following me as I make my way to the patio doors. I prop them open, allowing the warm breeze to pass through the room, and plop down on the bed, staring off at nothing.

A few minutes later, I hear his shoes drop and the bed dips next to me.

I let my head fall to his shoulder, and his warm arm wraps around my back, pulling me closer.

"My parents are dead," I blurt out.

"I figured they were."

"Wanna know when they died?"

"If you want to tell me," he says quietly.

I nod against him. "Two years ago, Hero. Exactly two years ago…"

"Fuck," he mutters, his hand coming up to swipe down his face.

Yeah...fuck.

I bet that's what Nate's doing right now.

"Ever heard of Patty Loveless, Hero?"

"No, Lolli," he whispers, his arm around me tightening. "I haven't."

"Get on your phone and look up 'How can I help you say goodbye.'"

He shifts on the bed, forcing my gaze to his with a gentle touch to my jaw. I look up into pinched, sorrow-filled blue eyes.

"Please?" I beg, in a voice so low and broken, I want to hide in shame.

He nods, reaching into his pocket to pull out his phone.

"The song; it's about a girl. Life throws different challenges at her. Some sad, some heartbreaking, but they all feel like the end of everything when they first happen." I close my eyes. "But someone is there after each event, helping her move on, say goodbye. Letting her know that everything she's feeling is okay, normal even." I look up at Parker.

His eyes are locked on me, his finger hesitating over his screen.

"Press play, Hero," I whisper.

He's already shaking his head before I've finished, silently begging me not to make him, but when I don't look away, he releases a heavy sigh, pressing play with a shaky finger.

When I first met Nate, I knew he was trouble. It was written all over his dangerously attractive face. He was everything fathers warned their daughters about. The bad boy with good looks. Athletic and strong, with a fancy ride and nice clothes.

Too bad I didn't have a dad when I met him.

I was doomed from the start.

If only he ended up being just those stereotypical things. If only that's all there was to him; looks and football. If only he truly was bad. Then maybe it wouldn't hurt so much. Maybe my lungs wouldn't tighten with every breath I take, my eyes wouldn't burn with every blink.

Nate was so much more than I was ready for.

While he was cocky and egotistical, he was kind and gentle. Hard-headed and presumptuous, yet open and honest. He was everything. Perfect.

Mine.

"Parker..." I twist my body to face his. "I need you to help me say goodbye," I whisper, the plea in my voice carrying more weight than it should.

The look he gives me in return is uncertain, but he stands, lifts me into his strong arms, and moves to the head of the bed.

Gently, he sets me down, and rids himself of his belt, pulling his shirt over his head.

He reaches for me, a tight smile on his lips, and helps me out of my dress, then pulls his shirt over my head as gently as possible.

Parker pulls the covers back, slides under the sheets, then pulls me onto him, cradling me to his warm chest.

Once we're settled in silence, Parker whispers, "How can I help you, Lolli Bear?" His voice is so soft and caring, and the pain in my chest intensifies, seemingly crushing me from the inside out.

I lift my head from his chest and look into his beautiful ocean blue eyes.

He must see it, what I need, what I'm about to ask of him, because his face contorts and he winces, fear and unease washing over his features.

My heart beating double time in my chest, I murmur, "Kiss me."

His eyes flit back and forth between mine.

Brows pulled in, his hand glides along my spine, applying just enough pressure to pull my body closer. When he reaches my neck, his fingers spread wide, sliding up and into my thick, dark hair at the base of my skull. When he leans forward, I close my eyes, parting my lips for him.

His breath is coming in short pants, blowing softly across my skin, warming my alcohol-infused blood.

As his head moves closer, his nose slides against my own, the softness of his bottom lip feathering against my mouth. He holds still for a split second, before his grip in my hair tightens and his forehead drops to mine, a defeated sigh escaping him.

My lids lift, finding his tortured gaze on me. "I can't, Lolli," he apologizes, shaking his head back and forth. He pulls me in, his chest inflating. "I can't take you," he whispers, "and not have you."

My eyes pinch, my mind racing to understand him, but he shakes his head again, and tucks me back into him, holding me tight. When he pulls the covers over our bodies and kisses my hair, the pressure behind my eyes turns severe, moisture building at an unstoppable rate.

And then, I feel it... a single tear rolls down my cheek. The first tear I've shed since the day my family died.

My body flies upright. "Oh, my God!" I frantically wipe at my cheeks in horror.

Parker leans forward, gently wrapping his fingers around my wrists, and he pulls me in tighter, protectively.

"It's okay to cry, Lolli Bear," he coos, running a hand over my hair. "Say goodbye."

So, I do. With his gentle whispers of encouragement in a moment I need them most, I cry.

I cry for my parents, for my grandpa, for me. Even for the guy who broke me.

I cry until there is nothing left inside of me. And when I fall asleep, the last thing I hear is Parker's sweet voice, telling me everything will be alright.

"You're not going in there!"

"Bullshit, I'm not!"

"Just get the hell out of here! You've caused enough problems for now!"

My eyes peel open and I try to focus on the yelling coming from the hallway. Glancing up, I see Parker is still out cold. No doubt, he stayed awake long after I did.

"I only want to see that she's alright, Mia. Now get out of my way before I pick you up and move you."

"Oh, so now you care. Cool," Mia mocks.

Rolling my eyes, I slip out of Parker's embrace and stand, wincing as good ol' Mr. Daniels seeks his revenge.

I open the door, covering my eyes as the bright light of the hallway blinds me.

Mia flips around when she hears it open, giving me an apologetic smile. "Hey," she says softly.

The corner of my lip lifts, but that's all I got right now.

"Hungover?" she grins, her eyes roaming my face.

I scoff, wincing simultaneously. "Oh yeah. Jack has a nasty right hook, apparently."

Her smile widens, but her eyes stay soft. "I see that."

She's happy I'm making light of what I can.

I wink at her, then turn, forcing myself to look at Nate, but as soon as my eyes lock onto his, I have to look away. "What do you want, Nate?"

"Nothing," he says hurriedly. "Just had to be sure you made it back fine." When I return my gaze to his, he shrugs and looks down the hall. "You were wasted, so..."

I nod, leaning my throbbing head against the doorframe.

His eyes come back to mine and he does a double take, his nostrils flaring when his gaze drops to my chest.

Before I can even process, he bounds forward, shoving my door open. And last night repeats itself with a vengeful twist when a wide-awake Parker is revealed sitting up in the center of my bed, shirtless and under my sheets.

Mia gasps and my eyes fly to hers, finding her hand covering her mouth, tears in her eyes.

When Nate shoves past me, Parker flies off the bed, ready for his advance, but Austin pops in out of nowhere, wrapping his arms around Nate's body and neck.

"Get the fuck off me!" A growl rips from within him.

"No, man. Chill." Austin says calmly.

"This mother-"

"Look at him, dude," Austin states, jerking his chin at Parker, who's standing tall, waiting this out, a blank expression on his face. "He's still got his jeans on, man. Nothing happened in here." Austin turns his gaze to me, raising his eyebrow at me for confirmation.

I shake my head no and he nods. Pretty sure, had I said yes, he'd have let Nate go. Bro code and all that.

"Soo..." I look around at all the boys, then down at my bare legs. "You guys can go now."

Parker, the smart guy he is, heads out first. He kisses my temple, telling me to find him later and walks out, still shirtless.

Austin waits a good minute and a half to release Nate, then steps out. Mia disappeared long ago.

Nate stands in the center of my room, chest heaving, his eyes on the floor.

He looks up at me, his gaze tortured, tired.

When I give him nothing but a stone-faced stare, vacant and dead, his hands fly into the air, his head shaking back and forth. They come down, slapping against his sides, and he nods. Words are completely lost on him.

And I'm glad because I don't want to hear it. I can't.

He thinks I'm at fault for something, and maybe I am, but I'll never know because he didn't give me the chance to find out. That's on him.

With that, he walks out, closing my door behind him.

I shower and pack my bag.

Plugging my phone into the charger, I set my longest playlist on repeat, blasting it as loud as it will go, knowing no one will push too hard for me to open the door. At least, not today. That gives me a good eight hours. I place a note for Mia on the table and slip out my door.

I take the shuttle bus to the airport. I'm gone.

Done.

Chapter Thirty-Nine

NATE

Head down, I hustle into the gym before anyone spots me. I made it a point to get here extra early today, knowing less people would be around.

Dropping my bag on the floor, I set up some cones. For the next hour, I run through a few basic drills, my mind refusing to turn off.

Kalani, Jarrod, Parker, Kalani.

I sprint forward, dropping to touch the solid red line, and dash back, faster. Harder. Still, the past week's events are front and center, refusing to be pushed back.

Kalani.

Jarrod.

The recording.

Parker. His shirt on her skin, laying on her bare breasts, teasing her naked thighs.

My foot slips against the freshly waxed floors, and I fall on my ass with an echoed thud. Throwing an arm over my eyes, I lie there with my back against the floor, attempting to catch my breath.

Kalani on my porch swing, a smile so soft on her lips, her body leaning into mine. Breathing me in. Loving me.

A grunt leaves me, and my fist hits the ground.

Loving me, my ass.

She said it herself, on the recording. She didn't love me. It was all about what she could gain from me. What I could give her.

She already had all of me, why not have what is, or would be, mine, too? If that's what she wanted, my future, I'd have given it all to her. Hell, I probably would have begged her to take it.

If she loved me.

Did she not know I would have given her everything?

Did I not show her, make her feel, how much I loved her?

I'd have done more, had I known. Not that it would have made a difference.

And that's a bitter pill to swallow.

"The fuck you doing, man?"

I lift my arm, popping one eye open in time to see Austin step in front of me, an eyebrow raised.

I sigh, pushing myself into a sitting position, and rest my elbows on my knees. "Couldn't sleep." I shrug, averting my eyes to the retractable bleachers against the wall. "Figured I'd get here early, get a workout in."

"Avoid the piranhas?"

I nod, dropping my head to my chest.

"Let's go, man." He thrusts his hand into my line of sight. "Class is in ten."

I clasp my hand in his, allowing him to pull me up. We collect the cones and my workout bag in silence, then make our way to the locker room.

"You alright?" he asks, casting me a sideways glance.

"Yeah, man. I'm good." I toss my bag into my locker, pulling my wet shirt over my head. "Not looking forward to the awkward shit today's sure to bring though, that's for sure."

He drops down on the bench, leaning his back on the lockers opposite of me. "I hear that. You talk to her?"

"Nah, man." I shake my head, scrubbing my hands down my face. "It's done. None of it was real, so what's the point?"

"You wanna talk about it?"

I laugh lightly and say, "Nope," and he laughs in return.

"Then get your ass showered before we're late."

"You can go on ahead."

He smirks knowingly. "I'm good."

My lip tips up briefly. "Thanks, man."

He nods, looking down at his phone. "Hurry up."

I do and we're walking out of the locker room a few minutes later.

Thankfully, the halls are empty except for a few stragglers by the time we make it to Chem. When I hesitate outside the door, Austin steps to the side, leaning against the wall.

"Look," I shake my head. "I hate to ask and put you in this spot, but have you seen her? Kalani?" I ask him. "Or has Mia said anything? I just don't want to go in there unprepared." My shoulders drop, my head tilting to the ceiling. "I have no idea what to expect."

Austin's eyes narrow. "What are you hoping is gonna happen?"

"I have no fucking clue." And I don't. Not at all.

He sighs. "Sorry, bro, but I got nothing." He shrugs. "Haven't talked to Mia."

My head jerks back. "Whoa. What? Why?"

"We were just having fun, man." He kicks off the locker, clasping my shoulder as he reaches for the door handle, pulling it open.

He glances back at me. "Fun's over."

Damn straight.

When Kalani and Mia didn't show to Chemistry, I figured they were attempting to avoid me, which I was grateful for, but when lunch rolled around and they were nowhere in sight, it was clear they played hooky today.

I look to my left just as Liv squeezes into the seat next to me.

"Hey. How is everything?" Her hand comes to rest on my shoulder, her blue eyes bright.

I shrug her off and sit back, stretching my legs out under the table. "Fine. What do you want?"

I give her credit, she doesn't blanch at my abrasiveness, but smiles instead.

"Nothing, silly." She bumps her shoulder into mine. "Just checking on you. I know you cared about her and I'm really sorry she messed with your head the way she did. You know, lying about having feelings for you and all."

I scoff, pushing my chair back to stand. "Yeah. Right. Bye, Olivia." With that, I toss my untouched pizza in the trash and exit the cafeteria.

By the time PE rolls around, it's raining out, so class moves into the gym for free workouts.

After spotting each other on the bench press, Austin and I move to the ropes.

"You sure you're alright, man?" he asks, his hands gripping the knot of the hanging rope, giving it a little tug.

"Honestly, no. I'm not." I step back. "I gotta get outta here. I need to talk to her. She owes me an explanation." I take two steps, then Parker's in front of me.

"Yeah?" He steps into me. "She owes you an explanation?" His brows jump up his pretty boy forehead.

"She does! The shit she pulled on me." I push into him with my chest. "You really gonna stand there and act like you don't get some sick thrill out of this?" I accuse, narrowing my eyes. "You think you hide it, your feelings for her, but I see it. Seen it since day one." I laugh bitterly, taking a step back. "You can have the lying-"

I don't see it coming; his fist connects with my jaw, knocking me back a few steps.

Commotion roars around us, and the guys jump up, pulling us both back.

"You don't know shit, Nate!" he hollers, jerking his body in attempt to free himself from Jarrod's hold. "You obviously don't love her like you claim if you didn't even think to give her the benefit of the doubt!"

"Don't act like you know shit!" I scream, trying to advance on him, but Austin's grip tightens. "I heard what she said." His brows pull in slightly. "I. Heard. Her."

Parker's body relaxes and he yanks his arms free of the bastard behind him. "Fuck you, Nate. I know Lolli well, but I'm not stupid enough to think I know her better than you. I can tell you, though, no matter what you think you know, think you heard, you're wrong. Whatever it was, it hurt you. And the Kalani I know, would do anything to keep you from hurting. She'd never cause it." He shrugs unapologetically, confidently, and my chest gets tight.

"You fucked up. Plain and simple." He turns to leave, but stops, his jaw clenching. His eyes meet mine and he looks ready to throw another punch, but instead, he sighs. "She's gone."

My blood runs cold. "Gone. What do you mean, gone?"

He shakes his head, his gaze landing over my shoulder. "As in, gone. Not in Alrick." His eyes come back to mine. "And you have no one to blame but yourself." With that, he shoves through the nosy asses and exits the room, slamming the door behind him.

And I'm left standing there, more confused than ever.

N ATE

Chapter Forty

"Hey, honey."

I turn at my mother's voice. "Hey, Ma." Reaching into my closet, I grab the first shirt I come in contact with and pull it over my head. "What's up?"

She shrugs, her eyes following me when I grab my shoes and sit on the edge of my bed, slipping my feet inside.

"Going out again?"

"Yup. Party at Shawna's." I place a quick kiss on her cheek and squeeze past her.

"Nathaniel."

I stop halfway down the stairs, squeezing my eyes shut at her tone. Wishing she'd just be mad at me instead of sounding so sad, worried. "Yeah?"

"Baby, what happened?" she asks quietly. "With Lolli…"

"Ma-"

"No, Nate." She shakes her head, coming to stand beside me. "You need to talk to someone." Her brows pinch in the center. "What happened? All of a sudden, she's nowhere to be seen, and you're drinking and partying like you were before she came around. I don't like it."

"I didn't like it at first either, Ma." I shrug. "But it is what it is. She's gone and I get to go back to the way my life was before her."

She nods, crossing her arms over her chest. "And that's what you want?" She raises a dark brow. "To party every weekend? Get so drunk, you can't even make it home, let alone function the next day?"

"Yeah." I laugh, but it's hollow. "Nothing to worry about, no one to consult with. It's a pretty sweet deal."

She shakes her head, disappointment floating across her features. "You're graduating in two weeks, Nathaniel. Going all the way to California for college. I don't want to get a call that my son's body was found slumped over a steering wheel because you're making the wrong decisions." Her eyes get misty and I feel like a jackass.

"Look, it's fine. I'm fine." I shrug. "Just enjoying my final days as a senior."

"But every night, Nate?" she questions, her features growing more tense. "This behavior is far worse than it was before. You've been drinking and partying for a month straight. Your offer can be pulled from you at any moment. You know that, right? You're not making your workouts, you're ditching classes. You're at risk of losing ev-"

"I already have, Ma!" I shout, feeling my chest grow tight, my eyes widening. "I lost everything. She was everything." My chin falls to my chest and I hear a small sob escape my mother.

"Nate...what happened?" Her voice breaks for her broken son.

I sigh, making my way down the stairs. "She didn't want me for me, Ma." I look over at my mother, who is frozen in place by my admission. "She didn't care."

"Oh, honey, she does care. That girl loves you."

"She doesn't. She admitted it."

My mom blinks, whispering, "What?"

I nod. "Olivia recorded her. She admitted to everything. Played me for a fool."

The moment I say Olivia's name, my mom's eyes turn hard. Like me, she doesn't know the details, but is aware that there was a nasty fallout with Liv and my sister a year or so ago. Not to mention, she's been chasing after me for years. If anyone dislikes Olivia as much as me, it's my mother.

None of that matters though because this shit with Kalani? I heard it all.

I thought about what Parker said for days after our argument in the gym, replayed every moment with Kalani, over and over again in my head.

The good and the end.

But at the close of every drunken night I spend sprawled out on the empty football field, alone, the results are the same.

I heard her.

And I can't unhear her.

Chapter Forty-One

M IA

It's half past ten when Ashley, Alyssa, and I finally make it to Shawna's.

"Damn." Alyssa smooths down her silky black hair. "Guess the party started without us, huh?" she smiles.

I nod, my gaze sliding across the room to take inventory of who is and isn't here. "Sure did." My shoulders drop an inch.

"Come on guys, let's grab a drink." Ashley links her arms through ours and pulls us toward the kitchen.

We're about to round the corner when I hear Liv's hushed voice. Grinning, I pull both girls to a stop, covering my mouth with my finger, signaling for them to stay quiet.

They nod, Alyssa's eyes suddenly gleaming for gossip, and we lean in a little closer, trying to hear her better.

"Seriously, I don't get it," Olivia whines. "It's been over a month since Lolli took off. Why is he still denying that he wants to hook up with me?"

"Come on, Liv," someone says. "He's probably still hurt. I think he really was in love with her."

Alyssa pulls on my arm, so I look at her and she jerks her chin forward, signaling for me to enter, but I shake my head no.

Not yet.

"Please," Liv scoffs. "He didn't love her. And he shouldn't be sulking around. I showed him all the pictures."

Alyssa's head pulls back and she mouths 'pictures' to me.

I shrug, my own brows dropping low, having no clue what she's talking about.

"I still think he cared for her."

"You weren't there, Shawna. You should have seen his face when I showed him the photos of her and Jarrod in Mexico."

On my right, Ashley stiffens.

A cynical laugh leaves Liv. "He totally freaked, seeing Jarrod's lips on his precious Kalani. Not to mention, he was opening the door to her hotel room while his mouth was on her skin."

Before I can stop her, Ashley flies forward, shoving the swinging door open and rushing into the kitchen.

Alyssa and I look at each other, shocked, then rush in behind her.

"What did you just say?" Ashley's voice is different. I can't tell if she's about to flip her shit, or cry.

Neither reaction makes any sense to me.

Olivia straightens and Shawna dips away from us, squeezing her way through the door we just came through.

"What are you talking about?" Liv pops her hip out, trying to look careless.

"You said you have pictures of Jarrod and Lolli, from Mexico," Ashley questions her. "What do you mean? Pictures of what, exactly?"

Olivia relaxes a bit, which puts me on edge. "Oh, yeah. I guess

Nate hasn't announced what happened between them. Embarrassed or whatever. He, or I, caught Lolli cheating on him with Jarrod that second night."

"Bullshit," Ashley whispers, her gaze dropping to her feet. "She...I didn't listen...I..."

When my gaze shifts to her, I see tears in her eyes.

"Wait." Alyssa's palms fly up. "What's going on, Ash? Why are you upset?"

She clears her throat. "I, uh...I'm not. I'll find you guys in a bit."

"Ash!" Alyssa tries to go after her, but Ashley is already gone.

I turn back to Olivia, narrowing my eyes. "What are you talking about?"

"What, did she not tell you?" Liv cocks her head to the side, a sinister smile on her pursed lips. "Guess you weren't as close as you thought." She shrugs and saunters past us.

"What the hell is going on?" Alyssa asks, looking around with wide eyes.

"I have no idea."

"What does Lolli say?"

Before I can answer, my eyes find Ashley hidden in the corner.

Alyssa follows my line of sight. "What the fuck?"

Ashley is in the corner, tears running down her face, with Jarrod.

Panic fills his eyes and he glances around the room, his hands shooting out to attempt to calm her, but she hastily shoves him away.

It's obvious he's trying to soothe her, to get her to quiet down and step outside with him. But she's not having it and soon, they have everyone's attention.

"It was your fault, wasn't it?" she screams, fresh tears spilling over her cheeks. "Tell me she was wrong! That you didn't do this!"

Jarrod tries to calm her once more, stepping forward to whisper in her ear, but she shoves him again.

"Tell me, Jarrod! I deserve at least that much," she wails.

Nate steps up beside me.

"What's going on?" he slurs, peering around the rest of the nosy onlookers, trying to understand the sight before us.

"No idea." I shrug, not looking at him. "She overheard Liv say," I hesitate for a moment. "Say that, uh, Lolli and Jarrod slept together, and she freaked out."

Nate tenses beside me, then takes a step closer to the scene.

"Come outside with me, Ash." Jarrod steps closer to her, his face pinched. "Let me explain."

"Explain!" she sobs. "So, there is something to explain? I defended you when she said-" Her hand flies to her mouth. "Jesus Christ... I'm gonna be sick."

Nate scoffs next to me, then storms away.

I glance back at Ashley, then head in the direction Nate took off. Finding him on the front porch, I drop into the chair beside him.

He's quiet for a few minutes before he speaks. "Did you know?"

I look at him and he asks again.

"Tonight was the first I've heard." My heart hurts thinking about it. About all of it. I honestly had no idea. "She seemed to really care for you."

It takes him a second, but he nods, looking out at the yard. "None of it was real, Mia," he huffs. "She never really cared."

My chest caves in at the possibilities of what a truth to that could, would, mean. "I'm sorry." It's a lame response, but it's all I've got.

"I just can't believe she would go that far just to secure her future like that." His lip curls. "I mean, I get she has no family and all, other than you guys, but that was low, fucking with me like that."

"Whoa, wait. What?"

He nods again. "Oh, yeah. There's more. She said all she

401

wanted from me was a title." He shifts toward me. "A fucking title, Mia."

"Nate..."

"She wanted to be one of those plastic, real housewives of fucking football or some shit." He shrugs, pulling himself to the edge of his seat. "I don't get it-"

"Nate-"

"She's nothing like that! At least, I didn't think she was." He's talking to himself now. "Sure, her finances would be secure, and I'm sure that would be a huge relief, considering her situation, but-"

"Nate!" I scream, jumping from my seat to stop his rant.

He looks up at me, coming back to the present.

I raise my brows and he nods, sitting back.

"What the fuck are you talking about?" My eyes stay wide.

"All she was with me for was my future, Mia."

"Nate," I kneel in front of him, physically needing all of this to be a misunderstanding, needing our eyes and hearts to have played a nasty trick on us. "Tell me exactly what happened."

"She played me. Made me think she was opening up to the idea of us. I watched it all happen. Felt every moment of it." He hits his chest. "I thought I was watching a girl heal, open up to the possibilities of what her life could be. What we could be." He turns to me, his eyes low and lost, vacant. "I'd swear on my life I watched her fall in love with me, watched the haze in her eyes clear, and see me, feel me." He tosses himself back in the seat. "She didn't fall for me. She fell in love with what she thought she could gain from me."

"Oh, my God." I gape at him. "You have no idea, do you?"

His face hardens, his dark eyes narrowing.

"That day at my house when Lolli fainted... You said she told you everything." I shake my head. "I assumed you knew..."

"Mia," he growls.

"I don't know about all the other stuff," I tell him, lifting from my seat. "The cheating or her feelings, but I can guarantee you..." I pause, letting him know how serious I am, "she wasn't using you for money, or a damn title. She never wanted either." I stomp down the porch steps, upset by the entire situation, but stop a few feet away, spin on my heels and throw at him, "Do yourself a favor. Stop getting drunk long enough to work a computer. Google her last name, Nate. You won't get to the B before you shit your pants." I take off down the driveway, done with this party, and knowing damn well I'm a total fucking hypocrite.

Graduation day is a day for emotions to run high. It can be the happiest day for some and the saddest for others. It's a day where some take chances, others realize their regrets, and some just flat out get wasted and carry on like any other day in high school.

All I want to be is one or the other, but still, my mind hasn't settled on the right reaction, hasn't stopped to allow myself to process the events of the last few weeks. Why? Because I'm a weak bitch. Scared. Too afraid of the 'what if' to go after the 'what the fuck'.

When I reach my locker, I toss my purse inside. As soon as I shut it, I see Nate approaching. We've done a good job avoiding each other since the party a few weeks ago.

"Hey."

"I didn't know," he rushes out, sorrowful.

"I know."

His eyes pinch, and he leans his shoulder against the lockers. "I'm so mad at her, Mia."

"I know."

"If she'd have told me who her family was, if I had known all that, maybe I would have had the sense to run after her that day. She just took off, and I was so mad, I didn't really process what was happening in that moment, or how she felt. What she must have been thinking. All I could see when I opened that door was red, a million thoughts running through my head. I was such a dick. I knew I needed time to cool off." He sighs.

"I was gonna take off and get shit-faced and who knows what after that, but she showed up before I was ready to go, and..."

He shakes his head; his lost eyes roam the now thinning halls. "She's okay, though...right? I mean, I know she doesn't want me, but she's good, not like when she got here?"

I drop against the locker, sharing my secret for the first time. "I haven't talked to her," I whisper. "Not since that day."

When he doesn't respond, I turn to look at him.

"What do you mean?" His brows pull in, his body tensing, noticeably so.

I squeeze my eyes shut. "I...left the room that morning, and never went back to check on her until it was an hour before we were to load the buses to leave, days later. She was gone. Found a note and her phone, so I knew she was gone gone. Guess I figured if she really truly didn't care about you, then she'd suck it up and grace us with her presence when she felt like it, on her own time. The only way she knows." I avert my eyes, ashamed. "I don't know if she left right then, if she stayed, waiting...hoping someone would come to her. I... I don't know."

When his eyes widen, I hurriedly add, "My mom's talked to her, Nate. She's, well, she's safe. I know that much."

He nods, relaxing some, and an expression I can't read passes over him.

"What?" I tilt my head curiously.

A sad smile twitches at the corner of his lips. "I'm just," he sighs, almost sounding irritated with himself. "I shouldn't care, but I'm glad she talked to your mom. That's..." He groans, rolling his eyes. "That's good."

I nod, confused and unwanted tears clouding my vision. "You did that, you know?"

He shrugs, looking torn by the thought.

"No matter what happened between you guys, Nate, you helped her heal. Helped her realize that there was still more out there worth experiencing. I'm sure she'll be a little lost for a while, but she'll have a good life because of you."

"Without me." His dark eyes lock on mine and I see the crushed man inside them. He's doing nothing to hide it if he even can.

A somber smile is all I have to offer.

After a few seconds of silence, I whisper guiltily, "I haven't read it. The note. I'm not sure I can, to be honest."

He studies me for a moment and I let him, almost wishing someone could understand where I am in my head but refusing to give it away. Being carefree isn't as easy as Lolli made it seem.

He opens his mouth to speak, but Mrs. Evans makes an announcement over the loudspeaker, letting us know it's time. With that, we walk out to graduate with our fellow classmates, our loved ones looking on, and I couldn't give a damn about any of it.

I'm stuck in a place between my heart and my head, and I have no clue which way to go.

Chapter Forty-Two

N ATE

"Feel like some dessert?" my mom asks quietly, stepping out the door my dad has just opened for her.

"No thanks, I think I'll get changed and head out for a while." I give her a weak grin and shuffle past, choosing to use the back door instead of walking up that damn porch – can't stand the sight of that swing. But before I have the chance to slip away, my dad stops me with a firm grip on my shoulder.

"Walk with me, son."

It's not exactly a request, so I nod, letting him steer me toward the tree line.

When we reach the water, he drops to the grass and leans back on his palms. "Gettin' warmer." He looks around.

I loosen my tie and drop beside him.

After a minute or two, he sighs. "You remember that summer we met your cousins and their friends in Chicago?"

"Yeah." I pull a piece of overgrown grass and toss it.

"We went to that Bears game?"

A light chuckle escapes. "Yeah, and Mason got pissed when Ari's friend was flirting with me."

My dad shakes his head, grinning. "Then got mad when Ari started flirtin' with his friend."

I laugh, leaning back to match my dad's position. "I knew she had a thing for Chase. Mason put a stop to that quick."

My dad scoffs. "Or so he thinks. Ari's an amazing girl. I think Chase will see it eventually. Though, I'd hate to be the guy that falls for his best friend's little sister." He laughs.

I nod but can't find it in me to care right now.

My dad sighs. "That game we went to, Nate; the Bears played the Tomahawks."

My head snaps to my dad's, eyes narrowing slightly.

He watches me for moment, studying me. "It was a playoff game, remember?"

I nod, scanning his face.

"She was there, Nate. She and her family. Her dad was the one who took our pictures in front of the stadium."

"How the hell do you know that?"

He doesn't snap at me for my tone or my words, but looks away, guilt shadowing his features for a moment.

"I figured out who she was the day I met her," he admits quietly. "Put two and two together based on what I knew; her story and her name." He pushes up, lifting one knee to rest his arm on. "Didn't tie her to that event until you guys had your fallout, and I started to really think everything through."

I scrub my hands down my face, unsure how to handle this situation, confused if it even matters at this point. "Why you telling me this, Dad?"

He ignores my question. "Remember that quarterback camp you flew out to a few years back, at SDU? The one Mason submitted your highlight reel to, without telling you?"

"Yeah, Dad. I remember." I turn my scowl on him. "What about it?"

"Did you know that program was created and funded by the Tomahawks? Their head coach, Lee Embers, ran that camp. He took you under his wing that summer."

"Why are you telling me this?"

"Son, listen to me. What your mom and I have..." His dark brows raise and he nods. "It's special. As sad as it is, most people who have been married, or together as long as we have, don't have that zing anymore. They don't get their breath stolen from their lungs when their wives first step outta bed, get lost in her eyes when she looks up at them, or blinded by her smile."

I wish he'd stop talking.

I palm at my chest.

"Yeah," he chuckles to himself. "What we have is really something." He locks his eyes on mine. "But what you and Lolli have?" He raises a brow and I frown at him. "That's once in a lifetime. Once."

"Dad-"

"I'm dead serious, son. I've never witnessed the kind of connection you two have. Hell, I'm not even sure I believed in it until she came along." He shakes his head. "It's almost too much to watch you two together. You're so attuned to one another, it's as if you're one person. You know what she needs without her telling you. You have deep, meaningful moments with just your eyes."

"Dad-"

"And when that girl laughs, I swear to God, I can see it leave her and run through you. You live for it. For her."

"Yeah, well. Sucks to be me, I guess." I hop to my feet and start toward the house.

"Nate, damn it." He catches up to my quick strides. "Don't you get it?"

I stop, dropping my head back. "Get what, Dad?" I lift my face to see his frown mirrors mine. "Get that the girl I'm, as you just pointed out, desperately in fucking love with doesn't give a shit about me, and took off without caring to glance back? No, Dad, I don't get it!"

Again, I expect him to smack the shit out of me for talking to him like this, but it never comes. Instead, he squares his shoulders and stands tall.

"You don't find it weird that, throughout your life, you've had multiple opportunities to meet her, and never did?" He doesn't give me time to answer. "'Cause I sure as hell do. I think this is how it was all supposed to happen. Your lives have been mixed and intertwined for years without your knowledge, but the universe knew you two weren't ready for each other then. You needed to live, Nate. To screw up a bit before she came to you. Otherwise, you'd have never seen her worth, her particular type of perfection. Without your regret, you'd never have had something, or someone, to be better for.

"And, as messed up as it is, she needed to see what life was lacking, experience pain and loss, and figure out her own way of handling it before she had you to lean on. Or else she never would have needed you, never would have searched your soul for her safe place. She'd have gone through life taking it only as it came, never truly living, or loving. That's the only way it could happen; through her terrible losses."

His theory makes sense, in a fucked-up movie kind of way. She came here and shook me to the core, right when I needed it. I quit the partying that threatened to ruin everything, because I didn't like the way she looked at me, like I was a typical guy. I had a breakout year in football, earning pretty much my choice of schools because knowing she was sitting there, watching me, pushed me to work harder. To make her proud.

I didn't want to be typical to her. I wanted to be all she could ever want and more. I wanted to be her everything, like she quickly and without my knowledge, became mine. And I was so sure I succeeded. I was so sure she felt me with every cell in her body, like I do her.

I bite the inside of my cheek, my nostrils flaring, as I try to keep my emotions in check in front of the man I look up to. I lift my shaky gaze to his.

"I don't know what happened. Heard the bit you told your mom, but I can see it in your eyes; you're not convinced. I know you're scared of the truth, pissed and hurt, but ask yourself, Nate," he places a hand on my shoulder, his dark eyes locked on mine, "what'll be worse? Finding out it was true, that she didn't love you? Or never knowing for sure, always wondering if you still hold a piece of her, like she always will for you?"

My shoulders drop and I look off to the side.

"She was made for you, Nathaniel. The other piece of your soul. She came to you, was given to you, when you were ready for her, when you needed her. Way I see it, things are coming around now. It was only right something happened now, to test you, like she was tested." My gaze returns to his and he gives a resolute nod. "It's your turn now. Go to her when she needs you most.

Well, shit.

Chapter Forty-Three

N<small>ATE</small>

I don't know what I'm doing, but I'm running on edge, hoping I don't fumble. I need my dad's words to be true, need to prove to my fucked-up head that my beat-up heart is right. But right or wrong, the bottom line is I have to know what happened. I'm fucked up in a bad way. I only know of one person who can help me in the end, but first things first.

I hop out of my truck and jog to the door, knocking on it loudly. Sure, I could have used my phone, but chances are she'd ignore me, out of whatever fear is cookin' in her mind, so I figured just showing up was best.

As expected, Mia flings the door open with a scowl. "What are you doing here, and why are you pounding on my door like a damn sheriff?"

"Get your shit, let's go."

"Excuse me?" She places a hand on her hip and starts to argue, but I head back to my truck.

She groans, slamming her front door slam shut.

"And where exactly are we going?" Mia hops in, pulling the seatbelt over her.

"To figure this shit out."

I see her tense out of the corner of my eye.

"Nate-"

"Look, I need to know what the hell happened, if only for my own sanity. And if I have to face it," I stop at the stoplight and turn to her, "so do you. I don't know what your issue is, yet, but clearly you have one. So, we're going to figure it out."

"I don't think-"

"Save it, Mia. It's time."

MIA

Fuck my life.

This isn't happening. I don't know who lit the fire under Nate's ass, but nothing but pure determination is burning through his eyes.

He's pissed and, bystanders be damned, he's getting his answers tonight.

"How the hell are you supposed to find out?"

"Ashley."

My head snaps back. "What?"

He sighs. "We're late to the game, Mia. I don't know why I didn't see it before. The way she acted that day at the party...it was all right there. I was just too blinded by fury to catch it. By now, she and, if my suspicions are correct, someone else knows what the fuck happened in Mexico. Now it's time for us to take the steps to prove we care enough to figure it out."

Nate might as well be speaking French, because his "come to Jesus" moment he's going for is lost on me.

I have no idea what's happening.

I'm going in unarmed.

Again. Fuck my life.

It only takes about fifteen minutes to get to the bonfire the seniors put on every year after graduation.

Nate puts his Hummer in park and turns to look at me.

"You sure you're ready for this?"

"No, are you?"

I shake my head, then we both step out of his vehicle.

"Alright, don't get distracted. Let's find Ashley."

We walk around a bit, weaving in and out of the parked cars, before I spot her in a lawn chair, on Jarrod's lap.

Huh.

Nate sees her the same time I do and charges in their direction.

Jarrod spies us in an instant, quickly rising to his feet and setting Ash aside.

Her gaze follows his and she smirks.

What the hell?

"What can I do for you, Nate?" he grits out.

"You can shut your fucking mouth before I knock your ass out. I don't have time for your bullshit, but I do want to borrow your," he pins hard eyes on Ashley, "girlfriend."

"Leave her out of this." Jarrod steps closer to Ashley, and I step away from Nate when I see the deadly smirk he gives Jarrod.

He's not leaving without answers.

"What's the matter, Jarrod?" Nate inches closer. "You find a way to manipulate her into thinking your secrets are better worth kept?" He goads him and I watch as Ashley's face contorts with guilt.

He's onto something.

I step closer.

"Make her think it was over and done, and no one was looking for the answers anymore, so you don't have to live with the fact that you fucked both your girl, and mine, in the same night? Figuratively speaking, though, right?" Nate's steps even closer and Jarrod's body starts to shake with rage. "'Cause everyone knows my girl never wanted you."

I'm not sure if Nate believes what he's saying, but I think he's getting what he's looking for.

Jarrod pushes forward. "Fuck you, Monroe! You think you're hot shit 'cause you scored with the new girl, who has been run through who knows how many times?" I see Nate's hands flex at his sides, but he doesn't advance. "Well, I got the virgin!"

When Ashley gasps, Nate smirks at Jarrod. Realization sets in and Jarrod's eyes widen. He quickly shifts to Ashley and pulls her into him. "Ash-"

"Stop!" she croaks and he flinches. "Just... stop. I can't do this again. You're..." She sighs, her eyes glazing over. "You're everything I thought you were, Jarrod. Self-centered, shallow, and... mean."

She steps away from him and pulls out her phone.

"Ash, don't do this," he pleads.

"You did this, Jarrod." She shakes her head. "To them, to us."

She lifts her screen, silent tears sliding down her cheeks, and meets Nate's gaze with a guilt ridden look on her face. "I'm really sorry," she whispers. "I sent it to Mia. Don't listen to it here, Nate."

I whip out my phone, seeing a message from her on my screen.

I meet Nate's gaze to confirm.

He sighs. "I'm sorry, Ash, I had to..."

"I know. I was waiting." She smiles softly through her tears, almost seeming proud, and his lip twitches.

Wait, what?

He squeezes her shoulder, then we both dash back to his truck.

Once inside, we freeze, staring at each other.

"Did you see what it was?" His brows jump.

"No."

"Are you ready to?"

"No."

He nods, his gaze dropping to my screen.

I open the message, download the attachment, and open it.

My heart rate spikes when Kalani's voice plays through the tiny speaker.

"Excuse me?" Lolli's voice is low, lethal.

"Oh, come on. Share the deets on your grandfather's NFL status. A several million-dollar football contract that renewed every so many years, only increasing in numbers? Impressive."

Silence fills the air for a moment, and then...

"He earned it," Lolli defends. "The NFL pays high for recognizable talent."

"And the millions?"

"What about 'em?"

"You're a millionaire now, right?"

"Holy shit," Nate mutters next to me.

"Yeah, and?"

"So, he just gave all his money to a child?"

"It was his. Now it's mine. Big fucking deal."

"So why are you wasting your time on Nate, then? It's not like you care about him."

"Wh...are you fucking kidding me right now?" Kalani's tone is incredulous, but strong. "Not that it's any of your damn business, Olivia, but I love Nate."

"Oh fuck," Nate groans, dropping back against the door.

I pull my ear closer to the screen, hearing Liv's gasp in the recording.

"Yeah, I know. Just figured it out myself, but it's true. I love the shit outta him. It's you," Lolli shouts, the sound muffling in the weak speakers of my phone, "who doesn't care about him."

"What makes you say that?"

"Uh...because it's the truth!"

"Okay, Lolli. So, what do you think this is all about?"

Silence again, then...

"What are you doing right now?"

My brows pull in at Kalani's inquisitive tone.

"Wha...what do you mean?"

"You. These questions. I don't know what you're shooting for here, but know I'm not an idiot, Liv."

"I don't know what you're talking about."

. . .

My eyes fill with tears. "What did you do, Liv?" I whisper, seeing Nate's head swing my direction in my peripheral vision, but my gaze stays on my screen.

"I'll play along..." Kalani speaks again. "What do I think you're after? Easy. Money, a title, and a ticket. When it comes to you, Olivia, all that matters is a shiny multi-million dollar contract."

"You think money is everything to me?"

"Money is everything to you!"

Nate starts dry heaving next to me, his body trembling. With rage or fear, I haven't a clue.

"I get it. You don't like yourself much; maybe your home life is shitty, so you do your damndest to make everyone around you miserable, just to feel better about yourself. Well, I'm not like you. I don't need to tear someone down or take advantage of people to feel good. I have Nate. And, to a girl who is used to having nothing but money in the bank, he's more than enough for me."

"For now. What about when school's over and he's off to college? He could get injured or decide he doesn't want to play football, what then?"

"Are you not hearing me? I don't care about that shit! Football or not. I want him. That's it. Where he wants to go, what he wants to do, how long he wants to do it...I don't care! I just need him. And, as much as it ruffles your fake little feathers, I have him. Me. So back. The fuck. Off."

The recording ends.

417

We're frozen, staring at the blank screen in silence, for what feels like an eternity.

Nate claws at his chest, his face constricted with pain, sagging against his seat.

And me? I'm a sick bitch because my heart feels lighter than it has in weeks.

She loves him.

Kalani is in love with him.

This means she didn't, she wouldn't have-

Wait.

I hop out of the car and he follows.

"Mia?"

My brows pinch in the center. "Lolli...she said you were fucking Olivia that night." Slowly, I turn to face him. "Why would she think that Nate?"

Nate looks at me, his head shaking in confusion. Then, an instant later, his face falls, paling. "Oh, fuck."

No...

"She saw you two, didn't she?"

Nate groans, pulling on the ends of his hair.

"That means..."

Oh God.

"We have to go!" He rushes to his door, his hand freezing on the handle when he sees I haven't moved.

I bend at the waist, one arm shooting out to hold myself up against the bumper.

"I have to get to her. Now." He rushes to me, ushering me to the door, but I don't budge. "Mia, this has been fucking killing me. Killing me." He pushes on his chest. "Thinking she didn't want this. Didn't want me."

He's pleading, and while I should feel for him, my own issues, insecurities, and anger rear their ugly heads.

He's vulnerable and crushed, but I'm bitter and lost.

"So," I squint. "Olivia tells you some lies and you jump into bed with her?"

His brows jump. "I-"

"Save it, Nate. You're just as much to blame as she is, for her leaving." I cut him off, my voice growing louder. "You could have talked to her, asked her if it were true! Talked to her, like she would have if it were you!" I shove him. "If you would have trusted in her, she never would have seen you with Liv! She never would have needed anyone to comfort her!" I cry. "She never would have-"

I clamp my mouth shut tight, my eyes widening, but it's too late. He caught it and a deserved, condescending laugh leaves him as he shuffles back.

"Wow, Mia." He shakes his head at me, his dark eyes pinched, disgusted. "I thought maybe you were hurting because she was or upset with her because she took off and left you. And you're questioning me about not asking her, not believing in her?" He scoffs, opening his door. "You're as bad as I am."

"Where are you going?"

He stops and looks at me with narrowed eyes, but they quickly turn defeated. "To find out where she is. I'm gonna go to her and beg her to forgive me; to keep me."

My jaw begins to tremble as tears threaten to fill my eyes. "How are you going to find her?"

"By starting in the right place. The only place that makes sense."

My pulse starts pounding against my ribs. Already knowing the answer, I ask anyway, "And that would be?"

He gazes at me for a moment. "I'm gonna ask the one person who, as much as it kills me to say, I know would never turn his back on her, not like you and I did."

My breath is stolen from my lungs, and I'm left frozen in place, feeling more conflicted than before.

Nate's words ring true... he'd never give up on her.

NATE

With my truck in park, I sit idling in front of his house, wondering how the hell I let things get this far, if we can ever go back, and even worse, if I'm too late. If she's realized who else has been in front of her all this time.

"Fuck!" I hit the steering wheel, dropping my forehead to rest on the grip.

"You're not my type."

I jerk upright at the intrusive voice, finding a smirking Parker poking his blonde ass head in my passenger window, scowling when I realize what his comment was.

He laughs goodheartedly, holding his palms up for a moment before leaning into the truck window. "Too soon?"

I scoff, facing forward. "Yeah, man. Too fucking soon."

I look back at Parker and see the duffle bag around his shoulders. Glancing at his truck, I notice the few garbage bags and boxes in the back.

He follows my line of sight, and bobs his head, looking back at me.

"California?"

"Oceanside, to be exact." He studies me for a few moments, looking me over, before landing on mine. Waiting for the only question he knows I'm dying to ask. So, I do.

"How is she?" My chest tightens, anticipating his response.

Aggression, judgment, confusion, and years of friendship pass through his eyes, but ever the golden boy, he settles on relief, and understanding.

"Damn, man." Parker drops his bag, pulls the door open, and jumps into my passenger seat, throwing his head back against the headrest. "She's fucked up. Pretending she ain't 'cause I'm-" he winces. "'Cause no one's around. These last few weeks though, something's shifted in her tone. Still sad, but...something else, too, that I can't quite put my finger on." He looks over at me. "She won't say it. She won't lie, so I haven't flat out asked her. Don't want to force her to talk about it when I know she's not ready." His eyes don't narrow. They stay focused, clear.

Message received: She doesn't lie if you give her the chance to tell the truth.

I'm a fucking idiot.

"I can hear it in her voice, Nate. She's miserable." He looks away, not willing to show me the pain the thought causes him.

"Why didn't you say something to me, man?"

He gives me a sharp look. "She's better than that. Deserves someone who realizes it on their own. Not someone who has to be reminded or convinced."

I know he's right.

He laughs lightly, like a weight's been lifted. "I'm glad you're sitting here right now, though." He looks at me and an understanding passes between us.

He cares about Kalani. He'd protect her from anything he could. Even me.

"You didn't sleep with Liv that night, did you?"

"Nah, man." I drop my head against the seat. "I never touched her. Never even considered it. I didn't even know she was still in my room, let alone fucking naked, until I walked out of the bathroom to answer the door. Then, when I saw her lying on the bed, I...used it to hurt Kalani. To try and make her feel a fraction of what I was feeling. It was so fucked up, dude." I groan.

"Real fucked up," he agrees.

I explain that night in Mexico, and the mind games from Liv that led to it. I tell him about Ashley and Jarrod, and the recordings.

I pour my fucking heart out to the guy in love with my girl.

"Damn."

"Yeah."

The silence stretches longer than it should. Blowing out a breath, I turn to my friend. "I need to go to her, Parker. Talk to her, if only to say I'm sorry."

He stares at me for a few seconds, then steps out of the truck. "You're right. You do." He grabs his bag off the ground, turning back to me. His eyes give nothing away, but I know this isn't easy on him. If he helps me, he knows what that means for him. But again, he'd never do wrong by her, especially for personal gain. "She's perfect, you know that, right? You know she deserves so much more than the shit she's been dished?"

I nod. "I know. Trust me, Parker. Please."

He casts his eyes to the side for a moment, before bringing them back to me. "Can you be ready in an hour?"

My body tenses. "Don't fuck with me, dude," I plead.

He grins, but his eyes are sad. "Nate. I've been waiting for you to get out of your own head for weeks." He looks me in the eye, all joking aside. "I'm about to lock up. I'll meet you at your house.

Then, we're headed west." He smacks the roof and walks off, as a thought pops in my head.

"Hey!" I lean forward, shouting out the open window. "Can you help me with something?"

He nods, not needing to know what before agreeing, and disappears into his house.

Calling my dad, I tell him my plan and ask him a favor, then toss my phone in the middle console.

Within an hour, Parker and I are on the road.

"Get your speech ready now, Monroe." He turns up the radio and leans back. "It's a long ass drive, but that shit might take some rehearsal time." He cuts me a grin, quickly focusing back on the highway.

This is it, my Hail Mary.

I'm going to California.

"Shit."

KALANI

Checking my phone for the hundredth time in the past hour, I sigh when I see a blank screen. Still no text from Parker. He was supposed to let me know when he hit I-5, so I could plan ahead and be home by the time he got there, since the distance between the stadium and the beach house I purchased is a good forty minutes.

Now I'm not cookin' him shit.

"Whatcha huffin' and puffin' about over there, young one?"

Pausing the submission video, I turn to my CEO, aka my grandpa's oldest friend. "Just ready to see Parker today. I need someone to compare stats with, since you're goin' senile and all," I tease, offering him an overly exaggerated smile.

Last year, when I sat down with Mr. Marshall, he let me know he was too old, and too tired, to keep going any longer. Running the headlining sports photography company will do that to a man. Not to mention his standing in for me as the co-owner of a professional football team.

He nearly had a stroke when I told him I named my best friend, an eighteen-year-old high school senior – graduate, as of three days ago - his successor. But like he said, he's old, tired, and his wife wants him home.

He's never complained though, and the omission weighed heavy on his heart.

Mr. Marshall's round belly bounces, his laugh lines on full display. "You're a spittin' image of your mama."

I shrug, sinking behind my coffee cup, and press play on another highlight reel.

"You planning on watching all of those?" He motions to the box of sealed yellow envelopes sitting on the ground by my feet.

"It's only fair."

He nods proudly. "You're all heart. Just like your grandpa was."

I bite the inside of my cheek to keep in an irritated sigh in.

This sort of thing happens a lot. He never did it before, and while he means no harm, just the sentiment of an aged man, I'm not sure I like it. But the very day I decided to get to work, to get myself acquainted with what will be the rest of my life, he started making some sort of connection between me and my family on a regular basis.

I asked him about it once, in a moment of panic, and he said the second I walked through the door, he knew I was much lighter. He said my eyes no longer carried the weight of the ocean, but the breeze in the sky.

I'm not quite sure that's true.

I feel heavy.

Being here, at home, at the company, and on the field; it's a lot to take in. A lot to process when you've denied yourself the thoughts for so long.

Truth is, it fucking sucks.

I'm trying my hardest to push back the memories, but this entire place is full of nostalgia, and I can't shut it down. It won't work. The feelings, they won't go away, won't lessen, or give my mind a break. I run and run, and I still can't escape myself.

He opened me up to the good, the bad, the ugly. Gave me no choice in learning the great, all-consuming, soul-binding warmth I never knew existed. Never wanted.

Nate opened up every piece of me, forcing me to feel every single nerve in my body. Every beat in my heart.

And now I can't forget it. Can't turn it off.

I've got blisters on my feet and a hole in my heart. The only thing that helps in the slightest is pouring myself into other young and aspiring players while I wait. Dare I say, hope.

I shove some envelopes in my bag and shuffle toward the door. "I'll call you later, Al. Have fun with those."

I hear a deep laugh and a mumbled "Brat" on my way out.

Once in my car, I pull my phone from my pocket, and see a text from Parker, saying he's in town.

Smiling, I let him know I'll meet him at home.

It takes me forty-seven minutes to get to the beach house from the facility, so by the time I'm rounding the corner, Parker's truck is already sitting in the driveway.

I park hastily behind it, squealing as I rush out, nearly getting strangled by the seatbelt in the process. Running around the front, I find my blue-eyed best friend smiling at me. He holds his arms out and I jump into them.

He swings me around, squeezing me tight, and a chuckled sob breaks from my chest, causing him to squeeze me tighter.

"Ugh." I laugh lightly, pulling back to wipe at my stupid eyes.

"It's like, once the floodgates are opened, there's no stopping 'em." I smile through my slight discomfort.

Parker's chest inflates with a deep breath, and he nods, reaching up to run his knuckles over my cheek. His sky-blue eyes roam my features, too many emotions to name flashing across his face. "That's a good thing, Lolli Bear." He smiles. "I missed you."

I grin, going in for another hug. "I've missed you, too, Hero. So much."

"You look even tinier, if that's possible."

I shrug, pulling back. "Yeah, I've been runnin' a bit more than normal, I guess." When his brows pinch, I continue, "That's one of the reasons I got this place. There are always people running up and down the shoreline, no matter what time of day it is."

He nods.

I smile and shove his shoulder. "Stop it. I'm good, and now you're here, so I'll be better."

His eyes cut to the left then back quickly, a nervous air crowding him. "You will be better, Lolli." When my brows knit, he smiles, but it doesn't quite meet his eyes. He laughs, shaking his head. "Hey, what did you want to show me?"

A huge smile takes over my face. "Oh man, Parker, it's amazing." I walk past him into the house to set my keys down and he follows.

Walking backward, my eyes grow big. "The back patio is small, but a hundred yards each way is ours! It's the best view this side of the ocean. So open and free." I sigh, picturing it.

His steps are too slow to follow, so I walk to him, tuck my arm in his, and pull him along.

"It's so gorgeous," I push the sliding door open, not bothering to close it behind us. "Right off the porch, there's a small hillside that dips down into flat, white ocean sand, and get this -lavender! I think the previous owners must have planted it. I've been using it on my calves." We step off the first step and I lose some of my focus. "Um, there's this huge pergola covered in solar lights that turn on as soon as the sun starts to set over the ocean. I want to put some-" I stop short, halting our footsteps, and look around me.

Parker tenses slightly but nudges me forward.

My heart rate spikes.

When Parker winces, I look down to see my nails are digging in into his arm.

I stop.

I know this feeling. I recognize it in an instant.

The hairs on the back of my neck stand up, my pulse quickens, and I feel like I just got off a roller coaster. I force my breathing steady and mentally slap myself, commanding my feet to move forward.

Inhaling as much air as my deprived lungs will allow, I hold my breath, take the last step to the edge of the hillside, and my feet give way, my body dropping into the sand.

"Shit, Lolli!"

Right there, under my pergola, is a beautiful, aged white wood swing, held up by triangular posts on each side, two metal chains hanging from the small beam above it.

Nate's swing sways in slow, gentle motions, with the help of the soft ocean breeze.

I stand, holding a hand out to stop Parker when he tries to help.

Moisture fills my eyes for the thousandth time since I left, but this time for a very different reason.

I knew he'd come.

Both hope and fear swim through me.

I take hesitant steps closer, eventually making it to the novelty that feels like it holds all the answers.

Biting the inside of my cheek, I reach out and run my fingers over the wood, my throat burning.

"Lolli..."

The soft whisper from behind me has me squeezing my eyes shut, my fingers clutching at the seat.

Warm arms wrap around my stomach, and a soft kiss lands on my temple. "Don't be scared, Lolli Bear," he whispers, squeezing me gently.

My body shakes slightly.

Parker sighs, softly spinning me in his arms to look in my eyes.

He's right; I'm scared, but not quite for the reason he assumes.

"Do you trust me?" He tilts his head, his blue eyes clear and understanding.

I nod.

He smiles, pulling me in for a hug. "I love you, Lolli. Trust me, okay?"

"I do." The pressure on my chest builds.

"I'm going to take a shower and then take a nap."

I nod but grip his shirt tighter. He lets me hold on to him for a few more moments, then gently pries my fingers off the cotton material and steps back. He gives me a small nod, hesitates for a second, then walks back to the house. I watch him till he's gone, then turn back to the swing.

I wrap my fingers around the cold metal, closing my eyes as I lower myself into a sitting position.

Tears roll down my cheeks before I can stop them, and I don't bother to wipe them away.

For the first time in years, I feel like I'm home. Like right here, in this spot, is where I belong.

But now comes the part where I'm forced to face reality, face the scary parts of life head-on, completely unprepared and unaware of how things will go, or what will happen next. All the things I make it a point to avoid.

My problem is, I don't know where the line of deception and deceit meets loyalty and faithfulness, but I never pretended to know how a relationship worked. With Nate, I learned daily how to be with someone I cared about, but that doesn't mean I knew how to act in a moment of panic and tested trust. I didn't know that meant that staying and fighting, demanding to understand, was what I was supposed to do. I was so used to the fallout; I didn't know reconciliation was even an option. All I knew was bad shit happened and you dealt with it. My newfound emotions got the best of me, so I shut that shit down, made a bad move, and walked away without a fight, without showing him he was worth it. Worth more.

But once the fog cleared, it was so obvious. It didn't take long for me to put the pieces together. All the stolen glances, the deliberate touches and grins. The faux friendliness and playful banter.

Those fuckers set me up. Set us up.

Sure, we fell for it, but who wouldn't?

As soon as I stepped foot in the stadium, looked down from the owner's box at the empty grass, I knew I was caught in a twilight zone of fuckery. I knew none of the things running through my mind were true. There was no way.

Nate would never. The bitch obviously ambushed him in his room, made it seem like the unimaginable to me, and I fell for her illusion.

He may have not given me a chance that night, but I failed him in that moment, just as much as he failed me.

We got caught in the trap they set.

Clever fuckers, they were.

At that point, my only option was to figure out how to fix it. I thought about turning around and going back, but I couldn't. Not then. Not when it would have been a battle of doubt and betrayal.

First, I had to find out what had actually happened.

That took some serious digging, but after replaying some scenes in my head, I knew who to go to.

I never intended to ruin someone else's relationship just to save mine, but like I've always said, honesty is key. If you're a lying prick, then you should have to deal with the fallout from it.

Ashley cried when she figured it out. I hated to have to ask her, but I needed to know what they did to Nate. First, she got mad, called me a liar, and stuck up for her man, unlike me. Then she called me crying, apologizing for things she had no control over.

I needed her help. And she came through for me, ready to help me fix it.

I made her promise not to tell a soul. Even if he didn't come to her, she couldn't go to him. She didn't understand; not many people would, I guess. But I needed Nate to be the one to seek answers. I needed him to need me, as senseless as it may seem. Reluctantly, she agreed.

Deep down, I knew he'd make me proud.

The last few months, I've survived on the faith I put in a man who thinks I've fucked him over in the worst way. Hoping and praying to the football gods that he'd come to me, that he'd find himself so desperate for the truth, that he'd find it. Find me.

Will he hate me when he finds out I knew and didn't come to him? Will he understand why I waited for him to come to me? Will he even believe that I was waiting for him? Does he know how much my body aches for him to be near?

I can't begin to imagine what Nate's been thinking. What he's been feeling.

Am I as sick as Liv and Jarrod for knowing the truth and doing nothing about it?

The shuffle in the sand may as well be silent. I know he's standing in front of me. I felt him the moment he approached.

After a deep inhale, I force my lids open, my blue eyes crashing into a pair of dark, roasted espresso ones.

A broken cry escapes before I can stop it.

The face I've dreamed about for months is standing right in front of me, looking just as nervous and as unsure as I feel.

Nate takes a small step forward, but when I tense, he freezes, his face tightening around the edges.

In a wrinkled shirt and shorts, with dark circles lining his eyes, he wears a worn-out expression.

"You look like shit," I whisper.

He chuckles lightly, and like a California wave, the sound rolls through my body and I settle against the seat.

"I haven't been doing so hot," he admits, tucking his hands into his pockets, shifting his gaze over my shoulder.

"Oh."

His eyes lock on mine and I can't breathe.

"Kalani..." he whispers, and my eyes close. His voice is so low, so gentle and loving.

I feel him moving closer, the warmth of his large body approaching mine. I'm torn between running away or handcuffing myself to him.

His shaky hand closes over mine holding the chain. "Can you please open your eyes?" His breath fans across my face; he must be kneeling. "I need to see those blues, baby."

Baby.

I don't know if I'm supposed to correct him on that, but I don't. I love the way it sounds on his lips; love the way it feels against my skin. Raspy and warm. I think I'm supposed to have anger coursing through me, be mad at him, something, but all my heart is transmitting to my brain is relief.

My body makes the decision and leans forward. I don't wrap my arms around him, but I lay my head on his chest, needing to feel his heartbeat against my skin.

He, however, wraps his strong arms around me instantly, enveloping me, squeezing me tight. He takes a staggering breath, dropping his head into my neck as much as the position allows.

A deep gust of air leaves him and his body sags against mine.

"I'm so fucking sorry, Kalani. I..."

Pushing off his chest, I give myself some distance.

His head is tilted, with no energy to hold it up, and his brows are pinched, unsure and scared.

"I, uh, wasn't expecting this. Today." I look up to meet his sad eyes. "Like, at all."

"Neither was I, to be honest." When my brows knit, he continues, "I thought for sure Parker would tell me to take a hike." He laughs nervously, glancing back toward my house, then returning his somber eyes to me.

"But you're here."

He nods, his gaze roaming my face.

"I know Parker." His shoulders sag slightly and he drops his gaze to the concrete floor. "He'd never bring you here if it wasn't the right thing to do." He nods, as if trying to convince himself, his chin still against his chest.

"He'd never hurt you." His sad eyes lift to mine, but his head stays down. "Parker would never hurt you."

"I know." I nod.

I expect him to grimace, maybe look away, but he doesn't. He gazes at me, his soft eyes searching my face, and then, shocking the hell out of me, he smirks. And it's the all out, stop a married woman in her tracks, Nathaniel Monroe smirk.

What the...

NATE

I smirk, determination burning through me.

I fuckin' knew it.

I saw it on her face the moment I stepped in front of her, the nerves. She hadn't even opened her eyes yet and I could feel it. She was scared shitless.

There was pain coming from her, but not the kind a brokenhearted girl would radiate.

I drop onto the sand, watching her wide eyes fly across my face as I lift her by her hips, bringing her down to straddle me.

Her hands come out to rest on my chest, her blues narrowing.

I sprawl one hand across her tailbone, the other gliding torturously slow up her spine, and she shudders against me, her eyes growing heavier.

"Tell me something, Kalani..." I murmur against her skin. "What is it you're afraid of?"

"What did I tell you about playing games?" she whispers in a false bravado. "Ask me what you really wanna know."

Pulling back, I offer a soft smile, and I run my fingertips across her lips. "Baby, I don't have to ask. I already know." Her eyes roam my face and I dip my chin slightly. "I suspected it as soon as I allowed myself to hope. Once I stopped running from the pain, I realized what I knew meant what I thought wasn't possible."

"And what did you know?" she whispers.

I cup her cheeks and she gasps. "You love me. I knew it before you did, and felt it grow stronger every day. I knew you wanted my happiness as much as I wanted yours, and you'd never throw away what we had. I knew you craved me, like I you." When her lips start to tremble, I lean my forehead against hers. "Once I realized all that, I knew you'd have fought for me. There was no way you wouldn't figure out what really happened once you allowed yourself to think about it. And I knew you'd think about it because you can't shut me out. You've never been able to shut me out." I wipe away the tears that run down her cheeks. "Do you know why that is, Kalani?" I whisper and she shakes her head no.

"Because my heart beats in your chest, and yours in mine. We're blended in each other in deeper ways than even we understand." She's full-on sobbing now.

I pull back more, needing her to hear me. "I need you to know I understand. I get it. I also need you to know how sorry I am for not coming sooner." She tries to interrupt, but I don't let her.

"I never should have allowed my mind to get clouded. I should have marched straight to your room and demanded answers."

"I should have come to you when I found out. Should have fought for you."

My brows crinkle. "You did fight for me." When her brows pull in, I explain, "Baby, you made my being here right now possible. You put it all together and found the answers I was too afraid to look for. I know you reached out to Ashley long before I did, or she never would have had what I needed ready and waiting when I approached her the other night. You made this moment happen. You think Parker would have brought me to you had I not known the truth ahead of time?" I tease to help relieve some of the tension. It works, and she chuckles slightly, her body dropping further into mine.

"I'm glad you didn't come to me, Kalani. I needed to be the one to open my eyes and see. I failed you that night. Not the other way around." I squeeze her cheeks tighter. "I will never fail you again."

A sob breaks through and she wraps her arms around my neck, holding me as tight as her little body allows, and I wrap my arms around her.

We sit there, holding each other in the sand, for a long while, before she pulls back. "How long do we have before you have to leave?"

"I'm not leaving."

She scowls at me, as she jumps to her feet and starts pacing in the sand.

And now, I'm nervous.

When I stand, she stops, turning to pin me with a glare.

"Bullshit, you're not!"

"I don't understand." I frown.

"You're not staying here!"

What? "The fuck I'm not!"

She scoffs, crossing her arms over her chest. "I won't let you."

I'm about to lose my shit...

I rush her, stepping right in front of her so she has to tip her head all the way back to look at me. She's not intimidated.

"I'm not fucking leaving," I growl through gritted teeth, my heart hammering against my chest.

What the hell is she doing?

Her hands fly up in the air, coming down to slap against her bare thighs. "Well, you're not staying!"

"I-"

"No! You have to go to college, Nate!"

Oh. I get it now.

"You're going to do amazing things." She reaches up, placing her tiny hands on my face and I tilt my head, leaning into her touch. "I would love for you to stay but being here will ruin everything you've worked towards." Her voice drops to a whisper, nearly inaudible. "And I won't allow that. I'll be here, waiting for you, but you can't just stay."

"This is where I belong, baby. Right here, with you."

"No."

"Yes."

"Nate, please," she pleads.

"I signed with UCLA." My heart stops beating while I wait for her response.

She pulls her hands away from my face, slowly lowering them to her sides. "What?"

"In February."

"February." She frowns at my chest.

I nod.

"You didn't tell me."

"I didn't want you to try and talk me out of it. I had to wait until it was too late to back out before I said anything."

"February." She looks up at me.

"Uh-huh." I dare her to argue.

"Why California?"

435

"You really asking me that?"

She goes to speak, but nothing comes out. Her lips purse, her brows furrowing. I see it all over her face; she's doing her best to tell herself I'd never choose my path based on hers.

She's so fucking wrong.

"Yeah, baby." I lift my hand and her breath hitches. Then I do what I've been thinking about for months.

My calloused fingers graze her jaw, sliding up and over her ear, where I tuck her hair behind it. I let my hand sink further into her dark locks and bring my forehead down to hers.

"You're staying?" she asks quietly.

"You couldn't force me to leave if you tried."

A small chuckle escapes and Kalani shakes her head. She pulls back and turns to look at the swing. "Do you feel like I lied to you, about...me?"

I shuffle my feet. "I'd be lying if I said it didn't hurt to hear you kept those things from me. Then, to find out you told Parker; that was a whole other kind of feeling."

"I didn't tell you because I thought we were just fooling around. I didn't think it was going to become more. You were... you, Nate Monroe, the proud manwhore, and I was having fun. Then things shifted and I convinced myself it didn't matter. As far as telling Parker; I didn't tell him until way later, when I offered him a job. Not that that makes it any better, but still."

"I know, and I don't care anymore. None of that matters." I reach for her hand and she looks up at me.

Her gaze is tender. "We fumbled pretty good, didn't we?"

I laugh lightly. "Yeah, I guess we did."

I pull her to me and together we drop onto the swing. I help sway us, since her feet still don't touch the ground, and we watch the waves grow stronger as the sun begins to disappear.

"Why did you bring the swing here?" she asks, not lifting her head from my shoulder.

"For you, so when I'm in class or on the field, you can sit here and feel close to me."

Her body tenses slightly, so I glide my palm up and down her thighs. "Don't. This is it. Us. You and me?" I nod. "We're gonna make it."

She pulls back to look at me. We shift our bodies so we're facing each other.

"I'm going to be busy, Kalani. Real busy, but so are you. There will be times when we don't see each other as much as we want but hear me when I say I will be here, with you, every chance I have. And when I'm not, when I can't be...you have our swing."

"Our swing?" Her eyes glaze over.

I cup her cheek, gently tilting her head, forcing her to look directly into my eyes. "Never gonna be alone, remember?"

She nods, her eyes locked on mine.

"So, what do you say?" I whisper, my fingers brushing her neck, creating goosebumps all across her flesh.

"You do know the Tomahawks work closely with their local athletes, right? And that Embers Elite Exposures covers all home games for the University?"

A slow grin spreads across my face and she smiles back.

She shifts, leaning in, and my breathing grows labored when her lips are but a breath away from mine. "Chances are, I'll be there all the time."

My hand slowly sinks into her hair, the other coming to rest on her hip. When her eyes close, I don't wait patiently, but crush my lips into her full, soft ones, and we each let out a sigh-filled groan on contact.

As I scoot back, she slides one leg over, straddling me.

My hands slide down her back, cupping her ass with a gentle squeeze.

It's too damn easy to get lost in her so I pull back quickly.

My arms wrap around her, pulling her close, holding her tight against my chest.

MEAGAN BRANDY

"I'm not going anywhere. Ever. I'm gonna stay with you, love you, forever."

She smiles and slides her hands up my neck. "I know." She tilts her head and raises a brow. "Ready to show me what forever feels like?"

I nod.

She nods.

We're on the same page.

Two Months Later

NATE

"I like her." Mason jerks his head toward Kalani, who is whippin' his buddy Brady's ass at sports trivia.

I chuckle, taking a drink from my cup. "That's 'cause she's perfect."

"Ah, fuck man, don't rub that lovey shit off on me." He makes it a point to shudder and I laugh.

As soon as I took the time to process where Kalani's new house was, I realized it was on the same beach where my aunt and uncle, and their friends, owned property. Turns out, they just gave one of their vacation homes to their kids to share, so they're here spending their last free weeks of summer.

"Hey, think she can get us season tickets?"

"Really, Mase?" his friend, Chase, laughs, walking off to grab another drink from the ice chest. "She's already letting your sorry ass stay at her condo in Hawaii in a few weeks."

"Hey, I didn't ask to parade around on an island in a monkey suit while your sister says I do to a jackass."

I punch him in the shoulder.

"I'm fucking with you, man." He laughs, shoving me. "Kenra's dude is a jackass, though."

"Trust me, dickhead, I know. But, in case you want to know, Kalani already gave us passes."

"What?" His eyes shoot as wide as saucers.

"And she's arranged it so we can check out Aloha Stadium while we're there."

"Shit, maybe I should marry her."

When I glare at him, he winks, and takes a drink from his cup. He looks to his side in time to see Brady step away from Kalani and rush up to his twin, Ari, and her best friend Cam, tossing both girls over his massive shoulders.

Mason groans.

"Put her down, asshole!" he tells him, his tone flat, and Brady turns to him.

"Which one, Johnson?" He teases, a shit-eating grin on his face.

"Both of 'em, dickhead."

I can't help but laugh.

Mason has a thing for Cam but won't admit it. He's a fool like that.

We watch as Brady walks the girls over to the others, introducing them both to Kalani and Parker.

"What's the dude's story?" He nods toward Parker.

"What is it you're really wanting to know?" I ask without looking away from my girl, winking at her when she catches my eyes on her. She lifts her Polaroid camera and snaps a quick picture of me, sticking her tongue out before turning back to her conversation.

"Am I gonna need to tell him to stay away from my sister and Cameron?"

I sigh. "Nah, man. He's not interested in anything right now. He's up to his neck in school shit; summer and early courses even. Focused as a motherfucker."

"And you don't think a chick could break through that shit in an instant?"

"Nope. Not right now anyway."

He lets out a low whistle. "Damn, man. I gotta say, I don't know how you can handle your girl having an alright lookin' fucker as a housemate."

I get it, what he's saying. Parker isn't ugly and Kalani is fine as fuck. Their living together isn't ideal and, admittedly, it makes me crazy sometimes to know that he'll get to come home to her most nights when I can't, but it's not like that.

I've thought a lot about their relationship over the last few months, and sometimes, yeah, the insecurities come out, but I've decided Parker's got some shit going on he doesn't talk about. Something inside him needed the friendship she gave him. That 'no pressure, no questions' friendship, full of trust and honesty; loyalty that only she can give someone. And I get that. Respect it even.

I smile at my girl and our friend. "I trust him. And it's good she'll have someone there with her when I can't be."

"Way to look for the positives." He chuckles and I roll my eyes. "But good to know." Downing the contents of his cup, he walks up to the girls and smacks Cam on her ass.

She spins and smiles at him, before jumping on his back. "Let's go for a swim, big boy."

He charges for the ocean, Brady and Parker following behind.

I laugh, watching as Mason disappears under the water.

Soft, small hands wrap around my middle. I lift my arm and drag Kalani in front of me, spinning her to face the ocean.

She giggles when I dip my head into her neck.

"I like your family and their friends. Brady's my favorite."

"That so?" I growl into her skin.

"Mmm." She pushes her ass into me. "And I thought your shoulders were big..."

441

I bite her neck and she laughs. "You better quit it, baby, or you'll pay for it later."

"Is that supposed to be a threat, Handsome?" I can hear her smile, prompting my own.

"It's whatever you want it to be." I kiss her shoulder, then rest my chin on top of her head. "Heard from Mia yet?"

"Not yet." She shakes her head against me. "She has to work through her own shit first. She's in her own head and no one can change that but her. Shouldn't be too much longer."

"And Parker? Is he good?"

"Parker... needs someone to need him. So, 'good'? I don't think so, but I do think he's happier now, here, with us." She sighs. "But she'll come."

My brows pull in. "Who?"

She shrugs against me. "The one who needs a hero." Her words are so simple, so sure. She wants her friend to find what he's looking for; what she feels he needs. "Whoever that is... she'll come. And he'll be ready for her when she does."

I squeeze her tighter.

"Tell me their story?" She inclines her head toward Ari and Chase, sitting far too close to each other on a beach towel.

I glance toward the water, making sure Mason isn't about to charge.

"Arianna's had a thing for Chase since they were kids, but Mason won't allow it, if Chase is even interested. My dad seems to think he is, but Mason's his best friend. I'm not sure Chase is willing to risk that."

"Lose the friendship or lose the girl."

"Shitty, but yeah. I guess that's how his mind works."

"I wouldn't be so sure..."

I look back to the two, and my eyes narrow, watching as they lean in toward each other. "Mason will kill him."

"Doesn't look like either of them care right about now." She

442

laughs. "These next few weeks are going to be interesting for these guys. All five of them in one house, no parental supervision."

"Shit's gonna be a nightmare."

When she laughs, I reach down to thread my fingers through hers, lift her left hand to my mouth, and kiss the small diamond that rests there. She sighs and melts against me.

"Parker's leaving tonight." I whisper, kissing each knuckle. "I get you all to myself for three whole weeks."

Tilting her head up, she looks into my eyes, then she squeezes my hand.

Because she's here; she's got me.

And she does, all of me. Everything I am, everything I have or will have, is already hers.

This girl. This blue-eyed, black-haired girl, who had no one and wanted nothing, chose me. She let me in, let me love her.

And she loves me back just as hard.

She's my everything and I'm her only.

I squeeze her tighter, pulling her closer.

"I love you, baby."

She smiles, a big beautiful one she's only ever given me, and my heart stops. "I love you, Handsome."

She's so beautiful.

So perfect.

So... mine.

Quick note from the author:

(*Keep reading for a free first chapter*)
THANK YOU SO MUCH FOR READING FUMBLED
HEARTS!!!

Nate and Kalani's story is very close to my heart. I hope you felt
their journey just as I did!! Girl made him work for it, didn't
she? Lol.

-

Are you dying for Parker's story??? What About Arianna's??Both
are live!!
Find Parker's book here -> meaganbrandy.com/dh

Read the first chapter of Ari's book, Say You Swear, below!

SAY *you* SWEAR

USA TODAY BESTSELLING AUTHOR
MEAGAN BRANDY

Arianna

The drive to Oceanside is usually a peaceful one, but my brother, Mason, and his two best friends, Chase and Brady, came to an unspoken agreement last night that "one more" meant one more twelve-pack. So out they stayed, saying drunken goodbyes to our classmates at the very last summer party to be had in our hometown.

My girl Cameron and I knew better than to party hard the night before a drive, so we headed home early to finish packing for our final trip to the beach before college life begins.

A trip that *should have* taken no more than three and a half hours, yet we've already been in this damn SUV for five. We learned years ago that long drives with pouty, hungover man-boys are not fun, but here we are again, willing yet slightly annoyed participants in the 'how many times does one man have to stop to piss' experiment.

The answer is seven. We stopped seven times already, thanks to Brady's baby bladder.

At least they seem to have sobered up in the last fifteen minutes, finally allowing us to turn the music up loud enough to where we can actually hear it.

Honestly, I shouldn't complain.

Group car rides are pretty much the only time I get to feign innocence when I lean a little farther into the star player of my fantasies, more commonly known as my brother's best friend.

'Play but don't push' is the game I'm forced to settle for and I'm good at it. Probably because I've had the better part of six years to perfect it.

See, the day Chase and his family moved in across the street, I saw *him* first. It was as if an invisible stamp came down and pressed across his forehead, a big fat red label that screamed *mine*.

Sure, I was only in junior high, but I'd seen *The Boy Next Door*. I understood the power of obsession, and mine started the minute I laid eyes on him. Granted, mine wasn't the murderous sort and watching that movie gave me hardcore, unachievable body goals, but all that's beside the point.

Chase Harper had arrived in the neighborhood, and I was determined to be the one to show him around it, so I pressed the brakes on my bike at the edge of his lawn, gaining his attention.

The minute his brace face smiled at me from across the yard, my twin appeared out of nowhere, something he's inconveniently good at.

Mason rushed him, tackled him to the ground, and when he stood, he fed Chase a line I sometimes wish he'd choke on.

He growled, "*Stay away from my 'little sister!*'"

In horror, I watched as Chase hopped to his feet, literally, like some sort of spider monkey shit. I held my breath, readying for the fight I suspected to follow—yeah, my brother was known to knock a kid out when it came to me—but then Chase laughed, and we all fell silent.

The brown-haired, green-eyed boy turned to my brother with grass in his mouth, a grin curving it, and asked Mase what football team he played for. He was looking for one to join.

I huffed and rode off because I knew with that single question asked, Mason and Brady had a new best friend, and I was, once again, colored in red, an invisible circle-backslash symbol painted across me.

In the span of five minutes, my brother's duo grew into a trio, and our house became their hangout spot of choice. I never understood the whole forbidden fruit thing until then, how not having something only made you want it more.

It's a bunch of bull, if you ask me.

Unfortunately for me, no one did, so I sat back, forced to watch as the jocks of junior high became the hotties of high school.

Every girl wanted a bite, but who could blame them?

They were model students, star athletes, and undercover bad boys. No matter a girl's type, one of the three was sure to fit the bill.

I like to joke that they're every shade of Dwayne Johnson since he seems to be different yet extremely fit regardless of the role. Brady would definitely be the WWE version.

No, but really, all three were gifted with good genes. Mason, my overprotective twin, is tall and trim and could literally stunt double for a slightly younger Theo James. Brady's a bulked-out Ken doll, and Chase is, well, the epitome of perfection.

Unfortunately for me, *every* girl agrees.

He has the same height and build as Mase, but his brown hair is a few shades lighter. His eyes, vivid and upbeat, are a mix of grass and seaweed. He's kind, strong, and confident. Almost as bossy as Mason and Brady, but out of the three, he's the only one who cuts us girls some slack from time to time.

I've convinced myself it's his way of differentiating himself from protective older brother to a man with eyes and hidden desires, but I'm known to be a wishful thinker.

Nine out of ten times, I'm thinking about the man beside me.

It's the oldest cliché in the books to want who you can't have. Unrequited love for your brother's best friend, a brother who is insanely protective and, yeah, admittedly slightly psychotic when it comes to those he cares about. He can't help it though. As soon as we were old enough to learn how my dad lost his baby sister, Mason made it his mission to shadow my every step. Combine that with the death of our friend Payton's boyfriend a couple weeks ago, and he's a pile of paranoia.

The fact that Chase was passed out for most of the drive today likely saved me from a solid dozen glares through the rearview mirror. Pretty sure that's why Mase insists I sit in the middle every time we ride together, so he can keep eyes on me at all times.

It's sweet how my twin takes his 'big brother' role so seriously.

It's also really annoying.

Had we stayed on track this morning, we would have rolled into town around eleven, but here we are, turning into the long driveway of the beach house at a quarter to one.

Mason barely has time to put his Tahoe in park before Cameron is throwing her door open and hopping out. She runs halfway up the steps and spins on her bare feet, throwing her arms out with a smile. "Come on, you guys! Time's already ticking!"

"We have the rest of the month!" Mason shouts out his open window.

"And we're already down half a day!" Cam fires back.

I smile, patting my brother's shoulder. "Come on, Mase, we're a half day down," I tease, and my brother grumbles as I slip out the door, following Cameron along the wraparound deck.

She beams, hopping up to sit on the edge of the banister, so I join her, and Brady's stepping up in the next second.

"This is fuckin' insane!" Cam shakes her head, eyeing the area.

"Fuck yeah, it is." Brady faces the ocean with a grin.

Heavy footsteps behind us let us know the other two have walked up, and together, we spin.

The five of us stand there a moment, silently breathing in the fresh seaside air as we stare into the floor-to-ceiling window of the beach house.

Of *our* beach house, as of a month ago.

Mine, Cameron, and Brady's mom have been best friends since college, and before they even married our dads, they bought a beach house together. As the years went by, marriage and us kids

449

QUICK NOTE FROM THE AUTHOR:

followed. They kept that place as a spot to always come. Then, when we were young, I guess there was a crash in the housing market, and all our parents were lucky enough to snag vacation homes along the beach, and ever since then, this is where our families spent every school holiday. We never understood why, but they never did sell the original home they purchased, and that's the house we're about to enter, but it looks nothing like the place we saw as kids.

They had it gutted, parts torn down, and not only rebuilt but also added onto. It's completely renovated.

Coastal blue in color, the place is huge. It has a massive wraparound patio, leading to a massive back deck, the one we're currently standing on, and a private pathway leading to a beautiful dock surrounded by California poppies. There's even a full sound system with speakers embedded into the corners of the walls, patio, and wood paneling every few dozen feet—there isn't a single spot in or around the place the music can't reach. Being on the opposite side of the condo strip, it's more secluded, so the sound doesn't bother others who are trying to have a more relaxing vacation.

It's the perfect escape, a palace on the water.

And it was just given to us.

To *all* five of us.

Our parents surprised us at our graduation party, handing us a deed to the place, all our names listed as equal owners. They said they decided to do this for us years ago as a way to try and keep our crew close, no matter where life may take us after college, as the place did for them afterward.

Splitting it equally among us meant no one can decide to sell without the others, and should life take us away at some time, we'd always have this place to come back to at any point.

To say we were excited is an understatement, but for me, it also brought a hint of dread. It was sort of a depressing conversation, to be honest. I'm not so naive to assume that our lives would stay the same, that it would be us five for always, but it is kind of terrifying to consider the alternative.

New people will come into our lives. I know this.

Some might be for the better, others for the worse.

But what happens if one of our worlds is flipped upside down? What if we drown from the capsize?

If we lose each other along the way, who will be there to pull us from the water?

Maybe that's a little dramatic, but it's a real possibility. A shitty one.

Less than a month from today, the future begins.

My brother and the boys will head to Avix University for the official start of their college football careers, and Cam and I will drive home to pack, getting ready to meet them on campus a few days before orientation.

Leaving home is as real as it gets.

It'll be the first time my brother won't be a door away. While it's slightly terrifying, it's also a beautiful thing how the football house is on the complete opposite side of Cam's and my dorm. Meaning, Mason won't be able to "check in" on us as often. That alone is going to be worth celebrating on move-in day.

I love my brother but damn. Sometimes he needs to back off. He's lucky I didn't pick a college across the country.

He also knows there is no way I would have.

I don't do well without family being nearby. Some might call that being codependent.

I simply call it a twin thing.

"So, we're still good with how we picked rooms a couple weeks ago, right?" Mason breaks the silence. "Girls upstairs with the joining bathroom, leave the spare room, a spare, and us downstairs?"

"Mom decorated our rooms when she came to check on Payton and stocked the fridge last week, so—"

"No take-backs!" Cam cuts me off with a smile.

The boys laugh, and then Mason takes a deep breath, pulling the key from his pocket.

"No take-backs." He grins. "We ready for a do-over? No parents, no rules."

"No one left under eighteen this time around." Brady playfully shoves Mason and me since Brady, Mason, and I became legal three days ago.

I look to Chase, who happens to glance my way at the same exact time. He smiles, and I match his with one of my own.

"Oh shit," my best friend teases. "Things are about to get real up in here!"

I wish I knew how true Cameron's statement would become then, but I didn't have the slightest clue.

Ch - 2

Arianna

"Fridge is open, alcohol's in hand, so get your asses in here and let's get this party started!" Cameron repetitively knocks a bottle against the countertop and doesn't stop until we're rounding the corner into the kitchen to join her.

"Easy on the granite, Cami baby. Take it out on me instead," Brady teases, leaning on his forearms.

"Next time, Brady, next time." She grins.

As she starts pouring the shots into the glasses Chase helped her pull down, I let my eyes roam.

The kitchen is everything you'd expect in a beach home, light in color and wide open. The dining table is a large U-shape bench-style seat with white and light-blue pillows in the corners. It sits in front of the large bay window, allowing you to peer out over the beach and watch the sun set or rise without stepping foot outside. There's a large marble island in the center, the

"Give me that," Nate demands.

"Uh," I cut my glance to the side and back quickly, "no."

"Kalani," he growls. "Give me the bottle before I take the damn thing."

I tuck it into my chest, but Nate's quick, pulling it from my hands in seconds.

"I'll never let go, Jack..." I slur, laughing as he yanks the whiskey from my grip, the force sending me stumbling right back into Parker's arms.

"Come on," Nate grumbles, reaching for me. "I'll take you to your room to sleep this shit off."

A harsh laugh leaves me and I rip my arm from his, fire searing through my veins and threatening to set me aflame. "Get. The fuck. Away from me, you rat bastard." I shove him sloppily, as fruitless as it may be. "You have zero claim to me and zero right to worry about what I'm doing."

"Don't stand there and act like this is me!" he screams, his face inches from mine, his breathing out of control.

My foggy eyes roam his face, looking for nothing in particular, but finding the tick of his jaw, the vein at his temple protruding. His eyelids are even shaking.

He's pissed.

My hand twitches to reach out and comfort him, to wipe the frown away, but again, Liv's ass flashes in my head, along with the thoughts of what they probably did once I left, or before I got there.

The saddest part...that's not even what's killing me inside, him being with her.

Nate didn't trust in me. He didn't believe in me, at least not enough to stop and consider that maybe whatever the bitch threw at him was false. He could have – more than likely, did - fucked her repeatedly tonight, and it still wouldn't compare to the third-rate feeling slicing through me right now.

That makes two of us.

I go to step off the stool, but stumble, falling halfway to the floor before he catches me.

I laugh and lean into him, closing my eyes in attempt to block out the lyrics.

Just like in the song, I should have kept my mouth shut. I never should have opened up and allowed Nate to embed himself inside me, to wake me up and bring out all this cheesy, Lifetime movie shit. I should have stayed locked up tight, emotionless and empty. Life is so much easier that way.

"Lolli?" Parker whispers, his knuckle gently bringing my gaze to his when he feels my body start to quake. "You alright?"

I pull myself out of his arms, twisting to grab the bottle from the sticky countertop. Bringing it to my lips, I take another swig, watching Parker's brows drop in concern.

I push off the bar and take a few steps toward the dance floor but stumble again.

This time, four hands reach out to steady me, one set heating my skin despite the situation. I shove away from Nate and settle into Parker's tense arms.

Nate's head jerks back, shock flashing across his features before he erases it and scowls at Parker. "How much you let her drink?"

"None of your damn business!" I shout drunkenly, spitting on that stupid dress shirt that looks so good on him. "Don't fucking concern your piece-of-shit self with me, Nate."

His eyes fly to mine, and I think I see remorse in them, maybe a little confusion and hurt, but definitely a dash of uncertainty. Too bad my brain shuts that shit down real quick, and flashes a picture of Liv's perfect ass, naked on Nate's bed, in front of my eyes instead.

His gaze cuts to Parker. "She's trashed."

"You're the cause," he throws back, through clenched teeth.

"And I'm right here," I slur, bringing the bottle to my lips again.

stovetop, and double ovens circling behind it, which is where Cam's now perched, five shot glasses filled to the brim at her side.

She waits for us to claim a shot, seizing the last as her own. "Let's toast to all the stupid shit we are going to do while we're here and to the blast that we are going to have while doing it."

We laugh, and her blue eyes narrow with playfulness. "I'm serious, assholes. This little vacay is now officially going to be our last memory before our new lives begin. This is huge!"

"She's right." Chase steps beside Cam with a grin. "Let's make the most of it."

"When do we not go balls out and have a kick-ass time?" Brady reaches over, squeezing her knee. "We're about to run this beach, girl."

Cameron grips his cheeks, pinching his lips like a fish. "That's the spirit, big boy." She pecks his lips, downing her shot in the next.

The rest of us follow suit, knocking our shots back.

My eyes pinch from the burn of the liquor, and I laugh when Cameron shakes her head, her tongue sticking out.

"Okay, that shit's nasty." She laughs, happily passing the bottle off to Brady when he reaches for it.

"I'll meet you bastards at the beach. Mase, call your cousin, tell him to get his ass down here, and one of you pansies bring the football!" With that, Brady disappears out the back sliding door.

Cam turns to me, mischief written all over her. "Come on, girl, let's get changed. There's a gang of beach boys out there calling our names."

I wiggle my eyebrows up and down. "Maybe those Brazilians will pay off after all."

"Oh, fuck me, I'm out," Mason grumbles, rushing toward the patio door. He stops as he steps through, turning back to pin Chase with an expectant glare. "You comin'?"

At first, Chase doesn't move, but then he shakes his head, and

Cameron covers her laugh with a cough, knowing we've painted a mental picture in his head.

"Yeah." He clears his throat and snags the football from the bucket by the door. "Right behind you."

As soon as the door is closed, Cam and I bend over, laughing.

"That was gold." She high-fives me, and we quickly rush up the stairs, dragging our suitcases away from the wall where the boys placed them before disappearing into our rooms.

"I call hot pink today!" Cam shouts.

"I figured so! I think I'm going with my black one!" I flip open my suitcase, planning to unpack later and pull out my bathing suits.

I'm just getting the bows looped on the bottoms when she barges through our joining bathroom.

"Tie this for me." She gives me her back. "Also, I'm vetoing the black suit in favor of the red one."

I roll my eyes and fix her top as she looks over her body in the full-length mirror mounted to the wall in front of us.

"Thank you, Victoria, for your super summer sale," she mutters.

"She must be doing something wrong because I don't see any secrets in this thing," I tease, and she blows me a kiss.

My best friend has an amazing body, toned and tight in all the right places and nearly opposite of me in every way.

Cam is an easy five-ten where I'm pushing five-five. She's tall, fit, and model-like with crazy, crystal-blue eyes. While there's no denying it, she hates to be called thin.

Growing up, people would tease her for being *too tall* and *too skinny*. I mean, they'd then get beaten up by Mason or Brady, but still. It was bad for a while. The boys always tried to make her height seem insignificant, even when, for a minute there, she was taller than they were, but they couldn't take away the hurt the words of others caused her.

She's tried everything from all-carb diets to pharmaceutical drugs, even adding Ensure to her meals every single day for months and nothing. Her metabolism simply doesn't work that way. Now that we've gotten older, she's learned to own it, has filled out more in other areas, and is constantly going with the boys to the gym to keep the bit of muscle she's added to give her more weight. Regardless, she's always had a confident attitude, the 'never let them see you sweat' type.

Cameron throws her long blonde hair into a high ponytail and turns to me.

"Now." She tosses me my new red suit. "I'm dying to see how those babies look in this." She gestures to my chest.

"Seriously?"

"Oh, yeah, go hard or go home."

"Mason might just drag my ass home if I start with this." I scoff, picking it up, and look over the deep cut of the front. "This thing is like 'fifth date, trying to get lucky' worthy."

"You're talking like you didn't already undo your top to swap it."

"Touché." I strip out of the black suit, slipping into the tiny red one.

Cam sprawls out on my bed, quickly checking her notifications, but then faces me when I spin, giving her my best Marilyn Monroe pose.

"Whatcha think?"

"I think you better thank the big man upstairs on the daily for those Dolly Ds he blessed you with." She looks me up and down. "These new-gen *Baywatch* babes got nothing on you."

"Why, thank you, friend. Now let's go."

I head toward the door.

"Wait," she rushes, crawling to the edge of the bed. "Let's talk for a sec."

It's clear she's nervous about something, so I drop onto the mattress next to her, waiting for her to speak.

"Our last trip ended in a sad shitstorm with your cousin and

Deaton's car wreck. That was heavy, but this is our chance to end the summer on a good note."

"That's why we went home with our parents for a couple weeks, to press the reset button."

"No, I know, it's just now we're closer to the start of school, and once we get to Avix, our schedules are going to be all over the place. For the first time, we won't have a ton of free time together," she begins, a bit overly serious for her.

"Cam, we're roommates." I laugh. "We'll see each other plenty, and we'll always have the weekends."

"Yeah, but," she huffs. "I guess I just want to live it up, you know? This is the last time we'll have virtually no responsibility outside of not getting shit-faced and murdered."

I laugh, but she doesn't even pause.

"So, I vote we do like we did on our secret little trip and have some fun flipping invisible middle fingers at the boys along the way."

"We're gonna sunbathe topless, the boys be damned?"

An amused groan leaves her, and she sits up, shaking my shoulders. "I didn't say try to get them to murder us," she teases with a grin. "But yeah, same vibe."

The two of us laugh.

"So real eighteen-year-old fun, swim, layout, barbecue, drink, dance, flirt..." I lift a brow.

"Make out with a couple of beach boys we'll never see again," she adds with a shimmy and ends in a shrug. "The boys are going to, so if we want to do the same, we should. And the best part is no one here will be afraid of 'big brother and his boys.'" She grins.

Chuckling, I pull myself up, walking backward toward the door. "No overanalyzing, no second-guessing, just go with the flow kind of fun that we may or may not have to sneak around the boys."

"But if we can't..."

"Invisible middle fingers, and we do it anyway."

"That's *exactly* what I'm talking about. Screw these boys and their obsessive need to know! Let's have as much fun as possible and whatever happens, happens."

"Whatever happens, happens," I agree.

Cam squeals, hops up and tosses her watch onto my bed. "Now, let's go make some poor fools drool. We didn't spend the last four months in Booty Boot Camp for nothing."

She pushes her forehead into mine, and we smile at each other.

"It's game on, bitches."

***

We search the beach as we step off of the back deck, spotting the boys about thirty feet down the sand line, so we make our way toward them.

"Looks like Brady's already found the hottest girl on the beach to keep him occupied," Cam jokes, nodding her chin in his direction.

I squint, skimming over the small group, stopping on the gorgeous, tan-skinned, dark-haired girl perched on a rock, and a smile takes over my face.

Kalani Embers is her name, and she's definitely the most beautiful girl around, but she's not free for the taking. She's my cousin Nate's soon-to-be wifey, who we had a chance to meet and hang with when we came down to set up the house at the start of summer. She's also the only girl to ever beat Brady at sports trivia. He literally bought every game in the book to 'study' the answers, so the next time he saw her, he could take back his know-it-all title, but Kalani, or Lolli as we call her, was born into the game, her entire family having been a part of the NFL world, and stats are her jam. Poor guy doesn't stand a chance.

She's not only the youngest but the first female franchise owner in NFL history.

"Aw shit, here comes trouble!" Brady whistles, gaining the others' attention.

Mason groans, shaking his head, shouting across the sand. "You guys tryin' to see me knock a fucker out?"

"What's the matter, Mase, afraid someone might take the bait?" Brady throws back with a grin.

It's no secret Cameron has a thing for Mason, but none of us really knows how he feels about her. He does things like running off guys who try and talk to her and will hold her when she cries, but it's hard because that's who Mason is. Protective by nature. He looks out for her as he does me, is there for her when she might need him, as are the other boys. As I am. It's what we do. We're family, the five of us, and where we come from, that little fact trumps all else. It's also what makes it so tricky to understand. It's like I said, Mase treats her as he does me, so there's a chance there's nothing romantic about it. He doesn't know how to care a little; it's always with all of who he is.

It's a blessing and a curse sometimes because he stresses and overanalyzes more than necessary, but he can't help himself.

My brother is the toughest person I know. He's everything a father would hope for in a son and more than I could ask for in a brother. He's the most important person in my life, and if there's one person in this world I want to make proud, it's him. My twin is the other half of who I am, but that doesn't mean I understand his every move, even if I wish I did.

Either way, Cameron refuses to think on it to keep herself from getting her hopes up. She's not lovesick, by any means, and she doesn't sit around and hope like I might be pathetically known to do, but as it stands, she'd take his hand if he offered it in a heartbeat.

What makes it a bit more difficult is the fact that Mason is the biggest flirt known to man, possibly neck to neck with Brady, but he means no harm and would never intentionally lead her on, so I guess only time will tell.

I look to Mason as he flips Brady off, but Brady only laughs.

Lolli smiles, pushing off the rock she was sunbathing on. "Well, well, looking fresh as always."

I grin, reminding myself not to go in for a hug. Lolli isn't the touchy type. "Had to try and keep up with you."

"Girl, please. You should have seen the suit she tried to wear today. I had to sex her up myself."

"So Chase has you to thank, huh?" Lolli smirks.

I squash my lips to the side, and she laughs.

Lolli guessed my feelings for Chase the day we met, and she loves to pop off with off-color jokes to make the boys uncomfortable while still attempting to be stealthy, but only for my sake. She'd outright tell him to strip me in the sand if it were up to her. She's down like that.

"Have you heard from Kenra yet?" I ask about my cousin, Nate's older sister, as the events of a few weeks ago flash through my mind.

Kenra just got out of an abusive relationship, one that took a turn for the worse when her now ex-fiancé crashed with her and his younger brother in the car. He and Kenra made it out okay, but his younger brother, the father of Payton's unborn baby, wasn't so lucky. He was only seventeen.

Talk about a cruel mess.

"How's Payton doing?"

Lolli lifts a shoulder, glancing behind her, where I spot Payton walking down the beach. "I try not to ask. I'm better at entertainment, so I keep her busy when I can."

"I bet that helps more than you know." Cam smiles at her.

Lolli looks off, uncomfortable with the deep stuff, so I change the subject.

"So, what's the plan for today, or do we have one?" I ask, looking around at everyone.

Brady shrugs, tossing the football in the air. "I figure we'd start it off right, go out to eat, dance, get fucked up, then bum it and bonfire tomorrow?"

Cam and I nod. "Sounds good to us. Lolli, you guys in?"

"My man reports for practice in two days, so that would be a no." She smirks. "We'll be locked in our room all night, but we'll see you guys tomorrow, I'm sure."

"On that note..." Nate steps up, hugs us hello, and waves goodbye in the next second, quickly carting his fiancée toward their house.

"Well, okay then." Cameron laughs. "A night of dirty dancing it is, but first!" She takes off, charging right into the open waters, Brady on her heels.

"Hold up, I'm snaggin' Pretty Little." He jerks his head in the direction of Payton. "She could use a little distraction." With that, Mason jogs a few feet down the beach toward the young blonde sitting alone on a rock, searching for answers she won't find in the California waves.

Slowly, Chase and I make our way closer to the water's edge.

He bumps his shoulder into mine. "You happy to be back at the beach?"

"Always, you know that." I grin his way, but a heavy breath leaves me as I face forward. "Let's hope this time is less traumatic."

"Yeah." He nods. "I can't imagine what she's going through."

We glance Payton's way in time to witness her eyes widen, having spotted Mason coming at her at the last second. He bends, swooping her up with no effort, and she squeals into the air, making us laugh.

I smile after my brother, a calm only the ocean seems to bring me settling over my shoulders. "I think this trip will be different."

He glances over. "Yeah?"

"Yeah." I nod. "When we came at the end of June, it still felt like we were fresh out of school, you know? Like we had the whole summer ahead of us, but we don't anymore. Summer is almost over, and we're moving out on our own the minute we leave here. It's just... different. Like we're grown, and this is life now." I scrunch my nose and turn to look at him. "Don't you think?"

That one-sided smile of his I love appears. "Yeah. I guess it is different." He's quiet for a second before he adds, "Maybe a lot of things will be different now."

It's as if he's speaking more to himself than me, so I don't respond.

A moment later, he stops walking and faces me. He frowns at my swimsuit, and I can't help but laugh.

"Is there a problem?"

"Yeah." He nods, his eyes lifting to mine. His frown doubles, but not even a second later, a grin pulls at his lips, one I recognize.

"Chase," I warn, but before I can make a break for it, he's already tossed me over his shoulder and is running for the ocean.

The others laugh as I'm tossed on my ass and swim over to join us.

I wish I could freeze this moment, our entire crew enjoying the last bit of the summer sun because who knows what the summer's moon will bring.

I look to Chase, who smirks at me from across the water.

I, for one, can't wait to find out.

READ MORE RODAY—> Click Here For Say You Swear

–

Want to be the FIRST to know when I have a new release or news at all?

Sign up for an alert here: Meagan Brandy's Newsletter

461

Ways to Connect

Purchase EXCLUSIVE merchandise here:
https://www.teepublic.com/user/meaganbrandy
Private Facebook Group: Meagan Brandys Reader's group
Facebook Page: Meagan Brandy
Instagram: @meaganbrandyauthor
Amazon Meagan Brandy
Goodreads: Meagan Brandy
BookBub: Meagan Brandy
TikTok: @meaganbrandyauthor

My newsletter is the BEST way to stay in contact!
You'll get release dates, titles, sales, and MORE first!
Sign up here: www.meaganbrandy.com

Playlist

Wrong Way - Sublime
   Numb - Linkin Park
   My Immortal - Evanescence
   The Reason - Hoobastank
   Breaking The Habit - Linkin Park
   Just A Kiss – Lady Antebellum
   Ride - Somo
   Close - Nick Jonas
   Acquainted - The Weeknd
   Bring Me To Life - Evanescence
   Somewhere I Belong - Linkin Park
   Never Gonna be Alone – Nickelback
   Stay - Rihanna
   I'm yours - Justine Skye
   Just A Fool - Christina Aguilera
   How Can I Help you Say Goodbye - Patty Loveless
   Blurry - Puddle of Mudd
   Far Away – Nickelback

Acknowledgments

Hot damn! Where do I even begin? First, let me tell you how this story came to be...

About two years ago I started writing. I would write and delete and rewrite. The story was so clear in my head, but putting pen to paper was proving to be difficult. It wasn't giving me everything I knew it could, so I shelved it and decided to write something different. No plot, no end game, just write. And Fumbled Hearts was born.

I had no idea when I started this book that I would fall for these characters the way I did. As the words went on, I could feel the passion burning for this world Nate and Kalani and their friends were creating. And before I knew it the book was finished.

I didn't realize until it was done what I had actually written about – a stubborn girl who needed someone.

See, when I was young, there was a point when things began to spiral in ways I never saw coming. Then I met my future husband. At fifteen and sixteen, we were just babies, but somehow, we were exactly what the other needed. And here we are, three kids and fourteen years later.

This isn't our exact story, not by a long shot, but it's interesting that when I freed my mind from the stress of the book I wanted to write, it gave me this.

So, thank you to the man in my life who helped create a beautiful love story without even realizing it.

And now for my girls...

My editor, Jenn, thank you for challenging me. Thank you for helping me turn my book into something I could be proud of and for not yelling at me after we deleted 2,500 words only for me to add more than that back in other areas. Pretty sure I owe you a strong coffee.

My Proofreader, Cat, thank you for your kind words and extra eye. I look forward to working with you in the future.

Alexandrea D., my book soul sister, you have NO IDEA how much you did for me when you agreed to beta read. All your thoughts and play by play comments meant so much to me. The brutal honesty you gave and your questioning things was exactly what I needed. Thank you for rereading time and time again because you wanted to. Your dedication to helping me through the writing process did not go unnoticed. I hope to hug you in person one day.

My awesome beta girls, Lisa and Meagen, thank you for your comments and feedback. I am so happy you girls went on this journey with me. I hope we can do it again.

Rachel, my personal crisis center, thank you! Thank you for talking me off the ledge and pushing me to move forward when all I wanted to do was take a step back. Having someone who was at the same point as me through all the amazing madness has been invaluable. Thank you. Can't wait for our next lunch date.

SE Hall, you're likely to never see this, and I'm totally okay with that. But, seriously. I have no words. Just, from the bottom of my heart, thank you for everything. Thank you for the books you write that inspired my soul. Thank you for allowing me to see inside your world. Thank you for reading my book and helping make it all it could be. If, with my words, I could make one person feel the way I feel when reading yours, I'll have accomplished more than I ever thought possible. Thank you.

Melissa Fucking Teo – Bish! You're a rock star and a half and an all-around badass. If it wasn't for your detail oriented mind, I never would have noticed that Nate never actually confirmed he was a good boy and kept it in his jeans. And for all the behind the scenes stuff you helped me with -there was a ton- thank you.

My work homies, damn! Thanks for entertaining me and helping make Kalani who she is without even knowing it! Love your faces!

BookSmacked Promotions, bloggers, and reviewers, thank you for your support and helping me get Fumbled Hearts out there.

And to the readers, you taking a chance on a new author is appreciated more than you will ever know. I hope you enjoyed Kalani and Nate's story as much as I enjoyed telling it.

About the Author

USA Today and Wall Street Journal bestselling author Meagan Brandy writes New Adult romance novels with a twist. She is a candy crazed, jukebox junkie who tends to speak in lyrics. Born and raised in California, she is a married mother of three crazy boys who keep her bouncing from one sports field to another, depending on the season, and she wouldn't have it any other way. Starbucks is her best friend and words are her sanity.

Made in the USA
Monee, IL
26 December 2024